The Sovereign Road

Aaron W. Calhoun

THE SOVEREIGN ROAD

Printed in the United States of America

First Printing, 2016

ISBN-10: 1539087980
ISBN-13: 978-1539087984

Contents:

The Canticle of the Last Morning:

And it came to pass
As he stood at the end of all things,
That he saw all that is
In a grain of sand:
The world, and the seed of its desecration.

How with a million others its tale was set for nought;
Its grammar shorn of meaning.
Though the fractured virtue of the high places
Still strove beneath it yet;
The harrowing of the Pit.

A grain of sand
Glistening in the sun of the last day.
A rose wet with the final morning's dew.
A road splashed with drops of blood,
Ascending the mount of stars.

From the brink of holocaust he trod the path,
The skies a pavement to his feet,
To plead with the riven heart of the usurped king
That the fires of night be quenched,
And the morning come one more day.

The Cosmic Mountain

Prologue:

...As he slept, he dreamed. He dreamed of a road paved with stars that stretched beyond the walls of Time itself. He dreamed of a door past the edge of all that is, of all that could be. He dreamed of a map, ancient and worn...

The echo of those memories would not leave Garin's mind. He did not know what they meant nor whence they had come, yet their unearthly power rolled through his soul like an avalanche.

The ruins of a city lay before him, its stark, burned out buildings of steel and glass rising from the cracked pavement like fractured idols to long dead gods. He ran down decaying boulevards overgrown with tall, alien plants and forced his way through cramped alleys so narrow that the surrounding walls almost threatened to crush him. He ran hoping to escape those memories, but he could not, for it was the memories themselves that drew him on. Garin could no more flee their presence than he could flee the sky or the earth.

A few moments later the walls opened around him and he stood in a vast plaza filled with cracked masonry and crumbling columns. Night fell over the city with the violence of a thunderclap and brilliant stars flamed above, each a point of fire that seemed to dance beyond the edge of the world, a bright window in the ramparts of the universe. It was a sight at once foreign and comforting.

Garin had never before seen the stars.

Then, one by one, the stars fell to the pavement like shining dew. Where they fell a great road was born, its flagstones formed of starlight and darkness, the very fabric of the universe. In the end, only three stars were left in the

5

sky. With a sizzling flash one of them burned out, leaving only a grey cinder. The second followed, then the third, and a deep shadow descended upon the city. A sudden fear welled up within him and he ran toward the road, the only source of light that remained. Yet when he reached the edge he hesitated, his fear of the blackness that lay behind him balanced by his fear of the unknown that lay before.

Suddenly the road rose from the ground, transforming into a curtain of light. Through this veil Garin caught a dim glimpse of a small room, its walls and ceiling obscure masses of stained crystal, its sole contents an ancient map, ripped and worn.

"*Will you go?*"

The voice whispered through his mind, pressing the question with such urgency that to hesitate even a moment seemed tantamount to refusal, and an urge to rush though the curtain, his very motion an unspoken yes, surged within him. Yet as Garin began to step forward he suddenly knew with a certainty transcending all reason that continuing onward would change his life irrevocably, and he held back. Tense with indecision and fear, he instead leaned in cautiously, straining to see what was written on the map without making that final commitment. But even as he did so a powerful wind blasted him backward, casting him out of the light. Then the world shattered and he felt himself drifting upward, leaving the broken city behind. His last thought as the dreamscape dissolved into reality was of the memories that had driven him on: memories of the same dream night after night, memories that had filled him with both fear and hope.

Garin awoke, his bed sheets drenched in sweat.

Book One: At the End of All Things...

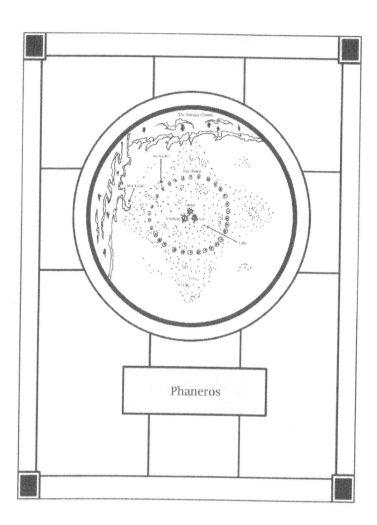

Phaneros

Chapter 1: The City on the Edge of Time

"And so," said the instructor as he paced the front of the ampitheatre, "based on the previous considerations we can easily derive the fundamental axioms on which the Conclave of Worlds is based. I wonder if anyone can name them?"

Trielle barely had time to consider the question before the silence was broken by a blue-feathered Garudan several stories above. It was not the first time.

"That matter gives rise to consciousness, and consciousness to meaning; therefore, meaning is subject and subordinate to consciousness."

"Correct," said the instructor, pleased by the quick response. Or so Trielle thought. In truth, she had always had great difficulty reading the facial expressions of Ixions. Centaur-like creatures from the cloudward rim of the Conclave, there was always a certain inscrutability in their features.

Probably all the facial hair, she quipped silently.

"And what is the corollary to these principles," continued the instructor.

"The universe means what we want it to," said the Garudan.

"Well," said the instructor after a brief moment of uncomfortable silence, "I would not phrase it quite like that. It is more accurate to say that the meaning of a life, of a world even, is imposed from within, rather than intrinsic to its nature…"

"Hence," said the Garudan insistently, "it means what we want it to."

"Er, yes," said the instructor, at last conceding the point, "perhaps one could put it that way. Thank you miss…?"

"Glerys," replied the Garudan. For a brief moment Trielle could hear the snapping rustle of Glerys' wings behind her, a smug, self-satisfied sound.

"The Universe's meaning is imposed from within," repeated the instructor, reverting to his preferred phrasing. "This is indeed the most profound understanding that can be drawn from the considerations of the past several days. It was this principle than enabled us to overcome the barriers between our myriad civilizations." The instructor continued, swiftly launching into a sociopolitical monologue on the founding of their common culture, that which allowed Humans, Garudans, Ixians, and countless other races to subsist in harmony. It was a speech Trielle had heard before, and one that she felt no qualms about ignoring.

She found great difficulty in according these facts the sacrosanct status that everyone gave them. She had been taught these ideas since birth, and to her they were as common as the air she breathed and the clothes on her back. She had even found herself once or twice questioning the logic on which they were based, but had quickly crushed those considerations. There was no value, after all, in being labeled a heretic at age sixteen. Still it rankled to have to sit through yet another year-long course in sidereal philosophy, memorizing the same time-worn arguments again and again. Her true interest, the sciences, would take up most of her classwork for the next several years, but for now she was trapped here.

"And thus, for the past several thousand millennia, our worlds, nay, our universe has known peace."

Good, she thought, *he's finishing up.*

"And as the end of all things draws ever nearer, we can enter that final night knowing that this universe, before its extinction, became all that it could and meant all we could make it mean. You are dismissed."

The last sentence injected a chill into Trielle's otherwise buoyant spirits. Quickly she gathered her things and left, hurrying from the Ampitheatre into the polished crystal hallway beyond. A short walk and she was outside, basking in the tricolor sunbeams of Scintillus' perpetual noon. As the warm rays suffused her flesh the chill left her and she felt her previous mood return.

She stood in a garden suspended halfway up the Arx Scientia, the central institute for learning on Latis. The edifice rose thousands of feet from the mist-shrouded ground beneath, a sparkling blade of fused crystal that pierced the mauve clouds above like a spear. And it was not alone, for in all directions similar spires soared upward, slender needles of red and gold and blue all interconnected by a Gordian Knot of delicate walkways. The city of Scintillus had always amazed Trielle. It was little wonder to her that it had been chosen as the capital of the Conclave.

She glanced at her wrist.

Garin still has a half hour of class. Good! I could use some time to myself.

A white railing warded the edge of the garden and Trielle walked lazily toward it, finally choosing a spot to lay in the grass. She gazed upward, her brown hair spread about her head like a fan, her green eyes drinking in the light of the three suns until they threatened to burst. Then she closed them, savoring instead the warmth on her skin.

As a child she had been told legends of the night sky, fantastic tales of the diamond-swathed blackness that used to cloak the worlds. She only half-believed the stories. No-one living remembered them firsthand and the skies

13

today were a far different entity. Only Vai, Verduun, and Vasya remained to lend truth to those tales, and, for her, that was enough. As long as the last three stars still burned, the end could not come.

It was well known that the three suns were senile, ancient stars well past their prime, but the skillful planning of the Council of Five Heirophants that governed the Conclave of Ten Thousand Worlds and the large-scale stellar interventions of the College of Gravitists had stretched the lifespan of these stars beyond all natural limits. By their predictions the three suns would last several more centuries, well past her projected life span. Trielle supposed that this should comfort her, and in some ways it did. Who, after all, would want to be the final generation, the ones who would stand helplessly by when the entropy clouds finally swept across the Conclave, erasing all existence in a flash of fractured space? Who would wish to watch as the Voidstars consumed what was left of the worlds and all matter finally dissolved into the night? No, she was glad that it would not be her. Still, every now and then its sheer inevitability weighed on her, and she could not bring herself to look out into the pulsing curtains of entropy that raged beyond the rim of the Conclave, held back only by the radiant pressure of the Three. Trielle shivered again despite the warmth of the afternoon sunlight. She did not like considering the end, which was one of the reasons Garin's current obsession with existential matters frustrated her so deeply.

Trielle felt a light touch on her forehead and opened her eyes with a near-audible snap only to find Garin's wiry form hovering over her.

"You're still supposed to be in class," she said. Then Trielle frowned, noticing for the first time his disheveled appearance.

"Sorry," he said with a grin as he smoothed back his sandy blond hair. "Gravitics ended early today. One of the laridian ring models they were using for the demonstration malfunctioned and liquefied half the wall."

"Was anyone hurt?" she asked, a wave of concern crossing her face.

"No," he replied with a laugh, "at least, nothing unrepairable. But the blast was fairly impressive."

Garin was in good spirits, and for that Trielle was glad.

She and Garin had been unusually close as children. Although he was only a few years older Garin had always displayed an uncommon maturity, a fact which their parents had often taken advantage of. Early in her youth, both her parents had taken scientific positions at the College of Gravitists and had quickly risen through the ranks of their peers. But this ascent came at a price, and Trielle's memory was filled with dinners eaten hastily late in the evening, unattended school programs at the Arx Scientia, and nights where neither returned home until the following morning. Yet those times had not been lonely, for Garin had always been there to encourage her when she had difficulty with schoolwork and entertain her when she was bored. He would even offer what small wisdom he had when she had problems with friends at school, although in these latter circumstances Trielle often found that she could come up with better solutions. As Trielle entered adolescence and her interest in the sciences grew, her father had begun to take a greater interest in her life and their relationship had improved considerably. But still, whenever she thought of companionship and love, it was Garin's image that sprung into her mind. At least it had until a few months ago. Since then, things had been... different...

Always a thoughtful individual, Garin had begun to prefer solitude. His mood, once quietly content, had become brooding and shadowed. Despite her pleas Garin would not open up. She knew him well enough to know that he was hiding something, and the fact that he would not share it, even with her, was more than a little disturbing. Still, the events of the afternoon had seemed to open a crack in his bleak exterior, letting a faint glimpse of the old Garin out. Trielle wasn't sure how long it would last, but she planned on making the best of it it while she could.

"Ready to go?" said Garin

"Yes," replied Trielle, rising to her feet. The pair strode back to the crystalline wall of the Arx Scientia and entered a transparent chamber that carried them downward through the bulk of the edifice, finally depositing them on a broad walkway of transparent crystal.

"So," asked Trielle as they walked onward, "How are things with Rakshi?"

"They could be better," responded Garin, his voice growing more subdued. "I'm getting the distinct impression that despite our feelings for each other, it probably won't work out."

"No surprise there, given your current moods," quipped Trielle in a sudden attempt pierce his shell. "I wouldn't be interested either, if…"

Trielle cut herself off as a pained expression grew on Garin's face. She had done it again, wasting what little time she had with the old Garin by trying to repair whatever was broken within him. After a few moments of silence Garin spoke.

"So how was class?"

Trielle allowed herself to smile faintly.

He's really trying today.

"Dull," she replied as she deliberately searched for words that would not stall the conversation again. "It was nothing I hadn't heard before, just a recounting of the Axioms and Corollaries... again."

Garin snorted. "It's almost as if they have to repeat them as much for themselves as for us." He thought for a second, then turned to face her, his cold blue eyes boring into her soul. "What do you think, Trielle, are they true?"

The suddenness of his reaction shocked her.

"Well, um, yes," she replied. She glanced about furtively, fearful of being overheard, and when she finally spoke her voice came out as the faintest of whispers.

"Don't you?"

Garin's face darkened, his thoughts momentarily focused elsewhere.

"Maybe not," he finally answered. "After all, here we are a couple of hundred years away from the end of existence, and what, in the end, do they tell us about ourselves, about the world, or about that existence? Next to nothing!"

As Garin opened his mouth to continue, Trielle inwardly rejoiced.

He's finally going to tell me something real!

Then a sound behind her caught her attention and a quick flick of her eyes revealed a group of instructors approaching from the Arx Scientia. She did not know what Garin would say next, but whatever it was would certainly be on the verge of heresy, if not outrightly so.

Though no law formally criminalized disbelief in the fundamental axioms, none were needed. Since birth, each citizen had been told the history of the Conclave of Worlds, of the endless wars and interplanetary conflicts that had raged as the aging universe shrank around them. All knew that the adoption of the Axioms had finally ended the chaos.

17

And now, with no real future left in which to formulate a better alternative, each citizen held onto those foundational beliefs with a strength bordering on fanaticism. To question them was to move to the margins of the great stream of thought that sustained their society. To deny them completely was to cut yourself off from the rest of the world in the time it mattered most to hang on. Though Trielle herself had often felt them to be questionable, she knew it was all they had.

"Garin," she interrupted," I just have to tell you about this Ixian I met the other day…"

Her voice, filled with trivial events from the past week, continued as if on autopilot even as her mind tracked the progress of the instructors. Only when they were far ahead, safely out of earshot, did Trielle stop her meaningless chatter.

Please Garin! she cried inwardly. *Say what you were intending to! Let me in!*

But Garin remained silent. The inner door he had been about to open was now firmly locked.

Trielle let out a faint sign of frustration even as she resigned herself to reality. She had done the right thing.

The road ahead continued to curve forward in a grand sweep that embraced the Arx Scientia's sister structure, the Arx Memoria, before diving into the bustling heart of Scintillus. Similar in size and shape, the chief difference between the two towers was the Arx Memoria's brilliant ruby red color, a rich contrast to the Arx Scientia's transparent purity. Within its crystalline bulk floor after floor of libraries stretched upward to the edge of space itself, the repository of the collected wisdom of the Conclave. Trielle was a scientist at heart, and the thought of access to that grand collection of knowledge almost made her chest ache with anticipation.

One more year, she said to herself. *Just one more year.*

Great crowds thronged about the Arx Memoria's base, and the pair slowed down considerably as they deftly weaved through the masses. The crowds quickly became too thick to penetrate side by side, and Garin, the taller of the two, took the lead. Silence hung between them now, any words sure to be lost in the chaos. Trielle hoped that once they reached the Kinetorium and started the journey home Garin would open up again. As the crowds thinned Trielle quickened her pace, then caught herself in time to avoid crashing into Garin, who had stopped several feet ahead of her.

"Garin, what…" she began in puzzlement.

Her voice trailed off as she realized that he was paying her no attention. Instead, his gaze was fixed on a man sitting crosslegged on the pavement ahead of them. He was dressed in worn robes, tattered and stained with grime. His skin was wrinkled, shriveled even, and his hair was a peculiar grayish white. Bewilderment crossed Trielle's face.

She had never seen age before.

In eras long past the ravages of time had been banished by genetic manipulation, and the toll the years could take on a body had long since been forgotten. Death was still unavoidable, but now individuals functioned as they did at their prime right until the last moment, the body shutting down and disintegrating in one painless, swift motion. Trielle could not dismiss the possibility that a group of individuals may have chosen to experience aging as a part of their own personal stories, perhaps to mimic and understand the aging universe. But if this was the case, it was a decision far beyond Trielle's comprehension. Feeling suddenly ashamed for staring, Trielle grabbed Garin's arm in an effort to pull him away but he shrugged her off.

19

Momentarily annoyed, she reached forward again but then stopped as she noticed the old man's eyes.

Dark pools shone within his wrinkled face, deep midnight wells that seemed to fall backward into some strange internal universe. Their blackness glinted momentarily with reflected light, and for a moment Trielle thought that stars burned in their depths. The old man's gaze was focused on Garin, who stood there as motionless as if he had been turned to marble. Suddenly the old man stood up, and Trielle stepped back in momentary fright as a wrinkled hand shot out from beneath the soiled robe and gripped Garin's shoulder with surprising force.

"Answer me young one, if you can," said the old man in a deep voice that belied his frail appearance. "For aeons men have told themselves stories about the world, but what is the story that the world tells itself?"

Garin opened his mouth as if to answer, but no sound came forth.

"Do not pretend that you do not know what I speak of," said the old man sternly, "Seek the road, young one, seek the road at the dying of the light." With that, the old man released his grasp and fled into the crowd.

For a long time Garin stood motionless, and when he at last turned toward Trielle his face was pale and bloodless.

"Come on Trielle," he said in a quavering voice, "Let's go home." Then he turned from her and set off hastily down the road.

Trielle's mind was exploding with a thousand questions. *How did that man know Garin? And what was that he had said about a road?* But as Garin's pace accelerated it was all Trielle could do to keep up, and she did not have the breath to ask any of them.

Chapter 2: Seeds of Doubt

The Kinetorium was a vast sphere of ceramic and green glass that hung jewel-like amidst the spires and roads of central Scintillus. Compared to the soaring structures around it the building appeared small and unassuming. But that impression was far from correct, for the Kinetorium was the city's transportation hub.

Few of the Scintillus' daytime inhabitants actually dwelt within the city itself, and for those myriads who did not the Kinetorium was vital. The very air surrounding the structure shimmered, energized by the countless distortions of space generated by the vehicles and transit portals within. Day and night, endless streams of citizens continually surged through its gates in great faceless waves. Trielle and Garin joined one of those surges, sliding into the crowd with practiced ease. Trielle had hoped that, once they slowed down, Garin might attempt to explain something of his reaction at the Arx Memoria. But those hopes were dashed as Garin continued to stare off ahead, his face an impassive mask. Frustrated, Trielle forced her way in front of him and stared him down.

"Garin," she began, "what was going on back there? I mean, I know that man's behavior was odd, but yours was inexplicable!"

Garin stiffened. His eyes softened slightly, and he gave Trielle a brief glance as he answered.

"I… I know it was. I can't even explain it myself."

"Try," urged Trielle. "Please try."

Garin sighed. "Have you ever felt that you were on the verge of learning something Trielle? Something that, if it were true, would contradict everything you ever knew? Only, you were sure that it wasn't."

Trielle nodded, more out of encouragement than understanding.

"Well," continued Garin, "did you ever wonder what would happen if, all of a sudden, you found out that it might just be true after all?"

Trielle's mind spun, her thoughts shattering into a thousand bright fragments as she tried to comprehend what Garin had said. Her eyes darted to his face, pleading for more.

"I don't understand, Garin. I want to, but you need to give me more. What might be true?"

Garin only sighed, his eyes again becoming hard and unreadable, his expression quelling the potential for further conversation.

"Never mind Trielle. Don't worry about it."

By now the ponderous movements of the crowd had brought them to a circular gate of white stone set in the equator of the Kinetorium, and they passed through into the space within. Inside, all remaining illusion of smallness was banished by the sheer scope of its contents. Tier upon tier of glassy walkways ringed the inside of its walls. From these, great translucent piers covered by a chaotic veneer of vehicles jutted into the center, ending a little over halfway in. The heart of the Kinetorium was occupied with a second sphere, its color a deep, impenetrable black. Within its shielded interior, twelve titanic laridian rings continuously distorted the fabric of space.

Named after Ronath Larid, a celebrated physicist from the bygone era of the Conclave's founding, these rings permitted the almost effortless manipulation of gravitational force, allowing ships to ride waves of timespace at superluminal velocity, wormholes to be called from the ether, and planets to be held in stable orbits at whim. These twelve were among the largest, and each served as an anchor for one of the twelve key timespace transit corridors of the Conclave. Each corridor ended in the Kinetorium of a distant world, from which another network of corridors then branched. It was said that nearly any world in the Conclave could be reached by seven corridors or less, although Trielle had never tested this for herself. In any event it did not matter today. The corridors were not their destination.

The inner walls of the Kinetorium were constructed of the same brilliant green glass as those outside, reinforced at regular intervals with great arches of wrought brass that soared between the walkways like the buttresses of a gothic cathedral. Each arch was inlaid with great cabochons of milky white imagnite, an artificial substance impervious to gravitic discharge. Although striking in appearance, Trielle knew that the arches were for far more than show, for they concealed a secondary network of laridian rings that, although less impressive than the transit rings in the center, were no less important. Each of the vehicles within was equipped with a set of smaller portable rings, giving them the capacity to generate their own small corridors for quick transit. But such capacities, when used by many vehicles in a confined area, carried the potential for larger scale disruptions to local gravitational geometry. It was this that the lesser ring network countered, stabilizing the structure of space and preventing unavoidable gravitic discharges from spilling into the public spaces outside.

The pair soon reached a glass capsule that carried them several stories upward, at last depositing them on one of the piers. A quick walk brought them to their vehicle.

As a child, Trielle had always been impressed by the large, decorative crafts of their neighbors. But as she grew, that love for the ostentatious has been replaced with a

23

quieter, more earnest interest in the machines themselves, and as Trielle and Garin mounted their ether chariot, she could not help but admire it.

Twin wings of milky white swept backward from an imagnite steering platform large enough for four adult passengers. The front of the platform was guarded by a crystalline balustrade in which the controls of the vehicle were set. The craft had no walls or roof, for upon activation the Chariot instantly surrounded its occupants with a focused gravitic sphere that protected far better than any physical shielding. To the rear were a series of laridian rings that provided the motive force for the chariot's metric drive, capable of accelerating the craft to near-lightspeed in moments and able to open a local wormhole in less time than that.

No, thought Trielle with more than a flash of pride, *it's certainly not the flashiest chariot, but it could get us halfway across the Conclave before these other ones even start up.*

With a few deft motions Garin activated the chariot, and the craft slowly rose from the pier. The air around them distorted momentarily as the gravitic shield formed, finally settling into a persistent blue shimmer thinner than a molecule but harder than granite. The ether chariot continued to rise, joining the great cloud of outgoing craft. The ascent seemed endless, but at last they crossed the shifting lights that marked the edge of the transit zone. It was there that the containment fields were focused, allowing for safe local wormhole creation.

Trielle stared through the shield, gazing at the constant shifting flicker of vessels appearing and disappearing, one crystallizing from the air itself even as another vanished like salt in warm water.

"Trielle," said Garin. "Ready to go?"

Trielle nodded, gripping the balustrade firmly as she did so.

Garin's hands flew across the controls, and a few seconds later Trielle heard the faint unmistakeable whine of the drive rings accelerating. There was a flash of brilliant blue and a churning maelstrom of distortion surrounded the chariot. Then they were swallowed up by a dark cloud rimmed with silver, falling into an endless mirrored void. A few moments later the void shattered and the chariot emerged above the dim landscape of Latis' nightside. Tidally locked in its orbit about the three suns, most residents worked in the perpetual day of Scintillus or another lightside city, but lived in the soft twilight that prevailed on the far side of the planet.

"Almost home," said Trielle.

The ground beneath was uneven: in some places forming tall mesas, in others sinking down in mist shrouded valleys. Atop each mesa stood crystalline monoliths arranged in patterned whorls, each ablaze with myriad pinpricks of light. Streets of silver stretched between the monoliths, running between the mesas atop arching spans. The entire scene was lit a soft ice blue by the countless worlds that drifted overhead in the vastness of space, gleaming with the reflected light of the Three.

As their chariot descended toward the monolith that they called home, Trielle risked a last glance upward. Her eyes quickly scanned the space between the worlds, searching for any sign of the entropy clouds inevitable advance, but the sky was a clear, twilit violet. Only a barely visible greenish flash seen once at the edge of perception marked the frontier.

***

"So does that make sense Trielle?"

"I think so," she said slowly, "but I still don't see where the rings get the energy to split the fields."

Garin sat in silence as Trielle engaged in spirited debate with their father about some basic aspects of gravitic science. Always the more technically minded of the two, Trielle had wanted to be an engineer for as long as he could remember. This suited their parents quite well. After all, his father was the current High Gravitist, one of the five ruling hierophants of the Conclave, and his mother was chief gravitational wave analyst for the Large Neutronium Antenna, the primary device used to measure the spatiotemporal activity of the three suns and of the entropy clouds. Both knew the importance of their work and enjoyed what they did immensely. Garin was thankful for this, although he knew that their dedication had often left Trielle and him to fend for themselves as children.

"It comes from the zero-point field itself, at least most of it does," his father continued, "although you're right to notice that there's always a certain startup cost. If you look at the mathematics, though, you can see that the deficit averages out over the bulk of the surrounding continuum fairly quickly. Think of it as generating its own fuel."

Garin watched as Trielle frowned.

"You always say look at the mathematics. I won't get to learn that for three more years."

"Well, I could always teach you some after dinner."

Unlike Trielle, Garin had never found the sciences at all intriguing. It was not for lack of trying. As early as he could remember the subtle pressure to excel in the sciences has been a part of his family. Never overt, he could see now that it came more from his parents' enthusiasm for their chosen field than any real desire on their part to direct their children's lives. But the hidden tug of their expectations, though innocent, nevertheless pulled at him like the gravitation they studied and controlled. As a child he had sometimes wished that he could generate interest at will, half-believing that it could somehow strengthen their family bonds. Now, as a young adult, he had all but given up on this, preferring instead the subtle reasoning of philosophy and its finely parsed arguments on the nature of existence as a whole. It was this path that had lead to his current predicament.

"So how were your classes," said his mother, jolting Garin out of his reverie.

"They were fine," he replied evenly.

"Fine?" said Trielle with mild shock, "since when is your instructor catastrophically remoldeling the lecture hall fine?"

All eyes were on him now, a situation he desperately wanted to avoid.

"Ah... I may have downplayed things a bit," he mumbled.

But Trielle was evidently not about to give up.

"Alright, well what about that old man who stooped us outside of Arx Memoria?"

Garin's face flushed, then drained of its color.
Why couldn't she just leave that alone!

Garin knew his sister's concerns. He saw them in her face day after day. Many times he tried to speak to her about the burden he carried, a few times almost succeeding. But each time there was something, some interruption, some unwanted presence or unforeseen event, that broke off the thread of conversation. And each time the interruption passed he had started to speak, only to find his confidence gone. He longed to open up, but, unlike the laridian rings his father had just been discussing, the startup costs of the conversation were simply too great. After all, how do you share with your family the growing conviction that everything your life was based on was a lie?

Garin did not think these things lightly. It had begun two years ago during the same sidereal philosophy class Trielle has just endured today. Unlike Trielle, he had enjoyed the class immensely. It seemed to mesh perfectly with his newly awakened interest in metaphysical reasoning. In the end, though, it had presented his mind with what he now believed was a fundamental contradiction.

As was the custom across the Conclave, the Three Axioms were taught with almost religious intensity; their necessity for proper societal function emphasized, their self-evident truth proclaimed. All held to them as fundamental, and in this Garin had been no different. Still, he had wanted reassurance that principles this basic were believed for good reason, and he clearly remembered the feeling of barely contained satisfaction that has filled him as the first lecture began. Perhaps how he would truly begin to understand.

But it was not to be. As their initial explanation had been advanced Garin could not help but see them as self-referential and hence fundamentally flawed. He vividly recalled the dull tension that had gripped his chest as the implications of his reasoning became apparent. He remembered leaving the class in a daze, his heart pounding as he struggled to enclose that understanding behind impregnable walls.

After all, he had reasoned, *the meaning of the Three Axioms are not the material of my everyday life, so why should these doubts affect me so strongly. What did they change, really?*

His initial attempts to quell his concerns had been successful, but as the year had progressed the walls he had built in his mind were systematically undermined by the very class intended to strengthen his faith in Conclave philosophy. As class after class passed, each painstakingly building the ideologic groundwork on which the Conclave was founded, he was forced to come to terms with the truth. Society was founded on the Axioms, the Axioms made no sense to him, therefore society made no sense to him. In vain he had hidden behind the last option left to him: the absurdity of the opposite view. After all, if matter did not give rise to consciousness and consciousness meaning then that implied meaning had an independent existence alongside the material world and there were deeper things in this universe than the mere interplay of matter and energy. Then the dreams came, and that last bastion had begun to crumble like a rampart under cannon fire.

"What man, Garin?" asked his mother lightly.

Garin took a deep breath, but before he could formulate a response Trielle had already started.

"There was an old man near the Arx, older than anyone I'd ever seen. He stopped Garin for a moment to talk to him and then ran off."

Garin's father narrowed his eyes in bewilderment. "Old age was conquered millennia ago," he said. "Are you sure…"

"Yes," responded Trielle

"Maybe he was a Selphidian," responded his mother. "They come from an ice-world near the Conclave rim. Their skin can become quite wrinkled during their adolescent years."

"Yes," said his father, "many of them do have similar pigmentation to humans from Latis."

"No," said Trielle firmly. "He was human! But his age is unimportant, what I wanted to…"

"He was a Selphidian," blurted Garin even as he focused his eyes on Trielle, trying to freeze her words in midair with the sheer force of his gaze. "I'd never seen a Selphidian before," he continued with forced calm. "But I

29

remember reading about their race in class. I think that is what he was."

Trielle's mouth remained open for a moment, then it finally closed as she accepted defeat.

The meal ended and Garin quickly ran off to his bedroom, giving a vague schoolwork related excuse for his quick departure. Only after he reached the relative safety of his bedroom did he let his guard down and begin to process the events of the day. Truthfully, he had no idea who the old man was, only that somehow he had known about Garin's dreams.

They had first started several months ago: unearthly visions of a ruined city, a worn map, and a road that seemed to be made of the sky itself. He had initially forgotten them as he had done with so many dreams before but this one had returned with maddening persistence, almost as if if were demanding his focused attention. There was something about this dream, some strange clarity that made it seem more than real, which made a final dismissal impossible. Beneath it all, he could not shake the thought that if meaning somehow really was independent of matter, what better way could there be for that meaning to make itself clear than in dreams? Or, he reasoned, he could simply be going mad. It was this internal conflict between a self-diagnosis of nascent insanity and the outlandish, but logically possible, chance that he was encountering something real that had led to his recent moodiness and withdrawal. Still, the possibility that some deeper reality was somehow involved here had remained that; a bare possibility, until today.

"The story the world told itself? The dying of the light?"

Garin murmured aloud the words that the old man had spoken, turning them over in his mind as he did so in an attempt to extract what meaning he could. A chill shivered though his body, accompanied by a strange sense of dread.

The old man had to know about the dreams, didn't he? How else could he have known about the road?

Chapter 3: The Dying of the Light

Trielle sighed as the sidereal philosophy instructor droned on interminably about the metaphysical principles that lay behind the War of Unification, a series of interplanetary battles that marked the birth pangs of the Conclave.

The morning had started off well enough with a sequence of lectures on the native biology of Latis and its relationship to structural aesthetics. Trielle's initial mild interest had grown into a deep fascination as she considered the millennia of biogeologic engineering that had been required to grow the city of Scintillus from the local silicon-based plantlife.

Found in the canyons of pre-human Latis, the organisms had originally looked like tall, thin spires of diamond-hard crystal that rose from the mist-shrouded depths like a forest of spears. Their metabolism was simple: chemical differentials between the canyon mists and the atmosphere above allowed the organisms to generate substantial electrical potentials along their lengths. The organisms then shunted this energy downward into their root structures via a complex web of electrically conductive tubules, using it to draw raw materials needed for growth from the soil by a process not unlike the electrolysis of water or salt. The first generation of humans to colonize this world quickly saw the potential of this somewhat unique ecology, and after substantial engineering efforts had been able to reconfigure the base lifeform into one that grew to gargantuan size according to fixed blueprints imposed while young. Soon Latis was filled with countless cities of towering crystal skyscrapers, each a self-repairing organism capable of living for centuries if not millennia. A few more minor biological alterations had granted access to the organisms' internal electroneural tubules, providing cheap electrical energy for the planet.

"Trielle!"

The sharp sound of her name snapped Trielle to attention.

"Yes," she responded, trying her best to recall the instructor's last point.

"I have asked you asked several times now about Xigris Nought of Axilar and, until this last attempt, you had elected not to respond. Perhaps you are unfamiliar with this historic figure?"

Trielle could hear the tittering of her classmates behind her, a curious polyphony of sounds given their substantially differing physiognomies. Fortunately this was a subject on which she had some knowledge. Her propensity to daydream during sidereal philosophy had, on occasion, lead to embarrassment. It would not do so today.

"My apologies," she said formally. "Yes I am familiar with him. Xigris Nought was a high-ranking member of the Puginihilist School. Believing, as he did, that all reality is fundamentally based in conflict and combat, he felt there was no inherent value to the joining of differing worlds in any kind of harmonious whole."

"Correct thus far," said the instructor with the hint of a smile. "Now, if you could inform us of the role he played in the assimilation of the Rodalan Hegemony, we would be grateful."

"Of course," she responded. "At first the initial Heirophants of the Conclave felt the Puginihilists to be a threat to their overall effort. After all, why would a group that based their entire understanding of the cosmos on conflict desire to assist their efforts at interplanetary unification. But when they turned their sights to the Rodalan Hegemony, Xigris' usefulness became apparent, as it seemed that the Rodalans shared a nearly identical philosophy."

"But how would this help?" asked the instructor dramatically, now warming visibly to the dialogue. "Surely life philosophies built entirely on conflict can create no lasting peace."

"While it does seem counterintuitive at first," admitted Trielle, "his interactions with the Rodalans proved transformative to his outlook, significantly widening the scope of his philosophy. Xigris was able to create a psychological bridge between the Rodalans' combat-driven worldview and the Conclave's efforts by recasting the Conclave's vision in terms of a large-scale conflict, one larger than he, or the Rodalans, had ever before considered. Essentially he realized that to extract meaning from a meaningless universe is the ultimate form of combat, and that the struggle between forms of life is nothing when compared to the struggle between life itself and entropy. It was this understanding that convinced the Rodalans"

"Excellent," said the instructor, "and also true in a most profound sense. Every day of our life is a battle to conquer the random forces of the world around us with our own will, desires, and truths."

Trielle feigned attentiveness as the instructor continued his monologue, only allowing herself to slip back into her daydream when he began to question another student. Class ended a few subjective moments later.

***

When she arrived at the hanging garden Garin was already waiting for her, seated in the sunlight-drenched grasses near the edge of the balcony. His face was drawn in a grim frown that was uncharacteristic, even for him.

"You're early," she said.

"I didn't have gravitics today," he responded.

"Oh, I forgot."

Trielle frowned. She could never keep track of his schedule.

"Today was paleoaesthetics," he replied

She nodded in response, now understanding the origin of his dour expression. Only a few, rare individuals truly enjoyed paleoaesthetics.

Trielle began to speak when a sudden change in the ambient light made her catch her breath. Puzzled, she glanced about, expecting to see the swiftly fading shadow of a cloud that had passed between them and the suns. But the same shadow hung about everything. No matter where she looked the light was trembling and dimming, its once-brilliant quality becoming somehow tenuous and strained.

"Trielle!" shouted Garin in alarm, his arm raised toward the heavens. "Look!"

Trielle looked skyward, expecting to see a fleet of etherships or some other rare sight, but the sky was empty of flying craft. Instead her eyes widened in horror as she watched the once fiery orb of Vai, greatest of the three last stars of the universe, flicker, darken, and die.

***

With trembling hands, Garin landed the ether chariot at the family's monolith.

The trip from the Arx Scientia to the Kinetorium had taken far longer than usual, the road obstructed by a swollen crowd of citizens in varying degrees of shock and panic. All eyes were focused skyward, as if none could believe that one of the three had been extinguished. At one point he caught a glimpse of the old man, but when he looked again he could see no sign of him.

The Kinetorium itself had been no better, with ether chariots and skyriders launching in frantic patterns that the laridian containment fields could barely accommodate. Erratic discharges of ungrounded gravitic potential flashed between the ships and the dome like sheet lightning, several of the larger ones striking with such force that it had seemed a near miracle the structure was not breached. When they had finally pushed their way through to their chariot Garin had sped off with as much velocity as possible, anxious to leave the turmoil behind. But when they reached the far side of Latis an even greater shock awaited them. The once-twilit sky now shimmered with a faint but unmistakable tinge of bilious green. A quick gasp from Trielle told him that she had seen it too.

The landing maneuver complete, Garin exited the ether chariot and rushed to the transit shaft with Trielle close behind. A few seconds later they reached the central living area and found their mother staring, white-faced, at the glassy cylinder of the monolith's core infochryst, its primary information processing unit. Wordlessly, Garin and Trielle joined her on the divan.

Within the holographic matrix of the infochryst Vasya and Verduun burned with supernal light, their surfaces ablaze with arcing prominences. Compared to their brilliance Vai looked like a rotten fruit, its cooling photosphere the mottled reddish-violet color of a bruise. Occasionally a dim red flare, the exhaust of now-extinguished fusion fires, burst from the surface of the star like the final exhalations of a corpse. The image of Vai was surrounded by a halo of constantly shifting data that displayed each stellar parameter in real time. Garin scrutinized the endless parade of figures, bringing what scientific knowledge he had to bear in a vain attempt to make some sense of them. It was a problem beyond his abilities.

"The Gravitic College believes it to be a spontaneous inversion of the radiative-core boundary," said a somber voice from the edge of the room, and Garin turned to see his father, still dressed in his robes of office.

"An inversion?" asked his mother? "Can it be corrected with a core agitation?"

"Possibly," Gedron said after a moment's thought. "But the metallic plasma density at the interface may be high enough at the inversion's base to cancel the effect. Still, we have devoted all of out infochrysts to the computation."

"Did you see the sky, Father?" asked Trielle anxiously. "It seemed greener to me…"

"Yes Trielle," said Gedron. "The entropy clouds have advanced." He did not speak further, but turned to the infochryst and gestured. The image within blurred, shifting from the core of the Conclave system to its outer fringe. The entropy clouds seethed with unnatural fury, their surfaces a shifting storm of nacreous green. Great filaments of acidic light erupted from them like the tentacles of a gaseous alien beast, tearing effortlessly through a cluster of gas giants and reducing them to a drifting cloud of disintegrating rocks and furiously churning vapor. Far away, embedded deep within in the shifting curtains, the black mouths of the Voidstars hung like gates into the final abyss.

Trielle hesitated for a moment, the asked in a quiet voice, "what about the end? Does this change the time table?"

"I… I don't know," said Gedron, "but I think we have to assume the worst. The date of final dissolution is likely much closer now that we thought, but it's hard to tell by how much. After all, Verduun and Vasya still shine. After the failure of Vai, though, I worry that we may not know as much as we think we do. But right now there are more immediate issues. This is by far the worst entropy storm I have ever witnessed. When Vai's radiation pressure failed, there was nothing to hold the clouds back."

He paused for a moment, a look of immense sadness on his face.

"We lost eighty-two worlds," he finally whispered. "Thirty-two inhabited."

Beneath the image a scrolling list appeared of the planets that had been consumed by the storms. Garin could see the color drain from Trielle's face. She had good friends on several of those worlds.

"I'm sorry I can't be with you all right now," said Gedron after a moment's silence. "I need to speak with the Photocanth and Chromatocron about how we should proceed." Unsurprised, Garin continued to stare at the infochryst as the data detailing the magnitude of the tragedy rolled onward.

Garin had never been close to his father. One of the five ruling members of the Conclave of Worlds' core technocracy, Gedron Donar has risen from relatively obscure beginnings to the heights of power through determination, focus, and a preternatural understanding of the laridian rings used to generate and manipulate gravitic fields. The story of his ascent was well known among the youth of the Conclave, and was frequently used by instructors, teachers, and mentors to motivate their charges to greater effort. And yet this determination had often meant long hours at the Arx Scientia, and later at the Omegahedron, the political heart of the Conclave; time not spent with Garin and Trielle. It was not that Garin did not love his father, but without that shared time and the memories that could have sprung from it his love often took on the crystalline fixity of a mathematical theorem, a truth that was known in the mind but did not make the vital descent to the heart.

After what seemed an eternity Garin's mother finally made the sign of cessation and the torrent of information pouring from the infochryst ceased. The family passed the next several hours in silence, each afraid to speak for fear that what composure they had would be lost.

For once I don't have to pretend to be in a good mood, thought Garin wryly, but even that internal attempt at levity failed to dull the impact of the tragedy he had just witnessed.

After the evening meal Garin excused himself and retired to his room. There his thoughts drifted back to the old man and his cryptic words. In the light of Vai's demise, both the old man's words and his dreams had begun to take on new meaning. After all, if the death of a star did not count as the dying of the light Garin did not know what would. He thought back to his dream, picturing in his mind the three last stars that hung above the shining road as they burned out one by one.

How long do Vasya and Verduun have?

An icy chill shivered through his flesh, and he realized that, whatever the nature of the connection between the old man, his dreams, and the stars, there may not be much time left to sort it out.

A soft bell announced that someone was outside his door.

Garin sighed. He has wanted to be alone.

"Come in," he said finally, hoping to sound irritable enough to drive whoever it was away.

The door slid open and Trielle entered.

"Garin," she said, "I need to talk to you."

39

Garin motioned silently and she sat down. She had a pressured look on her face, as if too many thoughts had built up within, all jostling for release.

"I… I don't know what to make of all this," she blurted. "I've lived all my life knowing that our civilization is doomed, but also knowing that I, personally, would never face it. I thought that we at least knew what was going on, how much time we had left."

"I know," he said quietly.

"I'd like to believe that this is a temporary setback, that Father can somehow restart Vai as he said," she continued, "After all, he did sound hopeful…"

"Yes he did," agreed Garin, and then paused, a frown on his face.

Within his mind a battle raged. The internal pressure to share the dreams with someone, anyone, had been building for the past week, and the encounter with the old man had only strengthened this urge. But still he hesitated. The words the old man has spoken were tantamount to heresy. Worse, they were an accusation of treason against the universe itself. After all, if the world told its own story then the citizens of the Conclave, in their ongoing attempts to stamp their own meaning onto a meaningless world, had placed themselves at fundamental odds with that world. But such concerns were abstract, ethereal. Just yesterday he had decided again not to share them, his reservations winning out over the desire to let Trielle in. But that was before Vai had burned out, and suddenly those reservations seemed a small thing.

He had to trust someone, and Trielle had always listened to him.

"I think…" he began, "I don't know, Trielle, but I think…" He hesitated for a moment before starting to speak. "I think there is far more going on here and around us than we have been led to believe. I've been having dreams: dreams of a planet on the edge of the Conclave, about to be consumed by the entropy clouds. There is a road there, Trielle, a road that in my dreams seems to lead... out..."

"Out, what do you mean, out," said Trielle, a frown crossing her face.

"Out of this world, out of time itself," said Garin carefully. "I don't know where it goes, but near the end of the dream the same thing happens. I can see a room ahead of me. There is a map in the room that seems to show how to follow the road, but I can't see it clearly. Then a man calls my voice, asking if I will go. I always hesitate though, and that's when I wake up."

"Garin," said Trielle, her face puzzled, "I've had hundreds of strange dreams. Even a few that reoccurred. But you seem to be putting this... dream... on par with Vai's failure." She paused in thought for a moment before adding, "I'm trying to see the connection but I can't."

"I barely know what I'm implying here myself," said Garin. "A few days ago I was still trying to dismiss the dream, but then I met that old man."

"Yes, who was he?" Trielle interrupted.

"Honestly, I have no idea," admitted Garin. "But what he said seemed to confirm that my dream meant something real. He told me to seek the road at the dying of the light."

"At the dying of the..." murmured Trielle. Then her eyes widened and the color drained from her face. "How could he have known about Vai?"

"Exactly," said Garin. "In my dream, right after the road appears, there are three stars left in the sky, then each burns out, one by one. I almost feel crazy for saying this, but I think those stars are Vasya, Vai and Verduun."

41

Trielle's face paled as she pondered the implications of this.

"I'm not saying I believe you yet," she said.

"That's good," said Garin. "Right now I'm not sure that I believe myself."

"But," she continued, "if there is any truth to it this could be the beginning of something much worse. If all three stars fail…"

Trielle's voice trailed off. As they sat in silence, Garin's mind wandered back to the images of the entropy storms they had both watched in the central infochryst. Then a troubling thought entered Garin's mind.

"Trielle," he said, "what did father say was the cause of Vai's death?"

"A radiative-core layer inversion," said Trielle. "Why?"

"Because," Garin said, "it makes no sense. The density of a star increases exponentially the closer you get to the core. By the time you get even halfway there all convection has ceased, the plasma is almost locked in place. Near the core boundary the density is even higher than gold. All the motions here are subatomic, there is no bulk flow of matter. And you need the ability to flow, Trielle, for any type of massive layer inversion to form."

Garin could see Trielle's mind race at the import of his last statement, but he did not pause. The words were welling up within him now like a fountain, and he feared that if he stopped them he would never again gain the courage to speak.

"There's more, Trielle. The old man told me something else. Well, he asked me a question really. He said 'For aeons, men have told themselves stories about the World, but what is the Story that the World tells itself?'"

Trielle thought for a moment about the cryptic phrase. "It sounds like he is trying to make you question the Axioms and Corollaries," she finally said.

"Well, I would say he succeeded," added Garin. He paused for a moment. "In truth," he said carefully, "I think there are many falsehoods about at present."

"What are you saying," whispered Trielle slowly.

Garin paused for a moment. Until now he had been afraid to make the leap from his questions to the inevitable answers, but now he saw no choice, no way to be true to himself and remain unchanged. And if his suspicions about the official explanation for Vai's demise were correct…

"I'm saying," he began deliberately, "that we have have been taught falsehoods about the nature of reality since birth. Whether inadvertent or deliberate I do not yet know. I am also saying that stellar radiative-core inversions do not, cannot happen, and that Father, given his training in stellar and gravitic science must know this. I am saying that Father, for whatever reason, is lying."

The silence that descended on the room was almost palpable, as if the air had been evacuated from the space between them leaving only a vacuum incapable of carrying sound.

"What do we do?" asked Trielle quietly.

"I'm not sure," said Garin with a sigh, "but I think it needs to start with me, tonight…"

Chapter 4: A Vision in the Night

Garin stood again in the ruined city of his dreams, the fractured buildings rising from the ground like the fragmented bones of a long-dead beast. Again he walked down cramped, shadowed alleys and soon reached the vast plaza overshadowed by the impossible vision of a starry night.

Although he could not say exactly what, something seemed different this time. He looked around, trying to identify the source of this feeling, but the plaza looked exacly the same as it had countless time before. Then he turned his scrutiny inward and understood. It was he who had changed.

Again the stars fell and gathered into the road of light and shadow, the last three flaring and dying in the empty sky above. Again the substance of the road surged upward as Garin approached, forming the curtain of starlight that guarded the way to the map room. Again the voice sounded, its deep tones echoing through the desolate city.

"Will you go?"

"Yes, I will go!" replied Garin firmly.

"Then come forward my child, Come and see…"

Abruptly the curtain of light parted, the innumerable stars that burned within it shifting and reshaping into a glittering archway. Taking a deep breath, Garin boldly strode through.

The crystalline walls of the chamber beyond were stained with ages of dust and grime, yet still they managed to catch enough of the light cast forth by the starry arch to fill the chamber with soft rainbow gleams. In the center of the chamber, upon a crystal dais, lay the map. Garin's eyes narrowed as he studied the convoluted symbols and diagrams that covered the ancient piece of parchment.

What is this? What am I looking at?

Then a troubling thought occurred to him.

How can I take this with me?

***

The next morning's trip to the Arx Scientia was pervaded by a quiet, desperate tension. Trielle's long-awaited conversation with Garin had failed to bring her the closure she had hoped for and left her with more questions instead. And behind them, drifting around the edge of her thoughts like wisps of dank fog, was the unshakeable sense of a universe spinning out of control. As the ether chariot phased into the Kinetorium, she found herself desperately hoping that somehow during their transit Vai had reignited and all would be as it was. But a swift glance skyward as they exited the structure only reconfirmed the harsh truth. As they walked toward the soaring crystalline mass of the Arx, Trielle tried to engage Garin in conversation. But he remained silent despite her prodding, and after a few attempts she lost the will to continue. A few moments later they parted ways.

Trielle began her day trying to pretend that all was well, but soon could barely muster the energy to go through the motions. As she sat through lecture after lecture a cold sense of apathy swelled within her like an abscess, an inescapable sense that the entire edifice of Conclave thought was built on a foundation of sand.

Eventually her classes ended and Trielle walked to the balcony, grateful for a chance to finally be alone. Instead she found Garin waiting for her with an exultant look on his face.

"Garin," she called out in surprise, "I thought you would still be in class."

"I didn't go today," he said. "There was something I had to do."

"What?" she asked with a puzzled tone. She had never known him to skip classes.

"Not here," he said, "Come on, I'll tell you later."

Trielle and Garin quickly descended the crystalline tower and made their way to the Kinetorium. A few moments later they were skimming toward their home on the far side of Latis.

"Garin…" began Trielle.

"Not yet," said Garin. "We need to find someplace isolated."

Garin abruptly twisted the ether chariot's control rod and the craft dove, dropping swiftly into a nearby canyon. After descending several hundred feet, he brought the craft to rest on a cracked ledge of reddish stone that jutted from the canyon wall and powered it down.

"Garin, why did you bring us here?"

Garin walked to the edge of the ledge and motioned for Trielle to follow. Together they gazed downward at the perpetual shroud of violet mist that filled the depths. Suddenly a cold wind swept through the canyon, stirring the surface of the mists into strange, fantastic shapes. Trielle shivered.

"You're starting to worry me Garin. Please tell me whats going on."

Garin did not reply, but instead reached into a pocket within his tunic and removed something, holding it with cupped hands. Trielle leaned forward and peered at the object. Within the hollow of Garin's palms lay a small diamond-shaped amethyst that pulsed and shimmered with barely trapped light, filling his hands with an unearthly glow.

"Is that an Oneirograph? Is that where you were today during class? The Oneirographicon?"

Over the past centuries, the noeticists of Latis had developed increasingly elaborate methods for reproducing intelligence and thought. Beginning with the same bioelectric crystal life forms used to grow the buildings of Scintillus, the noeticists had imbued a scion of these organisms with basic neural processing templates. By applying a firm but gentle selection pressure, their subsequent evolution had been directed toward forms more and more capable of generating the psychophysical energy patterns underlying rational thought. One result of this process was the development of the infochrysts: living crystals capable of analyzing data at almost any level of complexity. Within a century of their creation almost all the worlds of the Conclave had embraced the infochrysts as their primary computing technology. But the noeticists had not stopped with these devices. Instead they continued to relentlessly push the organism's evolutionary development until at last they had gained sufficient complexity to extract, shape, display, and alter the thoughts and dreams of living beings, and the psychochrysts and oneirochrysts were born.

Unlike the compact, solid neuroarchitecture of the infochrysts, both psychochrysts and oneirochrysts were composed of cloudlike arrays of microscopic crystalline filaments with a complexity exceeding that of a mammalian brain. When activated, rapidly shifting currents within these filaments generated a linked series of submicroscopic electromagnetic fields that permeate the surrounding space. These ever-shifting fields, once focused on the bioelectric currents of a living brain, created a reactive electromagnetic link between each neuron and corresponding fiber in the filament array, allowing for easy mirroring and extraction of the brain's contents. This information could then be interpreted, condensed and altered, used to reshape the subject's thoughts, or recorded for future consideration. Similar in overall structure, the only difference between psychchrysts and oneirochrysts was the type of mental activity they were intended to interact with; psychochrysts with conscious thoughts and emotions, and oneirochrysts with subconscious thoughts and dreamstates.

Trielle frowned. The power of oneirographic technology to reshape minds and thoughts had always disturbed her. Most justified its use by pointing to its obvious compatibility with the Axioms and Corollaries. After all, if the meaning of the universe depended solely on the thoughts of the conscious being within it, then technology able to record and shape thought could be used to clarify or even alter than meaning at a subject's whim. Still, Trielle had never been able to convince herself that the technology was entirely safe, and not without reason. Early in the history of psychographic technology a group of Gothrans had been rendered permanently vegetative by an oneirochryst. Relying as they did on quantum-entangled beta decay in biologically encapsulated actinide elements for their information processing, the highly correlated magnetic fields had induced a spontaneous, irreversible waveform collapse in their brains.

Sensing her misgivings, Garin sighed.

"I couldn't think of any other way to view the map," he explained. "And it's not as if I went to one of the cut-rate ones offworld, I used the one in the Arx Memoria."

Trielle paused. "What was it like Garin?" she asked finally.

Garin shuddered. "Like nothing I've ever experienced before. Imagine feeling as if there were two of you, but you didn't know which one was real. And then… Imagine someone, or something, literally pulling a thought

48

out of your mind. At one level you know it is alright, that you had gone there for that purpose, but on another level there's this instinct to rebel against the machine, this reflexive mental grip that makes it almost impossible to let go of the thought."

Trielle's face blanched. "Well," she ventured, "I hope it was worth it."

"It was," said Garin. "This oneirograph contains the extracted dream information. Look…"

As he spoke Garin held out the oneirograph, gesturing over it with his free hand. At once its glow increased, shifted, and finally leapt from the surface of the crystal in a perfect holographic representation of his dream.

Trielle was immediately enraptured as the dream's strange vistas, her breath catching in her throat when she saw the glittering sky, the road leading out of the doomed cosmos, and the shimmering archway leading to the chamber of the map.

Now I understand, she thought.

The dream was mesmerizing in its message, compelling in a way that, until this moment, she had not thought possible. And standing there beside Garin, sharing in his visions, Trielle felt the stirring of something new within her, the hope that things could be different. As the recording concluded Garin paused the display, lingering over the image of a worn and faded map.

"This is where I need your help," said Garin. "I tried to study the map as long as possible, to make sure that I had seen every detail. And believe me," he added, "there is more detail than might initially be apparent. Because of that I made sure that the oneirographer focused on this part of the dream."

Garin gestured to the device and the hologram expanded and grew, the image slowly rotating in the twilight air. The ragged edges of the map framed a rectangular space filled with the image of a vast mountain, its surface composed not of rock but of scattered points of brilliant light strewn through velvet blackness. The lights twinkled, seeming almost to flow through the substance of the peak.

Trielle frowned. Like the star-filled sky of the dream city, the substance of the mountain matched descriptions of the ancient cosmos from her paleoastronomy class. Yet this realization only added to her confusion.

What am I looking at? A mountain made of the ancient sky? It makes no sense...

Puzzled, Trielle took a closer look at the map. Five crystalline spheres, each filled with peculiar designs, were scattered across the mountain's slopes. The bottommost sphere contained a cross-shaped scattering of dark points surrounding a trio of bright spheres, framed on the top and left side by indistinct clouds of pale green. Trielle recognized it immediately as a planetary map of the Conclave and the nearest entropy clouds as shown from above the orbital axis of the three suns. The contents of the remaining spheres, however, were far more perplexing: a polyhedral construct of sharp crystal, a series of multicolored concentric circles crisscrossed with looping spirals, a geometric structure of spheres and multicolored lines arranged in concentric hexagons, an ivory city crowned by a crystal rose. The spheres were connected by a path of brilliant blue and red stars that ascended the mountain in a serpentine switchback, ending in a cube-shaped structure at the summit surrounded by a nimbus of golden light.

Trielle turned to Garin. "Is that the road that you've been talking about?"

"Yes, it is," he replied. "I've been studying this ever since I left the Oneirographicon. It seems clear that the lowest sphere is the Conclave, but I'm not sure exactly what the other spheres represent. Are they places? Concepts? And the road… It almost seems as if it leads out of the cosmos altogether. Also," he added, "look here."

Garin pointed to a shadow between the second and third spheres where the road seemed to momentarily vanish. The shadowed region formed a chasm that divided the bottom two spheres from the rest of the mountain, a rift in the otherwise smooth continuity of the image.

"I don't know what to make of this," he said with a frown, "but I think it's important."

Trielle studied the shadow for a few moments, then shook her head. "Garin, I'm sorry, but I don't know what to make of this at all. Part of me wants to believe that this map means something, but the only part that I can even begin to comprehend is the image of the Conclave at the bottom. If there is any truth to be learned here it was meant for you, not me."

Trielle paused for a moment. "Garin," she said finally, "are you sure, really sure, that this is anything more than an odd dream? And what if it is? How can we use it? Where does the road even begin?"

Garin stood in silent thought. "Trielle," he said at last, "perhaps I am going mad. Don't think I haven't considered that. Perhaps this map is nothing more than a foolish expression of my hope that this dying world is not all there is. But at this point, with Vai extinguished and the other suns on their way to the same fate, I guess I'd rather investigate a foolish hope than just give up. And if it is real, if there truly is a story that the world tells by itself, if the world truly does have some sort of intrinsic meaning, then we've lost something valuable and need to get it back. And," he added," we do know where the road begins."

Garin gestured at the image, enlarging and recentering it until the first sphere filled the entire hologram and the worlds of the Conclave lay stretched out before them.

I can see them all, she thought in amazement. *Latis, Garuda, Delphos… What kind of dream has this much detail?*

Then that she noticed the road. When the image was smaller the road had appeared to stop at the edge of the sphere that contained the Conclave, but now she could see that it continued inside it; smaller, diminished in both size and grandeur, but still intact. Trielle's eyes followed the road as it curved gently between the entropy clouds and finally ended at a small, nameless world near the outer rim.

"This is what I need your help with, Trielle," said Garin. "I need to get to that planet. If the road exists at all, it starts there."

Trielle thought for a moment. "All the worlds in the Conclave have at least one Kinetorium."

Garin frowned, considering this. "But this is an abandoned world," he said. "You saw the images from my dream: the broken buildings, the cracked pavement. Why would anyone maintain a Kinetorium there?"

"It might not be maintained," she said, "but it still has to be operational. Think about it," she continued. "The orbits that the Conclave worlds take around the three suns are artificial. It's one of the first things we learned in planetary kinetics. And the orbits are maintained by the interplanetary gravitic interactions created by the laridian rings housed in the Kinetoria. They're the largest stable ring systems on most worlds. I doubt there will be a direct route, but there should be a sequence of fixed transit corridors that can lead you there."

Garin nodded, the hint of a smile forming on his lips.

Chapter 5: The Edge of the Abyss

Garin and Trielle stood before the primary infochryst of the Scintillus Kinetorium. They left their home this morning as they always did, taking the ether chariot to Latis' lightside as if on their way to classes at the Arx. But here their paths would diverge; Trielle going about her usual day while Garin traveled the transit corridors in an attempt to look for a way to the nameless world.

If it even existed…

There was always the possibility of the Arx Scientia noting Garin's absence, but after discussing other possibilities it still seemed the best approach as it gave Garin an entire day to search the gravitic transit web before he would be expected back at home.

Standing before the infochryst Garin reflected on Trielle's final concern.

"What if it is real," she had said, "and you feel compelled to take the road. What should I do?"

Garin had responded in as reassuring a tone as he could muster. "Trielle, if the road truly leads outside of space, then it should lead outside of time as well. The trip may take no time at all from your perspective, no matter how long it may seem for me."

In truth, however, he was worried also. After all, he had no real idea of what relationships between space and time were even possible. They trip may take no time at all from Trielle's perspective, but he could just as easily envision the superspace and supertime that obtained outside their universe as being somehow slower and more unchanging. For all he knew, a minute there could take centuries in Trielle's framework.

53

I made a commitment, he told himself firmly, gathering his courage for what he had to do. *Even if it was only a dream. I have to look.*

"Garin," said Trielle, bringing his attention back to reality. "Look at this map. It's immense. How will we find what we're looking for?"

The infochryst displayed a rotating three dimensional map of the entire Conclave, nearly ten thousand worlds intricately arranged over a sixty-five thousand light-minute volume all orbiting each other in a vast puzzle of motion. It was relatively easy to locate Latis. As the most central world of the Conclave, and their home location, the map highlighted it in brilliant blue. Below the map, a projected box of text displayed the names of the planets immediately accessible by Latis's main transit corridors and offered to trace a pattern of corridors between Latis and any other world a traveler could name. And therein lay the problem, for the map of Garin's dream, while intricate in its detail, failed to provide the name of the world for which he searched.

Garin closed his eyes, summoning the image of the Conclave from his dream-map. Although he had brought the Oneirograph with him he did not wish to draw undue attention to himself before the journey actually began, and was thankful for the sleepless hours he had spent committing the portion of the map that depicted the Conclave to memory the night before. Looking again at the infochryst, Garin took control of the map's orientation from Trielle and began to rotate and resize it, shifting the image about in an attempt to orient it in the same way as the dream-map.

The enormity of the task quickly became apparent. The infochryst's map was three-dimensional and exhaustive, containing all the worlds of the Conclave, while the dream-map was a two-dimensional projection containing only a

54

small number of worlds. Even knowing that the dream-map was drawn above the rotational axes of the suns did not help as the Infochryst steadfastly refused to show the entropy clouds to which the dream-map had been oriented. The number of possibilities, while finite, was too high to be searched in a week let alone one morning.

Garin sighed in frustration.

"The world you seek is named Sha-Ka-Ri, first of the forsaken. But in aeons past it was known by another name."

The words startled Garin, and he snapped his head around to see who had spoken. Behind him stood the old man that had accosted him a few days earlier. He wore the same shapeless, tattered robe, its folds concealing all but his head, hands and feet. Though the material of the robe was still stained and dirty, Garin noticed that in several small patches the stains had been removed, allowing glimpses of the robe's original purity to show through. Despite his best attempts not to, Garin found himself staring at the man's face, wrinkled and timeless with the apparent burden of untold centuries. Then Garin noticed that not all of the wrinkles looked natural; some appeared too white, too linear, as if caused by an outside force.

Are those… scars?

The old man met Garin's gaze, the black pools of his eyes reflecting unseen lights, and Garin realized that his expression was quite different than when they first met. Lighter and more vibrant, it was as if the age he wore had somehow become a little less burdensome.

"Young one," the old man repeated with a stern but compassionate tone. "The time is short. If you would seek Sha-Ka-Ri and the Sovereign Road, you must do so now. It is later than you think!"

Caught off guard by the directness of the old man's approach, Garin could only nod wordlessly.

The old man began to move toward the infochryst with a swift stride that seemed somehow incongruous with his age.

"Wait," called Trielle, hints of concern and fear surfacing in her words. "What do you mean?"

"I mean what I say," said the old man sternly. "The time grows short and even now he begins to move against us. Soon the path will close."

With several deft movements the old man reoriented the infochryst map. He then entered a series of text commands, and in response a world on the very edge of the vast orbiting structure of the Conclave began to pulse with a dull orange light.

"That is Sha-Ka-Ri," declared the old man.

From the shining blue world of Latis, a series of linked lines began forming between worlds, inexorably leading to the orange globe at the Conclave's edge. The first four links were bright green, the next three yellow, and the last a dark red. Garin nodded, recognizing the color scheme. Green represented the mighty arteries of folded space-time that served as the main transit corridors of the Conclave, while yellow represented lesser paths that lead to worlds with minimal to no population. Red represented stabilization corridors, rough gravitic ties intended only to bind worlds together in stable orbits. They were never intended to handle living traffic.

Garin carefully examined the route, committing it to memory, then turned again to face the old man.

"This is not a path that the Conclave desires any to take," said the old man. "For although none but we know of the Sovereign Road, there are secrets on Sha-Ka-Ri and the other forbidden worlds that the Lords of the Conclave wish to remain buried."

"Secrets? Other forbidden worlds?" said Trielle. "If the Conclave is concerned about these worlds then why doesn't it simply release them from the gravitic web and let them fall into the suns or the entropy clouds?"

"Can a man ever truly destroy his own history?" asked the old man cryptically. "Now come! The time for questions has passed."

The old man swiftly strode from the infochryst and entered a nearby elevator, Garin and Trielle close behind. The elevator rose swiftly into the heart of the Kinetorium, depositing them on a broad imagnite walkway that led inward to the black sphere at the Kinetorium's heart. Ahead, Garin could see a circular distortion in space where the walkway met the wall of the sphere. A few moments later they stood at the foot of Angara Gate, a titanic whirlpool of darkness and blueshifted gravitic force that marked the entrance point to one of the great conduits traversing the Conclave: the first step to Sha-Ka-Ri.

Faced with the gate's immensity, Garin felt a pang of fear. He had used travel conduits before, of course. Almost everyone in the Conclave had. Yet he could not escape the conviction that this gate represented the first in a series of thresholds that would take him away from everything he had ever known. There, staring into that swirling vortex, he realized that everything he had experienced until now had been intellectual play, a dream that, had he wished, he could always wake from. But what lay beyond may well be the dream become reality, a reality that, once seen, could never be ignored again. He turned toward the old man, his eyes wide with apprehension.

The old man nodded, and placed his hand on Garin's shoulder. A curious strength seemed to flow from his touch, and the fear began to subside. Suddenly the old man seemed to grow taller, his form taking on a grave authority that seemed to fill the Kinetorium with its presence.

"Garin," said the old man in a thundering voice, "I charge you to seek the road and follow it to its end. Travel to Sha-Ka-Ri, there I will meet you and guide you to the Sovereign Road's beginning. Do you accept this charge?"

Garin looked quickly to the side, expecting to find a gathering crowd drawn by the strange proceedings, but the bustling traffic of the Kinetorium continued as if nothing were unusual.

Garin took a deep breath and nodded a wordless yes.

Trielle moved as if to speak, but Garin quieted her with a gesture.

"I'm going Trielle," he said firmly, "you and I both know that. I don't know how long I'll be gone, but please, wait for me."

With that, Garin turned and strode toward Angara Gate. Then he paused, facing the old man for one last set of questions.

"Sir," said Garin, "You never told us who you were. We don't even know your name. And… why do you call it the Sovereign Road?"

"You may call me Kyr," said the old man simply. "That will do for now. As for who I am… That must be discovered, not told. As for the road, it is called sovereign for it is the first road, and thus king and master of all roads. And," he added with the faintest hint of a smile, "it is in many ways the only road worth taking."

Inexplicably comforted by the cryptic words, Garin laughed briefly before giving a final goodbye to Trielle and stepping into the conduit.

***

Trielle watched as Garin entered Angara Gate. His image blueshifted, seemed to hang for a moment in suspended animation, and then surged down the conduit wreathed by flashes of gravitic flame. An instant later he was gone.

I hope, for his sake, that he is right, she thought absently, and then froze, a deeper understanding of what it would mean if he was correct suddenly trickling through her mind like an icy rivulet coursing across a melting glacier.

Suddenly something touched her and she jumped in surprise. Snapping her head around, she saw Kyr's bony hand resting on her shoulder. He was looking directly at her, the deep pools of his eyes filled with evident compassion.

"Young one," he said, "You do not need to speak of it for me to see the concern that you bear for your brother. If I could, I would allay those fears, but to do so would be a lie. Nonetheless he must be sent."

The words sounded warm and comforting, and yet the seeming callousness of their import coiled around her heart like a snake.

"You make it sound so easy," she said, trying to contain her emotions. "Why Garin? Why now? You've just told me that you've sent him into danger."

Kyr sighed, his eyes growing moist. "You do not understand as your brother does," he said finally. "He senses, even if he does not know why, that you all are in danger. And he is correct in this. I have sent him because he alone has the vision to see through the lies that surround you all and the courage to seek the truth."

Trielle shook her head. "The courage to seek the truth," she muttered to herself. "What is truth anyway?"

59

"You are not the first to have asked me that," said Kyr, his eyes distant, "though you ask it with more honesty."

"Well," she said, gesturing toward Angara Gate, "if he must go, then aren't you at least going with him like you promised."

"I am," Kyr said simply, "but I will not use the conduits. In truth, I would not have sent Garin by means of the conduits if there had been any other way, but the means by which I travel would be impossible for him in his current state. I would advise that the entire Conclave cease using them as well," he added, "for it is they, and other gravitic technologies like them, that are slowly unraveling the spacetime of your cosmos."

Trielle's eyes narrowed.

Surely this is too much, she thought. *Gravitics unraveling our cosmos? This is the very definition of madness!*

As she considered the possibility of Kyr's insanity the tension mounting within her drained away and she began to relax. After all, if Kyr was mad, then Garin was in no real danger and would return tonight with no more injury than a slight loss of dignity.

"You are skeptical of this," said Kyr, the hint of a smile forming on his face. "Good! You will need that skepticism in the days ahead, for true skeptics question because they desire the truth above all else, even when that truth contradicts their long-cherished notions. You see, young one, I have a charge for you as well. As your brother seeks to understand that which lies beyond and gives meaning to the world, you must seek out the truth of that which is poisoning it from within. You have both talked, have you not, about the lies surrounding the death of Vai?"

Trielle nodded, her eyes widening at the implications of his words.

How had he known?

"Then know also that these lies go deeper still. You have often questioned the workings of the laridian rings and other gravitic technology. Seek those answers now with open eyes and an open mind! Believe me when I tell you that behind Vai's death, the impending dissolution of this cosmos, and your Conclave's own past stands the same deception."

Trielle opened her mouth to protest, but was silenced with a gesture from Kyr's hand. His eyes flashed with blue fire.

"You may disbelieve me, young one, but I can see the workings of your mind and know you better than you know yourself. Search out the answers to prove me wrong. Search the answers to prove me right. It does not matter. In the end the truth will stand for itself. But do not ignore this charge, for when your brother returns he will have need of the fruit of your labors. How can he return and bring meaning to this world if there is no world left to return to?"

With that Kyr walked swiftly away. A crowd of travelers quickly surged into the gap between them, and when it had dissipated he was gone. Trielle sighed and began the journey to the Arx Scientia, alone with her thoughts. She did not know where to begin.

Chapter 6: All Skies Afire

With a sound like breaking glass the churning void surrounding Garin shattered, and he found himself once again in the light. A sickly, nauseous feeling flooded through him, and he dropped to his knees, breathing deeply as a red haze clouded his vision. After a few moments the feeling subsided and he rose again to his feet.

He stood at the top of a high hill, surrounded by the shattered remains of an ancient kinetorium that overlooked the dull green waters of a long-dead sea. An ancient highway led down the hill a short distance before curving around behind it in a long spiral, its surface fractured by the combined weight of millennia.

Is this Sha-Ka-Ri?

He had traversed the first four conduits easily. Connecting important worlds of the Conclave, these were major transit arteries with only a minimum of gravitic turbulence. He had not even needed to emerge from the kinetoria at each stop, as the next gate often lay right beside the one from which he had emerged. Vanth the golden, Shem-tov of the four moons, Moragoor of the emerald mountains; once he would have reveled in the opportunity to explore each, and if it wasn't for the haste urged upon him by Kyr he would have done so now. But his mission was clear. He did not know how much time he had before the entrance to the Sovereign Road was lost. Each moment counted.

The next three worlds had much lower populations, giving them the luxury of building their kinetoria at great distances from the main cities. Instead of the ornate gravitic containment domes of emerald and brass needed on the fully urbanized worlds, these were much simpler structures. Bowl-shaped slopes of unadorned imagnite opened heavenward, surrounding a ring of delicate buttresses that supported the central obsidian sphere like white hands holding out an offering. This open architecture afforded a marvelous view of the skies, and on each world Garin had stolen what upward glances his haste would allow.

Shar-apsu had skies of amber in which great swarms of golden-scaled winged wyrms flew among the clouds. The skies of Borag were filled with the planet's vast silver ring system, an impossible arch of metallic brightness that soared from horizon to horizon. Each world called out for Garin to stay, inviting him to explore its particular richness, but he resolutely maintained his pace.

Despite the openness of the architecture finding the next three conduits had been difficult. These were anchored by smaller laridian rings set in out of the way locations within the Kinetoria, places far from the central sphere. Traversing those conduits had been an exercise in fortitude, as the gravitic turbulence increased the further he traveled from the Conclave's heart. Each transit had left him dizzy and nauseous, a feeling that had often only begun to dissipate as he reached the next conduit.

But the final passage had been the worst. After what seemed like hours of searching he had at last found the anchor point in a utility sub-basement of the Xothian kinetorium. The laridian ring was cracked, in some places so badly that the glowing red mesh of spinning neutronium rings powering the device's field was visible. The mouth of the conduit was partially obscured by tidal distortions and the telltale jerking movements of advanced gravitic slippage. Unsure that this last gate was traversable by living things, Garin had stared for long moments into the erratically shifting vortex before finally plunging in. It had been, but just barely.

A hot, burning, wind blew against his face, bringing with it the mingled taste of salt and dust. Unsure where to go next, Garin stared out over the lifeless waters of the sea. As he watched its shining green surface pulsing and churning like iridescent poison, something about its color began to seem unsettlingly familiar. Then a wave of cold fear surged through his body as understanding dawned. Heart pounding, Garin raised his eyes to the heavens and saw the pulsing viridian wall of the entropy clouds spanning the skies from horizon to horizon. They seemed almost close enough to touch.

I'm standing on a condemned world, thought Garin, and he shivered despite the heat.

"You have arrived. Good."

The voice startled Garin, and he turned to see Kyr standing beside the laridian ring. Garin opened his mouth to speak, but Kyr silenced him with a gesture.

"I know that there is much you wish to know, but believe me when I tell you that now is not the time for such knowledge. You have no doubt seen the skies of this place. This world is but hours from being consumed. There is no time to…"

Suddenly Kyr was cut off by a shrieking sound that came from behind Garin, a sound like the wailing of a condemned soul. Whipping his head around, Garin's eyes widened in terror as a serpentine coil of flaring green light uncoiled from the main mass of the entropy clouds and shrieked downward toward the sea. It struck like the tail of a scorpion, a spear of violent force that at once collapsed the sea toward it and blasted it explosively away in a hurricane of vaporized water and rock. Waves churned. A fountain of water, steam, and magma spurted into the atmosphere out of

64

the void created by the entropy streamer. The clouds above seemed to boil with greater ferocity, as if driven by an unseen purpose, and Garin could not escape the sense that they were closer than they had been.

"He knows," said Kyr grimly. "He will try to keep us from the gate. We can afford to wait no longer."

Kyr strode from the Kinetorium, following the ancient road as it curled around the bulk of the great hill. He did not run, but Garin quickly found it difficult to keep up with his pace and soon was out of breath. As they rounded the hill a ruined city, vast and ancient, came into view. It only took Garin moments to realize that this was the city of his dreams. Seconds later another violent shriek sounded behind him and Garin turned to see the tail of a second entropy streamer as it crashed into the sea. A tremor shuddered through the rocks beneath him a few moments later, as if the streamer were burrowing through the planet's crust. Garin looked forward and saw that Kyr was already quite far down the hill; his distraction had already cost him needed time. Breaking into a sprint, Garin finally caught up to the old man as he reached the foot of the hill and together they entered the outskirts of the city.

Abandoned in an age long past, its buildings were gutted shells of shattered glass and twisted steel. Strange alien vines clung to the sides of the ruins, their tips covered in curious yellow flowers of a type that Garin had never seen before. They moved further and further into the city's heart, Kyr blazing a path through the twisting streets and alleys without a moment's hesitation. The ruins grew taller and closer together, seeming to intertwine into a soaring jungle of twisted steel, fractured concrete, and jagged shadow. Twice more Garin heard the shrieking wail of entropy streamers in the distance, but he did not stop again. Then a deep, low boom sounded behind them, followed by an actinic flash of blue light. Suddenly Garin felt an odd lurching sensation, as if the planet was shuddering on its axis. Kyr stopped and, without a word, pointed behind them in the direction of the now-distant hill from whence they had come. Garin turned and saw the fractured remains of the hill transfixed by a writhing spear of wicked green flame. A slowly expanding shell of shadowy gravitic distortion surrounded the fire, lit from within by flashing sparks of deep blue.

"He has destroyed the anchoring ring," said Kyr, "No time is left to us. We must run! Now!"

Garin understood the implications of Kyr's words. Without the laridian ring to anchor Sha-Ka-Ri to the Conclave's gravitic network, the planet would be cast adrift into the entropy clouds. He needed no further urging.

Garin broke out into a run, following Kyr through the twisting boulevards and alleys as the world continued to shudder and lurch around them. More than once Garin fell to his knees as the ground shook with tremors, each one stronger than the last. Above, flashes of viridian light burst and crackled like diseased meteors, and a dull wailing sound seemed to hover at the verge of hearing.

Then the fire-rain began, blazing orbs of flaring green light that fell from the boiling sky like hailstones. Their very touch negated any matter they contacted, explosively driving its subatomic components apart at superluminal speed. For a seeming eternity Garin twisted and turned, dodging cracked pavement, crumbing ruins, and the fiery exhalations of the angry heavens as he struggled to follow Kyr. Then the narrow confines of the streets opened into a wide plaza surrounded by crumbling pillars and walls of decayed masonry that somehow seemed even more ancient than the glass and steel ruins they had left behind. At the far side of the square stood a soaring edifice of brick and dressed stone crowned by two shattered domes of blue tile that flashed a pale turquoise in the unearthly light. The plaza was strangely free of the fiery rain, though the boiling energies overhead promised that this was at best a short reprieve.

Without breaking stride Kyr ran across the plaza and entered the building through an arched gateway. Garin followed close behind, and soon they had threaded their way through the dark entrance foyer and stood in a great hall. Here soaring pillars framed intricately carved statues and ornate frescoes, the fractured images depicting ancient men with golden light resting upon their heads, their hands raised in silent benediction. At the end of the hall a yawning archway opened into a vast rotunda that flickered with green light. Within this rotunda stood a smaller structure of carved stone festooned with gold and silver, its architecture strangely different from the rest of the building. A single, low door opened in its side, and moments later Kyr and Garin stood before that door, gazing at a weathered slab of cold stone that lay within. Kyr studied the slab intently for a moment, his eyes narrowed in thought, and then looked up through the shattered dome at the whirling maelstrom of destruction seething above. A single tear trickled down his face.

Garin stretched out his hand, touching Kyr's shoulder in a gesture of comfort. He did not know the source of Kyr's emotion, and could only surmise that some event of great import in his life had transpired here.

But surely this ancient city, this even more ancient building, came from eras immeasurably older than Kyr...

As Garin pondered this his mind was filled with a mixture of fear and wonder, and he realized how very little he knew of the one whom he had followed to this place.

Then Kyr stepped forward, entered the structure and stood before the slab of stone.

67

"At this site," he said sternly, "millennia ago, a great tragedy took place that brought hope to the cosmos. Here is the center of all worlds, the beginning of all true roads. The entranceway to the Sovereign Road lies before you. Now I ask you, son of man, do you trust me?"

Garin opened his mouth to speak and then hesitated as fear rose within him. Could he trust Kyr? How could he be certain? Then again, Kyr seemed to know so much about him. He had followed him this far. Could he even turn back if he wanted to? Another violent tremor shook the ground, and Garin jumped as tiles the size of dinner plates crashed to the floor from the shattered dome above. He had no choice; he had to decide now.

"I think so, yes," he said, his voice quavering with uncertainly.

Kyr stared at him for a moment, his eyes transfixing him with their piercing gaze as if he was somehow looking into the depths of Garin's soul. Then he nodded.

"It is enough."

Turning swiftly, Kyr knelt on the cold floor of the chamber, his hands raised skyward. Then he took a deep breath, opened his mouth wide, and began to sing.

The song erupted from his throat like a golden wave, its harmonies telling of a gleaming time long past when the morning stars cried out for joy and newborn worlds danced in their light. It rose in a vast crescendo, its power filling the low structure in which Kyr knelt with an almost palpable presence. Then the song surged outward in a great rush, bursting the structure apart before soaring upward into the tortured skies above the shattered dome of the rotunda. As the song ascended the light filtering downward through the shattered dome changed, the once furious green hue replaced with a soft silver gleam. In wonder Garin looked up and saw a velvet sky strewn with

68

stars, nebulae, and wheeling galaxies. The beauty of the sight smote Garin to the core, and he found himself on his knees weeping for what the worlds had lost. As in his dream, that sky descended around him in a soft silver rain of starlight and blackness, its substance changing and hardening into a pavement for him to walk on: the Sovereign Road.

Garin's eyes followed the road as it stretched toward the walls of the rotunda, and he realized that he could still see the road even when it traveled beyond them. It was as if the road was somehow more real than the matter of the buildings around him.

"Take my hand, young one, if you truly trust me," said Kyr as he rose to his feet. "If we hesitate longer, we will yet be lost. Only on the road will we be shielded from the entropy storms. Now run! Sha-Ka-Ri is lost!"

As if to punctuate his words the planet shuddered. Great cracks shivered through the stone of the floor, and a roar followed by a flash of green light blasted downward through the broken dome. Garin risked a quick glance upward. His eyes widened as he saw the death of worlds bearing down upon them, and without hesitation he took Kyr's hand and set off down the road.

As he approached the wall of the rotunda his body passed through it as if the stones were nothing but mist. With each step the tumult lessened. Around him the endless rain of green fire continued, dissolving ruins, stones, and the very air in its relentless onslaught, yet here he was safe, and the streamers of green fire seemed insubstantial as they passed through the flesh of his hands.

The road continued to double back, rising swiftly into the skies until the entire planet could be seen. Here the true size of the entropy clouds became apparent, a vast wall of destruction larger than a million stars. He watched as

Sha-Ka-Ri was inexorably drawn into the chaos, the planet slowly losing cohesion as its base matter dissolved.

"The death of a world is a thing of great sorrow," said Kyr as great tears rolled down his face. "It was never meant to be this way, you know. He tried with all his might to come against us this time."

"Who?" Garin asked. "Who is it that you're talking about?"

"The Shadow," said Kyr. He paused for a moment before adding, "if only he would come home…"

A few steps more down the road and the whole of the material cosmos receded from them like an ebbing tide. Soon Garin sensed the crossing of an unseen gate, a portal in some vast shell that surrounded the universe, then they were through into the space beyond, climbing an endless switchback on a mountain made of stars and darkness, the folded surface of penultimate time and space.

The road was sometimes difficult to see against this backdrop, its course only discernible by the marked contrast between the dimmer red stars that formed the bulk of its substance and the brighter blue and white stars of the mountain itself. After a time that seemed both longer than an aeon and shorter than the pause between heartbeats a crystal sphere appeared in the distance. With each step it grew exponentially larger, until at last its gleaming walls loomed before them like ramparts of diamond.

One final step and they were through. The walls fell away, and all around them was strangeness.

Book Two: The World, and the Seed of Its Desecration...

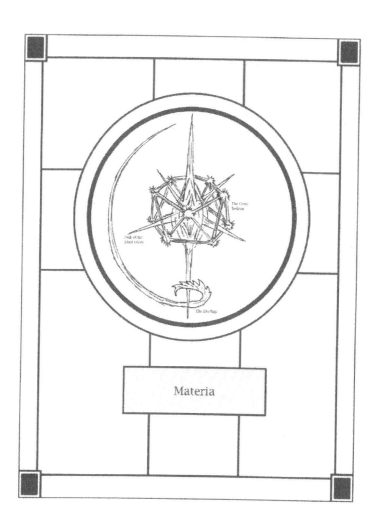

Materia

Chapter 7: Pawns of the Emptiness

The Omegahedron soared above the city of Scintillus. Grown from a single crystal of perfect obsidian blackness, the immense tower stabbed skyward from the surface of Latis like a sacrificial blade, its tip pointed at the three suns as if poised to eviscerate the heart of the cosmos. Within its highest pinnacle stood the throne room of the Five Heirophants, the rulers of the Conclave of Ten Thousand Worlds. Each throne was carved from a single gem, its color chosen to reflect the identity of the hierophant for which it had been made.

The thrones were arranged in a wide circle further surrounded by the ring of angular black pillars that supported the obsidian dome crowning the throne room. The pillars, floors, and walls were intricately interwoven with crystalline emission fibers extending from the Omegahedron's forty core infochrysts, transforming each surface into a three-dimensional display that could, at a gesture, spring to life with any sort of information or imagery that the Heirophants needed for their deliberations. Within the ring of thrones stood a low mass of amethyst crystal that shone with a strange writhing light as if a network of living fire burned just beneath its surface. This was the Great Psychochryst, a device empowered by the Conclave noeticists with the ability to instantly read and interpret the movements, expression, and thoughts of those who occupied the thrones, transferring them to the infochrysts below.

Gedron had always hated the psychochryst. It somehow left him feeling violated whenever he used it, as if he could not keep even the smallest thought to himself. But such was the price of being a hierophant.

With swift strides Gedron entered the chamber, dressed in the full regalia of a High Gravitist. His chest was adorned with a breastplate of blue crystal shaped like a manifold of hyperbolic curvature, the symbolic representation of the spacetime of the Conclave. His arms and legs were swathed in deep purple robes, and on his head sat the Miter of Hawking surrounded by a clear crystal torus, a stylized model of a laridian ring. He ascended a throne of purest sapphire carved with the myriad equations that defined the force of gravity and all its perturbations.

Named after the fundamental force of gravity, the High Gravitist was responsible for the laridian ring system that made interworld transportation possible, bound the worlds of the Conclave together in one immense yet stable system of interlocking orbits, and allowed for large-scale planetary engineering. Given the importance of the laridian ring system, the High Gravitist was often seen as the most powerful member of the Conclave, and Gedron had longed for the position ever since he learned of his particular gifting in the gravitic sciences as a youth. The ladder of power and success in the Conclave was both high and broad; all citizens could aspire to the highest office, but few had the intellect, skill, and tenacity to ascend its full length.

Climbing that ladder had taken almost the entirety of Gedron's life, and now that he had arrived at the top, he felt as if he should be more satisfied with his achievement than he actually was. As he considered the choices he had made to sit in the sapphire throne a parade of images flashing through his mind: Family events he had missed, friends he had ignored, holes left in his heart by stillborn memories that now could never be.

And now, Garin was missing.

Trielle had done her best to assure Gedron and his wife Dyana that Garin had left for completely legitimate reasons, but the lack of specificity in Trielle's words, coupled with her barely concealed discomfort as she delivered them, left Gedron with the clear impression that she was holding something back. Garin was of age, and the laws of the Conclave afforded him the right to take his life in whatever direction he desired, but Gedron still wished that he had at least said goodbye before departing. Still, he was not surprised.

If my father had missed as much of my life as I have of Garin's, I'd have done the same thing myself.

The writhing streaks of fire within the Great Psychochryst began to flare as the device performed its initial calibration. Gedron took a deep breath, striving to calm his mind in anticipation of the other Hierophants' arrival. It would not do to show weakness when their minds were linked in Conclave, not given the task that lay ahead of them.

A few moments later Erskilion of Garuda, the Photocanth, entered the chamber. His golden breastplate bore the Crest of the Dual Waves and his headpiece was adorned with a clear crystal pillar that crackled with trapped lightning. The Heirophant of Electromagnetism, the Photocanth was responsible for maintaining the Conclave's power and entertainment networks. His throne was hewn from a single topaz inscribed with the equations governing light and radiation.

The Chromatocron, Heirophant of the Strong Nuclear Force, entered next. His breastplate was of a deep red, bearing the Insignia of the Hexapolar Chromatic Field. Upon his head was a great shimmering disk that shifted between a spectrum of all colors and a pellucid whiteness. His throne was carved from three rubies of differing hue, each inscribed with the gauge equations describing the chromodynamic interactions that were the source of matter's fundamental cohesion. The philosophical leader of the Conclave, he was responsible for both the psychological forces that bound society together and the ongoing vitality of the three suns themselves: the physical heart of Conclave space.

Human by descent, his name was Tauron of Latis. Once Gedron had counted him a friend, but after Tauron's elevation to hierophant their relationship had soured. Now they subsisted in a weary competition, circling each other like moons in slowly decaying orbits, each waiting for the other to fall from the sky. Gedron sighed. Given the subject of today's deliberations, it would be impossible to avoid working with him.

Immediately following him was a small, furtive gelasian named Silindii: the current Ouranos Radii, Heirophant of the Weak Nuclear Force. As the representative of the cosmological force of transformation, the Ouranos Radii was the ultimate overseer of commerce, trade, and the biocomputational sciences. Strangely enough he also was responsible for the maintenance of the suns, as the fusion reactions that sustained them resulted from an interplay between both Strong and Weak Nuclear Forces. He entered the chamber wearing the emerald breastplate of his office upon which the Gem of the Four Transformations glistened with churning, clashing colors. Upon his head was a dull crown edged by two sharp spikes of transparent crystal, a shimmering energy field that split and shifted the ambient light like a desert mirage dancing between them. He crossed the chamber quickly and ascended a throne shaped from a curious amalgam of emeralds and gold and inscribed with the equations of nucleonic transformation.

Finally the last Heirophant entered the chamber. Known simply as the Entrope, he did not dress in the same manner as the others but instead wore a long black robe unadorned by any symbol or device. A dark cowl covered his head, partially concealing the gaunt and withered deathmask of his face, and in his hand he carried a bone-white staff whose tip burned with sickly green holographic fire.

Representative of Entropy, the relentless cosmic force of disorder that one day would sweep the works of the Conclave into the abyss, his position carried with it no societal responsibility. Rather, his role was to gaze, day after day, into the entropy clouds and draw from their chaotic violence some principle of guidance with which to direct the Heirophants' deliberations. Even his throne was built to embody that chaos, a throne not of gems, but of polished white bone inscribed with a scrawl of philosophical notations that embodied the essence of pure meaninglessness, the eventual state of all things.

Unlike the others, who had attained their positions through personal merit, no one knew from whence the Entrope came. Gedron had heard rumors from the others: rumors of a secret chamber beneath the Omegahedron where even now a child was slowly being prepared as the Entrope's successor, rumors of a pool of green fluid that suspended the faculties and poured information gathered from the entropy clouds directly into the brain, allowing the Entrope to commune directly with the destructive forces within them.

Gedron shuddered as the Entrope ascended his throne, remembering times in conclave when the Entrope had seemed to reach through the Great Psychochryst into his mind, infecting it with bleak, meaningless thoughts that had threatened to shred the very foundations of his sanity. While he knew abstractly that dissolution was the ultimate destiny of the universe, something within him still fought back and refused to accept it. Yet the Entrope seemed to embrace and glory in that dissolution. Gedron disliked the other Heirophants to some degree but at least he understood their ambitions and motives. The Entrope, however, was incomprehensible, even frightening, to him.

The psychochryst flashed one last time and Gedron felt the collective thoughtspace of the Heirophants form around him, veiling his perceptions in a mist of pure information. As he watched, softly gleaming halos that pulsed with rippling bands of color condensed from that mist around each of the Heirophant's heads: their emotions and thoughts given visible form. In the strange half-light cast by the halos each face seemed to unfold with new dimensions and nuances of meaning. Only the Entrope remained inscrutable; his face as still as a deathmask, his halo a featureless black.

"Colleagues, let us join our minds in conclave!"

Transmitted through the Great Psychochryst, the Chromatocron's call echoed in Gedron's head like a memory of thunder. It was soon followed by a rustling murmur of assent from the other Heirophants. Satisfied, the Chromatocron raised his right hand and the infographic surfaces within the chamber flashed, caught fire, and lit up with holographic radiance. The walls of the Omegahedron seemed to unfold around them. There was a sense of immense velocity, a vision of the blackness of space rushing past them like a dark wind, and then, brilliance.

The five thrones now appeared to stand on a ring of polished obsidian that slowly rotated at the very center of the three suns' orbits. Gedron was unsurprised; this was the typical place where deliberations began. But as the dark lifeless corpse of Vai slowly rotated into view an involuntary chill passed down his spine, and the color of his halo turned icy blue.

"You are disturbed, I see."

The words of the Chromatochron slid into his mind.

"And you are not?" answered Gedron, injecting a strong note of confidence into the transmission.

Focusing his attention inward, he forced the unease from his mind. As he did so his halo shifted in response, a deep red hue creeping along its outer rim and replacing the blue. It was time to take charge. Gedron turned his head, silently acknowledging the other Heirophants, and began his report.

"As is painfully clear to everyone, Vai has suffered a catastrophic failure of stellar energy production. I have spend the last few days examining the stellar corpse with all available instrument arrays, and our infochrysts quickly determined that the cause is at once simple, devastating, and, unfortunately, not unexpected. Given its current mass, Vai simply does not have enough fuel left to sustain fusion."

As Gedron finished transmitting his thoughts, his halo began to shine a deep gold, a color denoting both the gravity of the subject matter and the control he was now gaining over the attention of the Heirophants.

The Photocanth glared at Gedron, his halo a shifting combination of irenic green and accusatory vermilion.

"And how, might I ask, has this occurred?" he transmitted. "Prior to this event I, and the peoples of the Conclave, had understood that the three suns had enough fuel to last for centuries at the least."

Gedron sighed, his halo shifting to a dull silver as he steeled himself for what was to come.

"Unfortunately," he transmitted, "that has never been true. We have known that this event would occur within decades for some time now."

Though he transmitted no thoughts in response, the blush of fiery reds and cold blues that swept through the

Photocanth's halo betrayed his shock and confusion. His face remained impassive, but his eyes swept about the room, surveying the unchanged halos of the Chromatocron and the Ouranos Radii.

"You should not be surprised that you were not told this," transmitted the Chromatocron, his halo shifting to a pleasant green tone. "After all, yours is not the force that powers the suns. Indeed, we made certain that you did not know. How else could we be sure that knowledge of this was kept from the populace?"

The Photocanth was silent, his warring emotions sending brief slivers of sharp color through his halo.

"Very well," he transmitted curtly after a few moments. "And yet I will ask again. How is this possible? After all, surely you know the projected natural lifecycle of main-sequence stars. Long before Vai's fuel was exhausted it should have undergone the visible alterations brought about by helium fusion."

The Photocanth gestured briefly and a small, furiously burning model of a main-sequence star sprang to life in the center of the chamber. Another gesture and its evolution was accelerated a billionfold, the bright yellow orb rapidly swelling into a dull red giant before evaporating into a tiny, dense white dwarf.

"Vai," he added softly, "did not die in this way. Rather, it seems to have been snuffed out all at once, like a candle." As the Photocanth transmitted those words the white dwarf flickered and vanished like a flame assailed by the wind.

"You assume much."

The words had a peculiar quality, seeming at once uncertain and forceful. Gedron turned slighty and saw the halo of the Ouranos Radii spark with muted tones of white and violet.

"Surely you have been aware of the way in which these stars have been manipulated, their cores stirred by gravitic beams to generate an even mix of fuel. You must know this for it is your energy production needs that this process serves. Surely you know of the stellar mining, the removal of rich elements from the star's core for the development of the Conclave's outer worlds. How could you expect these things to have no effect on stellar evolution? No, my friend, there is nothing natural about these stars. Not anymore."

"Indeed," transmitted the Photocanth, his halo now shifting all the way to an angry vermillion. "I am well aware of this, but still fail to see how this could effect the lifespan of the star so profoundly."

The Photocanth gestured again and a web of complex calculations appeared in the air. The primary equations described the thermal equilibrium of Vai, the point at which gravity's inward pull was counterbalanced by the heat generated by fusing hydrogen at the star's core. A number of ancillary equations were arrayed around it, feeding historical statistics about the various elements mined from Vai's core over its lifespan into the main argument. The results were clear. The effect of this mining on Vai should have been minor.

Gedron raised his hand in response and a final term inserted itself into the equations. Variables shifted and numbers slid as the model integrated the new data until finally a new balance was struck, an equation that described a star with a vastly shorter life.

"Neutronium," transmitted Gedron flatly, his halo flashing with gold-streaked blackness. "The missing variable is neutronium. It forms the core elements of all laridian rings. Where else could we have obtained it except the cores of the three suns? Ever since we won our independence from the *Alapsari*, our society has depended on a small but constant supply of neutronium forged from stellar plasma. Observe!"

Gedron issued a mental command and the cold, lifeless orb of Vai erupted into brilliant light. He again raised his hands, this time bringing them apart in a quick motion, and the now blazing sun swelled to gargantuan size, the four neutronium forges that orbited its equator quickly becoming visible. Spherical metallic constructs the size of small moons, each forge contained compression vessels used to turn stellar plasma into primary fluid neutronium as well as the pion phase reactors needed to convert this unstable substance into its longer-lived crystalline form. A titanic laridian ring was affixed to the starward surface of each forge, its gravitic beam continually siphoning dense material from the star's radiative layer and feeding it to the compression vessels.

"I have returned this image to a point over three millennia ago," transmitted Gedron. "As we have extracted more and more plasma the overall mass of the star has diminished, decreasing the pressure at the core."

Gedron brought his right hand down in a slow cutting motion and half of the star fell away to reveal Vai's inner structure, a thin shell of convecting gases surrounding a much thicker layer of near-solid plasma denser than gold with an orb of fusion-fire throbbing at its heart. It was immediately apparent that this burning core was slowly shrinking.

"If Vai had been allowed to age via natural processes," he continued, "the neutronium mining would have already lead to its death. The mass limit needed to sustain helium fusion was crossed two hundred years ago. To prevent this the College of Gravitists initiated a process of stellar agitation using the neutronium forge mass drivers to distribute the helium ash across the body of the star, providing more raw hydrogen to burn."

As he spoke the image of the star responded, hydrogen and helium gradients now highlighted in hues of red and yellow. As the core fires shrank almost to the point of extinguishment, the neutronium forges shifted, releasing their columns of stellar plasma to fall back to the star's surface. A few moments later, beams of spiralling blue force stabbed downward from each forge, driving deep into the stellar core, mixing the hydrogen and helium throughout the bulk of the star. As the gradients dissipated, the fires in the star flared and burned anew."

"Yes," snapped the Photocanth, his halo a mix of boiling red hues. "Even the children know this. But it does not explain the current crisis."

Gedron's halo flared blue and gold, but he did not reply. Instead he gently pointed toward the image of Vai. Despite the now near-even distribution of hydrogen throughout the star, the fires had again begun to burn lower. Though more of the stellar hydrogen was now available for burning, the inevitable buildup of helium could not be halted. The Heirophants watched as the helium to hydrogen ratios inexorably rose and the core fires shrank in response until, finally, they died entirely and the star went dark.

All understood. A threshold had been passed from which there may be no return.

"What of the other stars?" asked the Ouranos Radii. "How close are they to a similar fate?"

"Closer than I would like to comtemplate," replied Gedron solemnly, "but they may have as many as two hundred years left. They are smaller stars, but are younger overall and were not as heavily mined for neutronium as was Vai. Thus their mass has not suffered the same rate of depletion."

"And what do the infochrysts say as to the possibility of reignition?" asked the Ouranos Radii.

"The lesser infochrysts were silent regarding this," transmitted Gedron, "and so I brought the matter to the Rhamachrond device."

At this the other Heirophants imperceptibly leaned forward, their halos flushing with inquisitive blues and greens.

"While it could not offer certainty," continued Gedron, "the device indicated a small but real possibility that Vai's energy output could temporarily be restored if we were to launch a massive circumferential gravitic volley from the Conclave's largest ships. Such a blast would almost certainly hypercompress the core and initiate helium fusion. Once the compression is achieved, there is a chance, but only a chance, that the neutronium forge mass drivers alone could sustain the compression and keep the star burning. There is considerable uncertainty as to the exact hydrogen to helium ratio at the core, and small variances drastically affect the outcome. There is also," he added, "the issue of enhanced entropic activity. This would be the largest single discharge of gravitic energy since the Philosoph War, and we would do well to remember the cost. The backlash might even be great enough to overwhelm the influence of the other suns, perhaps even the Guard."

"But if the ignition were successful," transmitted the Photocanth, his halo shifting to a hopeful, pastel mauve. "If Vai's radiation pressure could be restored…"

"Yes," transmitted Gedron, his halo fading to a deep shade of grey. "But success is far from certain, and failure will cost us even more worlds then Vai's demise."

"As will a failure to act," replied the Chromatocron crisply. "Do not think that our society's current complacence will last if we do not move swiftly."

The Chromatocron's halo grew in brilliance as his thoughts echoed throughout the chamber, a filigree of golden threads shot through with darkness. "I too have consulted with the infochrysts, running patterns and models of the social ramifications of both possibilities. The processing load was great, and even great Nagmochron was slowed by the noetic burden of the simulations, but, unlike the data you have presented, High Gravitist, the results were clear."

The Chromatocron raised his hand and, with a sweeping motion, banished the image of Vai. A crystal sphere coalesced in its place, its interior filled with shifting scenes from across the Conclave. From past gatherings Gedron knew these to be projections derived from sociometric data, raw numbers transformed into simulations of the broad future movements of society. Though each scene showed a different world, all predicted the same future. The populace, gripped by an exponentially growing fear of the coming night, would begin to abandon basic societal roles until the underlying structures of the Conclave dissolved and the worlds descended into chaos."

"The predictions of the Nagmochron infochryst were unequivocal," transmitted the Chromatocron grimly. "Though all know of our cosmos' imminent demise, few think of it frequently. And why should they? We have told them repeatedly that it is both unavoidable and several generations away, and thus does not directly affect them as individuals. Yet the death of Vai has changed this. Now the idea insidiously grows among the populace that this may be the terminal generation. You speak of the death of worlds, High Gravitist, yet I ask you whether it is worse to die unexpectedly in the infinite dissolution of the entropy clouds, or to die of despair while yet alive?"

Gedron was silent. He knew that in the end it would come to this. As he brooded, his halo thinned and darkened, seeming almost to vanish. "What of your considerations, Photocanth," he transmitted at last. "Do the information flows on the primary communications channels support the Nagmochron's prognostications?"

"They do indeed," replied the Photocanth. "Already there is a shift in the information content of most private transmissions away from the typical discussions of money and pleasure. More and more have taken a fearful and despairing tone. Even now I am receiving data from the Radithesia and Ionocaric infochrysts indicating that this trend is growing, and is projected to climb exponentially. No," he added after a moment, "the Nagmochron Infochryst's predictions do not surprise me in the least."

Gedron sensed that the tide was moving swiftly toward a decision, one with which he was not entirely comfortable. Despite his high office Gedron was a scientist at heart, and thought he understood their arguments, even agreed with them on one level, the sheer uncertainty of the outcome stood in the way of his assent. He knew that, in the end, it would fall on him as High Gravitist both to implement the plan and to deal with the results, whatever they might be. He also knew that if the gravitic discharge failed to stably reignite Vai and restore its radiation pressure then even more worlds, and lives, would be lost. Still, he could not help but wonder if the Chromatocron was right. As his thoughts wandered his halo lost definition, expanding into a ring of murky shadow.

"It appears that you remain unconvinced," transmitted the Chromatocron.

"Indeed I am," replied Gedron, his halo snapping back into sharp definition as he refocused his thoughts. "You present your concerns as if they render the outcome of our deliberations certain, even obvious. But let us make no mistake, in neither case can the outcome be termed optimal. In the end the substance of our decision devolves to which possible fate is worse, the near-certain degeneration of Conclave society if we do nothing or the near certain entropy storm that a failed ignition attempt will cause. And in all my projections," he added grimly, "the chances of failure are far higher than the chances of success."

At this the room fell silent. Gedron watched as the light of each heirophant's halo dimmed to a sullen red glow under the weight of his words and a strange mixture of satisfaction and despair filled him: satisfaction that his concern had prevailed, despair that his misgivings would be proved right. Then the Entrope raised his right hand in a gesture of command, and a thin, hissing voice filled Gedron's mind.

"You speak of fate and outcome, yet there is no possible outcome, no possible fate, but that which leads inexorably to chaos. You talk as if one or another choice were better, yet in the end all amount to nothing. Behold the reality of all outcomes, the fate of all fates."

With that the Entrope clenched his fist, and the chamber reeled. The suns shrank to the size of pebbles, a tiny trio of sparks whirling in the center of the thrones. Around them myriad worlds spun into view, each flying at breakneck speed toward the center of the chamber, and soon the entirety of the Conclave hung before them like some impossibly constructed armillary. Then a violent green glow erupted on all sides as the entropy clouds came into focus, the walls of their cosmic prison.

The clouds were at once sublime and horrifying: endless sheets of dancing green flame studded with gems of perfect blackness, boiling masses of plasma that churned and writhed in a sickening, almost biological, manner. There was a strange hypnotic quality to their movements, and several times Gedron found himself trying to trace the patterns that lay behind them only to fail as his understanding foundered against their inherent randomness.

"Do not fear the clouds, my friends," hissed the Entrope, "but instead gaze upon their glory. Here and nowhere else will all the plans made today end, for you know as well as I that at the final dissolution whatever is decided will be unmasked as meaningless no matter the choice. If all possible futures end in annihilation, how then can the sustenance of the Conclave for another year, another decade, or even another century truly matter? Indeed we must choose a course, but only by understanding the meaninglessness of the choice can it be appropriately made."

A palpable silence hung throughout the chamber as each hierophant contemplated the logic of the Entrope. Then the Chromatocron arose, his breastplate gleaming weirdly in the green light, his halo shining with clashing blues and yellows.

"If the outcome means nothing," he transmitted, "then this only affirms our need to attempt the reignition, for what else is left for us to value other than action itself, attempted for its own sake."

"Indeed," transmitted the Entrope. "The imposition of our will, our meaning, upon the chaos without until it overtakes us is all that we have."

"Then we are agreed?" transmitted the Chromatocron.

"Agreed," replied the Photocanth and the Ouranos Radii.

A few more moments passed before Gedron finally responded.

"Agreed."

At that the Entrope lowered his hand, banishing the vision of the entropy clouds and returning the chamber to its usual position within the orbit of the three suns.

"What resources will you need to attempt the reignition," transmitted the Chromatochron.

"The Worldship Gog," replied Gedron, "as well as the entire etherreaver fleet. The ships must be positioned at equal intervals around Vai's equator to generate the initial gravitic impulse. The neutronium forges alone can sustain the compression field, but I will need time to reconfigure their primary mass drivers and reorient them into polar orbits."

"How long will the reorientation take," asked the Ouranos Radii.

"Approximately eight days," transmitted Gedron after performing a quick calculation. Then he paused for a moment, his halo pulsing with violet sparks as a new concern arose.

"Even should the reignition succeed," he transmitted, "the initial discharge is almost certain to provoke a response from the clouds. We should consider evacuating the most rimward worlds as a precaution."

"Indeed," transmitted the Chromatocron, "and what do you propose to give those citizens as a reason? By revealing the margin for failure we will almost certainly incite panic."

Gedron thought deeply for a moment, his halo fading to a faint grey band.

"The entropy clouds have been in turmoil since Vai's demise," he finally replied. "This is known by all, as is the ability of the Ramachrond Infochryst to predict the effects of radiation pressure on the clouds. If we were to deliver an immediate forecast from the device predicting a severe entropy storm, the connection to reignition could be sufficiently obscured."

The Entrope's halo quivered with a phosphorescent blue, and a ghostly cackling filled Gedron's mind.

"Foolishness… Vanity… It matters not when a world dies, whether today or tomorrow or the next day. Such a paltry move effects nothing."

Gedron's halo flashed silver as he fought back a flush of anger. This was not the time to loose control.

"If, as you say, it does not matter," he transmitted smoothly, "then here is no reason not to do it. Did we not just agree that action is its own justification?"

At this the Entrope grinned, his mouth an array of bone-white teeth.

"Indeed," he transmitted, apparently conceding the point.

"So be it," confirmed the Chromatocron, golden light streaming triumphantly from his halo. Then he raised both hands as if giving a benediction and the chamber's point of view plunged downward into the darkness of interplanetary space, leaving the three suns far behind. A few moments later the spires of Scintillus rose up around them, the infographic surfaces darkened, and the walls of the Omegahedron again enclosed the throne room.

Gedron watched the other heirophants as the great psychochryst deactivated, their once expressive halos freezing in place and then dissolving into the air like mist in sunlight. One by one each of the Heirophants rose and departed until only Gedron was left behind. His last thought as he exited the chamber was of a world ripped apart by the entropy clouds, the blood of its inhabitants on his hands.

Chapter 8: The Geometry of Creation

Garin stood on a featureless plateau of gently curving crystal. Its glassy surface stretched several hundred yards in each direction before vanishing in a churning sea of azure mist.

Kyr was nowhere to be seen.

The strange calm of the scene was unsettling, a sharp contrast to the flaring green tumult he had just fled. He signed and walked toward the edge of the plateau. He had nowhere else to go.

"Garin."

The voice sounded softly in his mind.

"Kyr?" he asked. "Where are you? Why can't I see you?"

"I am above you, at a point just above the Xaocosmic Border. This world is different that the one below, and travel here is more a matter of comprehension than physical motion. The space in which you find yourself is an abstract one, imbued with powerful symmetries."

Garin frowned at the thought, his forehead wrinkling in puzzlement.

"I don't understand," he said.

"If you did," said Kyr, *"you would be at my side. I will wait for you at the border, for there is something there that you must see and understand. Seek the entities that call this plane home, one of whom is closer than you realize. But make haste, young one! We have not yet risen beyond the shadow."*

A chill swept down Garin's skin as Kyr's voice faded from his mind. He thought for a moment about calling out to him again, but something in Kyr's tone suggested that no further advice would be forthcoming.

93

Travel by comprehension? The very idea seemed absurd. How could knowledge and motion be connected, whatever the nature of this place? Garin glanced about, trying in vain to find some sign of a path. But there was nothing, only the hard crystalline ground and the soft blueness beyond. Unsure even where to begin, he sat down in frustration. It was then that he noticed the patterns.

He first caught a glimpse of them in the sky above, a strange shifting mixture of brilliant red and soft green hues. As Garin looked on, strange symmetries seemed to emerge in the swirling light only to vanish before he could gain a sense of their underlying order. But his attempts were not entirely fruitless, for at those moments when he seemed closest to grasping the pattern Garin could see a faint outlines of a shimmering bridge coalescing in the air before him, as if the sheer force of his thought was forging a pathway further into this world.

Travel by comprehension indeed.

Garin smiled, and set about the task of understanding the symmetries above.

He applied himself diligently for the better part of an hour, but despite his best efforts Garin could not get beyond those first shining glimpses of a deeper order. Eventually he was forced to admit that the patterns in the skies were simply too complex for him to grasp. Still, he refused to believe that Kyr would just leave him here with no hope of progress. There had to be something he was missing, some simpler pattern that was easier to understand. Somewhere that he could begin.

Garin walked to the edge of the plateau and stared into the cerulean mists below. Perhaps the patterns he sought were there. Within the mists strange lights glinted and swirled, tiny streaks of blue and violet that crackled like miniature lightning bolts. For long moments he stared at them, trying to see the hidden order. But the mists were even more inscrutable than the skies. In fact, there appeared to be no pattern at all, but rather a blatant randomness that seemed the antithesis of order. Garin sighed in frustration.

What am I missing?

Then a strange thought occurred to him.

Stepping back from the mists, Garin looked down and noticed for the first time that the crystal beneath him was not a plateau, but rather the outer layer of a vast glassy sphere. As he gazed into its depths, he saw that the crystalline bulk beneath him was aglow with a network of sparks that darted and wove about each other in a furtive dance. The sparks seemed to fly faster and faster as he watched, their movements tracing lines of fire that knotted and folded into a complex web of light that seemed almost alive. Suddenly he felt a strange sensation in his head, as if some invisible, incomprehensible force had reached inside and was gently shifting the contents of his brain. The feeling mounted until finally it resolved into words that resounded in his mind.

"Who are you, child of my scions?"

The voice seemed clipped and impatient, as if Garin's presence on this vast being's surface (for he realized now that the sphere on which he stood was in some way alive) was both a novelty and an annoyance.

"My name is Garin," he said, a note of fear creeping into his tone.

"Indeed," boomed the voice in his mind. *"Come closer, child of my scions, and we will speak of what brings you to this domain."*

The surface on which Garin stood abruptly began to sink. Curving walls of glassy crystal rose around him on all sides, encapsulating him in a transparent bubble. There was a falling sensation as the bubble plunged into the heart of the sphere. Then the walls dissolved and Garin found himself standing before something that he could only describe as a pattern, as pattern itself, come alive.

It seemed a multidimensional thing, an endless knot woven from strands of blinding golden light that looped and folded in ways that should not be possible, weaving in and out with an erratic, nervous energy. Each strand seemed to crackle with lambent force, sparks leaping along their lengths in brief, sharp arcs. Woven between these brilliant strands were threads of bluish darkness that gleamed dully like the night sky at dusk. Within its heart danced two spheres, one a large mass of pulsing golden brilliance, the other a small, orbiting satellite of deep blue. The spheres moved in an endless counterpoint, their motions driving the endless folding and unfolding of the outer strands, which in turn drove the movement of the entire figure as it spun about a hidden axis. Garin watched the shape make a complete revolution and was astonished to see that new features continued to be revealed. Only when two full revolutions were complete did the shape return to its original configuration. It was perhaps the most beautiful thing that he had ever seen.

"Well, Child of my Scions. Speak! For what reason do you tread the domain of the symmetries?"

The words resounded in Garin's head as if the shape had somehow formed them out of the matter of his brain.

Symmetries? Kyr also spoke of symmetries...

Garin framed his reply carefully, knowing that a careless thought by this entity could erase his mind completely.

"I came fleeing my world, the world beneath this one," he began.

"Yes, Yes, I know all of this," snapped the voice impatiently, interrupting Garin in midsentence. *"Do you not*

96

know that I can feel the very fabric of the matter composing your body, Child of my Scions, creature of Phaneros? Or are you perhaps unaware of what you are made of?"

As the entity spoke a strange half-formed thought flickered through his mind, a sense that he knew what this being was. Garin paused for a moment, trying to bring the idea into focus, but in the end it proved too elusive to put into words.

"I know, Great One, that I am a creature of matter," he replied uncertainly.

"Then you evidently know nothing, for even the simplest resonance of this domain can tell the difference between what they are and what they are made of," snapped the voice. Then, before Garin could respond the voice added, *"Do you even know whom you are addressing?"*

"No," said Garin, though the half-formed thought continued to teasingly dance through his brain.

"You begin to show understanding," said the voice. *"Know this, I am among the first to emerge from the blazing world-light of the origin-point. It is my scions that dance the cloud-dance about the innumerable hearts of the elements, bound by the symmetry of the two and one yet free to career through Phaneros, the world beneath. Know that I, as the father and homeland of my scions, have been called by many names throughout the worlds beneath, but here, in my primal domain, I am known as the Perichorr, he whose dance defines the nature of material things."*

Suddenly the strange half-thought crystallized in Garin's mind like ice on the surface of a freezing lake, an insight at once simple and impossible. His eyes widened in astonishment.

Could it be?

"Great One," he began, not wishing to offend this creature further. "In my world below, the world you have called Phaneros, we have for millennia understood that the elements are composed of atoms, and that those atoms, in turn, are composed of both nuclei and the electron clouds that encircle them. Am I to understand..." -here he paused for a moment- "that you are an electron?"

"*Correction,*" boomed the Perichorr, "*The Electron, the repository of the central being of each particle that bears my name, the fixed point around which the symmetry of their fields, and of all the fields that intersect them, reflects. Now that you know me, I ask again, Child of my Scions, why are you here? Or do you not know the strain that your material presence causes? It is as if I were bent in half when I see you, so distorted are the symmetries.*"

The Perichorr was sounding more impatient, even threatening, and Garin answered quickly.

"My world, Phaneros as you call it, is threatened by lies within and dissolution from without. I was shown the road and brought here by an old man named Kyr. I was told that I must follow him if I would learn the truth."

At the mention of Kyr's name the entity's motion seemed to cease for a second, as if it were consumed in thought.

"*So that is what he is calling himself among your people,*" said the Perichorr finally.

"Yes," said Garin. "Do you know of him?"

"*Child of my scions, all in this domain know him.*"

Garin frowned. Perhaps here was an opportunity for knowledge.

"How do you…" began Garin, but before he could complete the sentence the Perichorr cut him off.

"*Foolish child, know you so little of the nature of this domain and the worlds above. Here understanding and knowledge are of more worth than the accidental concatenation of my children that you call gold. There is no resonance, no leap to such knowledge beyond that which obtained by patient intellectual toil. Even were it my right to tell, and it most assuredly is not, I would not reveal it.*"

"I understand, Great One," said Garin, "but, if I may ask, he has brought me to this domain but I do not know the way forward to where he waits. When last I spoke with him, he told me to join him at the Xaocosmic Border. But I do not understand."

At the mention of the border a faint shudder passed through the otherwise free movements of the entity.

"*It is well that we do not speak of it at length,*" said the Perichorr, "*for it represents the frontier where the inner order of Materia, the name of this world in your tongue, strives against the exterior night which would extinguish the symmetries. There, only the Exofuge offers protection to the great 'hedron. But enough words. If Kyr has called you to the Border, then why do you not follow?*"

"I do not follow because I do not know the way," said Garin. "Kyr spoke of understanding as the road, but if it is so then I do not have the wisdom to traverse it."

At this a booming laugh proceeded from the shape. "*Foolish child, you do not know the symmetries. That is all the understanding that is required. Observe!*"

The endless jittering translations of the Perichorr froze and the shape unfolded to reveal a series of curved lines that radiated throughout it like a skeleton. As Garin examined these lines, he realized that their fixed curves somehow encoded the movements of the Periochorr in permanent form. Then a flicker of light at the edge of his vision drew his attention, and he turned to see the churning cerulean clouds that surrounded the crystal sphere begin to dissolve like mist in sunlight. More and more light broke through as the clouds fled, until finally the sphere floated free in a sea of brilliant clarity.

"*In this current configuration it is easy to comprehend the essential definition of my being,*" said the Perichorr. "*You have gained a measure of understanding, and because of this the path is now clearer. But there is more I would show you. First, direct your attention to what lies beneath."*

Garin looked downward. The same clouds that once surrounded them still boiled beneath the crystal sphere, but they seemed different somehow, brighter and less chaotic, and every now and then a brilliant shaft broke through them from beneath as if a hidden sun swam in their depths.

"What you see are the first intimations of the profound unity that undergirds all the symmetries," said the Perichorr. *"But you are not yet ready for this truth. Now, direct your thoughts to the walls of the sphere in which we reside."*

Garin obeyed, and saw that the wall of the sphere just to the right of the Perichorr was not perfectly smooth, but extended outward in a great glassy filament that crossed the cerulean mists like a bridge. Turning around, he surveyed the rest of the sphere and counted a total of four such bridges arranged at regular intervals. Suddenly he understood. The sphere of the Perichorr was not alone in this world but formed a part of a greater whole, a network that must have something to do with the symmetries it spoke of. Feeling sure that these bridges held the key to his progress, Garin focused on the nearest one, trying with all his might to see what lay at its end. But beyond a certain point the bridge just seemed to vanish into a thin azure haze. Apparently the mists had only been pushed back so far.

"You do not see because you do not comprehend the symmetries involved," said the Perichorr, *"and thus the paths are closed to you. Until you truly understand, the mists will continue to cloud your sight and impede your progress. Consider, though, this aspect of my being."*

As it spoke, several of the curved lines revealed by the Perichorr's took on a more brilliant hue.

"Observe these regularities, for they correspond to an essential component of my inner life. It is a strange property, known to those of Phaneros by the cryptic name of isospin but known to the denizens of Materia as an internal augmentation of the third glory of the fourth broken symmetry. View its essential configuration."

Garin did so, and, with a sense of surprise, realized that this abstract pattern was beginning to make sense to him.

"Now, picture a mirror in your mind, a mirror that does not reflect light as you understand it but instead reflects property and being. Then ask yourself this question, child of my scions, what does the mirror show when this aspect of my structure is placed in its view? I will assist you with the visualization of the mirror.

Garin's head throbbed with sudden pressure as the Perichorr reached into his brain. He could feel thoughts and ideas shifting about as the contents of his mind were forcibly rearranged. Then the pressure abated, replaced by the image of a polyhedral slab of silver rotating in empty space.

"I can take you no further," said the Perichorr. *"The understanding must come from you alone or the physical translation you seek will not occur."*

Garin nodded and focused his will on the image of the mirror, imposing the current shape of the Perichorr upon the gleaming surface. Slowly the mirror's peculiar properties took effect, and the bright curves within the Perichorr transformed into a series of pin-straight parallel line segments that rotated about each other like clockwork. He studied this change carefully, reflecting the form of the Perichorr back and forth in the mirror as he attempted to grasp the fundamental nature of the transformation. Suddenly his half-formed understanding reached critical mass and ignited in a flash of insight, flooding his mind with new light. Exultant, Garin surveyed his surroundings again

101

and saw that one of the bridges had taken on a new aspect, its length now shining with a fulvent glow.

"The symmetry you have comprehended has become a path for you to traverse," said the Perichorr. *"But there are other transformations you must master in order to reach the place of the Exofuge at the Xaocosmic Border. Beyond the symmetry-bridge is my brother. Seek his assistance in reaching the Peak of the Third Glory. From there you may reach the domain of the Exofuge. Now go!"*

Garin turned to the now-shining bridge and concentrated, mentally placing himself on the mirror and watching as the resultant transformation began. All at once, his body seemed to catch fire. He was surrounded by burning wind and light. Then a great force took hold of him, and, with blinding speed, he accelerated over the bridge into the unknown.

Chapter 9: Gravity's Shadow

The iris door opened and Trielle stepped into the central library of the Arx Memoria. Though Garin and her father had often described the library, the reality far surpassed her expectations. She stood at the edge of a vast cylindrical chamber, taller than most of the buildings of Scintillus and wide enough that the far wall could not be seen. The floor of the chamber was carved from a single polished amethyst crystal. The walls of the chamber were covered with an intricate weave of crystalline ramps and balconies that stretched upward from the floor into a brilliant obscurity far above. Countless library patrons moved up and down along these ramps, traveling to and from the data alcoves where the library's stored information could be accessed. In the very center of the library, soaring skyward like a pillar of spun glass and light, stood the Ionocaric Infochryst, chief data repository of the Conclave. Trielle stood for a moment and took in the scene, her eyes wide in awe. This was a day she had long waited for.

Gaining access to the Arx Memoria had been much easier than she had expected. The day Garin left, her sidereal philosophy instructor had announced an optional extracurricular research project on the Ardathan impressionistic concept of justice. The project was by application only, but included a period of time-limited access to the Arx Memoria. She had spend the entire night working on a proposal and, despite her instructor's surprise at her newfound philosophical interests, he had accepted it. Trielle grimaced as she remembered his confused look. He would have been less surprised had he known her true motives.

Since Garin's departure, Trielle's mind had wavered between doubt, fear, and resolve. Kyr's words regarding the Laridian rings, no matter how convincingly spoken, contradicted too much of what she already knew. And yet there had been something about the old man, some undefined sense of authority perhaps, that made it difficult to disregard his words completely.

Garin trusted him…

The thought of her brother called up a wave of sadness. Her parents had initially believed her explanation of a school assignment that required off-world travel, but now, three days after his departure, their questions were mounting and Trielle was increasingly uncomfortable with the ruse.

It was at least partially true, she reasoned. *In a way Garin is investigating the foundations of what we have learned, so it is school related, even thought they didn't sponsor it.*

The rationalization rang hollow as she rehearsed it in her head. She did not like misleading her parents. In the end, however, she felt that she had revealed all that she could, though if Garin did not return soon, the day was coming when she would have to tell the whole story.

Assuming he did return…

The thought left Trielle with a cold pit in her stomach, and she violently shoved it down. Worrying would not bring him back any faster, and she had her own charge to fulfill.

Taking a deep breath, Trielle strode confidently into the chamber toward the primary access ramp. The ramp's entrance was guarded by a tall Anvardian librarian, who scrutinized her intensely as she approached.

"You look somewhat young to be accessing the Arx Memoria," he said.

Trielle removed her personal infochryst from her robes and handed it to the librarian.

104

"I have a limited access dispensation for a class project. The approval files are on here."

The librarian scowled as he activated the infochryst and reviewed the files. After a few moments he handed it back to Trielle with an unpleasant grunt.

"Follow me."

The librarian lead Trielle up the winding series of ramps and balconies, guiding her at last to a secluded alcove about one third of the way up the library's wall. It contained a small seat and desk, both grown from the crystalline surface of the wall. On the desk was a small, gently pulsing structure of interwoven glassy spikes: an infochryst terminal. Open to the main chamber, the alcove's only illumination was the lambent glow of the Ionocaric Infochryst. Trielle hoped that the location was sufficiently remote from the main thoroughfares of the Arx to avoid detection, as anyone walking past would easily be able to see what she was doing.

The librarian gestured toward the desk and Trielle sat. He then hurriedly instructed her in the basics of infochrystic inquiry.

"Remember," he said sternly,"your pass is for limited access only, so please stay within the bounds of your subject matter or related material." His brow furrowed as he spoke.

"Yes sir," said Trielle innocently. She had no intention of following that particular stricture, but the librarian seemed a somewhat suspicious person. She knew she would have to be careful.

Raising her hands, Trielle began the sequence of gestures that activated the infochryst terminal. A hazy blue glow filled the air above the structure, coalescing into a complex network of nodes connected by glowing lines. Each node denoted a particular subject of inquiry while the lines represented relationships between them. Trielle quickly located and found the node for sidereal philosophy, a further network of information opening up as she accessed it. The Librarian grunted in approval as the network's contents narrowed down toward the subject of the Ardathan people and their particular judicial theories and practices. After watching for a few more minutes he turned and walked off.

Despite her newfound freedom from observation, Trielle adopted a cautious route as she navigated the forest of data before her. She first began by accessing introductory articles on Ardathan impressionistic justice, copying the obligatory images and descriptions into her personal infochryst with desultory sweeps of her hand. After fifteen minutes of this she felt that she had put on a decent show of research and began to search for specific legal cases tried under this judicial system, looking for logical ways out of this particular data tree into the subject of gravitic science. It took almost an hour, but eventually she uncovered a civil case concerning an iridium merchant who had inadvertently damaged the main Ardathan transit system by activating his ship's laridian ring too close to the mouth of an active conduit. The case was tedious, but eventually she found a portion of the testimony that involved the physics of two laridian rings in interaction.

Trielle thought that most people would find it reasonable if she investigated this particular bit of physics in order to better understand the case, but still she hesitated. As her fingers hung in the air, mere inches from the information node that concerned the laridian rings, a strange sense of dread washed through her. She knew that if she proceeded there was no way to turn back. Then the feeling passed, and she quickly reached out and accessed the information node before she could talk herself out of it.

Abruptly her view of the information scape contracted, and she was again among the brilliant nodes and interconnecting lines of the main information tree. The image panned and tilted, her point of view flying down a particularly bright line into a dense thicket of interwoven data that stood near the heart of the tree, the informational representation of gravitic science. Her point of view settled and the data began to unfold before her.

The first node gave a detailed schematic of laridian ring structure. Each consisted of an outer casing of imagnite covering a paired set of rings composed of fluid neutronium that rotated counter to each other at near lightspeed through the core of the structure. Wrapped around these larger rings was a series of smaller neutronium ringlets, also arranged in counter rotating pairs, which spun at a similar pace. Wire-thin but immensely dense, the naturally short lifespan of the neutronium in these rings was mitigated by the relativistic effects of their intensely fast rotation. When taken separately, the rotating mass of each ring produced a tremendous drag on the local space-time metric, but when summed together, the counter-rotation of each pair cancelled this effect to zero.

Trielle's brow furrowed in thought as she considered this. With a wave of her hand she enlarged part of the image and new structures became visible. A web of microthin wires, each composed of the more stable crystalline form of neutronium, connected the rotating rings to a series of crystals fixed to the outer imagnite casing. Trielle touched one of the crystals and the image enlarged again, this time accompanied by a wealth of new information. Her eyes widened in fascination.

Each crystal was composed of chromatically polarized crystalline neutronium and contained a high-pressure flux of relativistic mesons. When directed by the rings' internal infochrystic controllers, this meson flux could be routed through the wiring into any of the spinning neutronium rings. By canceling the minute quantum-chromatic polarizations that gave neutrons the bulk of their rest mass, the meson flux could selectively negate the frame-dragging effect generated by the ring's rotation. Effectively, the entire ring system was a directable source of gravitomagnetism, capable of sucking segments of space-time through its central orifice and spewing them back out in any desired direction.

The design was breathtaking, but her understanding was still incomplete. It was clear from what little she knew of gravitomagnetics that the magnitude of the frame-dragging effect was completely dependent on the total mass of the rings themselves, and, despite the immense density of the neutronium involved, they simply did not have the capacity to generate the wormhole-like effects that she knew the rings were capable of creating.

Then Trielle noticed a series of wires that were not connected to the neutronium rings, but instead extended to an array of small rod-like projections that ringed the inner aperture of the device. The accompanying description labeled these objects as chromomagnetic membrane generators, capable of creating an energetic field across the laridian ring's central orifice polarized to the strong nuclear force. Trielle frowned as she examined the strength parameters of this field. It was weak, so weak in fact that it would generate almost no effect on any matter moving through it.

Puzzled, Trielle dispelled the image with a wave of her hand and expanded the next node, which contained an animation of a functioning ring. Though it seemed promising, the initial segment of the animation did little more than confirm what she had already learned. But then the video shifted its approach and launched into a description of the structure of empty space. This material was new to Trielle and she listened carefully, drinking in each detail.

According to the animation empty space was not truly empty, but contained a large number of interacting quantum fields. These fields were not static, but possessed a certain amount of zero point energy that manifested as the short-lived particle/antiparticle pairs known as virtual matter. Additionally, each field could be classified according to the type of particle it was associated with. Fermionic fields were associated with matter particles like electrons and quarks, while bosonic fields were associated with force-carrying particles such as photons and gluons. The video then went on to explain that the zero point energy associated with each type of field interacted with the underlying vacuum in a different manner: fermionic fields tending to contract space and bosonic fields tending to expand it. All that preserved the relatively inert nature of space was the near perfect balance between these forces.

As Trielle considered this a glimmer of understanding sparked in her mind. She closed her eyes for a moment, picturing the balance of the vacuum, runaway expansion and contraction pulling against each other as if poised on a knife's edge.

But if those forces could be separated...

Trielle's eyes snapped open as the animation cycled into a new segment that confirmed her growing understanding. A schematic of a functioning laridian ring hung in the air above the infochryst terminal, its spinning neutronium rings actively pulling vacuum through the central aperture, the chromatic field blocking the fermionic fields but letting the bosonic fields through. She watched as a charge of virtual fermionic energy gathered on the near side of the aperture, an almost limitless amount of spacetime curvature capable of being further shaped by the finely balanced gravitomagnetic fields of the neutronium rings.

Trielle's mouth opened in awe as she understood the true power of the laridian rings for the first time. The design was elegant, a monument of mathematical and engineering triumph, and for a moment she forgot the purpose of her research. How could something so beautiful be destructive? The rings even appeared to generate their own operating energy by siphoning mesonic flux from the separated fields, using it recharge their internal storage crystals. It was almost as if...

Trielle's eyes narrowed.

Nothing is ever that perfect! These rings are being presented as if they were perpetual motion devices. No matter how elegant this looks, there has to be a cost...

As she pondered this, Trielle noticed the thick beam of virtual bosonic fields streaming unimpeded from the rear of the device. An absurd pleasure blossomed within her, and she smiled. Evidently Newton's Second Law still held after all. Then a troubling thought entered her mind.

What exactly does an unbalanced field of virtual bosons do? And how many fields like this exist? We've been using Laridian rings for millennia now!

The immediate effects were clear. If fermionic fields contracted space, effectively generating an artificial gravitic flux, then bosonic fields would create an antigravity field, a universal repulsion. But what then? Her brow furrowed in concentration as she considered the potential implications, but try as she might, she could not see beyond this fundamental insight.

The animation was complete now, and the final frames began to fade away, replaced by the nodes and lines of the datascape. Trielle gestured quickly, freezing it in place before it could vanish completely. She then touched the image of the ring's bosonic exhaust with both hands, attempting to access the most relevant explanatory links. The image stuttered for a moment and then dissolved, replaced by a new information node that expanded to reveal the image of an ionic waste disposal system.

Trielle frowned.

That can't be right… Must be a system error…

Trielle made a sweeping movement with her hands and instructed the infochryst to return to the previous node. A few seconds later the last frame of the laridian ring animation again appeared in the air. Trielle grasped the image of the bosonic field and gave a simpler command, instructing the infochryst to give a straightforward definition of the object. This time the animation was replaced by a primitive text article on stellar photonic emissions. Irritated, she tried a third time and then a fourth, but these attempts were also met with failure. Though she knew that a hundred innocent reasons could exist for unwanted redirections in a system of this complexity, the sheer persistence of the issue bothered her. Her eyes narrowed as she began to consider the unsettling possibility that it was deliberate.

Perhaps Garin and Kyr were right after all…

Chapter 10: Symmetry's Weight

Garin sped across the crystalline bridge. Around him the cerulean mists rose in great billowing thunderheads, their vast bulk lit from within by furtive crackles of distant lightning, hints of deeper symmetries yet to be uncovered. Between these massed clouds the bridge coursed like a bright sunbeam streaming through a darkened canyon, and Garin was a part of that light, his very being an interplay of thought and primal radiance moving with a velocity he never thought possible. Time felt somehow irrelevant here, as if the sheer speed of his transit had raised him to a transcendent state where each moment became infinite. Suddenly he felt a jolt that seemed to tear each particle of his body loose from their moorings, followed by a bright stillness.

"Then the rumors among my brethren are true…"

The sound entered his mind like the faintest hint of a whisper, as soft as the rustle of an ant's leg.

"Come closer, I wish to perceive you more clearly, thing of the lowest worlds."

An unseen hand grasped Garin, pulling him from the light. There was a momentary, sickening plunge and the world spun around him. When the sensation abated he found himself inside a dim sphere of immense proportions. In the center of the sphere hung a complex, whirling shape.

The outer layers of the shape were composed of a myriad of multicolored rods that shifted and danced in a jerking, stepwise motion, a staccato counterpoint to the graceful weaving of the Perichorr's filaments. Irregular fragments of shadow darted between the rods as they moved, their touch altering the colors of the rods and giving the entire shape a kaleidoscope-like appearance. Two

112

spheres of light danced a slow waltz at the shape's heart, their movements connected to the rest of the shape by long streamers of violet energy. The entire figure pulsed with strange, unearthly grandeur.

"Ahh, now my perceptions are clear. I know of your errand, composite one. My sister's interaction with you even now reverberates along the light that binds."

Garin strained to hear the words. The voice was almost inaudible. His heartbeats seemed like thunderclaps in comparison. The Perichorr, in contrast, had spoken in loud, almost deafening, tones, and Garin carefully considered the difference. Perhaps it meant nothing, but he was learning that he could take nothing for granted in this world. Any observation, no matter how insignificant it seemed, might be related to the next symmetry he must grasp to find Kyr.

"Great One," began Garin respectfully, "I can barely perceive your words. Why is your voice so soft?"

A low sibilant hiss filled his mind. Several moments passed before Garin understood what it was: laughter.

"Composite One," laughed the being, *"My sister speaks into your mind by manipulating the motion of her scions in the organ of instantiated logic that you call a brain. As her scions are the direct means of that organ's function she can do so with precision. But I am the father of different children. Deep within the heart of matter lay my scions, their movements only perceived in the fire of the suns and the decay of matter. Therefore they must exert their effects upon your brain carefully, lest they liberate a storm of radiation that incinerates your body from within."*

Garin stood in silence as he pondered this new revelation, struggling to grasp the nature of the being before him. As if reading his mind, the voice spoke again.

"Composite one, do you not yet know who I am? I am among the first to emerge from the blazing world-light of the origin-point. I am he whose children lie forever locked in the heart of the

elements bound by the symmetry of the three, the stable and fixed weight of all substances. I am the heart and telos of the endless dance of the Perichorr, the lodestar about which her countless children gather. I am First-Of-The-Bound. Do you now comprehend?"

Garin nodded. He needed no more explanation. If the Perichorr was the manifestation of the reality behind all the electrons of the physical universe, then this being was surely the reality behind their counterparts, the quarks invisibly buried within the proton and neutron cores of each atom. He now understood as well why First-Of-The-Bound could only speak in whispers, and shuddered at the thought of what could have happened had this restraint not been shown. He could almost picture it: the nucleons of his brain pulsing with new energy, countless gamma rays bursting from them as that energy was discharged, his brain liquefying within his skull under the sudden onslaught of hard radiation.

A soft chuckle sounded within his mind.

"You are learning fast, Composite One. Now, let us not tarry over these distractions. As I have said before, I know the reason for your presence. And yet, I would hear it from you."

"I seek the Exofuge, Great One," said Garin. "I have been told that his domain can be reached from the Peak of the Third Glory, but I do not know the way. I understand, however, that I must comprehend the symmetries of this place in order to progress. Your sister the Perichorr assisted me in opening the symmetry-bridge leading to your domain." Garin paused for a moment, and then added, "It was my hope that you could do the same."

"Indeed I can," echoed the voice of First-of-the-Bound. *"Yet before we speak of the symmetries, I must first know what it is you truly seek in this place. Why have you ventured from Phaneros to the higher worlds?"*

Garin told First-Of-The-Bound of his dream. He described the road paved with stars and his desire to know the truth of what, if anything, lay behind the doomed cosmos in which he had been raised. He told of how he met Kyr, and of his flight from the destruction of Sha-Ka-Ri. As Garin completed his story, the incandescent rods that formed First-of-the-Bound's body drew inward and their stuttering movements slowed. Then, after what seemed like an aeon of thought, the great being spoke.

"There is truth in your tale, for this much I have come to know from the Perichorr. And yet your story is incomplete. You speak as if it you are the only one who has received this dream. Are you so naïve as to think this is so?"

Garin was speechless. His mind raced furiously as he considered the implications.

Others had received the dream? Whom? When? Had anyone else responded?

"None but you have taken the road, composite one," answered First-of-the-Bound in response to Garin's unspoken question, *"None but you. And it is this that troubles me. Why you? Why now, when it is almost too late? We have called for so long! Are the people of the world below blind to the danger? Why! Why do they not care!"*

The whisper in Garin's head grew in strength as First-of-the-Bound's passion flared. He felt suddenly hot, and a burning pain began to rapidly build behind his temples. Garin pressed his hands to his head and fell to the ground.

"I don't know!" he cried, "Great One, please! I don't know!"

The pain soared, and a red miasma crept across Garin's vision. It felt as if the contents of his mind were evaporating. His last thought as his perceptions faded to blankness was of his father, and a dim pang of sadness gripped Garin as he realized that he would never see him again.

Suddenly the storm within his skull abated as First-Of-The-Bound fell silent. He lay there as the pain subsided to a dull ache, and his vision slowly returned.

"I ask your forgiveness, composite one." Said First-Of-The-Bound, his voice again a faint whisper. *"For a moment my anger overwhelmed my self-restraint. I have completed an inspection of the nucleons of your brain and can assure you that no permanent injury has been incurred."*

The pain had almost vanished now, and Garin slowly rose to his feet.

"But you must understand the shared nature of our peril," continued First-Of-The-Bound. *"The same dissolution that faces Phaneros affects our world as well, and yet my kind, for all our might, can do nothing to alter it. For a century of your years now the dream has been sent to your world. We know this for it is we who were charged by those of the higher worlds with inserting its content into the electromagnetic dance of your neurons. Many times the great 'hedron revolved around the central unity while we called, and each day the Xaos pressed further inward, yet no one answered. We had begun to lose hope. But now, against all hope, you have come, and I would understand why."*

As Garin considered First-of-the-Bound's question his thoughts inexplicably turned again to his father. But why? He had followed Kyr to understand the truth about their world, had he not? What did his father have to do with that? A rush of memories surfaced and he examined each one, turning them over and over like bright pebbles gathered from the seashore. Many were filled with sadness: long nights spent alone in his home while his father attended functions of the Gravitic College, anticipated family events cancelled at the last minute due to urgent meetings of the Heirophants. But not all were dark. Garin vividly recalled a time five years earlier when he had arrived home from the Arx Scientia in tears, having been slighted by one of his classmates. His father had been home that day, and he had sat with him until the pain had subsided. They had talked late into the evening, his father explaining bits of esoteric gravitic theory, Garin drinking in the attention. A sudden warmth filled him, and he realized that, despite the dark times, he still loved his father.

But in the end what did that love mean? If the axioms were true, then nothing, not even the deepest relationships, were anything more than the random collision of molecules. And once the entropy clouds had consumed the Conclave even these would vanish. It was then that Garin understood. He had ventured upon the Sovereign Road not just to find the truth about the world, but to find the truth about himself and his life. Like First-Of-The-Bound, there were things he simply needed to know as well.

"Great One," replied Garin with surprising confidence, "until now I thought that I was the only one who dreamed, and I confess that I cannot explain why I among all the others sought the road. But I do know this. For all my life I have lived in a world with no real meaning, a world where even the love between father and son was painted on nothing but an ephemeral canvas of dancing atoms. I believed that life was nothing but a long, slow slide into decay, and that someday soon all I cared about -my sister, my family, my world- would dissolve. But ever since the dreams came I have not been able to accept this. Not once I began to see that there might be real meaning after all.

A low hiss sounded in Garin's mind as First-of-The-Bound laughed.

"*Indeed,*" he whispered, "*there is more to your answer than you know. It is enough; I am satisfied. Now, Composite One,*

117

you must prepare to again traverse the symmetries if you would reach the Peak."

"I am ready to learn this new symmetry, Great One," said Garin.

"New?" laughed First-of-the-Bound. *"Why would you wish to learn a new symmetry when you have insufficiently comprehended the old? Observe!"*

The dancing rods that composed First-of-the-Bound's outer layers unfolded outward like the petals of a flower, revealing a weave of brightly shining threads. It only took Garin a few moments to realize that these threads somehow encoded the pattern of movements he had seen reflected in the mirror of the Perichorr.

"Great One," said Garin, "I understand. You are showing me those parts of your being that correspond to isospin, the symmetry that allowed me to travel here."

"It is so," whispered First-of-the-Bound, *"and yet I do not think that you understand fully. In what way did the Perichorr show this to you?"*

"The Perichorr assisted me by helping create a mirror in my mind where I could understand the transformation," replied Garin.

"Then you must return there in your thoughts," said First-of-the-Bound. *"I will assist you as I can, but as you know I cannot safely exert the same degree of force upon the substance of your brain as the Perichorr. Greater effort on your part will thus be required."*

Garin nodded and bent his will toward the task of recreating the mirror. After a few moments of concentration he felt a gentle pressure within his head (doubtless the subtle guidance that First-of-the-Bound had promised) and again the image of a rotating silver polyhedron filled his mind's eye.

"Do you see the mirror?" asked First-of-the-Bound.

"I do," said Garin with tension in his voice. He did not want his concentration to falter, not if it would require more intervention from First-of-The-Bound. That was an experience he did not wish to repeat. "I can see the transformation between your being and that of the Perichorr easily, but I see nothing new."

"Consider this, then," whispered First-of-the-Bound. *"With what sense do you see this transformation? How is it perceived?"*

Garin paused and considered this new question. Until now he had simply assumed that he was seeing the mirror with ordinary light, but he quickly realized that this could not be the case. After all, isospin was a concept, not a physical object.

But what illuminates a concept?

"*I can feel your bewilderment,*" whispered First-of-the-Bound. *"Yet in this bewilderment lie the seeds of understanding. Look closely at my shape and that of the Perichorr as reflected in the mirror, Composite One. Allow the similarities and differences to permeate your vision, your perceptions, and your thoughts. Consider them not as shapes, but rather as hues, shades of color that bear both similarity and opposing characteristics. Then ask yourself this, within what spectrum could these hues both dwell in comfort."*

Garin closed his eyes as he bent his will toward the task, aided by the faint but insistent nudge of First-of-the-Bound's mental influence. At first the image remained unchanged, the inner workings of First-of-the-Bound and the Perichorr rotating in reflected counterpoint, but then his focus deepened (whether from his own effort or that of First-of-the-Bound Garin could not tell) and the features of that counterpoint that had once seemed most opposed began to take on a certain similarity. It was as if those oppositions were but the endpoints of a deeper, more fundamental relationship that intimately linked the two beings. As Garin

119

continued to concentrate the connections between the Perichorr and First-Of-The-Bound became rays of light that reflected back and forth across the face of the mirror, growing in brightness until finally all was a blaze of white fire, an incandescent forge that created synthesis from opposition and unity from disparity.

"*Well done Composite One,*" whispered First-of-the-Bound.

Garin opened his eyes and saw that the once-dim crystal sphere in which he stood was now awash in radiance. He could see shimmering bridges extending in all directions from the curving walls of the sphere like filaments of spun glas, doubtless leading to the domains of the other entities that called this world home. The billowing thunderheads that had surrounded him on his journey were gone as well, replaced by a pellucid brightness stretching from horizon to horizon. Beneath the sphere the cerulean mists still churned, but these were distant now, further away than they had ever been since he had arrived in this world. And all around him, thusting upward from the mists like titanic shards of diamond, stood the mountains.

Each was a sheer pyramid of faceted crystal taller than any peak Garin had ever seen before. Their summits blazed like miniature suns, showering the slopes beneath with brilliant rays of golden light that caught on the crystalline facets and fractured into a thousand rainbows. One mountain was particularly close to First-Of-The-Bound's sphere, and the particular hue of the light streaming from its summit caught Garin's attention. A few moments later he realized that it was the same color as the light he had seen reflected between First-Of-The-Bound and the Perichorr in his mind only a moment before.

Could that be…

120

"*Yes Composite One!*" whispered First-of-the-Bound with a note of triumph. "*It is the Peak of the Third Glory, source of the symmetry that you have even now comprehended. Come! What bars your passage? You have simply to grab hold of the light.*"

Garin understood. After offering a word of thanks, he again closed his eyes and visualized the mirror. This time, however, he imagined his own body as it would look reflected from it. As the symmetry took hold, the image began to shift back and forth between its original configuration and a strange, inverted version. With each reflection the shifting accelerated, until soon neither the image nor its inversion could be seen, only a brilliant blur that grew brighter and brighter with each moment. Suddenly the light seemed to thicken and grab hold of him, and he was soaring through a blinding space on wings of thought. A few moments later the sense of movement diminished, the brilliance subsided, and Garin found himself at the top of a mountain of purest crystal. Before him burned the source of the light he had seen from below, a pulsing swarm of incandescent sparks that blazed like the surface of a star.

"*Welcome, Woven One. I am so glad you have found me.*"

The words seemed somehow seen and not heard, as if shaped from the effulgence that surrounded him.

Garin bowed his head.

"Great One, what may I call you," he said.

"*You may call me the Chromoclast, but it is of no concern. There is little time left, Woven One, and there is one thing more you must understand before the arrival of the Exofuge. Quickly, even now he comes! Look below and see that which you must understand.*"

Without hesitation Garin stepped to the edge of the peak and looked down.

Chapter 11: Gnosis and Epignosis

Trielle lowered her arms, her hands cramping from the repeated gestures needed to manipulate the data tree. It was as if a hole had been cut in the central database of the Ionocaric Infochryst, its edges a weave of tangentially connected data threads and sheared nodes. Her frustration was a palpable knot, a stone sitting solidly in the pit of her stomach. It was clear that she could progress no further.

She had initially approached the problem directly, but the infochryst had consistently redirected all attempts to directly ask for more detail about virtual bosons in gravitic theory to a variety of unrelated sources. Failing this, Trielle had instead attempted to trace the development of the first laridian ring prototypes, reasoning that at least some commentary might be present that discussed residual bosonic flux. At first this had looked promising, but as she followed the thread Trielle began to notice subtle breaks in what should have been smoothly flowing descriptions and animations -an elision here, a non-sequitur there- until finally she had hit the same barrier as before. Once she had found a promising description of the trial and error process the first gravitists had used to determine the correct rotational velocity of the inner neutronium rings, yet the next link had led her to a database containing designs for the atmospheric impellers used to stir the clouds of gas giants. And with each severed link, each redirected query, her initial suspicions had hardened into certainty. There was a secret behind that barrier, but she did not have the key to breach the wall.

Still, she reflected, the exercise had not been totally valueless. By carefully considering the pattern of links she had been able to make several reasonable inferences about where the missing information might be located. Although she had only been able to access a handful of truly scholarly materials on laridian ring flux, these repeatedly referred to a series of monographs by Anthron Rashavey, a human gravitist who had lived a millennia ago and had extensively studied virtual particle flux. If she could just locate those articles -articles that she could not, might never be able to, access- she was certain that she could find an answer. Frustrated, Trielle let out a loud sigh.

"Is there something I can help you with miss?"

Trielle quickly raised her hands thinking that she has enough time to shift the data tree back to the prescribed subject of her inquiry, but a few seconds later the futility of this gesture hit her like a punch in the stomach and she dropped them in defeat. She had been caught. Her time in the Arx Memoria was over, and all she had to show for it was the name of a monograph she would never be able to read. She slowly turned around, expecting to see the gangling form of the Anvardian that had admitted her to the Arx Memoria. Then her eyes widened and she exhaled sharply in relief.

At the edge of the alcove stood a young human no more than two or three years older than her. He was thin, and his eyes occasionally darted about furtively, yet his smile was warm and genuine.

"You look worried miss," he said. "I only came by to see if I could help."

"No," said Trielle, feigning confidence. "I'm all right. Thank you, though."

The young man stepped forward. His smile broadened.

"Forgive me if I persist, but our record of your activities indicates a persistent though unsuccessful attempt to reach certain data-points, and in such circumstances we are bound to assist."

Trielle's skin began to crawl as a new wave of panic swept down her body. A flood of frightened thoughts tumbled through her mind.

They've been monitoring! How could I have been so foolish!

Straining to control her emotions, she forced a smile.

"Well," she began, an air of feigned confidence in her voice, "perhaps you can be of assistance. I was attempting to research some specific Ardathan impressionistic case law, but may have gotten far afield."

"Indeed," said the boy, "quite far afield. We were notified by the Ionocaric Infochryst that, in fact, your queries had far more to do with gravitics than legal theory." His smile thinned and vanished as he spoke. Then, abruptly, he leaned toward Trielle, prompting an involuntary cringe.

"If it where any but me," he whispered, "you would have been ejected from the Arx Memoria hours ago. I hope this tells you that I may be trusted. Now, I ask you again, do you need my help? Or have you found what it is you are looking for."

Trielle could see no way out. Caught in the act of deception, the possible paths of escape were closing one by one. For one last moment she hesitated. Then her emotional facade crumbled as she saw that there was no way out other than the truth.

"No, I haven't. I want… I need… to get a better understanding of just how the gravitic ring system works, but I keep running into a wall. In particular, there is a series of articles about its basic function that I've been trying to locate, but they don't seem to be accessible."

The young man's smile returned. "Indeed, that is what I had thought. I can assure you that the articles you seek are in the system, but are accessible only to those with the highest clearance from the Gravitic Council. The contents were deemed too sensitive for public consumption." His eyes flickered back and forth before he added under his breath, "but there are other ways of obtaining the information you seek. Come with me!"

The young man turned and began to walk away. Trielle paused a moment, then switched off her personal infochryst and rose to follow.

The young man led her swiftly down the series of ramps she had ascended hours prior. Soon they neared the entrance, but instead of taking her toward the towering ruby portal the young man abruptly turned down a narrow hallway that lead away from the central library. The walls of the hallway were lined with iris doors and, after a few moments, he stopped in front of one of the doors and pressed his hand against it. The portion of the door immediately in front of his palm began to glow and a complex series of lines and shapes appeared in the light, forming an outline of his hand. A high, clear note sounded, and the door silently irised open, allowing them to enter.

Inside was little more than a closet, with rows of multi-hued robes electromagnetically suspended in the air. There was no exit.

Trielle's eyes widened in fear.

Seeing this, the young man sighed.

"Please relax," he said. "I really am trying to help. The information you need is in the Chthonic Archives and only those employed by the Arx can enter, so you'll need a set of official robes. It's not a perfect solution, but it should give you some time to search." The young man turned to the robes and studied them for a moment before selecting one. "Here, this should fit you," he said, handing it to Trielle.

Wordlessly, Trielle accepted the robe and put it on over her clothing.

"Thank you," she said, then paused for a moment before asking: "what is your name, and why are you helping me?"

The young man smiled. "It's Anacrysis. As for why... It will hopefully become clear in time. Suffice it to say I've been waiting for you."

Before she could speak more Anacrysis held up his hand.

"Not now! There is too much to be done. We will not have much time once we arrive at the Chthonic Archives, so you will have to work fast. They conduct security sweeps every fifteen minutes, and you don't want to be found near any unauthorized materials when that happens. You won't have time to read the articles there, so you'll just have to trust me that we're in the right section. Right now you are wearing a subaltern's robe. I'm a library subaltern, so it's all I have access to. Subalterns are only allowed into the Archives for brief periods, but if we get caught in a sweep near non-classified materials, we'll at least have a chance of making it out. Now, let's go!"

Anacrysis led Trielle back out into the hallway and deeper into the Arx Memoria. The hallway twisted left and right, frequently intersecting with other corridors, and Trielle quickly lost all sense of direction. Eventually their journey ended at a small blue-lit room containing a single glass cylinder. Anacrysis entered the cylinder and motioned for Trielle to follow. As she did so, a clear crystalline door closed behind her and the cylinder plunged downward. There was a brief moment of darkness and then the cylinder dropped through a round portal into a cyclopean chamber of dim red crystal.

Trielle gasped as she considered the scope of it. A red-lit domed space, large enough enough to hold an entire building, opened up beneath her. The floor of the room was filled with a maze of ruby spires joined together by a labyrinth of walls that pulsed and glimmered in the half-light. From an aperture in the center of the ceiling, a crystalline column descended a short way before fanning out into a spray of gleaming threads that arced downward, terminating on the spires beneath. The column flashed with brilliant blue-white light, as if filled with captive lightning.

"The core synapsis of the Ionocaric Infochryst," said Anacrysis, nodding toward the column. He then pointed at a specific thread. "Look closely at where that thread meets one of the spires. You can see the data exchange."

Trielle watched as a series of quick blue pulses traveled down the length of the thread. When the pulses reached the contact point there was a sharp white flash, and a wave of patterned red light descended the spire. A few moments later an answering pattern surged upward and jumped to the thread in another bright flash, sparking a second sequence of blue pulses that followed the thread into the core of the infochryst.

"Each thread is a hardwired dataport that actively searches for and collates information held in the archive below," explained Anacrysis. "Well," he added, "at least that's what happens most of the time… Look there!"

Trielle again followed his gesture, and noticed a single spire, close to the chamber's heart, that had no associated threads. Her eyes narrowed. It almost appeared as if the threads had been deliberately positioned to avoid it.

As if there was something there that was not intended to be accessed…

The capsule descended through a clear crystalline tube that guided it to a raised platform at the edge of the chamber. When it reached its destination, the door slid silently open and the pair exited.

Trielle frowned. The archive had appeared difficult to navigate from above, but here on the chamber floor the task seemed impossible. In the half-light, the spires rose about her like watchtowers and the walls like ramparts of darkness, flickering with blood-red light. Between the walls narrow corridors yawned like the alleys of some hellish city. A hot, stale breeze blew past them, carrying with it the acrid, inorganic scent of ozone.

"Follow me," said Anacrysis sharply, "the clock has already started," and he plunged headlong into the maze.

Trielle hurried behind him, her sense of time and direction quickly failing as he deftly led her through the corridors. As they ran, she noticed that the walls contained numerous receptacles filled with dully gleaming red datachrysts, the source of the flickering red light. Occasionally the scene would be lit by a white flash as a data request was transmitted from the core synapse far above and she would gain a better sense of her surroundings, only to lose it again as the light faded. After what seemed like an eternity, Anacrysis stopped.

"There," he said, catching his breath, "the information you need is in that storage wall."

Trielle examined the wall. There were hundreds of datachrysts.

"Which one is it in?"

"I don't know, you'll need to scan all of them and sort the data out later. Please start now, we'll need most of the time left to us to get back."

Trielle reached within her robe, pulled out her personal infochryst, and activated the scanning sequence. A bright fan of pulsating blue light radiated from the device. Carefully she moved it across the wall, each datachryst pulsing in keeping with her device as its contents were copied and verified. When she was finished, Trielle glanced at her infochryst and saw that 4,698 files had been downloaded. Satisfied, she turned to look at Anacrysis.

"Done."

"Good," he said, "because our time is almost up. The next security scan is in a few minutes and we don't want to be found here when it happens." With that he turned and hurried off the way they came, Trielle following close behind.

A few minutes later Trielle heard a faint whistling noise. At the same time, Anacrysis abruptly changed directions.

"What's that?" she asked, a pang of fear in her chest.

"We took too long," he said with a sigh. "The security drones are coming. Come on, we have to get out of this section."

The noise continued to build as they hurried on, rising to a constant droning buzz. Then Anacryis stopped near a wall only partway filled with datachrysts.

"Quick!" he whispered, "face the wall and start inspecting the empty datachryst sockets."

Trielle turned to face the wall and immediately began scrutinizing a hexagonal orifice. The buzzing steadily increased, and a few moments later she was bathed in pallid grey light.

"Keep to your work," Anacrysis said, his voice a slow, confident monotone.

The light played about them for a few moments and then abruptly vanished, coupled with a rapid diminishment in the buzzing. As the sound abated Trielle risked a brief sideways glance, and glimpsed a swarm of amorphous quicksilver droplets gliding around a nearby corner. Trielle turned to Anacrysis, but he was still focused on the wall, so she continued her pretended activities until she felt his hand on her shoulder.

"The sweep is done. Come on, let's go."

After another seeming eternity within the labyrinth, the pair emerged near the raised platform. They quickly entered the capsule and soon were ascending back toward the ceiling of the Chthonic Archives. Only then did Trielle realize that she was shaking.

"We're almost there. It's alright," said Anacrysis.

His tone seemed confident, but Trielle thought she detected a slight quaver in his voice. Despite the dim light she could see the pallor in his face, and realized that he was as frightened as she was.

"I know," she said reassuringly. "I gather you haven't done this before," she added after a brief pause.

"No," he admitted carefully, "but I have been planning this for some time. As I said before, I knew you were coming."

Trielle opened her mouth to ask how, but Anacrysis silenced her with a gesture. A few moments later the capsule arrived back in the blue-lit room. The pair stepped out and silently traversed the web of hallways to the storage room. They entered the room and, as the iris door slid shut behind them, Anacrysis gave his final instructions.

"You'll have to remove the robe and be ready to move on my word. I'll take you back to the main hall, but we have to maintain the appearance of innocence. Do not speak a word about where you have been. I'll handle any conversations. No matter what I say, you need to trust me. Oh, and don't come to the Arx looking for me once you've gone," he added. "I won't be here or anywhere else you would be able to find on your own."

A surge of emotions filled Trielle as Anacrysis spoke, a strange mixture of fear about what might happen next and sadness at the possibility of never seeing him again. The reaction surprised her with its strength, and, by the sudden look of concern on Anacrysis's face, she could tell he had noticed it.

"I know what you were going to ask back in the capsule," he said gently. "Believe me, I would tell you if I thought it safe. Suffice to say that there are things in motion that affect many lives, things I can't speak freely of here in the Arx. But if you keep following this path, Trielle, I promise that it will all become clear. And," he added with a smile, "you will see me again. Now, its time to go."

Trielle removed her robes as instructed and followed Anacrysis from the storage room. They walked swiftly down the hallway, and soon it opened up into the soaring cavernous space of the main library. Off to the right Trielle could see the entranceway and for a brief moment her fear lifted. She was almost free. Then it came crashing back as she saw the Anvardian librarian at his post by the main ramp and realized that they would have to pass by him to leave. She glanced briefly at Anacrysis, but his face was stern and impassive. Still, he had asked her to trust him. Taking a deep breath, Trielle steeled herself for the encounter.

"I'm sorry that we could not find the specific Ardathan case studies that you were searching for within the constraints of your permit," said Anacrysis in official tones as they approached the Anvardian. "I realize that your time with us is limited. Still, I hope that your visit has been of some use."

"Yes it has," said Trielle, struggling to keep her voice from shaking.

The Anvardian looked up from his podium, an irritated look on his face.

"We will need to see your infochryst before you leave," he said sharply. "Protocol dictates that those with limited-access permits submit for inspection any information that is to be removed from the Arx Memoria. We must assure that it falls within the boundaries of the original access agreement."

Trielle's heart raced. She had not expected this. Momentarily forgetting the injunction to keep silent, she opened her mouth to protest, but was quickly silenced by Anacrysis before she could say a word.

"Please surrender your infochryst," said Anacrysis, holding out his hand. "Don't worry, we'll return it as soon as the scan is complete."

Trielle stared at Anacrysis, searching his face for some sign that this would turn out alright, but his features were as hard as granite. Wordlessly she reached for the infochryst and handed it to Anacrysis. The Anvardian grunted in approval and moved to take it.

"Don't bother," said Anacrysis, "I will scan it myself." Before the Anvardian could object, Anacrysis brought out his own infochryst and held it next to hers. A brief volley of blue sparks coruscaded between the devices as the scan proceeded. Once complete, a holographic table of results appeared in the air above Anacrysis's device. He peered at the results, his lips a thin line, then gave Trielle an appraising glance.

"Hmmm… You were somewhat far afield in your search, miss?"

"Donar," she said. "Trielle Donar."

"Yes. Trielle," said Anacrysis. "Still, the bulk of these appear to be in order. I have removed all data from your infochryst that was not relevant to your initial query. You may go now."

"Thank you, sir," Trielle replied with a nod, then took the infochryst and walked swiftly through the main gate into the light of the dying suns. She did not risk even a single look back but focused instead on maintaining a calm, casual appearance as she moved into the city. Only when the Arx Memoria was far behind her did she stop to examine her infochryst. As she had suspected, the scan had been a sham. Nothing had been removed.

Trielle put the infochryst away and hurried to the Kinetorium, a smile on her lips.

Chapter 12: The Coil and the Fire

Below him stretched the shining mountain of faceted crystal, its very form a reification of the Chromoclast's brilliance. Its slopes coursed downward for miles until they vanished at last into the hazy cerulean mists far beneath. Raising his eyes, Garin saw in the distance the other crystalline mountains he had first observed from the domain of First-Of-The-Bound. Though he was no closer, from this vantage point it seemed almost as if he could reach out and touch them. Each was a different hue, a brilliant knife of color that, taken together, defined the spectrum of a strange, unearthly rainbow. Between the mountains the nodes and bridges from whence he had come stretched outward like a delicate crystalline lattice, its substance gleaming with reflected light from the peaks.

Then Garin noticed that the mountains seemed somehow misaligned, as if each were tilted away from him as well as from each other. Puzzled, he looked down again and saw that even the mists beneath did not form a flat plane, but gently curved away from him in all directions like the atmosphere of a planet seen from orbit. Seized by a sudden intuition, Garin reached within his clothes and pulled out the oneirograph. Accessing the map, he enlarged the image of the second sphere and stared for a moment at its complex geometry before turning to face the Chromoclast with a smile on his lips.

"You begin to see the full shape of the Great 'hedron, Woven one," flashed the voice of the Chromoclast. *"Now, do you know who I am? Do you know what I am?"*

"I perceive, Great One," began Garin, "that you are a manifestation of one of the great forces that hold my world, Phaneros, together."

"Manifestation indeed," flashed the Chromoclast. *"Like my brothers below, I am more than a manifestation! I am the reality of which the "force," as you call it, it itself an image. Must you persist in misunderstanding? I am the third reverberating radiance of the worldlight, fourth ray to separate from the sixfold emanation after the Exofuge had coiled his being around the nascent cosmos. Force indeed!"*

The words of the Chromoclast danced through Garin's field of vision, illuminated by a vibrating iridescence that seemed to suggest annoyance.

"I apologize, Great One," said Garin deferentially. "I only meant to use what understanding I brought with me from my own world to hasten my comprehension of the symmetries. You yourself have advised haste, and…"

"Indeed," flashed the Chromoclast, interrupting Garin's speech. *"Then tell me, Woven One, what have you learned?"*

"That you are, in all likelihood, the being or power behind what we call the weak nuclear force."

Abruptly the whirling light contracted, as if subdued. *"I have always hated that name…"*

For the first time since he had begun his journey, Garin laughed.

"You think this a laughing matter," flared the Chromoclast indignantly.

"No, Great One," assured Garin.

"Well then," flashed the Chromoclast, *"you are in fact correct. But come, there is no time left. Even now the Exofuge comes and you have not the understanding to rise to his side."*

Garin thought for a moment.

"In fact, Great One, I think I do. If you, the Lord of this peak, are the wea… I mean… if you are one of the nuclear forces, then the other mountains must each correspond to another fundamental force. On the map I recorded from my dream this world was portrayed as a single great crystalline shape. The mountains are parts of that shape, and thus the symmetry I must comprehend is that which unites you with the other forces."

"You have spoken well," flashed the Chromoclast. *"Stand fast now, and I will show you this symmetry."*

As the Chromoclast spoke a luminous darkness engulfed Garin: a vision of a multidimensional space, vast and empty, but pregnant with endless possibility. Then, in a burst of blinding radiance, the space was flooded with light. The light was bright and pure, rippling and coruscating in great waves like a mighty empyrean ocean as it expanded to fill the emptiness. But as the light expanded it seemed to become stiffer, brittler, until finally with a crack that seemed to shatter Garin's bones a vast colored shard split off from the light, taking some of its essential nature with it. Again the light shattered, this time into two essentially equal fragments that themselves split, one into two shards and one into three. Now the space was filled with a whirling clash of colors arising from the movements of these fragments. All sense of purity was gone, but in its place had been born complexity, movement, and relationship.

Garin pondered this for a moment.

"I see," he said finally. "The symmetry that I must comprehend is the nature of this primal shattering."

"Indeed," flashed the Chromoclast. *"Now turn again and face the 'hedron. Rise if you can. The Exofuge comes!"*

Garin turned and saw the same landscape, but this time through the perception of the Chromoclast.

He saw a landscape of fractured light, each mountain a shard of a greater unity. He became aware of a pulsating quality to the light, each mountain's brilliance beating like a heart, its rhythm a perfect counterpoint to its neighbors. The cerulean mists below him thinned, parting in places as great shafts of white effulgence streamed upward from the living unity that he now knew must lie beneath. Then a great sound like the rush of a thousand winds roared above him and Garin looked up to see a vast serpent, black as midnight, gliding through the heavens. Its head was a forest of spikes and its tail was long enough to wrap around all of Materia.

"He is come," flashed the Chromoclast impatiently. *"Go to him if you can!"*

With a cry Garin flung himself from the peak, grabbing onto one of the great shafts of light that rose from the mists with the pure force of his understanding. The light caught hold and he soared into the vermilion sky. Another moment of flight and he found himself atop the Exofuge, nestled between the crystalline spikes upon its head.

From his position, the Exofuge seemed endless in length, a near-infinite river of darkness as deep as the space between the stars. Its surface was at once solid and fluid: hard as obsidian crystal to the touch, yet able to flow and bend as the great being glided and coiled through the skies of Materia. It was like no other substance he had ever encountered.

Garin stepped to the edge of the Exofuge's head and hazarded a brief glance downward. Already the Peak of the Third Glory had receded beneath him, and he could see a sizable portion of the curved jewel that is the Great 'hedron, the world of Materia. Then he realized that, despite their obvious speed, he felt no movement. It was as if the Exofuge itself defined its own frame of reference apart from the external world. In wonder he turned back to the Exofuge and spoke.

"You seem to encompass the 'hedron, and yet not be a clear part of it. At least, not in the way the others below are."

At first, silence; a silence so long that Garin began to doubt the Exofuge was capable of response. But then the memory surfaced of an answer, a resolute "yes" that Garin could recall with clarity, yet never seemed to have been spoken.

Is the Exofuge altering the past?

A few moments later and he remembered an affirmative response to this unspoken question, followed by a memory that counseled patience. In response Garin wandered forward between the crystalline spikes until he could clearly see their course, and then sat down to wait.

The sky ahead pulsed with hues of crimson and muted green, the same pattern that Garin had seen when he first arrived in this world. But soon the pattern began to shift. Garin watched as the hues began to separate: the reds gathering together and sinking downward, the greens brightening and rising to fill the sky above. As the Exofuge ascended the greenness above them continued to brighten until at last it resolved into a shimmering membrane that stretched overhead like the surface of an ocean seen from beneath. Abruptly the Exofuge's movement hastened and they surged upward through the membrane in a shower of red light. Then the Exofuge came to rest.

"Is this the Xaocosmic Border?" asked Garin. A few moments later he remembered hearing that this was the case. Garin rose and again peered over the edge of the Exofuge's head. Below him lay a gently curving sea of vermillion effulgence within which swum a bright jewel. The heart of the jewel was still covered in mist, but its essential shape was now clearly visible. Above him stretched an endless expanse of green light that faded to a deep grey at the far edges of vision. Then Garin became aware of an indistinct human figure walking toward him across the surface of the red sea. A few moments later Garin's eyes lit up with recognition.

"Kyr!"

"Indeed," Kyr said softly. "I see that you were able to master the symmetries below."

"Yes," said Garin, "though I did receive assistance."

"It is well that you did," said Kyr with a smile, "for I instructed the denizens of this place to assist you. I would have been disappointed if they had not." Then Kyr's smile vanished as a thin bloodless shriek sounded above them.

"Step back young one," he said grimly. "There are things that you must see here, things that you must know. But understand… it is not safe. I have asked the Exofuge to protect you, but his strength is not as great as it once was."

His heart pounding, Garin backed up several steps. Then the shriek sounded again, followed by a rain of brilliant orbs that pulsed and seethed with poisonous green flame. Several fell into the red sea, consuming the water like acid before themselves being extinguished. Two were flying directly toward him.

His eyes closed, Garin put up his arms as if to ward off the inevitable, only to find that the promised destruction never came. Garin opened his eyes and saw that the forest of obsidian spikes atop the Exofuge's head had bent inward and woven together, forming a shield around him. Several of the spikes had cracked under the onslaught, and a few were being slowly dissolved by the sputtering bilious flames. A few moments later a powerful memory assailed Garin, a memory of crushing pain and vast loss. Under the weight of that memory, Garin felt small, alone, and vulnerable.

Faster and faster fell the orbs, now accompanied by strokes of brilliant lighting. The red sea below roiled with each blast, thrashing and churning as if it was being torn apart. From beneath, the Exofuge shuddered as if in agony. Then the green light above them visibly brightened, and Garin looked up to see an amoeboid mass of viridian flame approaching through the void.

Its surface writhed and convulsed as if woven of serpents. A corona of poisonous light surrounded it like the halo of a diseased angel. The shriek sounded a third time, this time clearly emanating from the thing. It was a sound of inexpressible rage mingled with notes of fear. Garin watched as the mass vomited forth another volley of putrid fire. Yet this time the Exofuge was not the target. Instead, the flames converged on the unprotected form of Kyr. Garin cringed in anticipation, but Kyr simply gathered the surging flames into his hand, squeezing them out of existence between his fingetips. Kyr lifted his eyes to face the thing, and Garin could see tears trickling down his craggy face.

"You forget yourself," whispered Kyr, his voice muted with grief. "Do you not remember the days of your youth, when we played together within the first light?"

"What good are memories of light?" answered the mass, its words sounding like cracks opening in the very fabric of space. *"The end comes and all you can speak of is this? Now I ask you, why have you brought one of them here? If there are any who deserve blame it is he!"*

The strength of the words struck Garin like bludgeons, and he fell upon his knees.

One of them? Does he mean… me?

As if in response to his unspoken question the mass unleashed another torrent of flame directly toward Garin. From beneath the Exofuge roared, and ribbons of black force surged upward from its surface toward the flames. The point where the fire and blackness met flared like the last convulsions of a dying star, a holocaust of power fierce enough to melt a planet. For a moment the green flames were arrested, but then the power of the Exofuge failed and Garin stood in the midst of a shower of green light. All around him the light burned away the smooth blackness of the Exofuge, burrowing beneath its skin like incandescent worms. The vast bulk beneath him heaved in untold pain. Only Garin was spared, still protected by the cage of black spikes.

"Stop this at once," cried Kyr, his voice ringing with sudden power. But the mass above only laughed with a sound like grinding stones.

"Do you truly think I can? Do you truly believe that he and all the diseased vermin in Phaneros beneath have truly left that open to me. Once I played with the children of the 'hedron, and our dance was bright and good, and the power of our tension gave life to the worlds below. But now the 'hedron is weak, and I have become bloated with strength. Once the Exofuge was my brother..."

As the mass's words trained off, his voice softened, losing its hard edge, and for a moment Garin was sure he heard the thing sobbing.

"Garin is not like the others," whispered Kyr. "He has come to seek the symmetries, to rise above the Shadow. I did not bring him here to torment you. I brought him so that he might understand. It is through his understanding that you can be set free."

Abruptly the fires died down.

"Free..."

At once Garin felt the intense attention of the thing as all its faculties turned upon him. For a moment his body seemed like a swirl of ink pained on a canvas that could at any moment be torn asunder. Then the terrible regard of the thing abated, and it spoke.

"Creature of the Under-of-Things, understand that my hatred for your kind has in no way diminished. Understand also that at

141

present I have little control over the assault that I will soon renew on the 'hedron. It pains me to do it, but it pains me worse to cease, so bloated I have become. Hear, then, my words. From before all things was I in tension with my brother the Exofuge and in that tension was the space of the worldlight, for it is in the nature of the Exofuge to coil and constrict, and it is in my nature to expand without end. In this tension there was joy, and that joy became the complexity that you call Phaneros. But now, through the works of your fellow creatures, that which was once in balance is now disrupted, and the dance between me and my brother has become disordered and destructive." The mass paused a few moments, then added: *"It pains me each time I give him hurt. But the time is soon coming when my strength will be boundless and his at its nadir. Do you understand, Creature of the Under-of-Things? If you do not, there is naught else I can teach. Now go, if you can, for even now I feel the pain building within me, and I must soon release the energies which I have held back these few moments."*

Garin looked down for a moment, deep in thought. Within his mind he could feel concepts orbiting each other like moons; complete in themselves, yet unattached. Then, unexpectedly, a moment of insight came. In his mind he saw the image of a great space, the space of all possible symmetries, the space in which the great 'hedron turned. He saw that space circumscribed by the power of the Exofuge, ever collapsing inward under its own weight. He saw that space supported and sustained in balance by an opposing force that held up the great arch of the Exofuge like Atlas lifting the sky upon his shoulders. All sense of danger forgotten, Garin stepped out from the protecting cage of spikes and looked down through the Xaocosmic Border in wonder.

Below him hung the Great 'hedron in all its marvelous complexity, a gleaming jewel set amidst a shimmering cagework of spun crystal. The last tattered shrouds of cerulean mist clung doggedly to the jewel as if trying to prevent some final revelation, but only for a moment. Then the mist was blown away in a mighty rush of wind and fire, and Garin saw for the first time the blazing heart of the Great 'hedron, the essential unity that gave it form and being. Armed with this new understanding, he turned upward again and saw clearly what the boiling mass that hung above him was: a primal force on the same level as the Chromoclast and the Exofuge whose task it once was to keep the 'hedron from collapsing, a force now so grossly swollen under the weight of its own power that every movement it made threatened the symmetries themselves. As he contemplated this, Garin saw in his mind's eye a wall of bilious green light sweep across the worlds below, erasing everything in its wake, and the last piece of the puzzle fell into place.

"You!" said Garin. "You are the one behind the entropy clouds."

"*No!*" the mass thundered, its form engorged with power. "*You are responsible, you and all those like you! My power was but the force you chose to corrupt! Now go! Your time here has ended.*"

Then the mass roared in pain, and a deluge of green fire rained down upon the world.

"Come," called Kyr urgently. "The Exofuge can protect you no longer."

Garin swiftly leapt from the Exofuge's head toward Kyr. For a moment he fell and then landed on a hard surface. Garin looked down in surprise, and saw that a pavement of stars and blackness had formed beneath him. A deep rumble sounded behind him, and Garin glanced back to see the Exofuge dive beneath the Xaocosmic border as it fled from the dissolving fire. Turning back to Kyr, he began to run.

143

The pair raced down the road as destruction fell around them. Soon they reached a place where the road curved sharply downward, diving steeply beneath the Xaocosmic Border. Garin hesitated for a moment, yet, urged by Kyr, took a deep breath and plunged over the brink. Despite its change in orientation, the road still seemed level to him; rather, it was the world about him that seemed to have shifted. They continued to run, passing the outer peaks of the 'hedron and the crystalline lattice in which the Perichorr and First-of-the-Bound dwelled, until at last they reached its blazing core and Garin felt the world around them begin to fall away.

"Take my hand," said Kyr. "Grasp it tightly! We must soon pass through the Shadow."

A few more steps and the 'hedron of Materia fell away completely, a dim sphere of crystal on the mountain of stars and blackness that held the worlds.

Chapter 13: Rumors of Holocaust

Trielle lay in her bed, feigning sleep. Though her door was closed a faint haze of light filtered beneath it, accompanied by the faint buzz of subsiding conversation. She was growing impatient.

Trielle had arrived home several hours ago and had patiently joined in the evening conversation, waiting for an opportunity to slip off and review her new treasury of information. It had been difficult. After the initial niceties, the conversation quickly turned toward Garin's disappearance. For the fourth night her parents asked if she knew anything more, and, from the strained look on their faces, she did not think they entirely believed her denials. In an effort to redirect the conversation Trielle had asked about the status of Vai. Unfortunately the news her father brought had only troubled her more. Apparently a stellar reignition was planned in seven days time. She had asked how much gravitic power such an event would take and it had taken a herculean effort of will to mask her concern when she heard the number. Even more worrisome was the brief flash of fear she had seen in her father's eyes.

Abruptly the lights beyond her door dimmed and the sounds of conversation ceased. Beneath the covers, Trielle clasped her infochryst tightly in her hands.

Just a few more minutes.

She waited until she was sure that her parents were asleep, then she drew the infochryst out from beneath the bedsheets and activated it. Within moments the device had drawn a holographic web of information in the air above her bed, a catalogue of the data she had acquired at the Arx

Memoria. Bringing up a query frame, she whispered the name of Anthron Rashavey.

The information web abruptly expanded as the infochryst pinpointed the object of her search. A few seconds later and the data she sought hung in the air before her: six augmented text files. The first two titles were quite abstract in nature and she did not know what to make of them, but the third immediately captured her attention.

Speculations on the Use and Cosmologic Consequences of Applied Gravitic Manipulation.

Trielle smiled and opened the file. Her eyes widened in bewilderment as she read the first sentence.

> For centuries now, preparations have been made for the coming inevitable war with the Dar Ekklesia, and yet the beginning of this necessary conflict has been delayed due to the travel and signaling advantages of the *Anastasis'* multidimensional biology. In addition, our sympathizers are outnumbered one thousand to one by the *Alapsari*.

War? thought Trielle. *What war? And who are the Alapsari and Anastasi?*

Puzzled, she read onward.

> Yet now this gross imbalance has been finally neutralized by new developments in applied vacuum engineering and the consequent creation of a prototype gravitic manipulation ring by Ronath Larid of D'zenohor.

The manuscript continued on, describing the function of the prototypical laridian ring system in some detail. Having already deduced much of this during her time

146

in the Arx Memoria, she rapidly skimmed the material until she reached a section titled *Possible Consequences of Long-term Use.*

> Even now, as we ready ourselves for the initial skirmishes, copies of this prototype are being crafted around the galaxy in the greatest of secrecy by Conclave sympathizers. Yet we must ask ourselves what the possible costs may be of this great advance. Larid's ring is currently hailed as a near perpetual motion machine, capable of generating any degree of gravitic disturbance with an easily replenished seed charge, but this is far from the case. As I have demonstrated, each use of a ring imposes an artificial separation between virtual bosonic and fermionic fields. While much attention has been given to the fermionic fields, virtually none has been given to the bosonic components. Instead, they are simply treated as exhaust, with the assumption that field dilution by normal spacetime will neutralize any untoward effects. Given the vastness of the Galaxy, and their expected lightspeed dispersion rates, this is not an unreasonable hypothesis. Unfortunately, it is also false.

Trielle took a deep breath. This is what she had been searching for.

> Over the past months I have conducted a number of experiments to investigate the nature and dissipation of unopposed virtual bosonic fields, and have found that this value is a gross overestimate. At its highest, I place the true rate at 0.25 the speed of light. My current hypothesis is that this

phenomenon is due to a residual stochastic attraction between the separated fermionic and bosonic field components. Given the relatively low energy density of the bosonic field, this phenomenon in and of itself is not a huge obstacle to the circumscribed use of Larid's rings. It does, however, place an upper bound on the amount of field separation that can be safely induced in a limited volume of space.

At its worst, unrestricted use of this technology could generate fields of sufficient magnitude to effectively separate that volume of space from the rest of the cosmos by creating circumferential regions in which $\omega < -1$, accelerating spatial expansion past the speed of light. To complicate matters, continued use of gravitic technology within that volume would cause rapid accumulation of additional virtual bosonic fields, eventually decomposing any and all matter within it via a phantom energy effect. Should this occur, the trapped bubble of normal space could be stabilized somewhat by the largely fermionic particle output of any enclosed stars, but this effect would only last as long as the stellar output remained above a critical threshold estimated at 4.2×10^{31} fermions/sec/cubic light minute of enclosed space. Fortunately, the level of ring usage needed to create this effect is extreme, far above what would typically be generated by routine uses.

Trielle looked away from the manuscript as a hard knot formed in her stomach. Though the mathematical terms were unfamiliar, it was easy to see the connection between Rashavey's description of unrestricted bosonic flux and the entropy clouds. A cold shiver ran down her back, and she suddenly became very tired.

Kyr had been right.

Still, she could not escape the sense that there was more to this that she currently understood. Rashavey had not expected this crucial tipping point to be reached by routine laridian ring use, so what had caused it? The references to war also puzzled her. After all, Rashavey had lived only a millennium ago, and the last wars recorded in her textbooks had been several millennia before that. Then a strange, unsettling thought rose in her mind. Touching the manuscript file's holographic icon, Trielle instructed the infochryst to display the date of the file's creation. Within seconds several dates appeared in the air. The first, 9,600 D.E., meant nothing to her, but the one below it, 11,700 A.D., did. The ancient dating system was still taught in schools that catered mostly to humans, even thought it had long been supplanted by one beginning with the founding of the Conclave. Trielle stared at the number in bewilderment.

Something is wrong here...

Gesturing to the infochryst, Trielle called up the current date and instructed the system to display it in both modern and archaic formats. When the date appeared it was as she remembered it: 5,361 I.C. (Inauguration of the Conclave). Translated into the ancient system, the date was approximately 15,000,002,314 A.D.

Trielle's brow furrowed.

If Rashavey lived a millennium ago...

There was no need to perform the calculation; by any measure the difference was immense. Filled with a growing sense of dread, Trielle closed the file and opened one of the others, quickly accessing its creation date.

11,650 A.D.

149

With a haste bordering on panic she instructed the infochryst to list all new files by the date of their creation. Though the numbers varied, practically all were dated to the 11th and 12th millennia A.D., one hundred thousand times younger than they should be. Trielle closed her eyes, trying in vain to clear her thoughts. The age discrepancy was troubling enough, but there was something more here that she could not put her finger on, something more crucial than the sheer difference in timescale. Then her eyes snapped open and she gasped in sudden understanding.

Vai! It's supposed to be an ancient star. But if this is true then it should be fairly young, not senile. It shouldn't have burned out at all!

A quick search on the aging patterns of main sequence stars confirmed her suspicion, and a wave of nausea swept through her as she considered the implications of all she had learned. Much of what she thought she knew about the history of the Conclave was false, a construct designed to hide the true origins of the threats that faced them.

Trielle contemplated the sheer magnitude of the deception. Such a lie would have required the alteration of records on an interplanetary scale as well as the consent of every living member of the Conclave. And even if this were possible, some must surely have passed on the true history if only to be sure that the lie was maintained throughout the rest of society. Then she recalled the uncharacteristic look of fear that flashed across her father's face as he discussed the upcoming stellar reignition, and the horrible realization of what that look meant gripped her heart like a fist of iron.

Filled with exhaustion, Trielle began to deactivate her infochryst, but then hesitated as a single anomalous file caught her attention. It was the only new file on her infochryst that dated from the current year. Puzzled, Trielle scrutinized the file more closely, and saw that it had apparently been created only hours ago. She touched the file and it opened to reveal seven simple lines of text.

> Trielle, by now you have discovered, or are about to discover, some long concealed truths. If you truly wish to pursue this path, you must travel to En-Ka-Re. Seek Tserimed on the fourth moon of Galed if you wish to know the way.
> I will be waiting for you.
> Anacrysis

After reading it several more times Trielle finally switched off the infochryst and placed it on the table beside her bed. The message had reignited a spark of hope within her, but it was a hope shot through with uncertainty. Where, or what, was En-Ka-Re? Finding the answer might take some time, and if what Rashavey had written was true then time was a commodity she had very little of. If the stellar reignition occurred as planned, they could be facing the worst entropy storm in history.

Chapter 14: Black Communion

In a vaulted cavern miles beneath the Omegahedron, the Entrope brooded upon a throne of black diamond. Despite the satisfying chaos produced by the death of Vai, a vague sense of unease veiled his thoughts. Even the prospect of greater destruction during the coming reignition attempt did little to soothe him. Over and over, his lips formed the same rambling series of syllables, a mantra intended to push away the intrusive emotion and fill him again with the sharp bliss of meaninglessness. The strategy was typically effective, but today the mantra seemed unable to penetrate his troubled mind. Instead, it flitted about the windows of his consciousness like an insect: clearly present, but unable to enter.

A brief spasm of pain assaulted his muscles and he snapped back to full alertness. Grimacing, he grasped his staff and arose, descending the dais on which his throne stood to the floor of the cavern.

Scoured out by magma aeons before, this cave system had been used by the Entrope and his predecessors since the founding of the Conclave. They appeared on no official records, although rumors of their existence occasionally circulated among the lesser officials. The Chamber of the Throne was the largest of the caverns. Its walls were forged of black basalt and its floor was rent by yawning chasms from which sulphurous vapors wafted, the final exhalations of the once mighty flames of Latis's core. A path paved with red marble and flanked by plasma torches ran the short distance between the dais and the nearest of these chasms, ending in a narrrow span that arched over the abyss into the darkness beyond. The torched flickered with furtive green light, casting venomous shadows across the cavern like a scene from a nightmare.

The Entrope strode down the path, each step sending electric jolts of pain up his spine. His memories stretched back to the foundation of the Conclave, but, curiously, he did not know his age, though he could tell from the way this body responded that the time for renewal would soon be upon him.

He crossed the bridge and came to a divide in the path. Briefly he looked down the rightward fork and traced the path as it spiraled outward to the edge of another abyss, crossed it in a shadowed arc, and disappeared into a tunnel in the far rock wall. At its terminus lay the Chamber of Rebirth, where the body of his successor floated in biosuspensive fluid. Cloned from a DNA sample taken from his original body millennia ago, the unstructured neurons in its brain were even now being reshaped into an exact replica of his by the ceaseless ministrations of the Irkallan Infochryst. When his time came to die a last cerebral transfer would be made, and his successor would awake with his thoughts and memories. He often wondered, in unguarded moments, if it would truly be him, his consciousness, in the new body after the moment of rebirth. And, as always, the conclusion was the same.

It did not matter.

There was no consciousness, and therefore the question had no meaning. If his neural patterns were successfully duplicated, allowing the new Entrope to continue the work assigned to him at the Conclave's founding, then nothing else was relevant. Despite this, the Entrope secretly hoped that this would be the last incarnation; that he, in his current body, would be the last man present in the heart of the maelstrom as the entropy clouds dissolved the remnants of the dying cosmos. It was an honor promised to the final Entrope alone. Then he remembered wishing for the same thing in his previous body, and a thin, almost absurd, smile parted his thin lips. But the smile was soon effaced as the unease he had felt earlier surged within him again. He would find no solace in the Chamber of Rebirth. His face grim, the Entrope turned and shuffled down the leftward path.

The path ended at the edge of a great chasm, descending into the depths of the crevasse via a narrow stairway carved into the cavern wall. He began the descent and soon was deep within the abyss, the sheer basalt walls rising on either side like geometric planes stretching upward to infinity. The stair seemed endless, twisting back and forth in sinuous curves. Only the light of an occasional plasma torch served to punctuate the growing darkness. Then the stairway leveled off, ending at a short bridge that crossed the chasm before disappearing into a deep cleft in the opposing rock wall. The cleft pulsed with a faint greenish glow. A small grunt escaped the Entrope's lips. He was nearing his destination, the Chamber of the Pool.

He traversed the bridge and entered the cleft, which quickly opened into a small cavern that seemed to have no floor, only a vast pit that howled with winds from the inner earth. In the center of the chamber, a great monolith of obsidian rose from the void, its surface dancing with an obscene green light. It was there that the pathway ended, bridging the void in a last arch, and soon the Entrope stood atop the monolith facing a shallow depression filled with luminous fluid that sputtered and flared with viridian fire. Thin threads of crystal hung from the ceiling far above, their tips trailing off into the pool like the taproots of a glass tree. Along their lengths faint blue sparks twinkled. The Entrope knew the pool was an artifact of Conclave science, a mass of seething nanotechnology into which realtime data from the entropy clouds was fed via the great infochrysts on the surface. Still, he always felt a tendency to regard the pool with an almost religious, awe, for a Presence dwelled, or seemed to dwell, within it. A Presence with which he would soon commune.

Trembling slightly, he stepped into the pool. For a moment there was nothing. Then the fluid flared with nacreous light, sending up burning tentacles that wrapped the Entrope in their fire. His vision clouded, his thoughts momentarily froze, and then his perceptions exploded outward as the vastening process took hold.

He hung in a great void, his body a representation of the worlds of the Conclave itself, and all around him burned and seethed the entropy clouds. Fixing his gaze forward he focused all his being on the clouds, drinking in their terrible might and letting their irregular surges define the rhythm of his thoughts as he sought the Presence that lay within them. He meditated for long moments, seeing and feeling nothing except the meaningless dance of dissolution that hung before him. Then there was a shifting, a parting of the veiling clouds, and a vague form began to take shape.

Its body was vast, obscured by the seemingly infinite folds of a cloak the color of midnight. Vaguely human in form, a great cowl covered its head leaving only the eyes and the bottom portion of its face visible. Though what he could see of its features suggested a beautiful, even noble, countenance, its eyes betrayed that beauty. Burning with a bizarre, alien fire, they seemed to suggest that the appearance he saw was a mask covering some incomprehensible force. An appearance, nothing more. And even now, after seeking the counsel of this Presence in this and countless other incarnations, he was still unsure exactly what it represented.

His pre-conscious mind?

The summed intelligence of the Conclave's infochrysts?

A bizarre manifestation of the existential hunger of the entropy clouds?

As with so many other things, the inexorable conclusion was that its true identity was irrelevant. Still, reflected the Entrope as he painfully knelt down within the green pool, one thing about it had always been clear; the Presence responded best when he assumed a position of submission.

The Presence smiled, and spoke to him in a rich, masculine voice.

"It has been long since we have communed, has it not?"

"Indeed it has master," said the Entrope

"And why have you come, my son?"

"Master," replied the Entrope, "in my meditations I have encountered a great sense of unease that does not seem amenable to typical psychomodulatory techniques. As always I have regarded it as illusory, yet it persists. As I serve the Conclave I see no reason to be troubled. Indeed, we seem closer than ever to the Great Dissolution you promised us. But I am still troubled."

The Presence's smile faded, replaced by a grim expression that sent a thrill a fear through the Entrope.

"This unease is not without cause," the Presence answered. *"Actions are afoot that would seek undo the great work, negating the dissolution altogether if it were possible."*

The Entrope gasped in shock at the reply, and the smile returned to the Presence's face.

"Ah, my son," said the Presence in soothing tones, *"our hearts are so cleanly linked that our desires are the same. Do not fear. The dissolution will come. No one and nothing can stop it now. Still, interference can occur."*

"Master," croaked the Entrope, "what must I do?

"Nothing that you have not already done and are not already doing," said the Presence softly. *"As you rightly said while in Conclave with the Heirophants, the planned attempt at reignition must occur, as should further attempts if the first should fail. You must focus all your efforts to assuring this comes to pass."* The Presence paused for a few moments as if weighing its words, and then added: *"I will deal with the interference in my own way…"*

The Entrope began to ask a final question but the Presence was already receding into the veiling curtain of the entropy clouds. Soon the entire scene dissolved, leaving the Entrope alone in the Chamber of the Pool. As he rose painfully to leave, this last unasked question echoed disturbingly in his mind.

Deal with the interference in its own way? How can the Presence…

But suddenly his curiosity dissolved in mid-thought, overwhelmed by his sheer conviction in the central truth he had held onto throughout his countless lives.

It does not matter… All is meaningless… All is vanity…

Book Three: How With a Million Others Its Tale was Set for Nought...

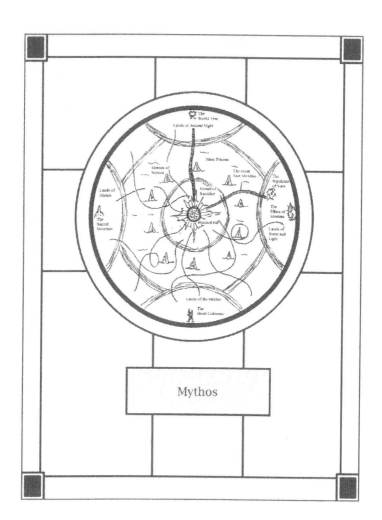

Mythos

Chapter 15: The Hand of the Shadow

The road mounted steadily upward across the face of the cosmic mountain, its course paved by points of deep crimson light. Garin climbed resolutely, Kyr's hand grasped tightly in his own. Looking heavenward, Garin could see nothing but a seemingly endless incline of stars and folded blackness ending in a dim expanse of sky that was no color he had ever before seen. It was almost perfectly quiet, the stillness broken only by an occasional rumble of distant thunder. Time itself seemed almost suspended in this place.

Then the road shifted, rounding a rugged spur brilliant with the trapped light of a thousand galaxies. Beyond the ridge the road ended abruptly in an obscure, inky blackness. It was as if the very fabric of reality was torn away, leaving a lightless, infinite chasm in its place. Garin squeezed Kyr's hand reflexively as a knot of fear formed in the pit of his stomach.

"It is the Shadow," said Kyr, his voice sounding strangely distant. "It has grown since I last trod this path. Come, we have far to go and we have no choice but to cross the gap." Then he turned, his eyes fixed on Garin. "Keep hold of my hand, and remember, the Shadow can hide the road but not destroy it." With that he turned and led Garin into the darkness.

A blackness thicker than any night Garin had ever known enveloped him. There was no light, not even the possibility of light, and a cold deeper than a polar winter settled into his bones. Then the winds began, a gale that assailed him with ever increasing ferocity until Garin felt as if he stood within a hurricane. The blasts tore at him like the hands of the dead: cold, unfeeling, and beyond mercy. So strong were they that, despite his best efforts, Garin's grip on Kyr began to weaken. Suddenly the assault abated, and after a few long moments Garin permitted himself to hope that they had passed through the worst of it, but as if from nowhere the black gale returned, bearing down on him with such force that it tore Kyr's fingers from his grasp and cast him screaming into the void.

His last thoughts before the darkness overtook him were of failure.

***

Garin awoke on a flat, cold expanse of ice swathed in great banks of clinging fog. His whole body ached.

"I'm so glad I found you," said a warm voice.

Startled, Garin sat up and saw an apparition approaching him through the haze. The figure soon resolved into the form of a tall man wearing a robe of deepest grey, his body concealed within its folds. A cloak the color of night hung from his shoulders and trailed behind him on the glassy pavement. His face shone like alabaster in moonlight and had the proud, noble bearing of an ancient king. A diadem hung on his brow bearing a single jewel that burned with pale fire.

Garin slowly rose to his feet, fighting off a wave of dizziness. "Where am I," he said warily.

"Khuliphoth, the Kingdom of Shells," said the figure. "It is the end of your journey. I have been waiting for you. Come, there is much to see."

The figure smiled broadly, extending his hand in greeting.

"Where is Kyr," asked Garin?

"He has gone onward," said the figure smoothly. "His work was complete once he delivered you to me."

164

The soothing words were slowly wearing down Garin's suspicion, yet the figure's curiously distant gaze prevented him from feeling entirely at ease.

"If I may ask," he said, "What is your name."

"You may call me Daath," the figure replied. "Now come!"

Startled by the abrupt shift in tone, Garin mutely took Daath's hand and followed him onward.

As they walked the fog parted around them to reveal a translucent plane of dull gray ice, the upper surface of an endless frozen abyss that stretched downward into obscurity. Great crystalline domes rose from the ice, their surfaces cracked and shattered like ruined glassware. Billows of glowing gas poured from the domes, rising in twisted spirals toward a hazy violet sky filled with tumbling shards of crystal. The entire scene had a surreal, unearthly quality to it.

"You stand in the forges of creation," said Daath. "Each dome is but the upper surface of a world-sphere like those that you have left behind. But these… these are different. The worlds you have left are consensus realities, formed from the massed belief of their inhabitants, but these are the creations of individual minds ensconced in the blissful contemplation of self. It is the ultimate destination of all thinking life, the final supremacy of consciousness over the material universe."

Garin could not put his finger on it, but Daath's words reminded him of something he had heard before.

Daath continued across the ice in long, confident strides that Garin, sore as he was, could barely keep up with. After a few moments it became clear that they were approaching the nearest of the domes, a fractured hemisphere of blood red crystal. Its sides were marred by gaping cracks and its topmost curve was shattered completely. The whole structure reminded Garin of nothing

165

more than a broken egg the size of a moon. As they walked onward the dome filled more and more of Garin's vision, until at last all sense of its curvature was lost and all he could see was the ice beneath and an infinite wall of fractured crimson. A few moments later they arrived at the wall near a point where one of the great cracks reached the surface of the ice. Daath turned and spoke, his eyes burning with a strange fire.

"You wish to know why I have brought you here? You should. You see, I know much of the inhabitants of the worlds below, and I know much of you. Go ahead, approach the sphere. Peer inside. View the world being created within! There is no danger."

The strange invitation both intrigued and frightened Garin, and for a moment he hesitated, but then his curiosity won out and he entered the crack.

The crack narrowed to a point just beneath his feet, leaving him little space to maneuver, and Garin was forced to brace himself against its walls and edge sideways to make progress. Smoldering embers seemed to dance just beneath the crystalline surface of the wall, and his hands felt as if they were on fire each time they touched it. A few more moments of struggle and then he was through into the darkness beyond.

Suddenly a barrage of images assaulted him. Memories of the sins of his childhood -friends he had wronged, promises he had broken- filled his mind with an uncontrollable flood of despair. Screaming, Garin shut his eyes, trying to block out the visions, but to no avail. The images were burned into his mind and there was no escape. He was caught in a universe of his own making, each memory of selfishness and betrayal an icy planet orbiting the black hole of his soul. Then a low rumbling sound like the clashing of icebergs grabbed his attention, and he opened his

166

eyes and looked upward to see the great cracks in the crystalline dome above him begin to close. Dimly he understood that Daath was sealing him in, and he realized the true nature of this place.

It was not the birthplace of worlds; it was their graveyard.

And then, off in the distance, Garin heard the mocking voice of Daath.

"What do you think of this world? I hope you like it. You see, it is of your own making. After all, does not matter give rise to consciousness, and consciousness meaning? See then the meaning you have wrought. Look below and gaze upon the glory of the Pit. It is Tehom, the Ancient Deep, source and end of all things."

Unable to disobey the words of Daath, Garin looked down and saw, far beneath him, an endless flood of black water that roiled and churned with sickening slowness.

His heart pounding, Garin struggled to turn and make his way out of the sphere, but it was like walking through molten lead. At each step the images tugged at him, dragging him downward into the boiling deep. Slowly his resolve wore down, until at last his strength failed. Gazing upward one last time, Garin saw the final cracks in the dome above him close, sealing him within himself forever, and despair rolled over him like a black wave. Then, as the images gathered around him for their final assault, a shred of memory drifted to the front of his mind. A memory of Kyr as they had left Sha-Ka-Ri, his weathered face downcast with profound sadness as he contemplated the wreckage of the world and the Shadow that was its source.

"If only he would come home…"

Garin's cold lips murmured the words almost unthinkingly, but the effect was instant. Suddenly the circling images became distant, dimmer, as if they had lost

167

some of their power, and Garin felt the inexorable pull of the deep abate.

"What did you say?" Daath's words were quiet but filled with venom, like an adder poised to strike.

Garin was puzzled. Why this effect?

"I said, if only he would come home…"

Was Kyr referring to Daath?

'It's you he meant, wasn't it?" said Garin. Sudden boldness seized him, and he thrust the question back at Daath like a dagger.

"Why won't you come home?"

There was sharp cracking sound, and the crystal shell that enclosed his private hell shattered like glass. Daath strode through the rubble, his eyes burning like perdition and his noble lips parted in a sneer. His cloak billowed behind him, and Garin could not shake the sense that its dark folds hid the coiling tail of a dragon.

"Come home?" he mocked. "And why would I do that? To render myself a servant again? Enslaved to the life of the Cosmos? Enslaved to Him!"

Garin was unsure what to make of Daath's words. Still, this distraction had bought him time. He did not know if escape from Khuliphoth was possible, but he was not going to waste the opportunity.

"What do you mean by servant?" asked Garin, attempting to keep the conversation going.

Daath laughed, seeming to regain some of his composure.

"How little you blind monkeys know of the nature of things, clinging to the surface of your precious worlds while the storm rages outside. You are the problem! It is you we were meant to serve! AND I WILL NOT DO IT!"

At this Daath seemed to swell. A vortex of darkness swirled around his form, flickering with tongues of lurid violet flame, and his face blazed with a black light. Snarling in rage, Daath lifted his hands toward the skies, summoning all the forces of Khuliphoth and releasing them toward Garin in a black wind of pure, unbridled hatred.

Garin knew he had little time left. The shattered dome had already begun to reform, and the images, infused with new strength by the power of Daath, were circling him once more. If he was to escape and find the road again, he needed to do it now.

Kyr said the Shadow could obscure the road but not destroy it. But how can I see through the Shadow when I don't even know what it is?

Even as he asked the question, his thoughts turned to the images circling around him and he finally understood. The Shadow was a reflection of his own self-centered choices, the central emptiness at the heart of a life that insisted on defining itself on its own terms.

Even when he had begun to doubt the Axioms, he had avoided the question of what that doubt implied about who he was. But he could do this no longer. If the Axioms were true then he had no intrinsic nature, no real heart or soul to speak of, only a fragment of the primal void masked by the endless succession of his life choices, the myriad meanings he had tried to make for himself in a meaningless world. But in a world like that no choice, no meaning, could ever rise above the level of pure self-centeredness, and those self-centered choices accumulating over years and years could not help but collapse into that void like a dying star forming a black hole, an endless abyss cut off from the rest of the universe. That was the true nature of his choices and of this place. He had built his life around self, and the combined weight of those choices was the source of the crystal sphere imprisoning him.

169

But if the axioms were wrong, what then? Garin drove his thoughts forward with all his might, straining to reach an answer before the fleeting moments left to him were gone. Then, in a flash of insight, he saw the alternative. If his heart was not a void then it had to be something solid, positive, and self-reinforcing instead, something that carried its own intrinsic meaning as a gift from a realm far above anything he currently knew or understood. And if this were true, then the Shadow could no more destroy that meaning than an eclipse could extinguish the sun. No matter how deep the darkness the reality must still be there, buried beneath it.

The shadow can obscure the road but not destroy it...

Was this the truth he needed? There was only one way to know.

Turning from Daath, he flung himself headlong into the black hole of his heart. The visions assailed him like a storm of knives, but he did not fight. Rather, he simply acknowledged them, accepting them as true in all their hideousness while seeking to find and surrender to the still deeper truth that they obscured.

Beneath the darkness, beneath all the selfish choices of my life, who am I?

It was enough.

In the heart of the void a light flared, a single red star burning amidst the darkness. Then another star appeared, and another, until soon the blackness looked like the skies of old. He had found the road. His feet touched the path and he began to run.

Behind him, he heard Daath roar.

"Do you think that you can flee by this path? Fool, I can tread it as well as you. Have you ever asked, blind monkey, why it is paved with stars the color of blood?"

170

Garin did not wait to reply, but sprinted faster. At once the shadow engulfed him, its chill blackness buffeting him like a thousand fists. This time, though, he did not falter, and soon the blackness gave way to the timeless, starry mountain that upheld the cosmos. The path twisted and turned beneath his feet, rising toward a mountain spur on which sat a vast sphere, the next world. Behind him, Garin could still here roars of anger.

He's on the mountain, thought Garin, and a shiver of fear ran down his spine.

Straining to the limits of his endurance, Garin summoned a burst of speed and soon reached the sphere. Without hesitation Garin flung himself headlong through its yielding surface. There was a brief sense of vertigo, and then a flood of light as Garin found himself in a valley of ancient stone lit by the blaze of the morning sun.

Chapter 16: The Frontier of Light and Darkness

Gedron sat alone in the High Gravitist's sanctuary. He was surrounded by a towering array of infographic crystals that displayed an ever-evolving series of equations and models, the ongoing output of the Rhamachrond Infochryst. Chief noetic device of the College of Gravitists, the Rhamachrond Infochryst's vast computational power was focused on a single goal, the reignition of Vai. Model after model flashed by, haloed by an abstract representation of the complex web of assumptions, variables, and relationships that formed their substrate. Each represented an iterative change in the reignition conditions that could be generated, yet each so far had ended in the same dismal outcome, an entropy storm bigger than any the Conclave had seen since the Philosoph War. In a few scenarios the storm had even reached as far as the Guard, the vast belt of brown dwarfs that served as the inner Conclave's last line of defense against the entropy clouds.

Gedron sighed in frustration. There was no way to make this work. He would have to summon the other Heirophants.

"I see you are preparing for the reignition. Good. Then my time will not be wasted."

Startled, Gedron turned to see the Entrope glide silently into the sanctuary toward the control throne on which he sat. His black robe, silhouetted against the actinic blue surface of the infographic crystals, made him seem little more than a shadow, an amorphous hole in the light.

"Yes," said Gedron tersely. "By tomorrow the neutronium forges will be fully realigned. Most of the

172

etherreavers are already in orbit around Latis awaiting the order to jump to Vai-space. My servants are readying the Gog's laridian drivers, and, even now, I am preparing the calculations for the gravitic burst."

"It is well that you have done this so swiftly, for I sensed hesitation at our last gathering and have come to encourage your work."

Gedron nodded in silent acknowledgement. He paused for a moment, then added, "In truth, these calculations trouble me still."

"Indeed," said the Entrope, taking an almost fatherly tone. "I am curious as to why this is so."

"Over the past few days new data have been gathered from Vai's convective zone probe network that allow us to more accurately estimate the elemental ratios present in the core. The helium levels are significantly higher than optimal."

"You do not believe that you can achieve reignition?" said the Entrope, his eyes narrowing slightly.

"That is not the issue," said Gedron. "With enough spacetime distortion I could turn Latis into a sun. The problem is sustainability. Observe."

Gedron gestured at the surrounding infographic crystals and two graphs appeared. The first was colored bright orange. It began at the zero point, rising in a steep curve before leveling out into a broad plateau. The second was colored a sickly green and was a near inverse of the other, starting at an initially low value and continuing there for quite some time before abruptly shooting upward exponentially.

"The orange graph represents the strength of Vai's stellar wind after reignition assuming different levels of hydrogen and helium in the core," explained Gedron. "The green graph represents the virtual bosonic flux created by the neutronium forge mass drivers when operating at the power levels needed to sustain fusion in Vai's core, again assuming different hydrogen to helium ratios."

Gedron stretched out both hands and brought them swiftly together. In response the two graphs merged, the lines superimposing one atop the other. He made another gesture and a vertical red bar appeared on the image.

"This bar represents the possible range of gas ratios in Vai. Look where it crosses the solar wind and bosonic flux lines. There is no way to use the neutronium forges to sustain Vai without strengthening the entropy clouds beyond what Vai's radiation pressure can hold. Even if we can sustain fusion, we will lose far more than we gain."

"I understand your concerns," said the Entrope in a conciliatory tone. "And yet we must proceed. After all, we have spoken of these possibilities already in council and I do not see how this changes anything. Still, these calculations are of interest. I will await your report after the ignition event."

"Entrope," said Gedron indignantly, "in fact you do not understand. If this ignition event occurs, half the Conclave may be annihilated and the end will be hastened, not delayed. We cannot go through with this!"

When the Entrope answered there was no trace of his former friendly tone. Now each word snapped like the crack of a whip.

"The Conclave has no choice! Despite the cost, despite the futility, we must act, for in the end blind action is all there is, no matter how meaningless. If we are to be destroyed, then what better way do we have to impress our own meaning on that destruction than to take it into our own hands. It is our most primal philosophy, our basic reason for continued existence."

"Or perhaps, High Gravitist," he added in a low hiss that somehow made Gedron's title sound like an insult, "you no longer believe in the Axioms?"

At the Entrope's words Gedron's resolve crumbled. His entire existence, his deepest sense of who he was, hinged on the Axioms. As High Gravitist he had sworn his unwavering loyalty to their tenets as part of the rite by which he had ascended to his office. To discard the Axioms would mean the abandonment of his very identity. Despite his misgivings, it was not a move he was prepared to make. Taking a deep breath, Gedron pushed back his doubts, covering them with a veneer of control and confidence.

"My apologies Entrope," he said. "You misunderstand me, and are of course correct. We must make what meaning of this event we can, regardless of the cost."

"Please, my colleague," said the Entrope, his pleasant demeanor restored, "no apology is needed. Sometimes we all need a reminder of what it is we have bound our lives to. I will leave you now to your calculations. Surely there is much left to be done."

"Indeed," said Gedron.

As the Entrope exited the room Gedron turned again to the infographic crystals. He sat for a moment in contemplation, then raised his hands and, with a flurry of movements, activated a noetic optimizing program and instructed it to search for the combination of ignition energies and neutronium forge mass driver outputs that generated the least bosonic flux. The program did not take long to complete its task, and in a few moments the requested parameters, complete with a simulation of the most likely outcome of their use, filled the display.

Gedron stared grimly at the simulation. It was better than some of the possibilities, but not by much. At least a third of the outer worlds were at risk from the initial gravitic burst alone, and the program gave a seventy-eight percent likelihood that the neutronium forge output needed to sustain stellar fusion would result in ongoing entropy cloud surges. Still, he reasoned, it must be done.

Gedron reached within his robe and removed a pale blue datachryst. He held it out at arm's length and soon the air was filled with pulsating blue light as the infographic crystals downloaded their contents. When it was complete, Gedron touched a jewel on the control throne. A few moments later a violet robed servitor, one of the High Gravitist's personal retinue, entered the chamber.

"Take this to Yithra-Gor, master gravitomechanist of the Worldship Gog," said Gedron as he handed the servitor the datachryst. "He is expecting this and will know what to do."

The servitor bowed briefly and left the room. After sitting in silence for a few moments Gedron rose from his throne and left the sanctuary, heading for the Kinetorium and home.

***

Trielle sat pensively in their central apartment, waiting for her father to arrive home from Scintillus. Ever since Vai had failed her father had worked long hours, often returning long after Trielle and her mother had gone to sleep. Tonight, however, was different.

For days Trielle had pondered the information she had uncovered in the Chthonic archives, trying to see some plausible means to explain away what she had learned, and had failed. Now, with Vai's reignition scheduled for tomorrow, she knew that it was time to put doubt aside and confront her father with what she was afraid tomorrow might bring.

A low whine sounded from below, the sound of an ether chariot powering down. A few moments later the door to the main transit shaft slid open and her father emerged, a worn look on his face.

"Trielle," he said softly. "I didn't expect anyone to be awake."

"I was waiting for you," she said, then added, "I need to ask you about something, about the reignition."

"Of course," said Gedron, sitting down beside her.

"It will take a lot of gravitic energy to restart Vai, won't it?" she said hesitantly.

"Well… yes," he replied.

She paused for a moment, steeling herself.

"How large of an entropy storm do you think that much laridian ring usage will cause?"

Trielle watched as fear and shock crossed his face. It was quickly replaced by a look of bewilderment and a reassuring laugh, but he had lowered his guard long enough to confirm the truth.

"I don't know what you mean," he said finally.

The blatant lie struck a spark of anger within her.

"Yes," she said grimly, "I think you do. I've read Rashavey's work, Father. I know about the consequences of unbalanced virtual bosonic flux. I know what we did to our universe, though why is still a puzzle to me, and I know what we are going to do to it again tomorrow!"

The color drained from Gedron's face, leaving it pale and cadaverous, and for the first time Trielle saw the toll the last few days had taken on him. For a long time he was silent, staring off into the shadows of their apartment.

"We have no choice, Trielle," he said finally, his voice barely a whisper.

"No choice?" she repeated in disbelief. "You are the High Gravitist. If anyone has a choice it is you!"

177

"Trielle," said Gedron sternly, "I do not know how you came across this knowledge. In truth, I do not want to know. But understand this. I am a Heirophant, and I have taken an oath not just to guide the people of the Conclave, but to uphold the principles it stands for, the Axioms on which it was built. Yes, we know the cost of gravitic technology. We have always known. Few remember why it is we chose this path and what we had to conquer to create the society in which we dwell. It is well that they do not. Now, you know in part, and I ask that you inquire no further. What happens tomorrow, happens because it must. It is better to act, and by that act to create our own destiny, no matter how dark, than to idly sit by and wait for the end."

"And so you act to hasten that end?" asked Trielle, her anger rising. "Father, these are not just principles we are talking about, but worlds, and all the living beings on them. If what you are saying is true then our civilization is founded on a desire for its own annihilation. It's no wonder Garin rejects the axioms!"

At the mention of Garin, Gedron's eyes widened.

"Trielle," he said, "do you know where he is?"

"No," she admitted, "but now I know what he is searching for."

"Searching?"

"Yes," said Trielle. "The last time I saw him he was heading through the transit system to the rim, trying to find out whether the Axioms you hold to so blindly are all that there is. And I hope he found the answers he needed, because if he didn't, tomorrow might be the last day he has to look."

Overtaken by sudden exhaustion, Trielle rose abruptly and gave Gedron one last, hard look. "Father, whatever you may think, you do have a choice!" Then she

turned and walked away, leaving Gedron alone with his
thoughts.

***

Trielle and Dyana had long since gone to sleep, but
Gedron could find no rest. He paced the floor of the
apartment, unable to reject the course he and the other
Heirophants had chosen, but unable to reject Trielle's words
either. Suddenly the walls felt too close, the ceiling like a
lead weight poised to crush him. He had to get out.

Gedron entered the transit tube and a few moments
later emerged onto a balcony of white stone that stood near
the top of the monolith in which his family lived. He took a
deep breath, letting the cool nightside air fill his lungs as he
gazed down at the crystalline towers and glass bridges of his
home. Despite the lateness of the hour, he could see the
occasional indistinct figure walking along the paths below,
enjoying the eternal twilight.

I have to proceed. I have no choice.

He repeated the words to himself over and over,
trying in vain to take some comfort in the inevitability of
what he must do. But somehow he couldn't quite bring
himself to believe them.

Sighing in frustration, Gedron leaned back and lifted
his eyes skyward to the myriad worlds of the Conclave.
Some were so close that Gedron almost felt as if he could
reach out and pluck them from the sky, others were mere
multicolored sparks burning amidst the dark abyss, but all
were worlds he had pledged to shepherd and protect. A
sickly green light flickered momentarily in the void, and
Gedron grimly wondered how many of those worlds would
still be there tomorrow.

Chapter 17: The Sepulcher of Suns

The valley's brilliance was such a contrast to the cool darkness of the mountain that at first Garin had to squint to see anything at all. Bur gradually his eyes became accustomed to the light and he was able to take stock of his surroundings.

He stood at the meeting point of four great mountain ranges that stretched off into the distance. The mountains seemed both beautiful and forbidding, their sheer granite surfaces shimmering with reflected light. Between the ranges stretched sterile valleys of stark, grassless rock. The sky above was a brilliant blue and seemed somehow closer than the skies of the worlds he knew, almost close enough to touch. Seized by a sudden intuition, Garin looked behind him, and saw, not more than fifty paces away, the great expanse of the sky curving down to meet the earth in a shifting sapphire wall. Embedded within this wall were two immense pillars of white marble, bigger than mountains, framing the blinding disk of a rising sun.

Then Garin felt a pang of fear.

Where is Daath?

Garin quickly glanced around, but could see no trace of him. Still, he did not wish to squander his lead. Turning back to the mountains, Garin quickly assessed each of the valleys, deciding eventually on one to the northwest (if the direction of the rising sun could be considered east in this place), and strode off resolutely.

The floor of the valley was level and its course straight as an arrow, so Garin had no difficulty in his travels. The bright sun rose quickly in the sky, washing the landscape with an endless cataract of light that seemed almost a solid thing. As he journeyed further from the world's edge, hints of vegetation began to appear. Never more than the occasional patch of grass and flowers, they still served to break the sublime monotony of stone and light. Finally, a little before noon, the valley opened up into a broad bowl filled with innumerable cenotaphs spaced closely at regular intervals. In the center of the bowl stood a stone hut, its architecture simple but elegant.

Garin paused for a moment, questioning whether he should proceed, but eventually curiosity overcame him and he proceeded to the nearest of the cenotaphs. A flat, rectangular slab of mirrored rock fully as big as Garin, its upper surface was inscribed with the image of a star surrounded by rays of light. Beneath the image, extending almost to the ground, were a series of inscriptions in every language and ideogram imaginable. Most were incomprehensible to Garin, but near the bottom he saw one in the common tongue of the Conclave.

> Alcyone: 13,885,032,211 to 14,000,012,650. Rest in peace my daughter...

Garin turned and looked at another monolith and saw the same starburst symbol followed by a similar litany. Only the names and numbers were different.

"They are the graves of my children. All but three are gone now."

The booming voice startled Garin. Lifting his eyes from the stones, he saw a titanic figure approaching him from the direction of the stone house. The figure was robed in white and bore a breastplate of burnished gold on which this insignia of a blazing sun was engraved. His eyes burned with a piercing brilliance, and he wore a jeweled crown that burned as if aflame, sending showers of golden light onto the landscape. As he approached the air grew warmer, as if his body contained an immense source of heat and power. The figure was majestic, almost godlike, and Garin found himself sinking to his knees in humility as the being drew near.

The figure laughed jovially.

"Rise, and pay me no homage. In the highest order of things, am I not a servant such as you? Be welcome here, creature of the lower worlds. I am Hyperion Starfather. Welcome to my home."

Starfather?

The word tugged at Garin's thoughts, and he turned again to the monoliths that filled the valley, scrutinizing the inscriptions one by one.

Alpheratz, Wezen, Adhara, Menkalinen, Deneb...

As the unfamiliar names rolled through Garin's mind a vision of the ancient night skies he had seen in his dream rose within him. Then he understood.

"The stars," he said softly. "These are the tombs of the ancient stars. They were your children?"

"Yes," said Hyperion, "and I loved each one dearly." A single, shining tear rolled down his face and Garin at once felt a sadness deeper than any emotion he had ever experienced before. They stood for a while among the tombs in silent contemplation of what the universe had lost, neither one speaking, neither one wishing to.

"Come," said Hyperion at last. "Join me for a meal in my home. Come meet my remaining sons and tell us of your journey."

Garin nodded, and followed Hyperion though the vast cemetery to the stone house at its center. Entering through a massive portal framed by slabs of granite and rock crystal, they passed through a grand hallway into a high-ceilinged great room lit by tall windows that flashed and sparkled in the noonday sun. A long table dominated half of

the room, laden with meat, bread and fruit. At the table sat
two frail, elderly men robed in grey. Their faces were
shriveled, and their eyes dull. In the corner of the room
stood three beds. Two were empty, but the third was
occupied by a near-motionless figure.

"Vasya, Verduun, how fares your brother?" asked
Hyperion.

Garin's eyes widened as he realized who these men
were.

"The same," whispered the nearest of the old men,
his voice barely discernable. "Vai barely moves now. There
is yet a faint spark of life within, but each minute he grows
closer to death."

Hyperion nodded gravely, then brightened.

"My sons," he said, "let us put this sadness aside.
We have a guest for our midday feast." Hyperion motioned
to Garin, who introduced himself. Hyperion then sat down
at the great table and bade Garin do likewise. After a brief
benediction, which Garin found both surprising and
strangely comforting, the feast commenced.

Garin had not realized how hungry he was, and he
ate with abandon to the bemused smiles of Vasya and
Verduun, who themselves consumed only a little bread and
wine. Hyperion and his sons waited patiently while Garin
refilled his plate a second and a third time. Only when it was
clear that he had eaten his fill did they speak.

"From whence do you come?" asked Verduun.

"I am from Latis, in the world of Phaneros," replied
Garin.

"Latis…" murmured Vasya, "All mesas and crystals,
is it not?"

"Yes," said Garin.

"I've always loved that planet," said Vasya. "I
remember when it formed from the dust, all heat and molten

rock burning in the void. It was one of my originals, you know…" Vasya's eyes closed for a moment in reminiscence, and Garin marveled at the immense age of the being he was conversing with.

"Many days I have stood in the city of Scintillus and basked in you and your brother's light," Garin said at last in reply. "I thank you for that."

Vasya nodded with a smile.

"What of Xhorhallas, the water world?" asked Verduun expectantly. "How fares it and its people?"

"I'm sorry," said Garin, a note of sadness in his voice. "It was destroyed in the last entropy storm."

"Oh," murmured Verduun quietly. He sat in silence for a moment. "It is a hard thing to hear of the death of your children," he said at last.

"Indeed," said Hyperion with a sigh. "But come, I would not hear of these sad events any longer. Rather, I would know what brings you to our valley, child of Phaneros. It is fortunate that you have come to us."

Garin took a deep breath and told them of his journey. Beginning with the day that Vai's light failed, he spoke of Kyr, Sha-Ka-Ri, the Sovereign Road, and his encounters with the beings of Materia. When he reached his confrontation with Daath, Hyperion's countenance darkened.

"You know of him?" asked Garin.

"Daath is well known to most who dwell in our world," said Hyperion grimly. "He has done much evil here and in the lower worlds. But I would know more of the being you call Kyr. I confess that I have not heard that name before."

"He is old," said Garin in reply, "older than anyone I have ever known, but he does not bear himself as if he was weak. His eyes seemed young and alive. It's hard to describe, but he seemed almost... authoritative, as if he were a Heirophant of the Conclave." He reflected for a few more moments, then said: "I don't know if this is important, but he had a strange pattern of scars around his forehead."

At the mention of the scars, Hyperion closed his eyes in recollection, murmuring to himself.

"So that is his name in this age of Phaneros..."

Suddenly Hyperion opened his eyes, a wide smile on his face. "Indeed I know Kyr," he said to Garin with a note of gladness. "I know him well, though when he last traversed Mythos he was known by another name. It is unfortunate you were separated from him by the Shadow. My council would be to seek him out with all your strength."

"Apart from fleeing Daath," said Garin, "that is my desire as well. But I do not know where to start. In fact, I do not know even know the name of this world. Did I hear you refer to it as Mythos?"

"Yes," said Hyperion, "and, as the word implies, it is the place from whence the stories that form the structure of Phaneros are derived."

As Hyperion spoke, Garin saw in a flash of insight the common thread that linked the Conclave with the higher worlds. If Materia was the reality behind the physical substrate of the universe, then Mythos was the reality behind its ongoing narrative. But if that were true, and the Shadow lay between them... Suddenly the implications struck him with almost physical force.

"Daath," said Garin in horror, "he's trying to sever the material universe from its purpose, to make it into a world of meaningless matter in motion. He's trying to make the Axioms become reality!"

"Yes," said Hyperion coldly. "That has always been his aim, and it is why he pursues you. Now that you understand you have become a danger to him, for his strength lies in blindness and ignorance."

"But I lost him when I entered Mythos," said Garin.

"No," said Hyperion, "the entrance into Mythos only split your paths, as it also split your path and Kyr's. For each of you is on a different meridian."

Seeing the look of confusion on Garin's face, Hyperion rose and left the room, returning a few moments later with a large blank parchment and a quill pen. Clearing a space on the table, Hyperion flattened out the parchment and drew a series of five concentric circles. He then drew four smaller semicircles within the outermost circle at the four points of the compass.

"This is the basic structure of Mythos," explained Hyperion. "Each circle is a movement, a chapter in the grand narrative of the cosmos. The outer circle is that of beginnings, and each of the cardinal directions represents a type of beginning that influences the lands around it."

At this he indicated the four smaller semicircles.

"My house stands in the Sepulcher of Suns, a great valley in the Lands of Stone and Light to the east. You arrived in Mythos through the Columns of Morning at Worlds Edge, a place not too far from here. To the north, at the base of the World Tree, lie the Lands of Ancient Night. The Lands of Silence and the Sacred Mountain lie to the west, and the Lands of the Hidden and the Great Colossus lie to the south. When a conscious being arrives at our world the choices they have made, the overall direction of their life's path, determine the location where they first enter. Even Daath is bound by this this law, for despite all his power he is still subject to the Great Story. When he has come to Mythos in ages past he has entered through the Lands of Ancient Night."

"And what of Kyr," asked Garin, "where does he enter?"

Hyperion laughed. "Child," he said, "the one you call Kyr can enter wherever he wishes. Those who tell the stories are not subject to them, unless they so will it."

Hyperion's words puzzled Garin, but before he could ask their meaning Hyperion had begun to draw again, filling the image with an array of lines. Each started at the outermost circle and continued inward until it reached the very center of the image. Some curved gently like the course of a meandering river, others twisted and looped in dizzying spirals. None were straight.

"These are the Meridians," explained Hyperion. "They are the only way to successfully traverse the circles of this world. I have drawn each circle as a finite space but in reality each extends forever, just as each page of a book represents a fixed but infinite section of the time and space of the story it contains. To turn the pages is to move through the story, and so it is with the Meridians. Each reflects a particular narrative connecting the circles; only by submitting to its flow can one travel."

The sheer complexity of the diagram threatened to overwhelm Garin, and he sat back in his chair with a discouraged sigh.

So many paths...

"Do not be troubled," said Hyperion. "Did I not say that it was fortunate you came to us?"

Hyperion marked a small circle within the northwestern portion of the Lands of Stone and Light, next to one of the larger, straighter meridians.

"The Sepulcher of Suns lies close to the origin-point of the Great Eastern Meridian. If you leave this valley in the direction of the setting sun you will soon come to the shores of Mare Primum, the universal ocean that once deluged the worlds beneath in judgment. There you will find the Mariner, who is also called Unapishtim, Atrahasis, Mano, Deucalion and Noah. Even now he completes the great Ark with which he seeks to cross the floods. Go to him and seek passage, for his ship travels the meridian."

Garin stared at the map, examining the gentle curve of the Great Eastern Meridian. It did seem to be a more direct route than many. He traced its lazy arc as it crossed the inner circles before ending deep in the heart of Mythos, the place where all Meridians met.

"Hyperion," said Garin, "All the meridians begin in different places, but they all seem to go to the same place. Where do they lead?"

Hyperion sighed. "To the end of all stories, Garin," he said cryptically. "Once the heart of Mythos was a paradise, a mountaintop garden filled with beauty and delight that grew in the light of the Trees of Life and Wisdom. In those days the Beloved dwelt there in splendour and all journeys ended with her embrace, but since the coming of Daath all that has changed. Paradise has withered, leaving only a bloody mount of sacrifice rising above the corrupt city of Hyrosol Eld. Few from the Lands of Stone and Light travel there in this age and so I have little knowledge of what you will find when you arrive, though what rumors have come to us are filled with shadow and terror. But this I do know. If there is any place within our world where you might find Kyr again, it is there. Now come, our meal is over and you must prepare for your journey."

Hyperion, Garin, Vai and Verduun rose from the table and began to exit the room. Suddenly a piercing scream rent the air, freezing them where they stood. As one they turned toward the source of the screem to see Vai convulsing upon his bed, surrounded by a nimbus of ghostly blue light.

188

Hyperion and his sons stared, their eyes widening in fear as Vai screamed again, and Garin suddenly realized what he was witnessing.

"It's Father!" said Garin. "The Gravitic Council is trying to reignite Vai!"

Chapter 18: Anastasis Astrae

The Worldship Gog hung in the skies above Vai's darkened orb. Shaped like a titanic golden lotus the size of small moon, the craft spanned one thousand miles between its furthest reaches. Each petal of the lotus, strengthened against its own weight by an infrastructure of pion-energized neutronium spars, carried more laridian rings than entire worlds. The petals joined together at the central ovule of the flower, which housed the ship's mighty engines. Its primary reactor was fueled by a blazing mass of neutronium slowly being converted into strange matter, a process capable of producing millions of petajoules of energy, enough to power a planet.

The long, tapering column of the flower's central pistil extended outward from the engines. Crafted of noetic crystal and imagnite, this structure housed the computational and navigational infrastructure of the worldship, as well as the quarters of its crew. At its very tip stood the bridge of the ship, a vast tiered platform of gold covered by a canopy of reinforced crystal. The bridge was filled with mounting ranks of infochryst terminals operated by the elite of the College of Gravitists. In its center stood Gedron, clad in the formal raiment of the High Gravitist and surrounded by his personal retainers. Though his face was stern, his heart was heavy. The time for reignition was at hand.

"Sir," said a red faced Gerellian, his three eyes blinking asynchronously, "Shemyazai, Armaros and Turiyel are now in position. That accounts for all etherreavers. The equator of Vai is encompassed."

"Thank you Yithra," said Gedron. "And I see that the neutronium forges have reached polar alignment."

190

"Yes sir, replied Yithra-Gor.

Gedron nodded in silent acknowledgment, then lifted his hands in a formal gesture of summoning. Three infographic crystals silently rose from the platform in response. Within seconds, each crystal was alight with shifting images and symbols, the sum total of the current available data from the Ramachrond and the Ionocaric Infochrysts regarding the state of Vai.

"The deep probes have reached the core-radiative boundary," said Yithra-Gor after scrutinizing the data. "We can prepare no more."

"Indeed," observed Gedron, "we begin now."

Gedron raised his right hand in preparation for the first gesture of command, but then hesitated at the last moment. Instead, he called up an additional data stream that appeared on the peripheral infographic crystals: a realtime image of the state of the entropy clouds. Yithra-Gor examined it for a few minutes and then looked to Gedron questioningly.

"To remind us of what we are fighting," said Gedron in response, though the words rang hollow. Then he steeled himself, raised his hands again in a gesture of declamation, and gave the first commands.

"Accelerate laridian rings, initiate fermionic field charging process!"

Transmitted ship to ship and magnified by a thousand relays and amplifiers, each crewmember of the massed reignition fleet heard Gedron's words as if he were standing beside them. Within moments the petals of the Gog had taken on an eerie, almost ephemeral quality as their surfaces shimmered with concentrated gravitic force. Angry blue discharges crackled across the hull. A flood of data from the infographic crystals confirmed that the etherreavers and neutronium forges were in a similar state of readiness.

Gedron glanced one last time at the image of the entropy clouds. Although there was some new agitation, they had not changed position.

Gedron opened his mouth to give the word to continue, but choked at the last minute, so that it came out not as a command, but as a whisper.

"Begin reignition…"

The petals of the Worldship Gog erupted in searing blue fire.

***

Ten thousand spikes of sharp blue incandescence lanced through Vai's darkened atmosphere, driving deep into the star's core like adrenalin-filled needles aimed at the heart of a dying man.

And Vai convulsed.

Rivers of red flame larger than worlds flashed through the dead star's bowels as helium ash, crushed beyond thought by the gravitic pulse, began to fuse. The streams of burning plasma expanded, mixing and churning the cooling gases of Vai's mantle until at last they reached the surface, erupting from the photosphere in great gouts of hellish light like blisters of flaming blood. And deep beneath it all a subsonic cry of pain echoed throughout the remains of the cosmos as walls of green flame collapsed inexorably inward, annihilating all the worlds in their path.

***

In the House of Hyperion, the body of Vai writhed upon the bed. Now swollen with power, the nimbus surrounding him pulsed with an unholy radiance. Garin watched in horror as tendrils of spectral light reached inward from the glowing cloud, penetrating the flesh of Vai's chest. Suddenly the light flared, each tendril becoming as bright as a lightning bolt as arcs of actinic blue flame raced down them into Vai's faltering heart. Vai's body stiffened, his eyes snapped open, and a cry of such agony issued from his mouth that Garin thought his heart would break.

Hyperion rushed to the bed and dropped to his knees.

"Vai! My son! What are they doing to you?"

Vai continued to convulse violently as the cataract of lightning poured into his chest, and an alien radiance began to burn in his sightless eyes. Seeing this, Hyperion cried out again with a deep wail of lament and prostrated himself before the bed. Vasya and Verduun stood behind him with bowed heads, weeping silently but with no less sorrow.

Suddenly overcome by the scene before him, Garin screamed.

"Father! Father please stop!"

Then he too fell to the ground sobbing, his words a muted whisper of pain.

"Father, please stop!"

***

Aboard the Worldship Gog, Gedron stared grimly at the data pouring in through the infographic crystals.

The initial surge had worked as expected, and Vai now burned with a sullen red glow. When the first flames had pierced the star's surface, a great cheer had erupted from the Gog's crew.

But at what cost...

Sixty four worlds lost to the entropy clouds in under five minutes. Only his command to stop the barrage once the first signal of ignition reached the Gog had halted the storm. Still, he reminded himself, these casualties had been expected. The forecasts had been sent as planned, and he desperately hoped that their inhabitants had possessed enough caution to heed them. They, at least, would have had a chance. He was more concerned about what would come next.

Sighing, Gedron turned his attention to the two infographic crystals directly in front of him. Each held the image of a neutronium forge depicted against the backdrop of Vai's north and south poles. With a gesture, Gedron summoned the governing infochryst of each forge, and the images were replaced by two expressionless crystalline faces framed by glassy feathers.

"Harut, Marut, have you had sufficient time to calculate the needed field strength based on the parameters of the initial burst?"

The infochrysts responded with a barrage of statistics and models, their equivalent of a yes.

Gedron glanced again at the image of Vai. The photosphere already had begun to cool, its ruddy light now shot through with growing patches of shadow. There was no time left.

"Harut, Marut, commence stellar sustenance protocol."

From high above the poles of Vai, two tubes of blue gravitic flux shot starward from the neutronium forges. As the flux tubes met and stabilized deep in Vai's core, the surface of the star ceased cooling and once again began to burn. At this a cheer rang out from the crew, and Gedron permitted himself to smile. Then a series of bright flashes from the peripheral infographic crystals drew his attention, and his smile froze as he saw the entropy clouds erupt with poisonous fire.

Sickly green prominences of destructive force arced from their surfaces, tearing through planets, moons and asteroids like scythes through wheat. Gedron watched for what seemed an eternity, hoping that Vai's renewed solar wind could hold back the storms, but the clouds were already advancing faster than they ever had before, crashing down upon world after world in a vast boiling wave. Within a few moments it was clear. Vai's radiation pressure was not enough. His models had been accurate. His worst fears were now a reality.

Already the crew of the Gog knew that something was wrong. He could see a few of them casting furtive glances toward the infographic crystals that showed the entropy clouds, their expressions thick with worry. Gedron glanced sideways at Yithra-Gor, who met his gaze with a similar look of concern.

It's not too late. I can still stop this.

The thought rose unbidden, only to be overwhelmed by the memory of the Entrope's accusation of treason. Gedron turned again to the image of the entropy storms, his mind a whirlpool of indecision. As he watched yet another world be consumed by the storms he suddenly thought of his son, alone on the outer rim, adrift in a cosmos dissolving because of his actions. The whirlpool abated, and a slim crystal of icy conviction began to form in his heart.

"The Axioms be damned," he growled. "Harut, Marut, initiate laridian ring deceleration protocol and full shutdown sequence." Gedron paused for a moment, then added, "And delete all stellar maintenance protocol data from long-term memory!"

The emotionless faces of Harut and Marut nodded and vanished. A few seconds later the gravitic flux tubes projected by the neutronium forges dissipated. Gedron watched as the surface of Vai cooled, the red flames sputtering and vanishing, vast patches of shadow spreading across the star like a fungus. Soon the orb was again cold and dead. Gedron glanced at the auxiliary infographic crystals and was relieved to see the entropy clouds slow and stop, their violence abated. Gedron lowered his arms and the infographic crystals that surrounded him slid slowly into the platform beneath. Suddenly overcome by weariness, he took a deep breath and addressed the crew of the Gog.

"College of Gravitists and crew of the Worldship Gog, we have failed in our efforts to sustain the reignition of Vai. I ask that you now set a course for high orbit above Latis, though it is with profound disappointment that we return to our families and homeworlds."

His speech completed, Gedron stepped down from the platform and left the bridge. Even now the Heirophants were meeting in Conclave, expecting him to join them after a successful reignition.

They would not be pleased.

***

Like mist dissolving in the light of the rising sun, the nimbus surrounding Vai began to disperse. Soon the violent convulsions subsided and the strange light faded from his eyes. Garin watched as the last of Vai's muscles relaxed, and as Vai slipped into a deep slumber he rose to face Hyperion and his sons.

Their eyes moist with tears, Vasya and Verduun held their breaths in fear of another assault, but as it became clear that this was not forthcoming their tears abated and their shoulders sagged with visible relief. Hyperion remained motionless, kneeling in silent contemplation beside the bed of Vai. His heart troubled, Garin walked to Hyperion's side and laid a gentle hand on his shoulder.

"They will try again, Hyperion," he whispered softly.

"Why?" answered Hyperion in anger. "Is it not enough that the rest of my children are dead? Now they must torture those that are left in their final hours? What good does this serve? Can your people not accept the fate they have chosen for themselves?"

"No," said Garin gravely. For a moment his vision turned inward as he contemplated the crystalline shell in which Daath had attempted to imprison him: his own personal world, a black hole of purposeless self-reference.

"My people have lost the ability to see anything beyond the surface of their own dying cosmos, beyond the meaninglessness they consider their only true inheritance."

Hyperion pondered this for a moment.

"And what of you, son of man?" he said finally. "You have done much to come this far, and you speak of the shortsightedness of your race, but can you truly see?"

"I know now that this blindness is the work of Daath…." began Garin.

"No!"

Hyperion rose to face Garin, all traces of his previous good natured demeanor gone. His face burned with imprisoned heat like the surface of the noonday sun, and his eyes flashed with righteous wrath.

"I will not allow you the refuge of that half-truth," Hyperion shouted. "Daath's evil is vast, but you bear as much blame as he. Though his power is great, it is your choices that have granted him the authority to exercise it."

As Hyperion spoke, Garin immediately saw the truth of what he said.

"You are right, Hyperion Starfather," said Garin, bowing his head his head in humility. "Though I was brought up in darkness, it was still my choice to remain blind. There is much that I do not know, and many things I do not yet understand, but I have seen seen enough glimpses of the light to know that I never want to go back to that darkness again."

Hyperion's features softened.

"Such words are the beginning of wisdom," he murmured. Then he rose and motioned Garin to follow him from the room.

"Come, you will need provisions for your journey."

After outfitting Garin with a traveling cloak and a pack of food, carefully wrapped so it would not grow damp as he sailed the stormy waters of the Mare Primum, Hyperion lead Garin from the house and into the valley outside. The sun had already moved past the zenith and was beginning its descent through the western sky. Hyperion pointed to the far side of the valley where, in the afternoon light, Garin could just make out a rift in the surrounding mountains.

"There," said Hyperion. "That pass is the beginning of the Great Eastern Meridian. Mare Primum lies only a short distance past the mountain wall. Travel with all haste, though, for even now the Mariner completes his ship and makes ready to sail the flood at sunset."

Garin nodded, then paused as a question rose in his mind.

"Hyperion," he asked, "if the Mariner is he who sailed the great flood, how is it that he only completes his ship today?"

Hyperion laughed, his good nature returning.

"Child of Phaneros, do you think that time only flows one way? He sails the flood every sunset. In Mythos, each week contains all the ages of the Cosmos. Now, go with my blessing."

Garin turned and, with resolute steps, strode toward the mountain pass.

Chapter 19: The Price of a Cosmos

A great crowd gathered amidst the towering spires of Scintillus' central plaza to watch the reignition of Vai. The local businesses, seeing an opportunity to enhance their wealth, had grown booths and arbors from which to sell their wares out of the local crystalline substrate. The entire atmosphere was festive and bright.

With eyes turned skyward at the appointed hour, the crowd cheered wildly when the pale disk of the dead star burst into crimson light. Even when the light failed a few moments later, and the star faded again into the skies of Latis like a ghost, the crowd's enthusiasm remained undimmed, a testament to the almost childlike belief that in this endeavor the Gravitic College could not fail.

Then the first reports from the Worldship Gog began to filter into the crowd. They came slowly, one personal infochryst at a time, but soon the news was spreading like a virus and a tone of uncertainty began to replace the crowd's once ebullient mood. Uncertainty quickly gave way to shock and then despair as news of the first entropy storms arrived, and cries of panic rose from a few isolated pockets as citizens from the outer rim realized that they now had no homeworld to return to. At last, like a wave withdrawing from a beach at low tide, the crowd began to drain away.

Trielle stood with her mother beneath a translucent arbor at the edge of the plaza, taking in the bleak expressions on each face as they filed past. Dyana had wished to meet after Trielle's morning classes at the Arx Scientia so that they could watch the event together and she had agreed, more from a sense of duty than anything else. It was hard to be enthusiastic about something that was doomed to fail.

As the first new light from Vai had washed over the crowd, Dyana's countenance had lit up like a star, and Trielle had found herself hoping against all logic that her father had succeeded after all. But as the light dimmed, reality had reasserted itself. Now, as Trielle watched the last guttering embers vanish one by one from Vai's darkening surface, she struggled to feel something, to share in the emotions that she was witnessing, but she could not. She had known what was coming.

What did I expect...

"Trielle, I need to get back to the antenna."

Summoned out of her reverie, Trielle looked at her mother. Though Dyana's voice was calm and measured, her face was as pale as ice, and her hands trembled slightly as she spoke.

"The College will want to see the gravity wave readings from the ignition event as soon as possible. Perhaps they will be of help to Gedron. Do you have more classes this afternoon?"

"No," said Trielle, "I'm finished for today. You go ahead. I'm going to stay here for a while."

Her mother nodded wordlessly and joined the crowd as it poured from the plaza."

Soon the last dregs of the crowds had drained away, and, apart from a few stragglers, she was alone. She did not know how long she stood there in the eternal noon, staring absently into the sky, pondering the cost of her father's actions, but at last weariness overtook her and she too left the plaza, making her way to the Kinetorium and her waiting ether chariot.

***

The Heirophants were joined in Conclave, but instead of their typical vantage point in the midst of the three suns, their thrones now seemed to hover mere feet above the blackened photosphere of Vai. The gases below them churned sickeningly, pools of ash and dust larger than worlds.

Gedron was disturbed by the choice of venue, but not surprised. It was, he reflected, a fitting location for his chastisement.

"Even now the rimward information-flows are fragmenting," transmitted the Photocanth, his halo flushed with sullen reds and oranges. "The populace is in turmoil. Already a migration from the rim begins, and there is not enough room within the Guard to accommodate it. Observe."

The Photocanth raised his hand and a cloud of glimmering spheres sprang into existence in the space between the thrones, each representing a planet of the Conclave. Above each world hung a column of bright light, and spider-thin threads wove in between them.

"The glowing columns represent a combined sociometric integration of each planet's current available resources," explained the Photocanth, "and the threads represent movements of people and goods. Before the failed reignition, the system was stable, but this is no longer so."

Gedron watched as the model swung into motion, the planets accelerating along their vast orbits, the transit lines arcing between worlds shimmering like gossamer threads in sunlight. Above the worlds, the columns undulated up and down in a seemingly placid dance of economic stability. All was peaceful.

Then the worlds along the edge of the model began to darken and vanish one by one like the embers of a dying fire. Dense webs of shimmering thread burst from each world in its final moments, a representation of those who were able to flee the destruction to the relative safety of the Conclave's dense heart. Soon the worlds had ceased disappearing, but despite this the bundles of thread continued to erupt from the rimward planets, and as they did so the economic dance was disrupted. The resources of the outer worlds stagnated, the bright columns above them shrinking to mere fractions of what they were, while the inner Conclave quickly became overburdened, their resource-columns rising uncontrollably and one by one taking on the ominous red hue that denoted unsustainable economic strain.

"The last moments of this are a simulation," stated the Photocanth flatly, the fiery red tones of his halo deepening to a solemn umber, "but the sociometric calculations employed are straightforward and unquestionable."

"My servitors have concurrently measured a sharp drop in short-term measurements of trade," transmitted the Ouranos Radii. "Electrophotonic currency exchange is a fifth of what it was this morning."

The Ouranos Radii gestured, calling into existence the image of a vast green sea that hung in the space beneath the Photocanth's simulation. The sea roiled and churned, its luminous crests and troughs representing rates of fiscal expenditure. It did not take long for Gedron to see that the levels of the central part of the sea were falling.

"Even now the rates of exchange continue to drop among the central worlds," he continued, "and if this stagnation continues, it will only exacerbate the resource drain caused by the migration.

As he spoke, the model continued to evolve. Once free waves of economic activity began to circle the central depression, transforming the image into a violent accretion disk, its center a dark abyss. Above this void, the inner worlds of the Conclave glowed the deep crimson of complete financial collapse like stars caught in the eternal redshift of a black hole's event horizon.

"It appears that the potential for profound social instability that was outlined when last we met had become our new reality," transmitted the Chromatocron gravely, his halo a subdued grey. He paused a moment before adding, "I trust the reason is clear to all…"

As his words rang throughout the collective thoughtspace of the Heirophants his eyes turned and fixed on Gedron, the weight of their gaze boring through him like high-energy lasers. A brief spark of anger rose within Gedron's breast and briefly threatened to become visible in his halo, but he fought it down and regained his composure. Nothing could be gained here by rash words. He had made his choice, now he must defend it rationally. He only hoped the other heirophants would listen.

Gedron took a deep, calming breath. His halo flashed with mingled gold and sapphire hues as he willed himself into the state of confidence and composure that he needed.

"I can only assume your last reference was to the unsustainable nature of the ignition event," he transmitted smoothly. "As you must certainly understand by now, the waste bosonic flux created by the neutronium forges significantly exceeded the radiation pressure Vai could generate in its reignited state. After the sustenance protocol was initiated it quickly became clear to me that the initial entropy storms would only accelerate if we continued and had a reasonable likelihood of overwhelming the Guard and breaching the inner Conclave. Prudence dictated that we cease our efforts."

"Prudence!" transmitted the Chromatochron, his halo flickering with angry vermillion. "And what did this prudence you refer to tell you about the effects of your failure on Conclave society as a whole?"

Gedron's halo flared with brilliant gold and black. "Do not take me for a fool, Tauron! Of course I considered the sociometric ramifications. Still, the cost of continuing was too great. Hundreds of worlds would have been extinguished. We could not go on!"

"No," transmitted the Chromatocron, "you both could and should have continued, and your error in this is grave. Observe what might have been!"

The Chromatocron gestured toward the still-evolving sociometric simulation, his movement causing it to rewind to the time just before the ignition attempt. Then, with a flick of his finger, he set the model in motion again. Again the outer worlds began to flicker and vanish, again the waves of migration fled each planet before it died. But this time the death of worlds did not cease; rather, it accelerated.

Faster and faster the worlds vanished, each representing millions of lives extinguished like sparks falling into water. At first the migrations continued, but eventually the wave of entropic activity caught up with them and the lines representing transit and flight died in the surging storm, countless lives erased in the very act of seeking freedom. When the entropy storms finally abated more than two thirds of the Conclave had been annihilated, along with the bulk of those fleeing the destruction. Only a fraction of the migrants had survived. Brief waves of economic disturbance initially fractured the calm of the remaining worlds, but these quickly subsided into a new equilibrium quite similar to the old.

"Do you now see?" transmitted the Chromatochron.

"I see the death of worlds," transmitted Gedron, the light of his halo flaring in barely restrained anger.

"And what is the life of a world, or even a hundred worlds, to the stability of the Conclave as a whole?" responded the Chromatochron. "Or have you forgotten the contents of the oath you took before us at your ascension?"

Summoned by the Chromatochron's words, memories surfaced in Gedron's mind like revenants called up from the grave: A dark chamber buried in the heart of the Omegahedron, a tablet of green crystal blazing with words of fire, the skull-like grin of the Entrope as he pledged to uphold the Axioms and the Conclave before the gathered Heirophants. As the words of the oath filled his mind, the fiery light of his halo died away.

No part of it had been to protect the worlds of the Conclave.

"Ah," transmitted the Chromatochron, "I see that you remember. It is well that you do, for otherwise precious time would have been wasted. Now, we must develop a strategy to salvage what we can."

Though the indignation that once fueled Gedron's words had been all but quenched, a small fragment of resistance still remained.

"I would discuss this further before we proceed," transmitted Gedron, his halo gleaming with frigid, icy hues. "You say that the oath I took was to the Conclave as a whole and not to its people, yet surely the citizens are the substance and body of the Conclave. Surely it is their lives that we are here to defend!"

"While your words are true," transmitted the Ouranos Radii in response, "you are mistaken as to the nature of that defence. What is life without power, without the ability to impose our own desires on the world around us? It is the life of a slave, a life not worth living. It is this principle that the Axioms guard. It is this collective way of life, and not the mere survival of the worlds and their populace, that we have pledged our lives to safeguard."

"Well spoken," transmitted the Entrope, his halo a thunderhead of impenetrable blackness, "and it is in this that the violation of your oath is most clearly seen, for what are the Axioms if not the assurance that each life is its own and can act as if unbound to another. You have all witnessed the economic devastation that the High Gravitist's actions have precipitated, now hear what I foresee in this."

"I see citizens forced to forsake their homes to accommodate the migrants. I see wealth and abundance vanishing as individuals begin to use their resources on each other. I see an abandonment of the blessed selfishness of the Axioms as men and women cease to impose their own individual meanings on the chaos of their lives and are forced instead to invest in the meanings that others have made. I see the ancient heresies of the *Alapsari*, so carefully eradicated from our cosmos, rising again even as the end draws nigh. No, better to amputate the limb so that the patient can survive. Better to allow the death of half the Conclave so that the survivors may preserve their way of life."

As the Entrope's thoughts rang throughout the Hierophant's collective thoughtspace a horror of great darkness descended upon Gedron as for the first time in his life he truly saw the nature of Conclave society. It was no society at all, but rather an endless whirlpool of selfish individuals imprisoned in beautiful, glittering cages of their own making, each swirling downward into oblivion. He too had lived his entire life like this -never hearing, never seeing- and with this new insight rose the certainty that he could no longer do so. He knew that this course could only lead to the destruction of his reputation, his career, everything he had spent his life building, but he also knew that he could not go back.

"I see you are troubled, High Gravitist," the Chromatocron transmitted, and Gedron realized that he had allowed too many of his true thoughts to surface. His halo had grown turbulent, filled with clashing colors that mirrored his internal distress. Now, of all times, he must maintain control. Taking a deep breath, Gedron brought all his willpower to bear, driving the raging storm of emotions deep below the surface of his conscious thoughts in one swift act of mental discipline. Within seconds the turbulence had dissipated, the riot of colors fading to a pellucid blue. He was on dangerous ground, and needed to proceed with caution.

"No Tauron, only momentary confusion," transmitted Gedron. "You are, of course, correct regarding the content of the oath. Thank you for the reorientation."

The Chromatocron frowned at this, and Gedron wondered for a moment whether his apparent change of heart had been too abrupt. Then, mercifully, the frown faded, and the Chromatocron's halo brightened with reds and golds, the colors of authority.

"At this point," the Chromatochron continued, "I believe that there is little else that can be done other than attempt the ignition of Vai a second time. Fortunately, I have run multiple sociometric simulations of the impact of a second ignition attempt using the Nagmochron infochryst, and for most permutations the results are favorable. Given the positioning of the neutronium forges, we should be able to attempt re-ignition within the day."

"Unfortunately it will not be that simple," Gedron transmitted, his halo dark with foreboding. "There were... errors... in the initial stellar maintenance protocols that will require full scale rewrites of the major information flows to correct. Harut and Marut, the infochrysts who operate the forges, are even now undergoing data-core formatting in preparation for the parallel evolutionary computing sessions needed to address the issue, but it will take at least two weeks for the process to be completed."

"It is fortunate then," transmitted the Chromatocron, "that the Ouranos Radii and I have developed an alternative means to achieve sustained ignition that does not require the forges."

A brief white spark surged around Gedron's halo as his eyes widened in shock.

"Come now, High Gravitist, surely you did not think that you alone possessed the tools to avert this crisis," transmitted the Ouranos Radii, his halo suffused with a smug coppery glow. "Yours was a more… direct… route, I will admit, but while you were preparing the neutronium forges, the Chromatocron and I were able to complete a prototype vacuum sculptor.

Gedron frowned. He had heard proposals for devices such as this in the past, but had not realized that their development was this far advanced.

The Ouranos Radii gestured and the image of an intricate device appeared in the space between the thrones. The vacuum scupltor was shaped like a bluish, elongated diamond capped on each end by a silver cylinder. Within the diamond was a nest of interlocking rings that swerved and gyrated like an armillary sphere. Across the center of the device ran a thin filament that glowed a dull red.

"The central armature uses adapted laridian ring technology to create a pocket of abnormal extradimensional space within the core of the device," explained the Ouranos Radii. "By tuning the rotation of the rings within the armature, this space can be made to take on some of the characteristics of the more abstract symmetry group spaces postulated by our unified field theory. In these spaces, subatomic particles can be converted one into another interchangeably. The glowing filament traversing the core is an extremely thin wire of crystalline neutronium maximally charged with pi mesons. Not only do these mesons stabilize the neutronium, but they give it the ability to minutely polarize the false vacuum within the device by attracting virtual quark/antiquark pairs. This polarization then skews the properties of the symmetry space within the armature, causing it to preferentially generate particles that interact via the strong force. At each end of the device is a traditional laridian ring, positioned so that its output beam is focused on the core armature. As the beams enter the skewed symmetry space they are converted into a cloud of virtual quarks which the device then releases into the surrounding environment."

Gedron frowned, his halo darkening to an obscure gray. The device was certainly an ingenious creation, but how could a surge of virtual quarks affect a dead star? Then his halo visibly brightened as a glimmer of understanding flashed into his mind.

"You're trying to shift the balance of forces within Vai's core to permit helium fusion without external compression!" he transmitted.

"Correct, High Gravitist," transmitted the Chromatochron. "The primary barrier to reignition is the inability of helium to fuse at Vai's current internal pressures. As this is ultimately dependent on helium's atomic binding energy, then locally enhancing that binding energy should enhance the fusion process, should it not?"

Gedron pondered the Chromatocron's words. The propensity of an atom to either fuse or split depended on the tension between the forces within the nucleus: the strong force binding it together, the electromagnetic force

209

attempting to push it apart. The balance of these forces was such in the helium nucleus that sustained fusion could not occur at Vai's current mass; the force of gravity simply could not generate enough pressure to sustain the reaction. But if the strong force could somehow be magnified?

One significant effect of the virtual matter that filled the vacuum was the way in which it modulated the relative strength of the fundamental forces. In the case of electromagnetism this virtual matter, once polarized by the field, had the net effect of diminishing the force between two charged bodies. But in the case of the strong force the opposite occurred and the polarization of the vacuum actually enhanced the strength of the field. By flooding Vai with virtual quarks the tendency of the helium nuclei to bind would be increased and the compression needed to sustain fusion would be lessened considerably. Gedron's halo flashed blue and gold as he marveled at the design.

Perhaps we really can reignite Vai without another entropy storm!

The sheer beauty of what was being attempted almost overwhelmed Gedron's prior misgivings. Still, a small part of him remained uneasy.

"I can see we have impressed you," transmitted the Chromatocron. "Excellent! Even now the corona of Vai is being seeded with the devices."

As he spoke, the Chromatocron stretched out his hand and touched the image of the vacuum sculptor. The image shrank rapidly in response, until it was no bigger than a grain of sand, and came to rest in the Chromatocron's palm. Raising his hand to his lips, the Chromatocron gently exhaled and the tiny, sparkling mote that was the vacuum sculptor drifted downward toward the simulated surface of Vai. The device began to multiply exponentially as it descended -one becoming two, then four, then eight- until finally a cloud of gleaming dust had enrobed the surface of the dead star. Each grain began to pulse with soft blue light as the vacuum sculptors activated and a few moments later the star responded, its surface blazing with new life.

"In two day's time they will be ready," continued the Chromatocron, his halo shining with golden light, "and Vai will live again."

As Gedron watched the simulation his sense of uneasiness mounted, at last resolving into a single, disquieting thought. A chill rippled through through his flesh.

"Ouranos Radii," he asked. "Have these devices been tested?"

"Only in simulation," transmitted the Ouranos Radii. "That is why we did not offer this approach during the first ignition attempt. There are a number of unknowns, of course, but during perilous times such as these such risks must be taken."

Gedron's halo darkened. Reaching down toward the now-incandescent surface of Vai, he called up the simulation's source code, which appeared in the air as a table of obscure numbers. With a flick of his finger Gedron highlighted the value corresponding to the strong force binding coefficient, altered it by a millionth part, and restarted the model. This time the scintillation of the vacuum sculptors was followed by the brilliant flash of a supernova as the star's entire helium content fused catastrophically. His face grim, Gedron raised his hands and Vai fell away. Higher and higher the thrones rose, soaring upward from the three suns' orbital plane until at last the entire Conclave lay spread beneath them. From this vantage point the Heirophants watched as the shockwave from the exploding star disrupted first Vasya and then Verduun before finally sterilizing the worlds of the Conclave in a blast of searing radiation. A few moments later the planetary remnants were consumed by the surging tides of the entropy clouds.

"We have covered this ground already, have we not?" transmitted the Entrope, his halo a shifting mass of vermillion and nacreous green. "We know the tolerances are small, but better the Conclave be erased than the principles by which we live be compromised."

"Indeed," transmitted Gedron, his halo an inscrutable grey. "I was merely being sure our brethren were aware of all the potential consequences of our actions."

"I assure you they are," transmitted the Entrope. "Now that we have established this, High Gravitist, I assume that you will not object to assisting the Chromatochron and Ouranos Radii in their preparations for the next attempt."

Gedron nodded imperceptibly as his halo faded to a featureless black. The implication of the Entrope's words had not been lost on him.

Their discussion concluded, the Chromatochron raised his hands in the gesture of completion. As the last vestiges of the Heirophant's collective thoughtspace faded away, Gedron allowed himself to release the emotions he had been holding in check. He felt as if he were drowning, buried alive beneath a crushing wave of defeat. With his authority removed, what power did he have to prevent the catastrophe he had just witnessed?

He did not know what to do, and had little time in which to do it.

Chapter 20: Rumors of Wars

Trielle's ether chariot emerged from its corridor of twisted space into a tumultuous sky. From horizon to horizon, the eternal evening of Latis' far side was crisscrossed with threads of light. Trielle stared at them for a moment in confusion before finally realizing what they were.

Ships, fleeing the destruction of the outer worlds.

The Kinetorium had likewise been congested, but this dwarfed what she had seen there by an order of magnitude. The sight filled her with an aching sense of dread, an unshakeable sense that the life she had known was drawing to a close. She arrived home a few moments later and found her father sitting alone in the central apartment.

A sharp, hot anger flared within her.

"I see that you attempted the reignition," she began, then her voice trailed off as she saw his grim, haggard expression.

"Attempted and aborted," said Gedron finally. "I could see the storms raging, the worlds dying, from the bridge of the Gog! I couldn't continue, not knowing the cost! For all I knew, Garin could have been on any of them…"

His eyes were moist, as if he had been weeping, and Trielle's anger died away at the sight, leaving an empty, hollow feeling in her chest. She stood there for what seemed like an eternity, not knowing what to say. Finally, she sat down beside him.

"You aborted the ignition deliberately?"

"Yes, Trielle," replied Gedron. "The Heirophants and I called for a limited evacuation of the outermost worlds when we planned the ignition. We never revealed the real

213

reason. We told them that it was due to the higher risk of entropy storms caused by the loss of Vai's radiation pressure. But I always knew that the inhabitants of the outermost worlds had a chance. It was after I initiated the sustainment protocol, after I realized that the resulting entropic activity would almost certainly wipe out everything and everyone outside the Guard, that I halted the process. The other Heirophants were not pleased. Still, you said I had a choice, and I made the only choice I could, though it's not as if it will make any difference in the end."

A wave of conflicting emotions surged through Trielle, a volatile mixture of hope and foreboding.

"What do you mean, Father? Surely you have the ability as High Gravitist to prevent another attempt."

"Not anymore," said Gedron grimly. "When I aborted the protocol I erased it from the core memory of the neutronium forge infochrysts. I thought that would buy me time to think, to sort out what to do next. But the Chromatocron and Ouranos Radii have developed an alternative approach that doesn't directly involve gravitic manipulation, and so it falls outside of my jurisdiction. I've been asked to assist them, but it is in their hands now."

"An alternative approach?" said Trielle. "But surely that is in our favor. If it doesn't use laridian ring technology then perhaps Vai can be reignited safely."

"Unfortunately, that is not the case," said Gedron. "The new approach involves an experimental device called a Vacuum Sculptor, which uses a modified version of laridian ring technology to manipulate the binding values of the Strong Force over limited volumes of space. The new values allow helium to fuse at a lower pressure, bypassing the need for external compression. They're planning to seed Vai's atmosphere with a swarm of them."

"So this swarm will still generate excessive bosonic flux?" asked Trielle. "Is that the issue?"

"Unfortunately it's much worse than that," said Gedron. "By themselves the vacuum sculptors will generate some increased entropic activity, but not nearly as much as the stellar maintenance protocols, and if reignition can be achieved then Vai's radiation pressure should be enough to counter it. The real problem is that much of Vai is made of helium now. If the adjusted binding coefficient is off by even a millionth of a decimal, every atom in the entire star could fuse simultaneously."

Trielle's eyes widened. "You're saying Vai could go supernova?" she asked.

"I'm saying that Vai could experience a helium flash of such magnitude that a supernova would be benign in comparison" said Gedron. "And if it did, the resulting shockwave would almost certainly annihilate the rest of the Conclave."

"How likely is the helium flash scenario?" asked Trielle

"It's hard to say," answered Gedron with a sigh. "I haven't had time to run enough simulations. But my best guess is at least fifty percent."

Trielle sat in pensive silence, her mind struggling to grasp the sheer scope of this new threat. "How long until the devices are ready?" she asked finally.

"Two days at most," said Gedron with a sigh. "The Chromatocron and Ouranos Radii have been working on them for some time now, and I suspect that the bulk of them have already been fabricated. If that is true, then at this point it is mostly a matter of calibration."

"I don't understand, Father," said Trielle, her voice filled with sudden frustration. "Why would the Heirophants

215

take such a reckless course? Isn't it their duty to protect the Conclave?"

"The Conclave, yes," said Gedron, "its structure, ideals, values, everything but its people. Trielle, the Heirophants care more about the Axioms and the philosophy they represent than they do about lives of the people they rule. Until today I only understood this dimly. I thought it was my job to preserve the citizens of the Conclave. Evidently I was wrong."

"It always comes back to the Axioms," muttered Trielle angrily. "That's what Garin was so disturbed about before he left."

"What do you mean?" asked Gedron, a puzzled look on his face.

"Before he left," said Trielle, "Garin was incessantly questioning the Axioms. He said they no longer made sense to him. At first I thought he was being foolish, but not anymore."

"Trielle," said Gedron, a hungry look on his face, "what do you really know about where Garin has gone."

Trielle closed her eyes as a shiver of fear ran through her body. Should she speak? How much would he believe? How much could he accept? He was, after all, the High Gravitist. Then she opened her eyes and saw the expression of concern on his face. There was no trace of duplicitousness, only the unmitigated concern of a father for his son. Trielle took a deep breath, and told him the story. He listened patiently as she recounted Garin's dreams, their chance meeting with the old man, and Garin's trip to the Oneirographer. Throughout the narrative his expression remained largely one of patient concern, though the occasional brief frown crossed his face, as if he found certain aspects of the tale unbelievable. Suddenly, as she told him of Garin's departure from the Kinetorium, his eyes opened wide in a look of mingled astonishment and fear. His hand shot out and almost painfully gripped her shoulders

"Trielle," he said slowly, as if fighting back the urge to panic. "What was the name of the world where Garin was heading?"

"Sha-Ka-Ri," said Trielle.

Gedron fell back and slumped down in his chair. His evident fear was contagious.

"What's wrong?" cried Trielle.

"Sha-Ka-Ri was one of the names of the early human homeworld. It was destroyed by the entropy clouds a week ago. If Garin was heading there…" His voice trailed off in despair.

"Father," said Trielle sharply, "Garin went there in search of something that seemed, that still seems, impossible. But… our homeworld? There are too many coincidences."

Gedron lifted his eyes, and Trielle was surprised to see tears. "What was it, Trielle, what was Garin looking for exactly?"

"A way out of this life, this existence," she said. "Something beyond the Axioms." Trielle paused for a moment, then said, "Father, you know that I have read Rashavey's manuscripts. Anyone who can add can see that the official timeline of the Conclave is false. I think whatever Garin found is somehow tied to that. Father, you need to tell me the truth!"

Gedron rose and began to pace the room, his brow furrowed in evident thought. Trielle waited patiently, fearful that any stray word she spoke might undo the progress she had made. At last he stopped and stared at her, his gaze as intense as a laser. His lips were tight. She could see the evidence of mental struggle written on his face. A few more moments passed, then his features relaxed and he nodded.

"Yes, Trielle, I do. Thought I have sworn an oath to keep these things concealed, apparently not all oaths can be kept."

Taking a deep, weary breath, Gedron sat down next her, and began.

"The true history of the Conclave of Worlds begins a little over two thousand years ago on Sha-Ka-Ri, though in that era it was known as Terra, or Urth. For thousands of years our race fought, lived, and died on that world. Though we had colonized our moon, as well as a few of the neighboring planets in our star system, we were really no closer to interstellar travel than when we first crawled from the caves of our race's infancy. It was a difficult time. The natural resources of our world had been all but drained by industrialization, and the planet's environment had been severely damaged by a series of deep cometary impacts. Wars and famines were commonplace, and the society of that time had nearly given up. Then… It came…"

"It?" asked Trielle, jarred from the story's rhythm by the obscure reference. "Are you talking about first contact?"

"In a manner of speaking," said Gedron after a brief pause. "By then we had we had caught the radio signature of several different civilizations within our galaxy, and many of us thought that the arrival of alien life was inevitable. But this… creature… claimed to be something else entirely… On the surface it looked as human as you or me, but it possessed power far beyond anything we had ever seen, beyond anything our science had even predicted as possible. It was as if it was subject to a different set of physical laws and constants."

"What did it want?" asked Trielle.

"Nothing less than the world," said Gedron grimly. "It promised that the transition process would be peaceful, but the combined governments of Terra were not willing to simply cede the planet. Many thought that by casting this creature as a common foe they could reunify the nations and end the ongoing wars. Needless to say, its demands were met with near-instant retaliation. We turned all our weapons against it, but they failed. After withstanding a barrage of atomic missiles, particle beams, and free-electron lasers, it opened what seemed to be a portal or gateway to wherever it came from and our planet was overrun with an army the likes of which we had never seen before. The battle was over in moments, and our world surrendered. Within a few days, the creature and its army had taken control of the planet. Not long after the surrender the first colonies of humans were transported to nearby star systems, and in a few months those worlds were already seeding others in an exponential pattern of growth. That was the beginning of the Galactic Empire of Dar Ekklesia, what we later began to call simply the Dar."

"Months?" interrupted Trielle. "You said humanity did not have the ability to travel interstellar distances?"

"Transluminal flight was a natural ability of the creature and those humans that swore fealty to it," said Gedron. "And with the lightspeed barrier torn aside there was no limit to how far the Dar could reach. Even death itself did not deter them. Our scientists were never able to explain it, but somehow the creature was able to reach back across time and recover the noetic patterns of those dead that it deemed worthy, reincarnating them as the *Anastasi*, the elite generals of the empire."

Trielle nodded her head silently, remembering the strange term from Rashavey's manuscript.

"As the Dar spread from Terra," Gedron continued, "it began to encounter other alien races. Some responded with force as we did and were conquered just as quickly, others were... well... different."

219

"Different? How?" asked Trielle, a bewildered look on her face.

"It's hard to explain," said Gedron after a moment's thought, "but they just didn't act like inhabitants of the other worlds. They seemed almost welcoming, almost as if they were waiting to be conquered. Eventually, when the wave of colonization had covered the majority of the galaxy, the Dar moved their seat of power from Terra to the galactic core."

"What was life like under the Dar Ekklesia?" asked Trielle. "With the continual expansion it seems that Terra would have been stripped of what few resources it had left."

"Actually, worlds under the rule of the Dar seemed to prosper," said Gedron. "One of their first actions after arriving on a new planet was to restore its ecological health, and soon the inhabitants would begin to experience enhanced lifespans and freedom from disease. But psychological health was another matter."

Trielle's eyes narrowed. "What do you mean?"

"Many of the more independent worlds, despite their prosperity, grew to resent the rule that the Dar imposed. After all, a prison, no matter how well furnished, is still a prison. Regardless of how good our lives were, we knew we were still slaves. And so, as the centuries drew on, small insurrections began to flare up on various worlds. But none of these ever succeeded, and none were ever able to combine their efforts"

"Why not?" asked Trielle. "Surely their goals could not have been that incompatible."

"It had nothing to do with goals," said Gedron. "Remember that only the Dar could surmount the lightspeed barrier. It is not as if their technology could simply have been stolen by rebel groups; it was native to the biology of the creature and those it transformed. And because of the immmense distances between them there was simply no way for the groups to band together and combine their efforts. But then Ronath Larid and Anthron Rashavey of Terra developed the first ring prototype. We knew about the potential risks, but these seemed remote compared to the possibility of finally having an advantage."

Suddenly Trielle understood. Despite the danger the new technology presented, it was better than servitude to the Dar.

"The first laridian rings were built in secret, and used only to connect resistance groups from different star systems," continued Gedron, "but it wasn't long before they realized that the rings could also be used as weapons. As the individual rebel groups banded together, their scholars developed a philosophy to embody what it was they were fighting for: the freedom of personal choice the Dar had taken from them. We know that philosophy today as the Axioms and Corollaries. Eventually a critical mass was reached and the resistance, now calling itself the Conclave of Worlds, launched simultaneous assaults against the forces of the Dar on a thousand different planets. Larid himself coordinated the first attacks. It took the Dar by surprise, but they quickly mobilized and the Philosoph War began. That war lasted for over two centuries."

As Trielle considered Gedron's words a vague suspicion began to form in her mind. "How long did it take for the entropy clouds to form?" she asked coldly.

"About a century," said Gedron quickly, as if he had been anticipating her question. "You have to understand Trielle, they weren't visible as clouds initially. Instead, we gradually lost the ability to see distant parts of the universe. First the superclusters vanished, and then the galaxies of the Local Group. Even when Andromeda, our closest sister galaxy, disappeared, no one gave the phenomenon the consideration it deserved. The leaders of the Conclave were

221

aware of Rashavey's projections, of course, and were suspicious about the new astronomical observations, but the war was in its hottest phase and the laridian rings were the only real weapon we had against the *Anastasi*. Rashavey himself urged their continued use. Then the green mist coalesced around the outer fringes of our galaxy, consuming the stars of the rim one by one, and we couldn't ignore it anymore."

"We tried to preserve as many worlds as we could, Terra included, by gathering them in great super-systems and herding them toward the center of the galaxy, even thought that meant a massive use of the laridian rings. Most of the Conclave was based in the outer rim, and abandoning those worlds would have meant losing, so we had no choice. At least, that's what we told ourselves."

"How did the war end?" asked Trielle.

"Eventually the Conclave and its armada of worlds reached the Dar Ekklesia's fortress-capitol of Hyrosol Neos, a golden city the size of a moon orbiting within the accretion disk of Sagittarius A* (the voidstar that used to exist in the center of the old galaxy). The Conclave never hesitated. We turned the full force of the rings onto the fortress, hoping to drive it into the voidstar and end the war. The battle was catastrophic. Space was twisted and warped by our laridian ring-based weaponry as we fought the *Anastasi,* and even with these devices we were outnumbered. Then… it… entered the conflict."

"You mean the creature?" prompted Trielle.

"Yes," said Gedron. "There are no surviving images of the last battle, those were all destroyed over a thousand years ago, but the one surviving description of the creature's appearance is truly frightening. A vast shape like a man the size of a world, ringed with countless burning eyes. Six wings of flaming crystal stretched wider than a solar system.

A face of living solar plasma, blazing with terrible light. Just as our despair threatened to overwhelm us, it is said that the creature cried a single tear of white fire and vanished, taking with it the *Anastasi* and the bulk of its armies. Then, Hyrosol Neos and Sagittarius A* vanished as a burning green curtain descended on the battlefield. We won, but paid a tremendous price."

"The galaxy was gone, wasn't it?" asked Trielle softly.

"All but three stars and a sixty-five thousand cubic light-minute volume of space had been lost to the entropy clouds," said Gedron grimly. "But we were free. We set up gravitic nodes on each world and used them to combine the separate super-systems of worlds into one great structure of interlocking orbits, the Conclave as you know it today. Although the vast majority of those loyal to the Dar Ekklesia had either been killed or had vanished with the creature, a small remnant had been left behind. They were given the choice to either join the Conclave or be confined to a reservation, unable to ever leave. To a one they chose confinement. We established a new government based on the Axioms and moved the three remaining stars to the center of the Conclave in hope that their combined radiation could slow the advance of the clouds. The leaders of the time knew that most Conclave citizens did not understand the real reason for the entropy clouds' existence and embarked on a plan of suppression, blaming the weapons used by the Dar in the last battle. Eventually it was decided to alter the historical records even further, removing any references to the Dar in the name of freeing us from even the memory of their tyranny. All agreed. After all, the Corollaries say that the world means what we want it to. From that time on only the highest leaders of the Conclave, the Heirophants, were told our actual history. Now you know as well. Not that it will make a difference."

Trielle's mind raced. Though there was still much to learn, some things were finally beginning to fall into place. She thought back to Rashavey's manuscript, its odd terms and phrasing, and smiled grimly at her naiveté as she saw for the first time what it really was: a military briefing. Then she remembered Anacrysis' note, and a new question formed in her mind.

"Father," said Trielle, "you mentioned a reservation where remnants of the Dar Ekklesia were confined. Does it still exist?"

"Yes," said Gedron. "It is located on a barren moon that circles one of the brown dwarfs of the Guard."

"Is its name En-ka-re?"

"How did you know that?" asked Gedron, his eyes wide with shock.

"It doesn't matter," said Trielle as she swiftly rose to her feet, "but I know where I have to go."

"Trielle, En-Ka-re is heavily guarded by Conclave soldiers," said Gedron. "Only the Entrope has access."

"Somehow I think I will make it," she said, the hint of a smile forming on her lips. "But I need your help, Father. Can you delay the deployment of the Vacuum Sculptors?"

"I don't have as much authority as I once did, but I can try," he said with a sigh. "Though I don't see what difference such a delay will make."

"Please trust me, Father," pleaded Trielle as she ran to the transit tube. "Someone I trust said that when Garin returned, he would be in need of what I found. I need time to finish that task."

As the transit tube doors closed around Trielle, the last thing she saw was a faint gleam of hope in her Father's eyes.

Chapter 21: The Cities of the Plain

The blazing afternoon sun beat down upon the dusty plains with almost physical force. The air was dense and still. With dogged steps, Garin drove himself forward toward a faint dark line that loomed on the far horizon.

The accursed city of the plain: Hyrosol Eld.

He did not know how long he had been traveling. It felt like months since he had dined with Hyperion, but time was fluid in Mythos, and the sun had risen and set only once since he had found the Mariner. His eyes momentarily lost focus as he recalled the journey.

***

The far pass from the Sepulcher of Suns had lead to a broad valley festooned with flowers. The valley sloped gently downward through the mountains, eventually opening though a gap in the foothills onto a broad strand of grey sand at the edge of a dark ocean. The waters were an ominous violet, but by this time the sun had neared the far horizon and its evening rays painted the surface of the water with flashes of joyful orange fire that almost concealed the inscrutable depths beneath.

At the edge of the sea, amidst the swirling breakers, stood a great black silhouette framed by the rays of the dying sun, its front lit only by a bright red spark that danced and leapt against the dark backdrop. From the distance he heard a strange, faint susurrus of animal sounds. As he approached the shape resolved into a towering ship of cyclopean dimensions, a vast deep brown slab of wood and pitch, and the sounds increased in volume, transforming into a bestial cacophony. The red spark was revealed to be a campfire beside which stood a tall, bare-shouldered man wearing a deep blue loincloth about his waist decorated with stylized images of waves. Garin felt certain that he had found the Mariner.

The Mariner proved to be a man of few words, but he had made it clear to Garin that he was welcome here. After Garin had eaten his fill from the remnant of the Mariner's evening meal they entered the ship, and the door shut behind them of its own accord. They swiftly climbed a rugged wooden staircase through the lower decks, which were filled with vast open pens occupied by every conceivable type of animal. The boat began heaving as they ascended, and Garin wondered what was happening outside.

"It is the first winds of the Judgment Storm," said the Mariner in answer to Garin's unspoken question. "Soon it will be upon us. We must be off."

As they reached the upper deck the storm's full fury broke upon the ship. The once-peaceful skies were now filled filled with billowing dark clouds illuminated by a near-continuous volley of lightning bolts, and an icy rain lashed the boards of the deck. Across the horizon, great waterspouts launched skyward from the ocean into the tempest. There was no land to be seen, only the boiling watery wasteland of the Mare Primum.

"I must go to my family now," the Mariner stated flatly. "The price of your passage along the meridian is your service as lookout. Do you agree to this cost?"

Garin quickly nodded yes and the Mariner left with a grunt, leaving Garin to his work.

He watched for what seemed like weeks, holding fast to his post amidst the driving rain, but the sun never rose and the storm never lifted. Then a row of looming shadows appeared on the horizon. Garin waited a few moments before descending to report.

"Good," the Mariner grunted. "We have reached the Mounts of Nomos, the place where the Laws of Heaven are writ upon the bones of the Earth. The Judgment Storm is a thing of Chaos and should abate beyond them. You have done well. Now, return to your post."

Garin climbed the stairs to the deck and was greeted by an uncanny sight. To the port and starboard sides of the ship loomed great masses of rock: sheer vertical columns, slick with rain, which rose from the swirling ocean currents like the watchtowers of a submerged citadel. Atop each stood a stone pillar inscribed with words that burned with strange fire. As the ship passed between them it was as if some invisible thresholf had been crossed. Then the churning of the sea ceased and the clouds overhead swiftly dissolved, leaving behind the pure brilliance of a night sky strewn with billions of stars. Garin's eyes widened at the sight of them and for a moment he forgot his quest, captivated by a beauty beyond anything he could ever have imagined as for the first time he understood how much light had been lost to the entropy clouds.

Garin passed what seemed like aeons that way, his gaze fixed on the glittering canvas above him. Then the sky lightened and soon the morning sun rose in a rush of gold and ruby effulgence, revealing a low, dark coastline to the west. Fulfilling his duty, Garin ran downstairs to report what he had seen, and soon the Mariner and his family were rushing about the craft making preparation for landfall. The great ark finally ran aground on a rocky beach covered with slime and seawrack. After the gangplank had been lowered and all the penned animals had disembarked, the Mariner turned to Garin and asked where he was traveling. He frowned when he heard the name of Hyrosol Eld.

"The place you seek was once grand and glorious," said the Mariner, "and the gleam of its towers was the pride of Mythos. Yet it has fallen into corruption, the bleak enslavement of the Once-Men. I dare not guess whether the one you call Kyr will be there when you arrive, but if he is you will likely find him in the Shattered Temple, once called the Temple of the Beloved, that lies near the city's heart."

Then the Mariner gave him a leather sack filled with gleaming white shells that sparkled in the sun like gemstones. "These are quite common along the shores of Mare Primum but for some reason the Once-Men find them valuable. This should be enough to quell any questions regarding your presence there and provide for your entrance. Now, farewell, and I pray that you find the one you seek."

After thanking the Mariner, Garin had continued onward from the shoreline. The rocks of the coast soon gave way to grassy hills, and the hills gave way in turn to the bleak desert in which he now wandered. As the endless miles had slid by, Garin had pondered the words the Mariner had spoken with little insight to illumine their meaning.

Once-Men? Shattered Temple?

The phrases seemed strange and forbidding, imbued with meanings that Garin could only guess at.

***

A low rumble sounded in the distance, and Garin awoke from his reverie to see that the dark line had resolved into a vast battlement of cracked black stone. Behind the wall, jagged towers in varying states of disrepair pointed at the sky like broken fingernails. Above the city churned a massive thunderhead, a vortex of tense black cloud that threatened to break open at any minute.

He had arrived.

The great gate of the city, framed by two gray towers of crumbling stone, stood open less than thirty paces away. Guarding the gate was a squadron of soldiers that broke formation as Garin approached the gate, blocking his path.

"State your business, traveler."

The words sounded peculiarly hollow, as if they had somehow been emptied of life and vitality, and a strange wave of fear coursed through Garin. Though he did not wish to draw undue attention to himself, he risked a glance at the guard who had spoken.

The soldier was clad in armor of black iron, unadorned save for an emblem upon the breastplace in the shape of a fist closing around an open eye. In his hands he held a halberd that seemed little more than a jagged fragment of metal affixed to a long shaft of grey wood. The visor of his helm was open, revealing a face as pale as marble, but otherwise human in appearance. Then Garin gasped as he saw the guard's eyes. There was neither sclera nor iris, only twin holes that seemed to drop forever into an impossible void. Suddenly Garin knew what a once-man was.

"I repeat, state your business! Why have you come to Hyrosol Eld?"

In response Garin held out the bag of shells and opened it just enough to give a glimpse of its contents. Though his eyes were unreadable, the guard grinned wth avarice.

"I come from Mare Primum to trade in the Great Market," said Garin.

"Indeed," replied the guard with a humorless laugh. "There is much that you could purchase for what you hold. Yet what value is it if you do not reach the market?"

Deliberately, slowly, Garin let his shoulders slump forward. He had expected this, and in truth did not care how much of a bribe was required. Above all, though, he knew that he must appear genuine.

"What is it you would require to ensure safe passage," said Garin carefully.

"Normally two shells would suffice," said the guard with a smirk. "Each," called out another, followed by nods from the rest of the squadron.

"Yes, each," he continued. "But today we have orders to turn away all merchants in preparation for the coming of Lord Daath."

At the mention of Daath, Garin's heart quailed. *Am I too late?*

Still, there was nothing to be done about it. He had to press on. Gathering his courage, Garin continued the negotiation, hoping he had successfully kept his fear from showing.

"Lord Daath," he said, "This is indeed a glad day. I would greatly enjoy being present for his arrival."

"As would most," said the guard, nodding his approval at the response. "But you, of course, can now see the position in which this places us."

"Perhaps additional shells could relieve that difficulty?" suggested Garin, his heart pounding.

"Perhaps they could," said the guard with feigned thoughtfulness. "Ten each should be adequate."

The other guards nodded in response.

"If the initial price was two," said Garin, "would not five be a more reasonable sum?"

At this the guard frowned, and a lump formed in Garin's throat. Had he pushed him too far?

"More reasonable, but not what we require," said the guard sternly, all trace of humor now gone. "Still, we would be willing to accept seven, but no less."

The tone in the guard's voice told Garin that further haggling would not be tolerated, and he wordlessly opened the sack, giving each their required bribe. After it was done the guard grunted and moved to the side.

"Safe trading to you," he said, a sarcastic edge to his voice. Garin nodded and proceeded through the gate.

At once the stench of the city hit him, a smell of mold and decay like that of a mausoleum. He stood on a broad avenue paved with cracked flagstone stained almost black by ages of soot and grime. On either side of him towered great crumbling edifices of masonry and rotting wood that blocked the light of the afternoon sun and cast the streets into thick shadow. And all around him surged the crowds of the Once-men. Though they conversed and traded as if nothing were amiss, to Garin they looked like animated corpses, undead revenants merely going through the motions of bodily life. He could almost feel the combined weight of their blank gazes, like a hundred thousand gates into the outer darkness.

He proceeded as swiftly as he dared, taking time on occasion to trade a few shells from his bag for the trinkets sold in the stalls that lined the street. As the shells traded hands he could see furtive glimmers of light flash in the black eyes of the merchants, and with sudden insight he saw that the shells' purity, their almost gemlike brightness, was the only fragment of beauty within this city of living death.

The road sloped upward as Garin moved further into the city: at first gently, but then with increasing steepness. Ahead he could see the sprawling mound that Hyperion had called the Mount of Sacrifice, its summit circled by towering walls of red granite, its slopes deep in shadow. As the road began to ascend the lowest reaches of the mount it abruptly curved to the left, coiling around it like a serpent. Here the buildings were better kept, a seemingly

endless array of decadent palaces and citadels peopled by
Once-men clad in ermine robes and jeweled finery. Yet as
Garin stared into the absence that was their eyes, he realized
that the deadness and corruption ran even deeper here than
in the more visibly decayed regions he had just passed
through. He walked for what seemed like an eternity,
treading an endless spiral up the side of the mount, until at
last the road ended in a vast plaza filled with a crowd of
Once-men.

Built upon a terrace that stretched outward from the
wall surrounding the mountain's peak, a pavement of black
marble ran to a sheer drop that loomed over the city below
like a cliff face. From that edge, two great staircases
supported on buttresses of black iron coursed downward to
Hyrosol Eld's northern gate. At the back of the plaza, built
into the red granite surface of the wall, stood a tumbledown
edifice of stained rock and obsidian pillars capped by a
metallic dome. The surface of the dome was dark with dirt
and tarnish, but in places its original luster still gleamed
amidst the filth. The center of the dome was marred by a
great gash. Almost instinctively, Garin knew that this was
the Shattered Temple.

"He comes!"

The cry rose from a bearded seneschal who stood in
the center of the plaza. His arm was outstretched and his
fingers pointed to the north. Gripped by sudden fear, Garin
turned and saw a dark mass of boiling vapor shreiking
toward the city. He did not have much time. Quickly he
skirted the crowd, angling toward the dark entrance of the
Shattered Temple. As he reached the door, he risked a
glance backward and saw the shadowy mass as it winged
over the city wall like a vulture and began its decent toward
the plaza. There was a deafening crash as the sky was rent
by a searing bolt of lightning. A black rain began to fall, and

a loud shout rose from the crowd as the Once-men proclaimed the arrival of Lord Daath. Without hesitation, Garin turned and ran through the entrance.

The inside of the temple was a shadowy vault filled with curving rows of marble pillars lit by the furtive gleam of countless torches. In the smoke-filled darkness of the temple's heart, robed figures bowed and danced in a strange ritual around a dim sacrificial flame. Beyond the fire, Garin could just make out a towering bronze door set into the back wall, its surface gleaming dully in the half-light. Though unmarked, he felt sure that the door led to the Mount of Sacrifice's summit. The door was shut tight, sealed with a bar of iron.

Garin shifted sideways into the shadow of a pillar, his eyes scanning the dark alcoves and colonnades. There was no sight of Kyr, and at once Garin was struck by the impossibility of a man such as him ever finding comfort in such a vile place.

"They used to call this the Temple of the Beloved?" he whispered to himself, as if saying it would somehow render it more believable.

Then a shout from the center of the temple drew his attention. The priests, finished with their strange leaping dance, were now filing down the nave of the temple in a double procession, crying out in unison.

"He comes! He comes! Let Lord Daath find the priests of his temple faithful."

Garin's heart withered in his chest, and a sickening numbness took hold of his limbs as he realized why Daath had chosen to make his arrival here. Of course he would come to the temple. Trying to hold his fear in check, Garin slowly slid behind the nearest pillar, his eyes always watching the priests. Seeing their attention was elsewhere he backed away from the entrance, crouching behind nearby pillars whenever it seemed they might turn his way, seeking to lose himself in the gloom. All at once he was met by a hard, cold surface of granite. He had reached the inner wall. There was nowhere else to go.

A tumult began to rise outside the temple, and Garin could hear the footsteps of a multitude approaching. Suddenly a great weakness descended on him and he slumped over in exhaustion. He was trapped, and there was little he could do about it. Then a curious image upon the tiled floor caught his eye. In the dim torchlight it was difficult to see clearly, but Garin could just make out the outline of a woman. To the side of the image, a strange mosaic of white tiles set in what once must have been a deep blue background was visible through the soot and grime. His eyes widened as he realized that it was an image of the Sovereign Road.

The image gave him hope, though he could not explain why, and it did not seem right to leave it in this state. Garin began to brush away the dirt and soot, and as he did more of the mosaic came into view. The woman was depicted wearing a golden robe with a stylized sun emblazoned across the breast. Her eyes were blue, and a smile was on her lips. The road began at her bare feet and swept about her body in a great spiral before at last ending in a circle of stars that hovered over her head like a coronet. As Garin examined it more closely he noticed an irregularity: a single red tile in the portion of the road near the top of the woman's head. Puzzled, Garin touched the tile and felt it move. Suddenly he heard a soft click and looked up to see a low section of the nearby wall swing open. Garin stared for a moment in disbelief, then quickly scrambled through the opening, pulling the door shut tightly behind him.

He found himself on a broad landing overlooking a deep chasm lit by a soft azure light that welled up from the depths. From the edge of the platform a series of stairs descended into the cool abyss, and Garin, having nowhere else to go, began the descent. The stairs ended at a golden door inset into the sheer rock face of the chasm wall. The surface of the door was elaborately worked with the image of a woman crowned with stars, a mirror of the one that lay above. Garin placed his hand upon the door and it swung open easily.

Beyond was a spacious chamber that gleamed with gold and silver. The chamber's alabaster walls were covered in bas-relief carvings depicting scenes from an ancient garden. In them a man and woman walked amidst trees and flowers followed by a leaping cascade of birds, deer, lizards, and all other kinds of animal. Between them stood a strange figure the likes of which Garin had never seen before: its body covered in robes, its head replaced by a starburst. It reminded him somewhat of Hyperion, though it was clear that the image was not meant to depict him specifically. Midway between the walls and the chamber's center stood a ring of broad pillars that supported the high vault of the ceiling. Each was covered images of vines, fruiting plants and trees. Worked in pure silver, these images seemed almost to pulse with life, as if they not been carved so much as transmuted directly from living plants by some subtle form of alchemy. In the heart of the chamber, shining with a holy radiance, lay a sarcophagus of pale sapphire. With halting steps Garin approached the sarcophagus, then stopped and gazed in awe as he saw what rested within.

The sarcophagus was occupied by a woman of surpassing beauty clothed in robes of purest white. The robes were fastened about her neck with a clasp of bright gold bearing the image of a lamb. Encircing her hair was a coronet of lapis lazuli, inlaid with hundreds of silver stars. Her eyes were closed, though in sleep or death Garin did not know. In only one place was the perfection of her figure marred: in the center of her chest, a deep red bloodstain bloomed upon her robe like a crimson flower.

Garin sank to his knees in wonder and sadness at the sight: wonder that such beauty could exist, sadness that it had been wounded. For long moments he wept, unsure of why he did so but simultaneously knowing that it was the only right response. Rising back to his feet, Garin noticed something that he had not before: a square of parchment sitting atop the sarcophagus. With trembling hands, he picked it up and began to read.

> Garin, by now I have passed beyond the circles of Mythos to the worlds above, where I trust you will soon join me. Understand that I waited as long as I could for you here at the tomb of my Beloved. Long I gazed at her beauty: she who once was the crowning joy of the worlds, now a victim of the shadow. How I yearn to free her, to raise her again to life, but that time is not yet come.
>
> Know, my child, that the Shadow is soon to arrive on this world. It is for that reason that I must leave. I do not fear him, but my continued presence here would certainly draw him to the path you must travel, placing you in danger. Know that as long as you stay within this chamber he cannot find you. Oh, he yearns to know where the body of my Beloved lies, but he cannot, must know, be allowed to enter, for if she dies the final death all hope dies with her. You are safe here, but you must not tarry.
>
> The road between worlds touches Mythos at the pinnacle of the Mount of Sacrifice. In this world the

pathway only opens to those who give of themselves freely. Remember, you have not yet resisted to the point of blooshed. Fear not! We will soon meet again.

Kyr

Garin's heart was filled with a mixture of hope and confusion.

Not yet striven to bloodshed?

The words were confusing to him. Still, the message had been clear about his goal. Steeling himself, Garin turned and left the chamber. Soon he had ascended the stair and stood again before the concealed door that had gained him entry to this place. Placing his ear to the wall, Garin strained to hear what lay beyond. There were no shouts of pursuit, only the faint sound of muffled chanting. Careful to make as little noise as possible, Garin gingerly pushed on the door, allowing only the smallest crack to open in the wall. Though it was difficult to see anything in the darkness beyond, there was no one immediately visible through the opening. Taking a deep breath, Garin quickly slipped through and shut the door. At once he dropped to his knees, willing his breath to slow as he carefully listened for footsteps. For a few long moments he knelt there until he was sure that his emergence had gone unnoticed. Only then did he stand and carefully creep further into the temple. Reaching the innermost row of pillars, Garin hid behind the nearest one and, with careful movements, peered around its edge in an attempt to see the events transpiring within the temple's heart.

The priests had returned to the central altar upon which now smouldered the remains of an unknown sacrifice. They lay prostrate before it, chanting strange prayers to the Shadow in an unknown tongue. Joining the priests in their worship was a larger throng of Once-men, presumably those that had had awaited the coming of Daath in the plaza outside. Garin carefully scanned the crowd, trying to catch a glimpse of Daath himself, but he was nowhere to be seen. Satisfied that the attention of the group was occupied, he turned to the bronze doors and was surprised to find them already unbarred and open, presumably as a part of the rite he was witnessing.

Quickly he turned back to the group around the altar, scrutinizing each face to see if any eyes were upon him or the door, but all eyes were closed as the priests intoned their black prayer. He knew his chances were small, but he also knew that no better time than this would come. Without a moment's hesitation Garin darted from the pillar to the back wall of the temple and quickly edged his way around and through the posts of the great gate, only daring to breathe when he had reached the other side.

Ahead of him rose the summit of the Mount of Sacrifice, a slope of gravel and withered trees crowned with an obscure mass of mingled of gold and darkness. A mirthless laugh sounded.

"Blind monkey," the voice hissed, "so I have found you again, and without Kyr to protect you."

All around Garin shadows rose and congealed, revealing a squadron of Once-men. Their weapons were drawn and a ghostly blue fire burned in their empty eyes. In their midst stood Daath, his black cloak billowing behind him, a cruel smile on his noble face.

"Have you seen the Beloved?" whispered Daath. "I can see by your eyes it is so. Good! Then you have something of worth to offer me."

The Once-men closed in on Garin, bound him in shackles of rusted iron, and led him up the mountainside.

Chapter 22: The Altar and the Oath

"So... The reignition attempt was aborted at the crucial moment?"

"Yes, master," spoke the Entrope, a wave of shame washing through him.

He had been summoned from his sleep by an inexplicable sense of urgency and now stood within the Chamber of the Pool, surrounded by clouds of boiling green flame.

Surrounded by the burning embrace of the Presence...

"Do not think that this failure has gone unnoticed. Perhaps the time of your successor's awakening is closer than you reckoned."

The Entrope's heart sank within him as the Presence spoke, even as his mind involuntarily chanted that this, too, was meaningless.

"Nevertheless," continued the Presence, *"I did not call you here to chide you, but rather to share my imminent triumph. Rejoice, Servant of the Void, for the disturbance has been localized and even now is facing termination at my hand."*

"Disturbance?" asked the Entrope. "You spoke of this when last we met, yet I must confess the nature of it is still unknown to me."

The eyes of the Presence flashed with mirth at the Entrope's words, and its mouth opened wide in silent laughter.

"Almost you sound like those we hate," it answered. *"We would not speak of natures but rather of perturbations of the primal void, false faces placed upon the nothingness from whence all springs and to which all in the end returns."*

The Entrope shuddered, mindful of the precipice at which he stood. Such ill-considered expressions had been the downfall of many a prior incarnation. He knew that the human mind was neurologically predisposed toward certain false teleological perceptions; perceptions that were ultimately responsible for the tendency to see reality as an ordered purposeful whole rather than the froth of chaos that it truly was. Only by relentless application of certain psychomodulatory techniques could the tendency be held at bay, and this not for long. He had held on longer than most of his past versions, but eventually each had begun to succumb to the delusion of purpose and had willingly submitted to the Rite of Dissolution, transferring their memories to the blank slate of their successor's brain before being disassembled into their constituent elements. Though reluctant to undergo the rite, the Entrope knew that his time was soon at hand.

But not yet…

"My apologies, master, for the unfortunate way in which my thoughts were phrased. I sought only to determine how best to assist in the great work of eradicating this and other disturbances like it."

This time the Presence laughed audibly, with more than a hint of scorn.

"Servant, you do not grasp your limitations! In this you can do nothing. The disturbance is located in a place you cannot reach. But I can. Even now I hold its squirming form in my grip. You need only watch. I will give you my eyes so that you may see my deeds in the outer realms."

At once a torrent of images overwhelmed the Entrope: a storm-wracked sky, a rocky hilltop swathed in shadow, a procession of guards holding the shackled form of a boy…

***

The barren hillside sloped steeply upward, its surface a rough mass of uneven boulders occasionally breached by the twisted corpse of a tree. Above, clouds churned and writhed as if in pain, showering the ground beneath with a freezing, bitter rain. More than once Garin tripped on a rocky outcropping only to be roughly pulled back to his feet and forced to march on by the Once-men guards. Then, abruptly, the ground leveled off. They had arrived.

From the rocky summit of the hill two great trees stretched skyward into the storm. One gleamed brilliantly as if wrought of living gold, its bows laden with silver apples that twinkled like stars. The other seemed less a physical object than a tree-shaped hole in space, a towering mass of inky blackness that was difficult even to look at for long. Between them lay an altar of black stone, its cracked surface stained with the blood of countless sacrifices.

Daath, who until now had led the procession, turned and stepped aside, gesturing toward the altar.

"The Place of Sacrifice! Gaze on it well, blind monkey, for if you choose poorly it may well be the last sight your eyes perceive. Now, I ask you again. Where is the Beloved!"

A wave of fear surged through Garin, his mind assailed by a billion thoughts of failure and pain, yet he held his tongue.

"So be it," said Daath. "Bind him!"

At once the closest soldiers grabbed him by his shoulders and laid Garin flat upon the altar, binding his limbs to the cold surface. Above him the branches of the trees entwined in a subtle weave of mingled light and darkness. The weave pulsed like a thing alive, and for a moment Garin thought he could see in its complex pattern

242

the history of all things: the eternal balance between what was, what could be, and what, erased by corruption, could never be again. Then a crash of thunder drew his attention, and Garin turned his head to see Daath approaching, his black form momentarily silhouetted by lightning. In his hand was an iron spike.

"You do know what this place is, do you not?" asked Daath mockingly. "It is the Garden spoken of in all the earliest tales of the worlds of Phaneros. Here the ancestors of your people, of all peoples, once payed fealty to me, and it is here that that fealty will again be renewed. The stone beneath you thirsts, blind monkey, it thirsts for the blood of those who bound it over to me. And today it will drink of yours if you do not speak. I am willing, oh, so willing, to slay the Beloved in your stead, but I am prevented from discovering her. Ah, but if her location were to be willingly revealed... Speak, blind monkey! Where is her crypt! I know it must be on this mountain."

"You... you would free me for this knowledge?" asked Garin, his mouth dry with fear.

"I would," said Daath smoothly. "Is this act so large a price? Come, you do not even know her. Why give your life for hers? What love do you hold for her?"

"Kyr loves her," croaked Garin.

"Indeed he does," replied Daath, "hence my desire to slay her. For I would strike him a blow from which even he cannot recover. But what of you, child of man? Why should that be of comfort to you? Have you even seen Kyr since entering my domain below? I am sure you have asked why he has not come for you many times. Or has that thought not occurred to you in your ignorance? Why do you persist in protecting the beloved of one who has so clearly abandoned you when I am offering your release in return? Do you not wish to see your sister again?"

243

At the mention of Trielle memories flooded Garin's mind: the look in her eyes as she laughed, the way she would listen to him no matter the concern. Grief surged through him, and he felt the last dregs of his resistance begin to melt away. Then another, more recent memory surfaced: the memory of a face so pure that it outshone the stars, of a form of surpassing beauty, marred by a mortal wound, and from far away he could almost hear the words Kyr whispered so long ago amidst the ruin of Sha-Ka-Ri.

"Son of man, do you trust me?"

"Hear me Daath," he said, surprised at the sudden strength in his voice. "You may tempt me with memories of my family, of my life before this journey began, but I have seen the Beloved and I know that she must live again regardless of the cost to myself. So come, slay me if you will, but I will not give her into your hands!"

Daath's noble mouth opened in a wide grin.

"So be it, blind monkey!"

In a single, swift movement Daath raised the iron spike and struck downward toward Garin's heart. Garin closed his eyes, waiting for the impact.

He felt a pinprick on his chest, nothing more, and opened his eyes to see the face of Daath contorted with effort as if all his strength was being brought to bear upon an impossible task. Garin looked down and saw that the tip of the iron spike had just broken his skin. Despite Daath's obvious exertions it would go no further. A single drop of blood ran from the wound down the side of Garin's chest.

You have not yet resisted to the point of bloodshed...

In a blast of light and heat the iron spike ignited with white-hot flame. A cry of pain escaped Daath's lips and he released the spike, but it never fell. Slowly at first, and then with increasing velocity, it rose into the air, a blazing arrow shooting skyward as if loosed from the Bow of

Apollo. There was a moment of silence as it pierced the roiling underbelly of the storm, and then a thunderous sound like a mountain shattering rent the air as a great gleaming crack split the clouds in two. And through that crack poured the brilliance of the stars.

All around Garin the heavenly light fell. It rained down around the two trees in great shimmering sheets, illuminating the ruined garden with soft brilliance. It touched his bonds and they dissolved away, crumbling into dust. He rose to his feet, blood still streaming from the puncture wound in his chest. Enraged, Daath moved as if to seize him, but to him the lambent starlight was a wall as hard as diamond, a ward that surrounded Garin, protecting him from harm.

Lifting his eyes skyward, Garin watched as the last vestiges of the storm boiled away into nothingness, replaced by the naked effulgence of the night sky. And from the velvet darkness between the stars came a wind of light and power that descended in a great spiral to encompass Garin, forming into a road of stars beneath his feed. Joy swelled within his heart, and with a glad smile he stepped forward and tread the path that stretched between the worlds. His last sight of Mythos as the walls of the crystal sphere parted before him was Daath: his fists pounding on the walls of light, his proud mouth opened in a scream of primal rage and loss.

***

The Entrope pressed his hands to his ears but could not drown out the awful scream. All around him the chaos ripped and tore at his body like a hurricane of knives. Whether the onslaught lasted for minutes or millennia he could not tell; he only knew that after what seemed like ages of suffering the storm abated and the boiling entropy clouds again parted to reveal the shadowed form of the Presence. The Entrope opened his mouth, but was silenced by a searing wave of fire, like liquid pain, that stabbed from the Presence's blazing eyes.

"Do not presume to speak, blind monkey," said the Presence angrily. *"The time for speech has long past. The disturbance grows greater now, and has strength that I did not anticipate. But it matters not, for he is yet within my reach. Soon he will reach the Primal Wound, the ancient seat of my strength, and it is there that he will be consumed. In the interim, servant, there is a task for you to perform. Shepherd the Heirophants, cajole them, do what is needed to hasten the next reignition, for if the disturbance cannot be quelled in the high realms, the only recourse is to assure that the dissolving husk of a dead cosmos is all that remains on his return. Do this and I assure you that you will be the final Entrope, the one to see with his own eyes the nameless abyss from whence the cosmos sprang and to whence it will inevitably return."*

The green fires vanished with the suddenness of a thunderclap and the Entrope found himself standing alone within the Chamber of the Pool. As he stepped from the pool and painfully began the journey back to the Omegahedron, his lips split apart in a narrow grin as he contemplated the promise made by the Presence.

The final dissolution was near, and he would be the one that would herald its advent.

Book Four: Though the Fractured Virtue of the High Places Still Strove Beneath It Yet…

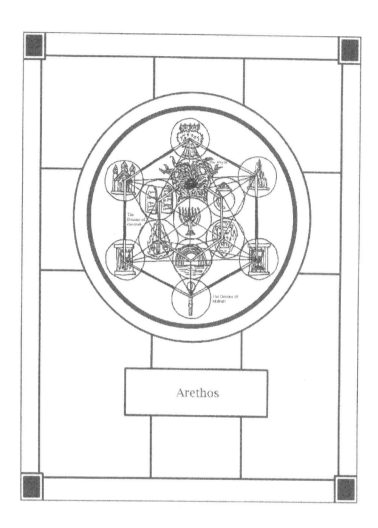

Arethos

Chapter 23: On Ancient Wings

      With a flicker of blue lightning Trielle's ether chariot crackled into existence in the space around Galed. A small gas giant swathed perpetually in azure storms, the planet boasted more natural sattelites than any other world in the Conclave, earning it the nickname "Galed of the Sixty Moons." Trielle gestured to the ship's infochryst and a hologram of the Galed lunar system appeared in the air before her. While the first three moons were small, little more than captured asteroids really, the fourth moon appeared to be one of the planet's larger sattelites. Reaching forward, Trielle touched the image of the fourth moon and it enlarged to fill the hologram. A few seconds later a halo of abstract white lines appeared around it, each a link to information about the moon's internal structure, possible origin, orbit, and other physical parameters. Trielle gestured at the first of these, and a block of illustrated text sprang into the air above the image.

      Trielle's eyes narrowed as she read. Evidently the moon was largely composed of iron and nickel with a relative lack of crustal silicates. The surface was covered with a shallow, acidic sea, stained red by iron oxide and broken only by a range of low mountains. The sole solid ground on the moon, the mountains meandered northward in a series of great, lazy arcs from their origin point near the equator. The atmosphere was thin but breathable, with a relatively high oxygen content that made up for the low barometric pressure. There were no indigenous lifeforms and no listed inhabitants. Trielle was tempted for a moment by the next link, which promised to give a convincing account of the moon's origin as the captured core of a nearby gas giant that had lost its atmosphere due to some ancient stellar catastrophe, but eventually she turned away. She was not here to explore planetary geology.

Bringing her hands together, Trielle shrank the vast globe to more manageable proportions and plotted a course that would skim the ether chariot along the tops of the mountain range. Unless Tserimed was an aquatic creature that could swim in rust, she reasoned, he would have to be on one of the peaks. A few moments later the ether chariot sprang to life, its laridian rings carving a flickering gorge in spacetime, and within moments she was soaring above the blood-red sea.

The sky above was a deep violet speckled with the twinkling light of the closest moons. The western horizon was dominated by Galed itself, a massive cerulean dome banded with wisps of white cirrus. A soft tone alerted her that the craft was approaching its first stop, and she looked northward to see a jagged gunmetal gray pyramid rising from the murky waters. The ether chariot slowed down as it neared the peak, and Trielle scrutinized the slopes to see if there were any signs of habitation. There were none, and Trielle soon moved on to the next mountain.

Several hours later Trielle gestured for the ether chariot to stop. With a weary sigh she sat back in the control chair, exhausted from the search. So far she had scrutinized less than a sixteenth of the mountain range, and was far from sure that she had not missed something crucial. Filled with a sudden, overwhelming sense of futility, Trielle gazed off into the distance at the seemingly endless ribbon of mountains. Then a curious feature caught her eye. While most had sheer, jagged peaks, one far-off mountain rose instead to a high, flat plateau. She did not know what to make of it, but after hours of work it seemed her first real lead. Reaching forward into the hologram, Trielle altered her ether chariot's course and a few moments later was hovering high above the strange mountain.

From this close, its artificial nature was readily apparent. The plateau was almost unnaturally level, as if the entire mountain top had been sheared off by a titanic blade, and though she was still several hundred feet above its surface, Trielle thought she could make out the faint greenish tinge of vegetation. But what drew her attention most was a circular cluster of oblong white shapes near the plateau's heart.

Are those buildings?

If so, then this worldlet had secrets even the Conclave infochrysts did not know.

Trielle landed the ether chariot near the edge of the plateau. There was a momentary pain in her ears as the gravitic containment field dissolved and the air within rushed out into the tenuous atmosphere. Trielle took a deep breath, and then another. Thin, but breathable, as she had expected. Still, she would not be able to exert herself here.

The edge of the plateau was composed of a rough mulch of gravel and loose boulders, but this quickly gave way to grass covered soil as she moved toward its center. As she approached the cluster of objects, Trielle could see that indeed they were buildings. Organized in a half-ring around a central courtyard, the majority were little more than cubes of grey stone pierced by a single door and a single window. Near the courtyard's center, however, stood a much larger structure that was quite different from the others. Though built from the same grey stone, this building had been created with more artistry, and was adorned with a myriad of stained-glass windows that gleamed like rainbows in Galed's light. A tall, narrow door stood open at its front. Trielle scrutinized each building, looking for any sign of their inhabitants, but all appeared empty. A thin, chill breeze began to blow, carrying sharp scents from the sea far below. She stood in silence as the cold began to seep into bones. She did not know what to do.

"You really should follow me inside. This icy air could be the death of you."

Startled by the voice, Trielle snapped her head around and saw a white-haired man approaching her. He was dressed in brown robes and carried a large pack slung over his left shoulder.

"My apologies if I frightened you," the man said, laughing. "I was out gathering vegetables from my garden. May I welcome you to the Abbey? It's not much to look at, but it suffices for my needs."

"Thank you," said Trielle, willing her voice to remain steady and confident despite the lingering feelings of shock. "My name is Trielle, and I am looking for Tseramed. I was told to search for him on the fourth moon of Galed, and this is the only settlement I have seen so far. Do you know of him?"

"Indeed I do," said the man, his eyes sparkling. "In fact, I have known him my whole life. I, my dear, am Tseramed: Abbot, and currently sole member, of the Holy Order of Gatekeepers. Now I would very much like to know why it is you search for me, but I will not ask you to tell your tale out here in the cold. Come inside! There is a fire by which we can warm ourselves as we speak."

Tseramed lead the way into the nearest of the buildings, a cozy dwelling lit by a leaping fire. A cauldron of some dark metal hung over the fire, the steam wafting from its interior heady with the aroma of roasting vegetables. Near the fire stood a table with three chairs, and Tseramed motioned Trielle toward it. As she sat down, grateful for the warmth, Tseramed took an iron ladle and filled a bowl with some of the cauldron's contents.

"I hope you don't mind me having my dinner while we speak"? he asked as he sat down beside her. "I find that I can focus better on matters at hand when my stomach is at least somewhat full. Would you like some? There should be enough for both of us."

Trielle shook her head in a gesture of polite refusal.

"Alright then," said Tseramed goodnaturedly. "But feel free to take some later if you decide you are hungry after all."

As Tseramed began his meal, Trielle studied his face. In the flickering firelight, the deep wrinkles that furrowed his skin stood out in sharp relief. His aged appearance seemed almost youthful next to her memory of Kyr. Still, the idea that age had been banished from their society had taken such deep root in her mind that she could not help but widen her eyes in surprise.

At this Tseramed put down his spoon and chuckled. "Not used to the elderly, eh?"

"No," Trielle admitted, "though I have seen age before."

"Really?" said Tseramed, his eyebrows arching with skepticism. "You look like to you come from one of the inner worlds, either Latis or Ravallon I would guess. No one has aged naturally there in centuries."

"I know," she replied, "but, well, that's how this all started. Not long ago my brother and I met a beggar in the streets of Scintillus. I never asked his age, but by his appearance he was much older than you."

A look of bewilderment crossed Tseramed's face as he considered her words. "Both poverty and age," he said at last. "I would think it quite unusual to find these things on Latis, thought I have not visited the inner Conclave for decades."

"His appearance wasn't even the strangest part," replied Trielle. "As we passed by, he grabbed my brother and asked him about the story that the world told itself."

Suddenly Tseramed's goodnatured smile vanished, replaced by a stony, guarded look, and his once mirthful eyes became distant and shadowed.

"Where I come from," he said warily, "we have a saying, a question used to instruct the young and instill in them the beginnings of wisdom. For aeons, men have told themselves stories about the World, but what is the Story that the World tells itself. Think back! Is this what the beggar said?"

Trielle nodded in silent affirmation.

His dinner forgotten, Tseramed leaned forward. She could feel his breath on her face.

"Trielle," he asked slowly, "What was the beggar's name?"

"Kyr," she said.

Tseramed sat back, lost in thought. "I think you had better tell me the whole story," he said at last.

Trielle nodded and began her tale. She left nothing out, telling of the beggar, the dream, and the map. She told of Garin's departure and the new discoveries she had made in the Arx Memoria. She told of her father and his role in the failed reignition of Vai. When at last she finished Trielle sat back in the chair; exhausted, but strangely relieved, by the telling. For a long time they sat together in silence: Tseramed staring absently into the flickering firelight, lost in thought, Trielle waiting patiently for his response. Then his lips parted in a near-inaudible whisper.

"From the brink of holocaust he trod the path, the skies a pavement to his feet…"

Suddenly Tseramed turned to Trielle, his eyes bright. "I think, nay, I know, child, that your tale hints of events that we have long awaited. As I have said before, I am of the Order of Gatekeepers, a long-lived and noble monastic brotherhood that has existed since the Great Loss. As a gatekeeper it is not my place to give you the knowledge you seek; rather, it is my job to protect the path to the Beloved. Know this, young one! If you continue through the door I will show you, there is no return. To enter will mark you as an enemy of the Conclave forever. Therefore count the cost, young one, before you make your choice."

Trielle knew that the words were meant to caution her, but curiously she felt no fear, only a mounting confidence that she was exactly where she needed to be.

"Tseramed," she said, "My brother risked his life to find something I am still not sure even exists. In the face of his courage how can I remain in safety and risk nothing myself? Besides," she added, "If even half of what I have learned is true then the Conclave has taught me nothing but lies my entire life. And if that is so then in my heart I am already their enemy."

"So be it," said Tseramed. "Come."

The pair exited the house. The azure sphere of Galed was setting in the west, casting the plateau into an eerie twilight. The sky above was almost black, lit only by the glimmer of a few distant moons. The wind was stronger now, and the cold it carried was almost a palpable thing, a living presence that invaded her body and pulsed through her veins like a heartbeat of ice.

They quickly crossed the courtyard and entered the large building she had seen earlier. In the half-light the stained glass gleamed softly, sending strange multicolored shadows skittering across the interior walls. The building was dominated by twin rows of wooden benches. An aisle stretched forward between the rows to a raised dais upon which stood an altar draped with a cloth covered in

257

unrecognizable symbols. Two lit candles and a large bell rested atop the altar.

Tseramed shut the door behind them and led Trielle down the center aisle, indicating that she should sit upon one of the benches nearest to the dais. As she rested there, watching the soft glow of the candle flames as it played across the bell's bronze surface, Trielle found herself strangely comforted, as if a part of her had always been waiting for whatever unknown experience would come next.

"I ask that you be silent and focus solely upon the altar during what is to follow, Trielle," said Tseramed as he ascended the dais. "Though the prayer is not long, it does require a degree of concentration."

Without waiting for her answer Tseramed stepped behind the altar, raised his hands skyward, and began to chant. The language seemed a mixture of words she partially recognized and words she had never heard before, almost as if the tongue in which he spoke had split at some point in the not too distant past from the common speech of the Conclave but had since evolved in near isolation. Straining to catch a few phrases, Trielle was left with the clear impression that this speech was an invocation of sorts, calling on supernatural powers (or was it one power?) to come to his aid. Abruptly Tseramed ceased chanting, raised a metal rod, and struck the bell once.

Trielle frowned. Had it made a sound? She thought she had heard something, but could not be sure. It was as if she had felt the ringing directly in her mind. For a few moments there was an absolute silence so dense that Trielle was uncertain if any sound could possibly end it, then the building was filled with a roaring, surging tumult of wind that rose, peaked, and died in the space of a heartbeat.

"You have called, my brother, and I have come."

The voice seemed familiar. Forgetting Tseramed's injunction, Trielle rose and turned, a smile blooming across her face as she saw who had spoken.

"Anacrysis!"

"I see you received my message," he said with a look of utmost seriousness. "Then you truly wish to see En-Ka-Re and know the truth of things?"

"Yes," said Trielle resolutely, her smile hardening into a look of steely determination.

"So be it," said Anacrysis. "But first you must understand the truth about me as well. I'm afraid I couldn't be entirely forthcoming with you in the Arx Memoria..."

"I don't understand?" said Trielle, her eyes narrowing.

Anacrysis said no word in response, but instead crossed his hands in front of his chest and closed his eyes. A few seconds later a soft light began to shine through his skin. Like a candle wick catching fire, the light grew in intensity until his form was surrounded by a brilliant nimbus of golden effulgence, and from his back two great wings unfolded like sails made of beaten gold, transparent as glass.

"What are you?" said Trielle as she took an involuntary step backward.

"I am one of the *Anastasi*," said Anacrysis. "Don't be afraid, Trielle."

As the initial shock of his transformation subsided, Trielle realized that she felt no fear at all, only a baffling sense of calm. "I... I'm not," she said. "I can't explain it, but somehow this doesn't strike me as surprising." She paused a few moments, then said: "My father told me about the *Anastasi*. Were you truly created from the noetic patterns of our dead ancestors?"

"After a manner of speaking," Anacrysis replied. "My mortal life was almost twelve thousand years ago. My name then was Saturninus, and I lived during a particularly dark period of Terran history." His eyes closed in remembrance. "I was only twenty three years old when they came for me."

"Who?" asked Trielle.

"The provincial governor Hilarianus and his soldiers," said Anacrysis. "There were six of us in all. They tried to make us recant but we held fast, even when they led us to the stake to be burned. The pain only lasted a short while, though, and soon we were welcomed into the Presence."

Trielle's eyes widened. "You remember your death and... the time after?" Her words trained off as she grappled with this new revelation.

"Oh, quite well," said Anacrysis. "I also remember the day when my body was called from the dust and I returned to this realm. That is what *Anastasis* means: resurrection. But enough for now. Time grows short, and there are things that are better seen than spoken of. Come, I will take you to En-Ka-Re."

Anacrysis stretched out a shining hand toward Trielle and a brief flash of warmth passed between them as she took it. Drawing Trielle close, Anacrysis folded his wings about her, transforming them into a sphere of translucent gold that surrounded Trielle like a shield. There was a sense of swift motion, and then the world around them fell away as they were borne aloft, caught on a flaming wind that blew from a mountain of stars and blackness.

Chapter 24: The Vessels of the Everlasting Light

Garin stood on a wild, windswept plain amidst a gloaming twilight. Overhead, violet clouds raced across the face of a low crescent moon that filled over half the sky. Although no-one was in sight, Garin could not dispel the sense that someone, or something, was watching him.

The transition to this world had been different than the others. As before he had approached the crystal sphere, and as before the sphere had opened, falling away to admit Garin to the world within. But then everything had changed. The new world's reality collapsed around him almost immediately, trapping him within a rigid crystalline matrix like a fly in hardened amber. He tried to turn, to escape, but to no avail. He could not see. He could not move. He could not even draw a breath. It was then that he heard the voices. As soft as whispers, their words seemed to reverberate through the crystal that surrounded him. He could not hear everything, and some of what he could hear was incomprehensible to him. Still, he was able to grasp fragments of what was said.

"Shall we deny admittance?"
"The World-Fracturer follows on his heels."
"He cannot move yet within the matrix."
"I will translate him."
"He must begin the ascent!"

As the voices trailed off a strange vibration surged through his limbs. For a moment he feared that he would be shaken apart, but as the sensation mounted he realized that he could now move again. Suddenly the pressure surrounding him abated and his vision cleared, revealing a vast crystalline matrix filled with scintillating patterns of light. When he looked down Garin barely recognized what he saw, for his body had also been changed into a pattern of scintillations. He had felt a mighty tug, followed by a sensation of falling as he plunged through an iridescent membrane. A moment later he had arrived at his present location.

Garin looked about the bleak landscape, unsure of what to do next. The plains were empty as far as his eyes could see. Indeed, there seemed to be no landmarks at all save for the glaring sickle of the moon. And so, lacking better options, he began to walk toward it. A few moments later he realized that the moon was larger than it had been. With each step it continued to grow, as did the strange sense of being watched he had felt on his arrival. Then a booming voice sounded across the barren plain.

"You may approach me, small one, though indeed you seem to be doing so already…"

"Please," said Garin, a cold pit of fear forming in his stomach. "Who are you? Where are you?"

The voice laughed jovially.

"I am the Lord of this domain. As to where I am, I thought you already knew, small one, given the course you are now taking. But no matter. I will make things clearer for you."

The ground convulsed with sudden violence as a double row of jagged stone pillars erupted from the violet plain, forming a pathway toward the cloud-swathed moon. Garin proceeded between the monoliths, the moon growing higher and larger until at last it was directly overhead, its luminous crescent filling the entirety of the sky. Standing beneath the moon, Garin felt as if an immense weight were pressing down on him, the regard of a presence as vast and massive as a planet.

262

"*Ah, that's better,*" said the voice. "*Now tell me, what business do you have in the Cube of Cubes?*"

"Cube of Cubes?" asked Garin.

"*Hmmmm,*" mused the voice, with more than a hint of mirth, "*you are lost then… Do you not know where you are?*"

"I know that I am in the world above Mythos, on the Cosmic Mountain," said Garin. "But of this world I know nothing. It was my hope to find someone who could tell me of this place."

"*Ah, then you are not entirely without knowledge, or at least you know what it is you seek. It is of no matter. In the end, these things are the same. I will give you the information you require. You travel in the lowest sphere of Arethos, the world of the Arethoi, also known as the Cube of Cubes. Now I must ask why you are here. My brethren will not forgive me if I fail in this. Indeed, some of them were against me translating your form into the language of the crystalline matrix at all.*"

Garin pondered this for a moment.

"So it was your voice I heard when I was trapped in the crystal?"

"*Yes,*" replied the voice.

"I thank you then," said Garin, "for I do not believe that I could have survived that way much longer."

"*In that you are correct,*" replied the voice. "*The crystalline matrix in which you were trapped is the native form of Arethos and is the substrate out of which the Cube of Cubes is constructed. Before you could exist here, you form had to be translated into the language of that matrix and integrated into its flow. From there it was easy to bring you to this place, which in fact is but an expression of my mind as it stands in connectivity with the Cube. All this is but a small task for the Arethoi, but the need for it serves as a barrier to keep those from our world that we wish to deny entrance.*"

"Who could come here that you would wish to deny?" asked Garin in bewilderment.

"The servants of the Fractured One, whose name once was Daath and Gnosoi, giver of the knowledge of good and evil."

"It is Daath I am fleeing," said Garin, his heart racing at the mention of his adversary. "He attempted to slay me in Mythos, but the sacrificial dagger broke in his hand and allowed me access to this place."

"Indeed," said the voice with sudden interest. *"We Arethoi are always interested in news of Daath's activities, shameful thought they are. He was once one of us, you know, but was not content to remain in his appointed place. Instead he rose in anger against the throne of He Who Is, and for that act of treason his crystal mind-shell was cast forth from Arethos, leaving only a fracture, a wound, in the fabric of the Cube of Cubes where his domain once stood. You must tell me of your journey,"* the voice added after a brief pause, *"for if Daath is pursing you even here to the site of his ancient power, then my brethren must know."*

Garin took a deep breath and began his tale. As he spoke the moonlight washing over the stark landscape seemed to deepen, shifting from light silver to a brooding grey. There was a long silence after Garin finished, and when at last the voice spoke all traces of mirth had vanished.

"Child of Phaneros, I see now why you have come here, perhaps even more deeply than you do yourself. The worlds below approach the zenith of their corruption and the time of the Apocatastasis may at last be at hand. I perceive that you have no small role to play in this but the time for your journey grows short."

"All denizens of Phaneros who enter this world must pass through my domain, which in the lower worlds is named Malkuth and Kyriakos, for all the light and wisdom of the realms beneath is but the reflected sovereignty and love of He Who Is. In the Cube of Cubes all things are connected, for the minds of the Arethoi are an ever-vast assembly of bright vessels endlessly refracting and mirroring the Uncreated Light. Yet for those of the lower realms only certain of these paths can be safely traversed, for your minds are too fragile for many of

them. But know this! All paths open to you must cross the Abyss, the Primal Wound in the cosmos created by Daath's betrayal. It is to there that you must go, and quickly, for I perceive that the Brightness of the Uncreated Light also moves within the Cube. Here then are the paths that you may tread."

There was a pulse of moonlight followed by a great cracking sound as three tall slabs of translucent crystal burst from the ground. Each was easily twice Garin's height. Their surfaces gleamed with inner radiance, and within them Garin could see swirling visions of strange, unearthly scenes.

"To your left is the Slab-Gate of Glorious Judgement, in the center lies the Slab-gate of the Foundation of the Stone Rainbow, and to the right is the Slab-gate of Eternal Mercy. All lead to the Garden of Creation's Beauty and from thence to the wound, but it is up to you to decide which gate you will take. Choose well, child of Phaneros, for some paths are bright yet endless in the undertaking, and some are dark and terrible but strangely easy because of it. Remember always that each sphere, like myself, is a living intellect, and that your journey through each depends less on the sphere through which you move and more on the virtue of the one who is moving."

Taking a deep breath, Garin studied the Slab-Gates more closely. The central gate seemed to beckon to him, its surface ablaze with images of endless adamantine plains and arching rainbows. But the longer he gazed at it the more remote and forbidding the landscape seemed, as if he could wander forever across those bright fields before reaching the end. Filled with a strange sense of dread, Garin turned away to the Gate of Eternal Mercy. This one was filled with soft visions of golden pillars overseen by a shining face whose eyes danced with kindness. The entire scene glowed with calm and peace.

Surely this is the right path, thought Garin, and he took a step toward the gate. Then he paused as he remembered the warning the voice had given. Could he truly pass this way safely? If the success of the journey depended on the virtue of the traveler, was he merciful enough to take this road? Had he ever really shown mercy at all? Then he realized that the face within the Slab-Gate was watching him. Suddenly its humanity vanished, replaced by a leonine visage framed with wings of fire. Its eyes flashed with a piercing light that cut to the very core of Garin's being, and he knew that he could not go that way. His mercy was too weak and broken to survive an encounter with whatever it was that dwelt atop those golden pillars.

With a sigh, Garin turned to face the last Slab-Gate. Here terrible images danced: cloud-swathed brazen pillars that rose to cosmic heights, a chaos of fire burning in the heart of a dark sky. As he considered these scenes, he thought of the people of Phaneros as they faced the destroying fire of the entropy clouds. He thought of the realm of Daath, filled with the innumerable prison spheres of those that had fallen to selfishness and despair. He thought of himself, standing here as the representative of an entire cosmos, a cosmos that deserved judgment for what it had allowed itself to forget. Then he understood.

Though he did not wish face judgment there was no way it could be avoided. It was the very reason he had come.

"I choose the Slab-Gate of Glorious Judgement," said Garin resolutely.

"*Really*?" said the voice with a note of surprise. "*Are you sure? Few children of Phaneros have ever climbed this far, and none have ever chosen that gate.*"

"Did they make it through?" asked Garin uneasily. "The ones who chose the other gates?"

"*Oh, one or two did,*" replied the voice, "*though it took them both a millennia to make the journey. The rest, as far as I can tell, are still on the road.*"

266

Choosing to take the cryptic response as encouragement, Garin offered a word of thanks and stepped through the swirling surface of the Slab-Gate. There was a flash, a strange sense of dissociation, and he was back in the crystal matrix.

The cloud of scintillations that formed his body flashed down a pathway of purest diamond, moving at a near-impossible velocity. Garin glanced around him as he flew, trying to gain a better sense of the medium through which he traveled. At first he could see nothing but endless miles of glittering crystal, but then he began to perceive the outlines of a vast geometric form, larger than worlds, and began to understand what the voice had meant when it spoke of the Cube of Cubes. Ahead loomed an iridescent membrane, a curvilinear defect in the otherwise angular facets of the crystal matrix that grew larger every second. Suddenly it was upon him. He was overcome by a feeling of disorientation. His vision swam, and when it cleared a few moments later Garin found himself standing on a ledge overlooking an abyss of swirling cloud.

Overtaken by vertigo, Garin took several reflexive steps backward only to be stopped short. In surprise he turned and saw a sheer wall of bronze. Its surface radiated a dull light as if it had just been removed from a furnace, yet curiously it was cold to the touch. Garin cautiously stepped back from the wall, his eyes following it upward to where it vanished amidst a vortex of fiery red vapors. Then he noticed that the wall was not flat, but gently curved away to his left and right. As Garin pondered this, he realized that this was not a wall at all but rather the base of the pillar of bronze he had seen in the Slab-Gate, a structure so vast that it dwarfed the Arx Scientia by at least an order of magnitude.

Garin sat down, leaned against the frigid surface of the pillar, and considered what to do next. He was certain that his goal lay at the top, but was equally uncertain of how to begin the ascent. Then a deep bell-like tone sounded and he felt a faint vibration from within the column. The air seemed to thicken around him, and again Garin had the overwhelming sense of being watched.

"Hello?" said Garin. "Can you hear me? I must ascend the pillar, but I don't know how."

At first there was no answer, but then the tone sounded again, this time gaining in volume until the entire pillar was visibly resonating. There was a succession of sharp reports, like stones cracking under a hammer, and a series of bronze cubes thrust their way out of the surface of the pillar to Garin's left, forming a crude staircase.

Rising to his feet Garin approached the first cube, a ponderous block of metal as high as his waist. These stairs were obviously not meant for humans, but there seemed to be no other option. Taking a deep breath, Garin hauled himself atop the first block and began to climb.

Chapter 25: Forces in Discord

In a cold room lit by the rhythmic flicker of countless holographic displays, Gedron, The Chromatocron, and the Ouranos Radii worked to calibrate the vacuum sculptors. Each heirophant stood at a raised crystalline podium surrounded by concentric circles of infochrystic workstations occupied by the highest ranking members of their respective colleges. The podiums were thought-responsive, allowing the heirophants to transmit their ideas and wishes to their colleagues near-instantaneously.

In the center of the room rose four multifaceted columns of sapphire that shone with a spectral azure glow. Between the columns, three holographic images hung suspended in the air. To the left was a stylized representation of the turbulent plasma flows of Vai's surface. Based on a series of mathematical models composed by the Ouranos Radii, the turbulence map enabled the heirophants to simulate the effects of different vacuum sculptor distributions on the ignition process. To the right rotated a detailed schematic of a working vacuum sculptor, its central neutronium filament glowing an iridescent red as beams of virtual quarks played about it. This image was linked to both the Chromatochron and the High Gavitist's infochrysts and showed the effects of minute adjustments in the filament's pion resonance frequency on the particle distributions in the underlying false vacuum. A full simulation of Vai itself hung in the center.

Gedron watched the simulation at it cycled through yet another iteration, its evolution defined by the shifting parameters of the models to each side. As the image brightened he entertained a brief hope that this one might be successful, only to be inundated by a wash of disappointment as the star flashed into a brilliant supernova. That run had been his best attempt thus far at reproducing a successful ignition. But like so many others, it had failed.

Many of the early models had resulted in asymmetric explosions that propelled Vai onto a collision course with the worlds of the Conclave, but these had quickly disappeared from the simulations when the College of Cosmic Change (the servants of the Ouranos Radii) finally developed a series of vacuum sculptor distributions that were able to avoid large-scale ignition asymmetries. The results had seemed promising even to Gedron's jaded sensibilities and he had briefly wondered whether his initial concerns about the vacuum sculptors had been unfounded. But the subsequent simulations had not been as encouraging. Some had resulted in successful reignitions, but most still led to supernovas.

He had first attempted to improve success rates by rebalancing Vai's density gradients, hoping that a simple solution was possible, but this approach had not been as high-yield as the Ouranos Radii's efforts. The extensive gaseous mixing the heirophants had used to prolong Vai's life had already smoothed out most of the irregularities in the distribution of stellar plasma and there was not much room for improvement. In the end he was only able to increase success rates by five percent using this approach and was forced to conclude that the vacuum sculptors themselves were the real issue.

Gedron had worked with the Chromatochron for the rest of the day to find an optimal resonant frequency for the central neutronium filament, but as the long hours passed he had watched with growing horror as values that worked in one iteration of the model would result in failure in the next and supernova in the third. The source of the unpredictability was clear. The enhanced strong force binding energy created by the vacuum sculptors ultimately depended on the ability of the core filaments to precisely manipulate local virtual quark concentrations, but due to the inherent instability of the quantum vacuum the degree of control required was simply impossible.

With a sigh of frustration, Gedron called up a table summarizing the results of their work. So far the best resonance settings resulted in a fourty percent success rate, with none offering less than a fifty five percent risk of helium flash. With a flick of his wrist he sent the table to the Chromatocron, who immediately frowned.

"I am aware of this, Gedron. Do you take me for a fool?"

"Far from it Tauron," said Gedron. "I merely wished to point out that to date our most successful simulations are still worse than a coin flip."

"And yet we must proceed," replied the Chromatocron. "Surely you are aware that our activities here are being monitored, and we have received no message to cease our attempts."

"You have less backbone than I thought," said Gedron with more than a hint of anger, "to so blatantly admit your lack of authority here."

"Oh, come," said the Chromatocron with a dismissive laugh. "You knew also - you had to know - that the Entrope was truly in control. How could we expect less? He is the symbol, after all, of the entropy clouds, and we but representations of the lesser forces of a cosmos soon to be destroyed, or have you somehow managed to miss the real point of the elaborate play we Heirophants perform each time we gather in Conclave?"

The Chromatocron paused for a few moments, his eyes closed in thought. "Gedron," he said finally, "I too enjoy the pleasures of existence, but these cannot be maintained unless the society that supports them continues in its present state. Surely this point is not lost on you. Besides, you know as well as I that if the Entrope were directly exerting his power we would not be engaged in our simulation game here at all and Vai would likely be nothing more now than an expanding shell of incandescent gas and radiation. I still have a great deal of authority over this process, and there is work to be done."

Before Gedron could respond the Chromatocron's attention was diverted by a series of diagrams and notations that abruptly appeared in the air before his podium. After a few moments of silence The Chromatocron turned back to Gedron with a smile.

"Ah, now here is an interesting possibility. A member of my college has postulated a resonance frequency with an additional degree of freedom that opens up strange phase space to the sculptor. Perhaps a change in quark flavor balance will improve things. Observe."

The Chromatocron transferred a copy of the diagrams to Gedron's podium and quickly began feeding the specifics into the main simulations. As the model of Vai again began cycling through its vistas of creation and destruction Gedron considered the data before him. By opening up strange phase space a number of higher energy virtual quarks entered the equation that seemed to have a small, but real, stabilizing effect on the background vacuum energy. It was an admittedly elegant approach, though he was still not sure it would make a real difference. Then an additional feature of the model caught his eye. By enhancing the creation of virtual matter bearing the strange quantum number, the resonance also opened up the possibility of a larger array of meson subtypes participating in force exchange. Kaons, in particular, seemed to receive a probability boost. Intrigued for reasons that he could not yet clearly articulate, he called up a subwindow containing the quantum properties of the meson particle family. He rapidly scanned the list, searching for the K-meson subclass, and as he read their particular properties his vague curiosity suddenly crystallized into a moment of pure insight.

Gedron looked up at the flickering hologram of Vai; the virtual star had already gone through four hundred thousand ignitions. A plan had already begun to form in his mind, but he needed more time to analyze the model and the simulation run was almost complete. Trying his best to be discrete, Gedron reached into his robes and removed a small personal infochryst, concealing it in the palm of his hand. He waited a few moments, eyes fixed on the diagrams of the altered vacuum sculptors in feigned concentration, and then casually reached out toward the model as if he were considering some specific feature, scanning its contents into the infochryst as he did so. As the infochryst flashed with the telltale blue sparks of data transfer, his heart raced with fear. He quickly glanced around, searching for signs that someone had noticed his actions, but all eyes were fixed on the simulation of Vai. When the data transfer was finished Gedron pointing to a few more features in the model to complete the deception, then dropped his hands to his sides and pocketed the infochryst. If his speculations proved valid, he might now have what he needed to defuse the vacuum sculptors.

"Gedron!"

The words startled him, and a deadly chill crept down his spine. Had he been seen after all? Taking a deep breath, Gedron steadied himself and turned to face the Chromatocron.

"Yes?" he said smoothly.

"Have you not been following the simulations? I would think you would be interested in the outcomes of the run, given your prior concerns. In any event, here they are."

With a gesture, the Chromatocron sent a statistical summary of the simulation to Gedron. Both the reignition and supernova rates now approached forty-five percent. The results were better, but not by much.

"You see," said the Chromatocron with a laugh, "Now our chances are better than a flipped coin."

Gedron frowned at the Chromatocron's mockery of his previous concern but after a few moments nodded in grudging agreement. Satisfied, the Chromatocron turned back to the simulations, leaving Gedron to his thoughts.

***

A few hours later, Gedron climbed the spiraling ramps of the Arx Memoria in search of a private place to work. Though he was sure that most would not understand what he was doing, given the stakes he could not afford to take unneccesary risks. He soon found what he was looking for: a dark row of secluded alcoves near the top of the main library. Far from the bustling activity of the floors below, here there was little chance of arousing suspicion. Gedron glanced around one last time to be sure he was alone, then sat down at the desk and removed the small datachryst from his robes, placing it as far from the alcove's primary terminal as space allowed. It would not do to have them communicating prematurely.

Gedron was sure the Entrope was monitoring him, and it was for this reason that he was not working at the Omegahedron or his home. Those infochryst terminals would almost certainly be under surveillance. Here he could be assured of some degree of protection, if he were careful.

Gedron waved his hands above the infochryst and it sprang to life. He first activated a group of subroutines designed to mask the identity of the device from the Ionocaric Infochryst and prevent the data stored within from being accessed beyond this particular terminal. Only then did he bring the two devices together. For a moment they communicated in silent, rapid flashes of blue light, then a shimmering information network coalesced in the air above them.

He worked quickly, first confirming his intuitions regarding the properties of Kaons via a search of the public physics databases. The results brought a smile to his face. One of the high-energy mesons, Kaons possessed weak isospin, a property that the ligher mesons did not have. In and of itself this was of little consequence, but when coupled with the Kaon's momentum this property gave each particle a chirality, a "handedness" to its spiraling motion that drastically changed its interactiveness with the weak force and hence its rate of decay. Known as CP symmetry violation, this effect was thought to be the primary cause of the dominance of matter over antimatter in the universe.

With this new information in hand Gedron called up the simulation of the redesigned vacuum sculptors, paying specific attention to the predicted balance of Kaon chirality that the devices would generate. It took an eternity to run the model on his tiny infochryst, but, firewall or not, he was not going to chance moving the simulation to the much faster public terminal. The results were more encouraging than he had hoped. Over eighty percent of Kaons generated by the new vacuum sculptor resonances were of the long type, a mix of chiral states that allowed for extended particle lives and a much higher effect on the strong force binding constant. All that was needed to disable the vacuum sculptors was to change this balance. If he could be sure that enough short-lived Kaons were produced then the danger of supernova could be averted.

Gedron leaned back and closed his eyes as a mixture of exhaustion and excitement ran through him. Changing the Kaon mix should only require a simple alteration in the neutronium filament resonant frequency. The greater issue was how to transmit that new frequency to the millions of vacuum sculptors that were even now being seeded in Vai's photosphere. He was still far from a solution, but he felt sure he was on the right path. He only hoped that Trielle was meeting with similar success.

And Garin, he still dared not think about Garin…

Chapter 26: The Forgotten Vale

The golden sphere skimmed across a gently curving expanse of translucent crystal. Beneath its surface Trielle could see the whole of the Conclave spread out like a map.

"We're currently skirting the edge of the world-shell that contains your cosmos," said Anacrysis, "a structure that I believe your cosmologists would call a five-brane. What you see beneath it is a multidimensional view of your universe's spacetime. But there is more you must see; lift up your eyes."

Trielle did so, and gasped as she caught her first glimpse of the mountain.

A series of crags made of stars and darkness rose beyond the expanse, culminating in a soaring peak crowned with terrible light. Upon its slopes rested four bright gems that gleamed with unearthly colors. Though they looked small from her current position, Trielle could not escape the sense that the gems, like the crystal plain beneath her, were large enough to contain whole universes.

"Anacrysis, what... what is this place?" cried Trielle, overwhelmed by a sudden wave of wonder and terror.

"Despite what the Conclave has taught you, Trielle," said Anacrysis, "your cosmos is not the only one. It is but the lowest link in the great chain of worlds. And this," he spread his arms to indicate the entire mountain, "is the foundation upon which they rest, the greater reality in which they live, move, and have their being."

Though she knew she had never seen this strange, otherworldly vista before, it still seemed somehow familiar. Then she remembered Garin's map, and rush of hope swelled within her.

"Anacrysis, is this where Garin went?"

Anacrysis nodded. "By now he is in the upper worlds," he said, pointing to the gems that rested on the highest slopes of the mountain. "A rumor has come to us that he was separated from the one you call Kyr, but even now they draw closer together."

It was as if a heavy burden had been lifted from Trielle's shoulders. She felt a great tension that, until now, had lay coiled below the surface of her consciousness suddenly rise up and give way, leaving only mingled relief and joy behind. For a few moments she said nothing, a wide smile on her face, but then her natural curiosity reasserted itself and a new question rose in her mind.

"Anacrysis," she asked, "how is it that you can travel like this?"

Anacrysis thought for a moment. "It is difficult to explain," he said finally. "Your scientists are used to considering the natural world, even space itself, as something inanimate that can be manipulated with tools such as the Laridian rings, but you must not think of it that way. The cosmos is not a dead thing but a living expression of the outpoured life of He Who Is, its Maker, and every thread of the world's being throbs with His heartbeat. The body that houses your spirit is, in its current state, like a poem or play composed of the ephemeral fluctuations that you call particles and fields. The *Anastasi*, however, exist at a deeper level. At the time of my resurrection the patterns that once were contained in the matter of my body was written upon the underlying structure of spacetime itself. Do not misunderstand, even in your present form you partake of the Life of the World, for there is one Life just as there is one Life-giver, but because my current body is essentially composed of pure spacetime I have much greater latitude in my relationship with distance. It is a state of being in which

278

all created beings were meant to partake. But we can speak of this later. We have almost arrived."

The golden sphere dropped downward, merging with the crystalline material beneath it like a bubble of soap alighing on a pool of still water, and the worlds of the Conclave unfolded before Trielle. To their immediate left hung a brown dwarf, its surface a churning soup of opaque gases and dully glowing plasma. Ahead lay a small planet pockmarked with thousands of craters.

"Is that En-Ka-Re?" asked Trielle.

Anacrysis nodded.

Within moments they were soaring over the planet's surface, the craters and fissures passing beneath them in a dizzying blur. At first she thought them natural features, but as they flew onward she began to notice a strange uniformity to their shapes and sizes, almost as if they were artificial. Then she understood. These were not natural features at all; they were the scars of war.

Ahead loomed a mountain ridge covered by a sprawling collection of technology - generators, pipes and electrophotonic architecture all feeding into a line of laridian rings that stood upon the crest of the ridge like sentinels. Although they were currently inactive, the rings appeared ready to spin up at a moments' notice.

"The Siegewall," said Anacrysis darkly. "It has been there ever since the war and the hiding of Hyrosol Neos. It keeps the Sur Ekklesia imprisoned within the valley beyond."

As they neared the ridge, Trielle saw a group of indistinct figures tending to the machinery.

"Those are the Entrope's personal guard," said Anacrysis, "an army of clones with altered brain strutures that carry all of his intelligence, but none of his will. He would trust no-one else with guarding this valley."

"Won't they see us?" asked Trielle.

279

"No," said Anacrysis. "Though we are close enough to the cosmos to see within it clearly, our bodies are still outside the world-shell, and they cannot detect us until we pierce it. An *Anastasi* re-entering normal space produces a specific pattern of gravity waves that is fairly easy to localize with the right sensors. While they expect to see that pattern every now and then within the Valley of the Sur, detecting it outside could trigger a massive retaliation. It is the sword that the Conclave has hung above our heads."

Trielle thought about this a moment.

"So is that why I had to meet you on the moon of Galed?"

Anacrysis nodded. "That moon is almost pure iron. It's one of the densest bodies in the Conclave. Combined with Galed's tidal forces, it fills that area of space with enough gravitational anomalies to confuse all but the most accurate sensor arrays. Still, it's risky to appear even there. Had I manifested as an *Anastasi* on Latis or one of the other inner worlds there would not have been a valley to return to."

As he spoke, a troubling thought arose in Trielle's mind.

"Anacrysis, I need to tell you something. My father is the High Gravitist of the Conclave."

"I know," said Anacrysis. "Most of the *Anastasi* know as well. We have been watching you and your brother for some time now. Our ability to enter the world-shell without fully translating into normal space has many uses."

Trielle could see the figures atop the ridge clearly now: their bodies covered in black and green armor, their faces obscured by featureless masks. They seemed close enough to touch, and for a moment she was afraid that they would be seen despite Anacrysis' assurances, but the golden bubble sailed by the guards undetected. Then the mountain

280

wall fell away behind them and they soared into the valley beyond.

Here the land sloped sharply downward into a deep bowl filled with a golden haze. The ground was covered in scrub grasses punctuated by the occasional twisted trunk of a tree. They were the first plants Trielle had seen on this planet.

"En-Ka-Re once had an atmosphere - thin, but breathable to most of the races that composed the Dar," said Anacrysis, "but the war changed all that. Now the only place with enough air to support life is this valley. Even if the inhabitants were permitted to colonize the rest of the planet, there is nowhere else to go. Still, the vale is fairly spacious and supports the remnant well enough."

The scrub grasses soon gave way to a patchwork ring of fields surrounding a collection of slender, transparent buildings that rose skyward like a glass forest. As they approached the buildings, their movement slowed until soon they hovered above a single structure. A few seconds later the golden bubble dove abruptly downward, passing through the structure as if it were a mirage. There was a blast of wind and a shattering sound as if they had crashed through some invisible barrier. Then the golden sphere unfolded and Trielle found herself standing next to Anacrysis on the cold stone floor of a basement chamber.

Despite its subterranean location the chamber was brightly lit by a number of lamps made of luminescent sapphires that hung from the ceiling. The center of the chamber was, save for them, unoccupied, but a table and several rude stools filled one corner, overshadowed by a gnarled plant wrapped in vines and crowned with golden-red foliage.

"Xellasmos," called Anacrysis, "we have come. There is someone here you must meet."

"Indeed," said a voice that sounded more like rough surfaces being rubbed together than an exhaled breath. To Trielle's surprise the gnarled plant turned and moved toward her, the vines wrapped about its trunks coiling and uncoiling to pull it across the ground. The bright foliage atop the plant fanned outward at it approached, revealing a central core of flowers that vaguely resembled a human face. The creature came to a stop several feet from the pair and for a long time stood immobile, as if staring at them. Then, with utmost graciousness, it spoke.

"And who might this be?"

The creature's speech was largely comprehensible to her, despite the raspy quality of the sound, but many of the words had the same odd divergent quality she had noticed in Tseramed's chant.

"Her name is Trielle," said Anacrysis, "and she had come to learn the true history of the Sur Ekklesia. But it is her brother that I think may be of most interest to you."

"Indeed," said Xellasmos after a moment of deliberation. "Have you brought him as well?"

"No," said Anacrysis. "Even now he ascends the road. He is the first to do so in millennia."

At these words a trembling thrill ran through the creature's foliage.

"Could he be…"

"Perhaps," said Anacrysis, cutting him off, "but the situation is more complicated than this. Their father is the High Gravitist of the Conclave, and Vai is in his hands. If we do not proceed with care, this could undo everything."

"It is worse that you think," said Trielle. "The last attempt to reignite Vai was unsuccessful because my father had a change of heart. He saw the destruction it was causing and stopped the process. When the other Heirophants understood what he did they stripped him of his authority over Vai. They have also developed another, perhaps even more dangerous, way to attempt reignition."

As Trielle told them about the vacuum sculptors Xellasmos' foliage began to droop and Anacrysis' lips narrowed in an expression of grim concern.

"This is indeed dire," said Xellasmos after she finished. "And you say that we have only a few days before they are activated?"

"At most," confirmed Trielle.

Anacrysis took a deep breath. "Though this is disturbing news, it is comforting to know that your father is no longer an enemy of the Sur Ekklesia. His aid may yet prove vital. Now is not the time for despair, but for knowledge and action. Trielle, you have been brought to Xellasmos to learn the truth. He is one of the foremost scholars of all the *Alapsari* races on the history of the Conclave."

"When I last spoke with my father, he told me of the founding of the Dar Ekklesia Empire by an alien extradimensional entity of some sort, and about the war…"

Trielle's voice trailed off as she saw a look of mingled amusement and incredulity in Anacrysis' eyes.

"Is that how they remember things?" said Xellasmos with a note of shock.

"If so, then the truth has been completely lost even among the Conclave's leaders," answered Anacrysis.

"Forgive my surprise," he continued, turning to Trielle. "I meant no disrespect, but it is both sad and amusing to hear He Who Is, Son of He Who Is, the very source and life of the Cosmos, being referred to as an 'alien extradimensional entity.' No, Trielle, it is the Conclave that is truly alien, for in their ongoing rejection of that life your people have alienated themselves from the very breath that sustains their existence."

Trielle's brow furrowed with incomprehension.

"Your father's story stands in relationship to the truth as a blurred, cracked mirror to the reality it reflects," said Xellasmos. "The actual story of your people, and by extension the story of the Conclave, extends ninety one thousand years into the past. I was then in my youth, and our race, the Ferisi, had just developed the technology to survey other worlds…"

"Wait," said Trielle in shock. "You are ninety one thousand years old?"

"Oh no," said Xellasmos with a grating sound that might have been a laugh. "Forgive me for the confusion. The youth of a Ferisi can last over ten millennia. My age is closer to one hundred and five thousand of your years."

Trielle's eyes widened in wonder and surprise. "There are hundreds of different races in the Conclave," she whispered, "and though some are longer-lived than mine, none have a lifespan past three or four hundred years. We no longer age, but death itself is still inevitable. How is it that your race is so long-lived?

Xellasmos foliage shook with evident dismay. "Anacrysis, she does not know?"

"It is part of the complex of falsehoods that forms the basis of their society," replied Anacrysis. "Trielle," he said, "I fear that you misunderstand. It is not that the Ferisi are long lived, it is that they do not die at all, at least naturally. Their bodies, of course, can be destroyed, as all material things can be. The first true Feris, born from the crawl-shrubs of their native world, lived for thousands of millions of years only to be slain in the Philosoph War. But left to themselves, there is no death among them or any of the *Alapsari* races."

"The death of a sentient being is a violation," said Xellasmos, "a severing of their tiny life from the greater life of He Who Is. Each race that is called to attain true selfhood is simultaneously called to submit that selfhood to He Who Is. By doing so they are joined to His life and share in His eternity. But if a race chooses otherwise…"

Xellasmos paused for a moment, his foliage drawn inward as if in deep thought.

"Perhaps it is best to show you."

The Feris turned and set off with long strides, the multiple trunks that made up his lower body shifting and knotting as the vinelike cords that evidently served as its muscles pulled them forward. They left the room and ascended a broad stone staircase that ended in an open glass atrium lit by the ember-like glow of the brown dwarf. From there a second staircase, this time made of glass, ascended further into the structure. After another short climb the trio arrived at a small chamber containing a podium made of bright silver metal. Atop the podium was a bowl containing a shimmering liquid that Trielle could not identify.

"Wait here," said Xellasmos, who left the room and returned a few moments later with a large woody bulb in his tendrils."

"Our race first developed the technology to survey other worlds almost one hundred thousand years ago. The photonscopes we then used not only permitted us observe these worlds optically but also to decode the entangled quantum information present in the captured light, allowing us to generate immersive simulations of the events we were following. Our planet of origin was only ten light-years from your world, so your race was the first we watched. Though I was young at the time my scholarly pursuits made it natural to include me in the observational team. During the first few years we saw little of note and spent most of our time experimenting with and refining the equipment. But halfway through the fifth year of observation our instruments picked up something different, something new."

Xellasmos dropped the bulb into the liquid, which quickly began to steam and froth. A few moments later a mass of gleaming microfilaments rose from the surface of the liquid and wove themselves together into a rough sphere. There was a burst of light from within the sphere followed by a flash of color that quickly resolved itself into the silent image of a jungle at night.

"This is your homeworld, known in this age as Sha-ka-ri, as it was before the emergence of your species," said Xellasmos.

"Where is the sound?" asked Trielle

"It is an artifact of the technology," replied Xellasmos. "The first generation devices could not extract sound wave information from the quantum entanglement data. Still, it is enough to show you what you need to see. Now, watch."

Trielle turned back to the image. The trees were massive, their trunks reaching skyward like the pillars of an ancient temple. The roof of the forest was dark with leaves, but here and there small holes in the canopy let silver shafts of starlight peek through, dappling the ground with a shifting pattern of shadow and soft iridescence. Then a patch of foliage at the lefthand side of the image began to rustle, and a few moments later the figure of a man stepped from the shadows. His body was covered in thick hair that barely concealed the massive cords of muscle rippling beneath. He wore no clothing, but carried a spear in his right hand. She could not see his face.

"Who is that?" asked Trielle.

"Right now he is nobody," said Xellasmos. "He is a creature with no no name, no identity. Look at his movements, consider the way he surveys his surroundings.

286

He is intelligent to be sure, but there as yet no sentience in him."

As that moment, as if on cue, the man turned to face them, and Trielle could immediately see that what Xellasmos said was true. The expression on his face was cunning, even feral; a mass of instincts given emotional expression. She watched as his eyes darted about in search of the next meal or predator, and realized that despite the creature's evident intelligence there was something missing in his gaze that was present in every other human she had ever known.

Intelligence without understanding; a mind without a soul.

A wind began to blow. It surged through the leafy roof, pushing aside the leaves and filling the forest with the soft gleam of starlight. Trielle watched as the light grew and realized that the wind itself, and not the stars, was its source. It seemed to pulse with a soft inner fire, a burning radiance that cast the colors of the trees and soil into sharp relief. Evidently the man noticed it also, for, confronted with the unknown, he began to run.

Their viewpoint followed the figure as he crashed through the jungle, pursued by the strange flaming wind, until finally it reached a clearing surrounded by scrub brush too thick to penetrate. In the center of the clearing stood two saplings. The man hid beneath them.

"Watch," said Xellasmos. "You are about to see the awakening of your race."

As he spoke the wind began to rise in fury, fire and light soaring high above the clearing in a hurricane of celestial radiance. Then, from the center of the hurricane, a gust of brilliance flooded downward to the cowering figure, caressing him with soft warmth. In wonder, the man lifted his head, breathing the light into his nostrils.

287

Suddenly his body stiffened. His eyes dilated momentarily, lit from within by the radiance that now flowed through him. Then they constricted and the man tilted his head upward, the light of the glory-cloud bathing his face as he opened his mouth in a soundless cry.

"Father," said Xellasmos in answer to Trielle's unspoken question. "He calls on his father. It is the first cry of all the awakened races. Charagon, our oldest ancestor, used to tell us of when the Root of Life was given to him. As his mind filled with understanding, he looked out on a world awash with a Presence beyond his comprehension, a Presence that was to him as a father to a son. This Presence has been given many names throughout the ages, and yet in the end they all carry the same meaning: He Who Is, the Self-existent One."

"Why does my race not remember this?" asked Trielle, shaken and amazed by what she had seen.

"Some still do," said Anacrysis softly. "You will meet them soon."

"Watch," commanded Xellasmos, "There is more to be seen and the time grows short,"

Xellasmos waved his tendrils at the image and it blurred momentary as time compressed. When it again came into focus Trielle saw that they were still in the clearing, but now the trees in its center shone with unearthly light. One pulsed with a golden glow; the other was wrapped in a nimbus of violet shadow.

"The Two Trees," explained Xellasmos. "Life and Knowledge, Self-Sacrifice and Self-Awareness. They are given as a gift to all awakened worlds and are the source of its lifeblood. It is said by our metaphysicians and hypernoeticists that each pair in this cosmos is but an eidolon, an image, of the true trees that stand in worlds above our own. But I do not know the truth of this."

288

Then the man reentered the scene, accompanied by a woman.

"He brings his mate," said Xellasmos

Trielle could clearly see the difference in their bearings. The man, now gifted with sapience, moved forward with deliberate, purposeful strides, while the woman seemed perpetually poised to run, her eyes darting back and forth in search of the next threat.

When the pair reached the center of the clearing the man raised his hands and suddenly the sky was bright again with flaming wind. His mouth moved rapidly, as if conversing with a silent partner. Then he gestured toward the woman and in answer the flaming wind descended upon the man, embracing his body and easing him to the ground. His eyes fluttered and then closed in a deep sleep. The womans's gaze darted about and her muscles tensed as if to run, but the wind encircled her also, soothing her with its warmth. Trielle could see her fear gradually abate until finally she walked toward the man and rested calmly at his side.

The wind gathered about them as they lay there, a cradle of glory holding them together with cords of light and power. Then, like the hand of surgeon, the wind touched the man's chest and brought forth a bright flame that pulsed like an incandescent heart. Carrying it to the woman, the wind pushed the flame through her skin and deep into her body. Then the wind vanished, leaving the pair alone in the light of the trees. A few moments later they awoke, and as the man and woman saw in each other's eyes the telltale gleam of life and understanding they leapt up and danced together.

"Thus far," said Xellasmos as the image faded away, "the awakenings of both of our planets mirrored each other, and my people rejoiced to see another world entering into the harmony of the deeper life. But several decades later we saw another scene that disturbed us greatly. Watch again Trielle, one last time."

Again the image blurred as an unknown span of time rushed by. When it cleared, Trielle saw that the two trees had grown tall in the interim, their branches weaving together in a glowing ceiling of bright gold and deep violet. The woman, looking somewhat older, rested beneath them. Then a curious red light began to play over her features. At first Trielle thought it was the wind again, but the color seemed off somehow, almost alien. As if in response to her unspoken question Xellasmos gestured and the aspect of the image widened to reveal a strange creature standing at the edge of the clearing.

Serpentine in form, the creature looked as if it were composed of liquid flame, a sinuous mass of burning redness almost as tall as the trees. Its reptilian face was surrounded by a mane that blazed like the suns at noon, and its head was crowned with ten horns that gleamed like brass drawn from a furnace. Its form seemed to swim in and out of focus as Trielle watched, as if in some undefinable way it wasn't really there. The creature and the woman appeared to be in dialogue.

"Such a thing also happened on our world," said Xellasmos. "Perhaps even with the same creature. After studying this image, most Ferisi metaphysicians have come to the conclusion that this creature is a three-dimensional manifestation of a being whose primary existence rests in a higher plane. Charagon himself told us of his encounter with the creature, thought he did not like to speak of it. He said only that it offered to somehow augment the root of life within him, to make him wiser. Such counsel seemed foolish to Charagon, and he refused. Would that she had done the same."

As he said those words the woman stood and walked to the trees. For a moment she stood between them, her head turning back and forth. Then she walked to the violet tree, reached out, took something, and put it in her mouth. Suddenly the woman looked about as if in fear. A wind began to blow, but there was no light in it. As the scene began the fade out, the woman shivered and her eyes filled with tears.

"Thus is a world cut off from the true life," said Xellasmos At first we continued to watch your world to monitor the effects of her choice, but when our monitor showed us an image of the mother of your race dying in pain we were so shaken that we could not look again. It was seven thousand years before another of the Ferisi dared to use a photonoscope. During those lost millennia we found that many new races across the galaxy had awoken to the deeper life. Some, like us, chose well at the moment of awakening and with these we communed. Others chose poorly, and whenever we looked upon those worlds we saw nothing but pain, destruction, and death."

"Then, tens of thousands of years later, an envoy of beings such as Anacrysis, those whom you call the *Anastasi*, came to our world. They told us that you race had not been left alone in their darkness, that a mighty work of healing had come to all those worlds that rejected the true life, and that the time had come for the entire galaxy to enter the deeper life as one."

"I remember those journeys," said Anacrysis wistfully. "The first time our explorations brought us to a world of the unfallen we rejoiced in wonder. Until then I had never dared think it possible that a race could remain uncorrupted."

"Then came the war," said Xellasmos with a note of sadness. "But now, with your brother's journey and your coming to En-Ka-Re, perhaps the time of our exile is nearing its end."

The weight of this new knowledge crashed down on Trielle with the sudden force of an avalanche. She had known that the Conclave's history was a falsehood but only now was the true depth of the deception apparent. And somehow she and her brother were expected to right the situation? The thought was absurd.

"What can I do?" she said finally, her words as much a plea as a protest. "You both know the strength of the Conclave; it shattered an empire and put you here. I don't have the power you think I have, and my brother, even if he returns, doesn't either. Perhaps my father once did, but not anymore."

"Power?" said Xellasmos with a rustling sound suspiciously like a chuckle. "Who said anything about power? The deepest wisdom of the Dar Ekklesia has always told us that all strength will one day fail and that true strength is only found in weakness. In the end, I have confidence that what you can offer will prove in the end to be sufficient."

"I wish I shared that confidence," said Trielle with a grim smile.

"Come Trielle," said Anacrysis, "There is one other you must meet before I return you to the Conclave. Perhaps he will make your path clearer. Thank you, Xellasmos."

Xellasmos' trunks shifted and creaked as he bent in a deep bow. Trielle and Anacrysis bowed in return, then descended the stairwell and exited the building.

Chapter 27: The Sword and the Lampstand

Fire, an endless storm of fire raging as far as he could see.

After the grueling climb up the column of brass Garin had hoped that the next domain would be more level. But this place only traded the sheer sides of the pillar for near-intolerable heat. Still, he could not help but wonder why he was able to survive at all amidst the burning clouds. It was as if the fire was a living thing that waited and watched, reserving judgment on his presence, holding back the full measure of its fury until some unpredictable moment when it would decide that he didn't belong and burn him to ash. He pressed on with dogged steps, marching forward across a plain of black obsidian that shimmered in the heat, hoping that his course was taking him closer to the resting place of whatever intelligence called this domain home.

He had chosen this path and was not turning back.

After what seemed like an eternity of wandering amidst the flames and black glass Garin thought he saw a dark shape ahead. He could not make out exactly what it was, only that it was tall and thin, and seemed to drink in the light of the surrounding blaze. The object loomed larger as he drew nearer, until at last the fires parted and Garin could see it clearly.

Within the eye of the firestorm hovered a sword, its upright blade a dull black and its hilt shaped like a stylized version of the scales of justice. Beneath the sword lay a circular pool filled with blood. Garin walked to the side of the pool and waited for the spirit of that place to speak. He did not have to wait long.

"Guilty or not guilty!"

The dolorous words crashed around Garin like a thunderclap and the fire-clouds seemed to whirl faster in response. He could not escape the sense that his answer might well determine the outcome of his journey. Still, the question was not entirely unexpected, and he was not entirely unprepared.

"Great One," he began, "I come as a representative of the lowest world, a world that has strayed far from the right path. A world that..."

"The words you speak are at best peripheral. Only one question matters. Guilty or not guilty!"

Garin was confused. Hadn't he been in the process of declaring the guilt of his world? He took a deep breath, and began again.

"Great One, my people have done many wrongs. I have come to represent them in..."

"Do not trouble me with irrelevancies! Now I ask again. Guilty or not guilty!"

With each word the fury of the fire-clouds grew until the heat became so great that Garin felt his skin would char. Yet still he remained unharmed.

What does it want? How do I answer?

"Great One," he whispered with a note of fear. "I do not understand."

"Then watch, and learn!"

A beam of brilliant red light stabbed from the tip of the sword, transfixing Garin's forehead like a red-hot nail and driving him to knees. A wave of pain rolled through him and a volley of images flashed through his mind. Faster and faster they came until at last they blurred together into a white haze. A moment later his vision cleared and he found himself sitting in the central chamber of their apartment on Latis, hard at work on the family infochryst. The kitchen door opened and his father stepped out. He was clad in his robes of office.

"Hello Father," Garin called.

"Hello," Gedron replied with a weary voice.

Garin rose to his feet in excitement.

"Father, I've been working on a new gravitics simulation program for school on our infochryst. It's almost done, but I was hoping you could help me."

"Garin," said Gedron with a dismissive voice. "Not tonight. I barely have time to eat. There is an urgent meeting at the College of Gravitists that I need to attend."

A wave of bitterness surged up inside Garin.

"You've had urgent meetings every night this week," he said in anger. "Father, I need your help with this! Can't you stay just tonight?"

"No," said Gedron with a touch of exasperation. "There are a number of resolutions that require my attention." As he turned toward the transit tube he added, "I need to keep up with these things if I ever want to be High Gravitist." Then, without another word, he left.

Anger and malice surged within Garin.

"I hate you Father! I hate you!" he called out, then his vision faded away into indistinct whiteness.

He stood on bridge of a golden starship the size of a continent, the flagship of a vast armada of stellar dreadnaughts and battleships. Before them, bathed in the light of the mighty accretion disk that churned at the galaxy's heart, hung a golden cube surrounded by countless smaller ships.

None were armed.

Malice surged within his heart, the same feeling that had filled him in the previous vision. Garin raised his arm.

"Fire all batteries!"

Each warship fired as one, and a wave of searing fire surged toward the golden cube, immolating the orbiting spacecraft like snowflakes in a blast furnace. Soon the space around the golden cube had been converted into an expanding shell of white hot plasma, and his field of vision again faded into blinding whiteness.

Garin felt a sudden weight on his body, and he looked down to see himself clad in armor. He stood in a company of soldiers atop a sun-bleached outcropping of rock at the edge of a sprawling city. In his right hand he held a hammer. On the ground in front of him was a naked man tied to a beam of rough wood.

"Well," said a soldier next to him. "Are you going to finish the job or should I."

"No, I've got this," said Garin with a harsh, guttural laugh.

Garin reached into a leather pouch on his belt and removed a long iron spike, the now familiar sense of rage and malice filling him again as he did. With a grin, Garin placed the point of the nail on the man's wrist, raised the hammer, and drove the sharp metal through flesh and tendon. Blood spurted from the wound, running hot and free across Garin's hands, and he laughed as he hammered the spike deeper and deeper. Then he glanced at the man's face, and the feeling of malice fled in a flash of sudden recognition. Though countless years younger, the outlines of the face were clear. As the vision began to fade one last thought hung in his mind.

Kyr!

Garin opened his eyes. He lay prostrate at the edge of the pool of blood. The sword hovered a few feet above him, dark and inscrutable. As he stared at the ebon surface of the blade a sudden wave of fear washed through him, and he finally began to understand.

All mankind hung together.

None were innocent, not even himself.

He was not here as a representative of his race. How could he even think to take on that role when his own heart contained the same darkness? How could he hope to survive the fire that would surely overwhelm him?

No, when the voice spoke of guilt, it was his guilt alone that was being judged.

"I see that you now understand. Good. Then we may continue. I ask again, guilty or not guilty? Answer swiftly, for it will be the last time the question is posed."

A thousand voices filled his mind: each an excuse, each a rationalization. Yet in the end he knew that none spoke the truth. He glanced one last time at the blazing clouds and then cried out in a loud voice as tears streamed down his face.

"Guilty! I am guilty!"

"It is so!"

The sword began to rise, its blade shining with a dull red glow like metal in a forge. Around him the burning clouds churned faster and faster, a cyclone of living flame. With a sudden rush the fire leapt inward, infusing the sword with its heat until it blazed like the heart of a star, and within seconds the skies were black and empty. All had faded to darkness except Garin and the intolerable fury of the sword. The fiery blade continued to soar upward, rotating as it ascended until its tip pointed downward toward Garin's heart. Then, without warning, it fell toward him like a meteor. Fear gripped him and he braced himself for the first searing pains of judgment, but they never came.

Instead the blazing sword plunged into the pool of blood. The dark liquid hissed and bubbled as it extinguished the blade's fire, sending great billows of acrid steam heavenward. A few moments later the darkness began to lighten, and a soft brilliance crept slowly across the empty landscape.

"Guilty you are," whispered the voice, *"but my flame has been quenched by the blood of another. Now go! The realm of my sister awaits."*

A long, thin slab of crystal rose silently from the pool, its surface flickering with soft candlelight.

"Thank you," said Garin.

"It is not I that deserves your thanks."

Garin nodded silently, then rose to his feet and stepped through the slab-gate.

Again he coursed down the crystalline pathways of the Cube of Cubes, his body a coherent array of scintillating light. Ahead loomed the iridescent membrane that enclosed the next realm. His vision blurred and spun as he passed through its surface, and when his eyes cleared Garin found himself in a verdant garden at twilight. Soft breezes, warm and fragrant with the scent of flowers, caressed his skin, and as the pure beauty of the scene took hold of him he was suddenly overwhelmed with exhaustion.

"Rest, my child. Rest…"

The voice was soft and gentle, with the soothing tone of a mother. How long had it been since he had last slept? Days? Weeks? Though a dim part of him wondered what spirit it was that spoke to him, Garin could not muster up the energy to respond, and instead lay down beneath a tall tree festooned with bright red blossoms and fell into a deep, dreamless sleep.

***

"Child, it is time to awaken."

The soft words slid into Garin's mind, gently arousing him from slumber. He sat up slowly, feeling more

298

refreshed than he had in a long time. Around him was the same soft twilight in which he had fallen asleep, but he was not particularly surprised. He had passed through stranger places on his journey than a garden of perpetual evening. Stepping out from beneath the tree, Garin saw a well-worn footpath that he felt certain had not been there before.

"Come forward child. We must speak soon, but your journey has been hard, and you must needs be refreshed."

The path lead through a dense forest of trees similar to the one he had slept beneath. The air here was thick with birdsong and the fragrance of flowers. As he walked onward he began to hear another sound, a gentle trickling like the chiming of bells. Then the forest opened up to reveal the grassy banks of a river. The water was clear and ran across the rocks of the streambed with an evident playfulness that kindled joy within Garin's heart.

"Bathe my child! Cleanse your body and soul!"

Garin waded out into the stream. The water was cool but not cold, the seeming embodiment of refreshment, and he scooped large handfuls onto his face and body. Each muscle relaxed as the liquid coursed over his skin, and a bright smile broke out across his face.

"Drink! Drink my child. It is the River of the Water of Life! Drink your fill and be satisfied!"

Garin bent down in joyful obedience and took a long draught. As he swallowed new vitality surged through him, as if the blood in his veins had been filled to the bursting with the pure essence of life. He continued to drink until his stomach could hold no more, and then waded back to shore.

"It is good! Now come. There are more trials ahead."

The path clung to the river's edge, following it upstream into a cluster of low hills topped by a dense mass of forest that glowed with faint light. At last it ended at a

299

large round pool backed by a cliff wall from which a cataract poured with great tumult. Garin scanned the scene, and spied a series of switchbacks cut into the cliff-face near the waterfall that promised access, albeit difficult, to the forest above. There appeared to be no other way forward, and so he quickly circled the edge of the pool and began to climb.

The slope of the switchback was steep, but surprisingly Garin felt no exhaustion. Indeed, new energy seemed to well up within him every moment, and he realized that something inside him had changed since he had drank from the River of the Waters of Life. Gaining the cliff top, Garin saw that the cataract was fed by a swift-moving rill that emerged from a dense wall of evergreen and fir. Shafts of red-gold light shone between the trees, as if a perpetually setting sun lay just beyond. Garin examined the treeline more closely and saw a break near the point where the stream left the forest, a living archway that penetrated the thick foliage like a tunnel.

"Come my child. Just a little way further."

Garin stepped through the archway and made his way deeper into the forest. The light streaming through the wood grew brighter as he walked until all was a chiaroscuro of dark trunks and beams of fiery brilliance. From somewhere nearby, Garin could still hear the tinkling, babbling sound of the stream. After a short distance the tunnel ended at a high hedge pierced by a single portal. Feeling sure that the intelligence of this domain must dwell within, Garin took a deep breath and entered.

The hedge enclosed a woodland glade filled with wildflowers. Within the glade's heart bubbled a crystal clear spring that seemed to dance with barely restrained life. A deep channel stretched from the pool to the edge of the glade, and through it the Waters of Life poured out ceaselessly into the forest beyond. In the center of the spring rose a mound upon which grew a tree made entirely of gold. The tree had no leaves, but from its trunk seven branches reached toward the sky, each bearing a single immense candle that burned with a brilliant flame. Dazzled by the beauty of the scene, Garin walked to the edge of the spring and knelt amidst the flowers.

"My Child, do not kneel to me. I am a fellow servant like yourself."

The voice whispered softly in Garin's ear, carried on a breath of warm wind that blew from amidst the candles and golden boughs.

"Who are you?" asked Garin as he rose to his feet. "What domain is this?"

"You have passed beyond judgment into the heart of the Cube of Cubes," said the voice. *"Here, all is beauty and joy, the ancient joy of creation that was sung by the morning stars before the worlds were made. I have many names, but in the realms below I am often called Tifereth or Kallos."*

Garin thought for a moment.

"Are you truly the sister of the one whom I met on the blazing plains?" he asked. "Your domain is so… different from his."

"After a manner of speaking," answered the voice. *"The Arethoi are not biological beings as you are; each of us sprang fully formed from the thoughts of the Ever-living One long before your world began. But as those thoughts co-inhere each within the other, so we are rightly called siblings. Even the fallen one, though his corruption has proceeded far, is still our brother."*

"You speak of Daath," said Garin with a shudder.

"He has had, and will yet have, many names," replied Tifereth, *"but in this life-age he calls himself by the name of his ancient domain in the Cube of Cubes."*

"Malkuth spoke of that domain," said Garin. "He called it the primal wound and said I would have to traverse it."

"*It is so,*" said the voice solemnly.

"Is there anything you can tell me about it?" asked Garin. "All Malkuth said was that Daath betrayed He Who Is and because of that treason he was cast out and his domain shattered."

"*You ask to hear one of the oldest and saddest tales of the Arethoi,*" replied Tifereth. "*Come, sit on the banks of the Spring of the Waters of Life and I will tell it to you.*"

Garin sat down amidst the flowers and listened intently as Tifereth spoke.

"*As I said before,*" she began, "*each of the Arethoi sprang fully formed from the mind of He Who Is. We are thoughts of His thought, finite expressions of aspects of His eternal existence. On the day of our birth we were given the City Imperishable for a habitation and the Cube of Cubes as the embodiment of our inmost thoughts and desires. In that glad time my brothers and sisters rejoiced in harmony and danced together upon the Cosmic Mountain. Beauty and Joy were at the center of that dance, surrounded by all the thoughts of He Who Is given form: Grace, Life, Sovereignty, Eternity, Strength, Mercy, Judgment, Wisdom, Understanding, Foundation, and Knowledge. Then He Who Is propounded a greater deed. By pouring His uncreated light through the Cube of Cubes, He would create worlds other than ours through our agency. We gladly joined in the work, and as His light pierced the crystal of the cube each of us reflected and focused that light, calling the lower worlds into being out of the deeps of Tehom. As we saw them take form we rejoiced in the order and hierarchy of creation, seeing ourselves as the vassal rulers of these new realms. But then life emerged on the worlds of Phaneros, and all was changed.*"

"*It began when the first races were raised to sentience from the lower animals,*" continued Tifereth. "*He Who Is started to lavish love and attention on them in ways that he had only done with us in the past. He walked with them, embraced them, and drew them closer to Himself. And as we watched His affection for these new creatures, we learned that our earlier picture of our place in the cosmos was… incomplete…"*

'What do you mean?" asked Garin.

"He Who Is came to each of us in a vision," replied Tifereth, *"walking with us in our domains within the Cube of Cubes and revealing His heart. He explained that the Arethoi were never meant to be the crown of creation but rather its pillars and foundation, eternally weaving His light into the fabric on which the cosmos rested in an endless act of self-giving. He gave each of us a choice, asking if we would freely devote ourselves to the ongoing nurture of the realms beneath, knowing that one day they would surpass us in glory. Though the thought was foreign to us, most of the Arethoi were captivated by the beauty of His plan and readily agreed. Most, but not all."*

Tifereth paused a few moments, and when she continued, Garin thought he heard a note of sadness in her voice.

"None knew exactly what transpired as He Who Is walked with Daath in the privacy of his own domain, only that afterward Daath came to each of us in secret, railing against what he had learned and calling upon us to join him in open rebellion. To a one we rejected his advances and soon he ceased speaking of it, but a day came when thunder shook the cosmic mountain and we looked to see Daath ascend its summit in anger, demanding sovereignty and lordship over the lower worlds. He stood before the gates of the Golden Temple, delivering accusation after accusation against He Who Is while all the cosmos waited in silence. Then the shining gates opened and He Who Is stepped forth. His brilliant face was downcast in grief, and he shook his head in sadness as Daath raised his hand to strike his creator. As Daath swung to deliver the blow, He Who Is cried a single tear of living flame that fell upon Daath with the force of a meteor, casting him down from the mountain into the boiling deeps of Tehom and shattering his domain within the Cube of Cubes. All that remains of it now is a gash,

a wound in the fabric of creation that may never heal. The shadow that has engulfed the lower worlds springs from this wound."

"I have entered that Shadow," said Garin sadly. "I suppose I grew up within it, not knowing the darkness in which I lived, but when I made the ascent to Mythos I saw its true form. Daath has imprisoned the spirits of all the races of the Cosmos within it: each walled off from the other, each endlessly dissolving back into the nothingness from which it came. I was nearly trapped as well."

"It is the most terrible truth of Daath's rebellion," whispered Tifereth sadly. *"To deny the reason for which you were made is to deny your basic being. And once that being has been denied, what is left except the endless emptiness of the void? Still, I would not leave you in despair, for rumors have come to us that He Who Is has entered the darkened spheres alone and wrestled with Daath amist the corruption."*

As Garin pondered her words, a memory of the ruined stone building on the shattered world of Sha-Ka-Ri surfaced in his mind. Kyr had spoken there of a great tragedy that had brought hope to the cosmos. But that conversation seemed like aeons ago, and Sha-Ka-Ri was now lost to the entropy clouds.

"I fear that the corruption is reaching its peak," said Garin, his voice choked with sadness.

"It is so," said Tifereth. *"Yet while Phaneros remains, the hope that moved you to seek the Sovereign Road is not yet dead."*

As Tifereth spoke, a crystalline slab rose silently from the waters of the spring. Its surface was a pure black deeper than night itself.

"Beyond this slab-gate lies the primal wound, the ancient domain of Daath. For all those touched by the shadow it is the only road forward. Even now I can feel great movements in the Cube of Cubes. Darkness gathers, a darkness that you have faced before and must face again."

304

As he stared at the flawless obsidian surface a chill shivered through his flesh. Still, he knew he had no choice but to go forward.

"Thank you, Tifereth, for the love and refreshment you have given me," said Garin as he rose to his feet. "Whatever may happen next, I am grateful."

"*Take heart child,*" said Tifereth. "*He Who Is has not abandoned you.*"

His heart lifted by the words, Garin stepped through the gate.

Chapter 28: Guardian of the Ancient Mysteries

Trielle followed Anacrysis down a broad street lined with low glass buildings. The mirrored panes gleamed in the murky red light of the brown dwarf as if the city were perpetually bathed in the last beams of a fading sunset. All around her was a sea of faces. Some were from races she knew, many, like Xellasmos, were from races she had never before seen, but all possessed a look of peace that contrasted sharply with the hurried, often frantic look of the crowds of Scintillus.

"There are fewer of us now than there used to be," said Anacrysis with a touch of sadness. "But despite this the joy of the Sur Ekklesia remains undiminished."

Trielle could not help but agree. Despite the sparse, twilit surroundings, she could not escape the sense that this place was somehow more alive than anywhere she had ever been.

The buildings grew in height as they neared the heart of the city, until at last the road ended at the doors of a vast structure that reached skyward with graceful towers of glass and stone. As Trielle considered the shape of the building a strange sense of familiarity grew in her mind.

"It reminds me of the place where you found me on Galed's moon," she said to Anacrysis at last.

Anacrysis laughed.

"Indeed, that building is an image of this one and others like it. You stand before the last Cathedra of the Dar. Once every world possessed one, yet now even their memory has vanished. Only this one remains."

Anacrysis stepped toward the door and gestured.

"Come Trielle, there are things inside that you need to see."

Trielle stepped through the doors of the Cathedra. She stood on a floor of polished marble, flanked by twin rows of slender glass pillars that formed a pathway into the vaulted space beyond. The pillars rose to a high dome that soared above her head like the sky. Both the walls and the dome above were covered with shards of colored glass arranged in a myriad of scenes. Although many of these were meaningless to her, she recognized a few from her father's description of the Philosoph wars. But even these were portrayed from a clearly different perspective: the forces of the Dar depicted in a sympathetic light and those of the Conclave shown as malicious. Then she caught a glimpse of the far wall of the Cathedra, and the rest was forgotten.

Stretching across the glassy surface was the image of a man shining like the sun and crowned with rainbows. Below, above, and all around him a myriad of strange creatures lifting their hands up in gestures of joy and honor. His arm was outstretched toward a group of figures dressed in rags, the palm of his hand raised as if in warning. Yet the figures appeared not to notice, but instead marched blindly over the edge of a dark precipice filled with smoke and fire. As Trielle gazed at the precipice a cold wave of terror shot through her flesh, and she looked away with a shudder.

Immediately below the image stood a raised dais and stone altar similar to the one used by Tseramed on Galed's moon. The altar was flanked by two great candelabras that burned with hundreds of bright flames, their radiance mingling with the dim light of the brown dwarf to fill the Cathedra with a warm glow. A vast multitude from all races and worlds gathered at the foot of the dais, their faces glowing in the candlelight like embers ready to burst into

307

flame. Then a bell sounded, and Trielle turned to see a figure robed in red and white step from a door in the far wall of the Cathedra. His head was crowned with a golden miter and a flowing white beard trailed regally from his chin.

"That is Yochenath, High Overshepherd of this Cathedra," whispered Anacrysis. "He is the one you need to speak to."

Trielle began to walk forward, but Anacrysis laid a restraining hand on her shoulder.

"Not yet," he whispered. "For now you must observe, and perhaps understand."

Trielle watched as Yochenath swiftly ascended the dais, raised his hands, and began to sing. A few moments later the congregation joined in and the space was filled with a soaring melody infused with beauty that Trielle had never before known. Like the prayer spoken by Tseramed when he had summoned Anacrysis, the language of the song was similar enough to her own that she could make out many of the words, although their meaning was often barely comprehensible to her.

"World without end…"

"Light from Light…"

"Begotten, not made…"

The phrases were strange and evocative, unlike anything she had heard before in the Conclave. Their very structure seemed archaic, as if lifted from ancient modes of thought beyond her understanding.

"The song invokes the presence of He Who Is," whispered Anacrysis in response to her bewildered expression. "They rehearse the stories of His great deeds in Phaneros."

"Like what Xellasmos showed us?" asked Trielle.

"Those, and others," said Anacrysis cryptically.

The song was followed by a responsive chant, and as the words flowed back and forth Trielle realized that she was viewing the reenactment of a conversation that had taken place aeons ago, an exchange of such importance to the Sur Ekklesia that its memory had been preserved in this shared ritual. Then a flicker of movement caught her eye and she turned to see a white-robed figure enter the Cathedra bearing a golden plate and chalice in his hands. The congregation ceased chanting and stood in silence as the figure ascended the dais and placed the vessels on the altar. Yochenath approached the golden vessels, raised his hands skyward, and cried out in a loud voice that seemed as if it might shatter the glass walls of the Cathedra with its power. Although he still spoke in the archaic language of the song one phrase stood out with crystal clarity, though she could not begin to fathom its meaning.

"Anacrysis," she whispered with a frown, "did he say 'sacrificed for us'?"

"Indeed he did," said Anacrysis with a smile.

"Who is he talking about?" asked Trielle. "Who was sacrificed?"

Anacrysis paused for a moment.

"He Who Is," he said finally. "He Who Is was sacrificed for us."

"But I thought you and Xellasmos said that He Who Is was the source of the cosmos?" asked Trielle, her mind reeling.

"So we did."

"Then how could He sacrifice Himself?" she whispered. "I don't understand!"

"None of us do," answered Anacrysis simply, "and yet it is the foundation of all things. Even now, even here, He gives himself for us." Anacrysis thought for moment, and then added, "Perhaps this truth is better seen than heard.

309

Prepare yourself, for I am going to show you a mystery."
All at once his wings folded about Trielle and she felt a
sudden lurch as they lifted free from the cosmos.

Hovering just above the frosted crystalline surface
of Phaneros' world-shell, Anacrysis and Trielle could still see
the ceremony within the Cathedra as it unfolded. Yochenath
was now holding up a white disk of what looked like bread
in one hand and the golden goblet in the other. Although she
could not hear his words, she could see the joy in his eyes as
he lifted these elements to the heavens. Then she felt
Anacrysis' warm hand on her shoulder.

"Behold, Trielle, He comes."

Trielle looked upward and saw the cosmic
mountain, the stars that formed its substance sparkling like
ice in the morning light. She saw the worlds nestled in its
slopes, each a crystal sphere that pulsed with life and
radiance. She also saw the shadow, a great serpentine mass
of darkness and fog that writhed and twisted up the sides of
the mountain in its attempt to strangle creation. But above
all, she saw Him.

Far above, at the mountain's burning peak, stood a
figure that shone like the noonday sun. He was surrounded
by rainbows as green as emerald, and in his hand he held a
bright star. Then the figure raised his arm and a beam of
brilliance stabbed downward from the star like a bar of solid
light, transfixing the worlds below with its power. It surged
through the crystal spheres one by one, each grabbing hold
of and magnifying it as a lens magnifies the rays of the sun,
until at last it reached Phaneros.

Even within the protective shell of Anacrysis' wings
Trielle could feel its heat, and she reflexively raised her
hands. But they did nothing to impede the brilliance, and
with wide eyes she watched as the burning light shone
through her flesh as if it were a mist.

"It's as if this light is more real than I am," she murmured.

"Indeed it is," said Anacrysis. "It is the life of He Who Is, the Eternal One."

The beam poured through the word-shell beneath them in a mighty cataract, falling on the bread and cup held in Yochenath's hands and inflaming them with its power. A few moments later the torrent ceased. Trielle watched as Yochenath set the cup down and broke the bread, the light still burning within them. One by one the congregation came forward, and as they ate the bread and drank from the cup the fiery light entered into their bodies and flashed through their arteries and veins, filling each of their cells with new strength.

Trielle turned to Anacrysis, an expression of awe and fear on her face.

"Come," said Anacrysis gently, "You have seen enough."

There was a sense of downward movement and a brief shudder as they breached the world-shell. Then the golden sphere of his wings unfolded and they were back in the Cathedra.

Though there was more to the service Trielle could not pay attention. Over and over again she wrestled with the implications of what she had just witnessed, at last surrendering in the face of realities much greater than herself. When her focus at last returned to the world around her she was surprised to learn that the ceremony had ended and the last attendees were in the process of filing our. A few moments later the Cathedra was empty save for Yochenath, who was carefully cleaning the altar vessels.

"Yochenath," called Anacrysis.

The robed figure stopped and lifted his head.

311

"I have someone here that you must meet." Anacrysis paused for a moment before adding, "The time of the Canticle appears to be at hand."

Setting the vessels down on the altar, Yochenath stepped down from the dais and walked swiftly toward them, proffering his hand in a gesture of greeting.

"Good day miss…" His voice trailed off.

"Trielle. My name is Trielle," she replied.

"Thank you," he said, then gestured toward Anacrysis. "I see that you travel in exalted company."

"You flatter me," Anacrysis said with a laugh, "but come, greater matters await."

"Yes, yes," said Yochenath dismissively. "You mentioned the Canticle, yet I seem to recall that we have trod this path before. You *Anastasi* always seem to think so… cosmically…"

"You say this after conducting the supper?" said Anacrysis with an air of feigned incredulity. "Surely there is nothing so cosmic as that? Tell me Trielle," he said, suddenly turning to face her, "what were your thoughts on what you witnessed?"

Trielle's eyes widened at her sudden forced entrance into the conversation. Unsure of what to say, she opened her mouth to speak in the hope that the right phrase would come out, but before she could utter a word Yochenath laughed and placed a hand on her shoulder.

"Our apologies," he said gently. "I have known Anacrysis my whole life. I find it difficult to have close friends in my current position, and his encouragement has always been a source of strength to me. Still," he added, "there have been many times over the past millennia that the Canticle has been invoked to explain this or that occurrence in the Conclave, yet this has never proven to be the case. I am curious as to what makes this time different."

As he spoke Trielle could hear the skepticism in his tone. Yet beneath this, an occasional flash of eagerness surreptitiously crept through.

Anacrysis turned to Trielle, all traces of levity gone from his face.

"Trielle, tell him about Garin and your father."

Trielle took a deep breath and began. At Anacrysis' encouragement she spoke slowly so as not to leave out any details, and as her tale unfolded the faint online of a smile began to grow on Yochenath's face. Twice Yochenath stopped her for clarification, his evident satisfaction growing with each answered question. When at last she finished, Yochenath raised his hands skyward and cried out in jubilation.

"Glory! The time is near! The end of the siege of the Sur Ekklesia is at hand!"

Abruptly his head snapped back downward, his piercing eyes focused intently on Trielle's face.

"Child," he said, "you have told me your story, now I will tell you one in return. It begins a little more than a thousand years ago by your reckoning. At that time a great empire spanned the galaxy that then was, ruled by He Who Is, Son of He Who Is."

"I know of the empire that was," said Trielle softly.

"Then you also know of the Conclave's rise and the war they began with the people of the Dar," said Yochenath.

Trielle nodded.

"The events I will relate to you occurred three months before the final battle," continued Yochenath, "at what would turn out to be the last gathering of the Seven Shepherds of the Dar."

Trielle's brow furrowed in confusion.

"I apologize," he said in response. "I have lived so long in this vale it is easy to forget that the children of the

313

Conclave know nothing of these things. The Seven Shepherds were the highest leaders of the empire, although empire is really the wrong word for what the Dar represented. Kingdom is a much better choice. Regardless, each shepherd oversaw the administration of one of the galaxy's spiral arms, ruling from their seats in the seven great Cathedra. This building," he added with a sigh, "is the only Cathedra left."

Yochenath's sadness at this prospect was palpable, and Trielle bowed her head in a gesture of respect. After a long pause, Yochenath continued.

"Even then it was clear that the weapons of the Conclave were having deleterious effects on space-time. Already the outer fringes of the galaxy were unravelling and the Conclave had begun herding its worlds toward the galactic core, leaving the worlds of the Dar to be swept up in the cataclysm. The seven shepherds gathered on Urien, the fourth world of the star Xecrux in the Sagittarius arm of the galaxy. The system was far from the primary battlefronts and the shepherds hoped they could meet there undisturbed. For seven days they prepared for their deliberations: seven days of fasting, prayer, and worship. They spoke to none, not even each other, as they sank deeply into the realm of the spirit, awaiting the word of He Who Is. But on the eve of the last day, the forces of the Conclave attacked."

"They seemed to come out of nowhere. One moment the skies were clear and in the next they were filled with shrieking trails of fire as a battalion of stellar dreadnoughts rained white-hot plasma on the planet. Four of the shepherds were killed outright in the attack, but the rest managed to flee deep underground into the network of tunnels and catacombs that riddled the Urien's crust."

"It is not the first time that the Ekklesia has been forced to gather in the catacombs," mused Anacrysis.

314

"Indeed," said Yochenath, "and like many of those ancient men and women it is only through what they have written and passed down to us that we know of their deeds. In this case, only one shepherd survived in the end. Wounded in the final assault and taken prisoner onboard the dreadnaught Achamoth, he knew that he was soon to die and recorded a testament of their final moments. Miraculously, the ship's surgeon was sympathetic to the Dar and carried his manuscript to safety. It is known by the Sur Ekklesia as the Book of Utohu, and is the last of the scriptures written during the Philosoph War. Many years ago it was given to my predecessor for safekeeping, and he, in turn, gave it to me. Come, I will show you."

Yochenath led them from the dais to a small door set in the rear wall of the Cathedra. Reaching into his robes, he removed a silver key, unlocked the door, and motioned for Trielle and Anacrysis to follow. Beyond the door was a narrow passageway with walls of polished marble and high, narrow windows. The floor seemed level at first, but as they proceeded it began to slope sharply downward. Soon the windows vanished and the smooth marble gave way to rough-hewn bedrock. As they walked onward, Trielle idly ran her hand across the cold pitted stone and wondered just how deep their destination lay beneath the planet's surface. At last the passage ended at a round antechamber lit by a single luminous globe suspended from the ceiling by a chain. Twelve stone doors lined the chamber's walls, each engraved with a different symbol.

"Beyond these doors are the Archives of the Sur Ekklesia," explained Yochenath. "All of our most sacred artifacts have been stored here against the day of our release."

Yochenath led them to a door with the image of a book etched into its surface. It opened at the touch of his

315

hand. Beyond it lay a small room containing nine lecterns, each bearing an ancient-looking book. Some were massive tomes, ornately bound with clasps of gleaming metal. Others were thin folios only partially protected by their time-worn leather covers. But of all the books one stood out. Little more than a sheaf of brittle yellow papers, it looked as if it might fall apart at the slightest disturbance. Although the lectern bore no label Trielle somehow knew that this was the Book of Utohu.

Yochenath reverently approached the lectern, unbound the papers, and began to search through them. He moved carefully, scanning each page and then gently setting it to the side. A few moments later he found what he was looking for. He glanced up at Trielle, as if giving a silent command to listen, then placed his finger on a line of script near the top of the page and began to read.

> For eight long nights we were sealed in the abyssal chapel of Dar-Em-Rhiolta with no food and little water. Still, the chapel was close enough to Urien's core that the planet's inner fires kept us warm. It was a small blessing, but one for which we were profoundly grateful. Each day the sound of explosions grew louder, and each day our fear grew that we would soon be discovered. But we had not forgotten the purpose of our gathering and desired that our time together, if it were to be our last, would not have been spent in vain. It was with this prayer in our hearts that we entered worship, and the answer we received exceeded our greatest expectations.

> It came as we laid prostrate in meditation. One moment all was darkness and silence and in the next

316

the chapel was filled with brightness. What happened then was little short of a miracle. One by one we rose to our feet as words came to our lips, words not of our own making that burned and smouldered in our souls long thereafter. These words I give to you now.

And it came to pass
As he stood at the end of all things,
That he saw all that is
In a grain of sand:
The world, and the seed of its desecration.

How with a million others its tale was set for nought;
Its grammar shorn of meaning.
Though the fractured virtue of the high places
Still strove beneath it yet;
The harrowing of the Pit.

A grain of sand
Glistening in the sun of the last day.
A rose wet with the final morning's dew.
A road splashed with drops of blood,
Ascending the mount of stars.

From the brink of holocaust he trod the path,
The skies a pavement to his feet,
To plead with the riven heart of the usurped king
That the fires of night be quenched,
And the morning come one more day.

And with those words came a revelation, a vision of an age of exile wherein the Dar Ekklesia would suffer in bondage to the powers of the Conclave.

Yet at the end of this time a child would arise from the darkened spheres, one who would ascend to the heights of creation and there be given power to speak and call the peoples of the Conclave back to their true place in the light.

"We call it the Canticle of the Last Morning," said Yochenath as he looked up from the text, "and ever since the fall of the Dar Ekklesia, and the beginning of our imprisonment, it has been looked to as a source of hope."

"But what does it mean?" asked Trielle in confusion.

"Literature of this nature often admits for multiple meanings," admitted Yochenath, "and this passage is particularly difficult. Still, our philosophers have agreed on some basic themes. Look here."

Yochenath pointed to a series of places on the page and Trielle's eyes narrowed as she tried to read the words. The script was ornate and the letters cramped and tiny, but surprisingly she was able to make out most of them."

"Sand, tale, virtue?" Trielle looked up at Yochenath in confusion. "But those are just metaphors, aren't they?"

"Perhaps to you," said Yochenath, "but to a philosopher who has devoted his life to the study of ultimate things, these words carry great significance. You see, for aeons men have debated about how reality is ultimately structured. Many theories have been proposed and many discarded, but one venerable approach sees a fourfold order to the causation of events in our world. Consider the lectern on which this book sits. Of what material is it made?"

"Wood," answered Trielle.

"Correct," said Yochenath. "Now, how did it come into being? How was it made?"

"I don't know," said Trielle. "I suppose it was carved by someone. But I don't see how that relates to…"

318

"Patience, Trielle" said Yochenath. "Again you are correct. In this case it was shaped by my predecessor Elinoh. Now, so far this has been relatively straightforward, but it is time to explore some deeper considerations. Tell me, Trielle, how do you know that this is a lectern?"

"I know it is a lectern because it looks like one," she replied, her confusion beginning to give way to frustration at the oblique line of questioning.

"Indeed," said Yochenath, "and many debates have been held as to how that act of knowing takes place. For the sake of brevity, however, please accept at least provisionally that this act of knowing can only occur because in fact there is a form, a pattern, in your mind to which the table corresponds. Now, bear with me for one last question. What is this lectern for?"

"Right now, it is for supporting the Book of Utohu," said Trielle, her frustration level rising.

"Yes," affirmed Yochenath, "its final reason for existence is to bear the book. Do you see now how these four causes - the material of which the object is made, the place it fits into the ongoing flow of world events, the pattern to which it conforms, and the purpose for its existence - cohere in the lectern in front of you?"

"I suppose so," said Trielle skeptically. "But I still don't see how this pertains to the Canticle!"

"One last question," said Yochenath, "and I promise that all will be clear. Consider this, Trielle. If these causes pertain to the lectern, how do they pertain to the cosmos as a whole, and, perhaps more importantly, from where do those causes originate?"

As Trielle pondered the question an image of the cosmic mountain flashed into her mind, the bright gems of the worlds perched on its craggy slopes.

Four worlds...

Then she understood, and her frustration was washed away by a flood of excitement.

"The worlds!" she said. "The worlds are the causes!"

"Ever since the first *Anastasi* stretched their wings and soared above the confines of the cosmos, we have known by sight what was long only suspected by faith and logic" responded Anacrysis.

"Our world, the lowest in creation, is the place where the rays of light shed by the higher worlds cohere and interact," said Yochenath. "And though their inhabitants are mighty and exalted far beyond the races of our cosmos, it has also been truly said that the higher worlds were created by He Who Is to be the foundation and substructure of our own. Thus the first shall be last, and the last first."

"But why was I never taught this understanding of cause and effect?" asked Trielle. "I can see why the Conclave would conceal knowledge of the Dar and of the war, but my father gave me no hint that they know of the other worlds, so why would they censor what from their perspective only amounts to a point of philosophy?"

"I think you know," said Yochenath darkly.

Trielle thought for a few moments. "It's the Axioms, isn't it?" she said finally. "The Axioms only allow for material causation, and so even the suggestion that there might be more to existence than matter had to be suppressed."

Yochenath nodded. "It is for that reason," he said, "that the vision accompanying the Canticle speaks of one from the darkened spheres ascending the heights of the cosmic mountain, for only one who has seen the worlds as they are could hope to break through the lies that have imprisoned the minds of your people."

"You see, Trielle, our aging cosmos will not exist forever. The Sur Ekklesia have known this for millennia and rejoice in that knowledge, for although we love this world we hope for a better one. Though the Book of Utohu may seem ancient to you, in truth it is the one of the most recent writings of the Sur Ekklesia. There are other, far older prophecies that speak of a time when the elements will melt with fervent heat and the universe be consumed in a conflagration from which none will escape. But those same prophecies also say that a new cosmos will be born from the ashes of the old, a cosmos in which darkness has been erased and the light of He Who Is shines through all things. It is for this renewal that we wait."

"It sounds almost too good to be believed," said Trielle.

"Several millennia ago I had the same thoughts about resurrection," replied Anacrysis.

Trielle nodded, deep in thought. After a long silence she spoke. "You think this child from the darkened spheres is my brother, don't you?"

Yochenath and Anacrysis nodded.

"Before the final cataclysm the cosmos will be given one last prophet, one final messenger of mercy from its Father" said Yochenath. "He Who Is does not wish that anyone be destroyed."

"That is why we need you and your father, Trielle," said Anacrysis. "If the Entrope succeeds in using the vacuum sculptors and Vai detonates then your brother will have no cosmos to return to, and those that might be rescued from the final cataclysm will be lost."

"Vacuum sculptors?" said Yochenath, "I fear that I am missing something."

"Tell him, Trielle," said Anacrysis.

Trielle quickly outlined the Heirophants' plans for the second ignition attempt and her father's concerns

321

regarding the vacuum sculptors. When she finished, Yochenath bowed his head in deep sorrow.

"Even how they oppose us," he murmured. "Not only do they desire their own destruction, but they would prevent others from escaping. What hatred!"

"Who are you talking about?" asked Trielle in confusion.

"The Entrope, child," sighed Yochenath. "The Entrope and the one that controls him…"

"There are forces in the cosmos that desire nothing more than the dissolution of all things," added Anacrysis. "You saw one of them in Xellasmos' photonoscope as he tempted the mother of your race to eat from the Tree of Wisdom. Many times I have watched from outside the world-shell as their master communed with the Entrope in secret, shaping his thoughts into an almost perfect contempt for existence. The Entrope has been deceived so greatly that he does not know he is as much a pawn as those he commands."

A sudden crack of thunder sounded in the antechamber behind them, followed by a rush of warm wind. Startled, Trielle turned to see the unfolded wings of a second *Anastasi*.

"Auriel," said Anacrysis with a look of concern.

Auriel bowed briefly toward Anacrysis and Yochenath. "My brother, High Overshepherd," he said in grave tones, "I regret the need to disturb the sanctity of this place, but time is now growing short. This morning, on my patrol of the inner Conclave, I witnessed an armada of etherreavers massing around the corpse of Vai. I fear that a second reignition attempt may be at hand."

Anacrysis placed a hand on his shoulder. "We thank you for this intelligence Auriel," he said softly. "Take five battalions of *Anastasi* to the space surrounding the three

322

suns, but do not breach the world-shell. The time may soon come when we must break the siege but I will not put the inhabitants of the valley at risk unless pressed."

Auriel bowed, then wrapped his wings about his glowing body and vanished with a rush of imploding air.

Anacrysis turned to Trielle. "Do you now see the importance of your brother's journey, and of your own?"

Trielle thought for a moment. "I don't know what I can do to delay the second ignition attempt," she said finally, "but if I see a way I will give my all to prevent it. I have to," she added, "now that I understand the cost."

Anacrysis smiled grimly. "Know that I will be following you wherever you go and will offer what protection I can. As I told my brother, we cannot breach the world-shell in the inner Conclave unless the need is great, but we will if we must, for if Vai becomes a supernova the valley is also lost. Come now, I will return you to Galed's moon."

Trielle nodded and then stepped toward Anacrysis as his wings unfolded.

"We thank you for your time Yochenath," said Anacrysis, "and I apologize that we must leave in such an abrupt manner."

Then his golden wings wrapped around her and once again they soared above the crystalline skin of the universe.

Chapter 29: The Shattered Sphere

Garin flashed through the diamond pathways of the Cube of Cubes. All around him was crystalline beauty, a cosmos of endless geometric perfection.

Then the pain began.

Cracks shivered across the surrounding matrix, dark discontinuities where light arced and crackled across fractured connections. Each spark wracked his body like an electric shock. His perspective began to twist, as if the geodesics of space itself were tangling in impossible knots. No membrane lay ahead, only bright shards that hung amidst a blurry void like a shattered pane of glass floating in the depths of space. As he hurtled onward the cracks around him grew larger and larger, and his body became an endless wasteland of electric agony. In vain Garin tried to cry out, but there was no voice in this place. Then there was a flash and a feeling like a million needles passing through his flesh. A moment later he opened his eyes on the primal wound.

He stood atop a cliff of glass beneath a storm-wracked sky filled with billowing shadows and crackling streaks of electric blue light. Great curving fragments of crystal tumbled overhead, each flashing with echoes of how this domain had once appeared: endless mountains bathed in brilliant starlight, a soaring tree wreathed in flames of rose and violet. But now all that was gone. Nothing remained but the abyss.

A vast shaft flickering with lurid fire stretched downward from the cliff's edge, a bottomless pit that pierced the heart of the cosmos, inexorably leading to the sickly boiling deeps far beneath.

Tehom…

Chaos…

Above the center of the abyss Daath floated on wings of shadow: his cloak billowing behind him, his noble countenance crowned by a black rainbow. In his eyes a cold light gleamed like foxfire in a swamp, a fetid harbinger of decay.

"Blind monkey!" he said with a horrible smile, "you have joined me at last. I thought the journey might prove too difficult for you. Tell me, what do you think of my domain?"

Curiously, Garin felt no fear.

"I see in the crystal shards above the beauty that it once possessed," said Garin, "and I am saddened that you have shattered that beauty."

"You think to lecture me on beauty!" said Daath with a flare of anger. "I who stood here before the lower worlds emerged from Tehom. I who have climbed the cosmic mountain countless times and have stood in the ancient councils of He Who Is amidst the stones of fire?"

"Until darkness was found in you," said Garin sadly. "Daath, I too have walked the worlds, and though I am from the lowest place in the cosmos, though you have power that dwarfs my own as the fire of a star dwarfs the flame of a candle, can it be that I see something you cannot?"

"And what is it that you have seen," said Daath, his words dripping with malice. "Please enlighten me."

"I have seen that none of us is our own," said Garin. "I have seen that the idea that each of us exists for ourselves is a lie. I have seen that the song of the cosmos is one of sacrifice."

"Sacrifice!" bellowed Daath as dark shadows writhed beneath his cloak. "You would have me uphold the vermin that crawl on the low worlds, freely giving them my amassed knowledge and expecting no glory or fealty in

325

return? You would have me veil my majesty, I whose might can crack a crystal sphere and cast a world out of the heavens? You would have me serve you!"

"And what would you propose in turn?" said Garin, amazed at his own calmness. "A world where each is walled up in their own nothingness? A world where the damned look only after their own pleasures, ignoring the cry of their father, their sister, their brothers? A world where we each make up our own story? No, Daath! In the spheres below I have learned at least a part of my purpose, and if it is truly my role to stand here in the heart of creation's deepest wound and deny your vision and claim over the races of Phaneros, then I will do so with all my strength."

"With all your strength indeed," said Daath with a laugh. "But whatever makes you think that will be enough… You have spoken of sacrifice, and sacrifice you shall have."

As Daath spoke a chill wind began rose, blowing his cloak behind him like the tail of a black comet. Beneath it the shadows twisted and grew, and a strange scent like burning sulfur began to permeate the air.

"Until now I have permitted you to call me by me ancient name among the Arethoi," hissed Daath. "Yet I have been known by many other names on many other worlds, names at which entire planets have trembled in abject fear. I think it is time you learned this fear, blind monkey! Some have called me Borog, the black cloud of hate. Others Choronzon, the tyrant of oblivion. On yet another world I was called Lukifell, the corrupted lantern. Yet on your ancient homeworld of Sha-Ka-Ri I was given perhaps my favorite name: Leviathan, the seven-headed chaos-serpent."

At those words Daath began to swell. His cloak seemed to grow into an encircling canopy of wings, merging with the black rainbow that crowned his head in a mass of shadow and cold flame. His noble face fell away like a mask and from the boiling darkness beneath spun seven serpentine necks covered in red and black scales, each ending in the fanged maw of a dragon. The dragon's heads were crowned with circlets of iron that burned as if just drawn from a blast furnace.

"Perhaps you will fear now, blink monkey," roared the heads in unison, and a pang of terror smote Garin's heart. Yet still he held fast.

"I will die, if I must, for the worlds below," said Garin. "I have already faced death in the desert of the flaming sword and fear it no longer."

"Death!" laughed the heads. "I will have nothing of death. Instead I will take you to Tehom, where the dregs of creation ceaselessly churn in undying agony around the void from whence all sprang!"

"Enough Daath! You will not claim this one, he is mine!"

The words startled Garin, and he turned to see the figure of an ancient man cloaked in white linen ascend the edge of the precipice.

"Kyr!" Garin shouted.

"It seems we have finally caught up with each other," said Kyr as he laid a hand on Garin's shoulder. Garin looked at that hand, marred with a single central scar, and for a brief moment recalled the vision granted by the black sword on the plains of fire. He could almost hear the sound of the mallet slamming downward, and as he thought on it a great sadness filled him.

"Be of good cheer," said Kyr. "I saw your stand for my Bride in the world below, your willingness to face death for me and those I love."

"Your Bride!" roared Leviathan. "I wonder how much you know of this bride you say you love. Do you know

327

of the countless times she has prostituted herself to me for power? Can you smell the stench of her sins rising to the top of the celestial mountain?"

"Yes," said Kyr, a tear rolling down his face.

"Then how can you still love her!" cried Leviathan. "Why do you still care for her when every deed she does binds her to death, to Tehom, to me?

"For the same reason I still care for you, my poor, lost son," said Kyr. His tears were flowing freely now. "It is in the nature of Eternal Love to Love. That is the music my Father and I have sung from before always."

Kyr paused for a moment, and then said, "you could hear the music again, my lost son, if you would only come home. Again we could walk like we did in aeons past…"

Leviathan screamed a cry of such primal rage that Garin thought his heart would stop.

"Never! I will never return to servitude!"

"Then you damn yourself," said Kyr softly.

Kyr turned to Garin. "When the conflict is done," he whispered, "you must ascend the road no matter what you witness. Regardless of how it appears, know that I will return to you on the third day. You must wait for me at the Rose."

Garin nodded uncertainly. "What are you going to do," he asked softly.

Kyr did not speak, but turned to face Daath and cast his robe aside. Clad only in a loincloth, Garin could clearly see the wounds that marked his body. Great welts furrowed his back, the remnants of a bloody beating in ages past. Each hand and foot was marred by a circular scar, and a deep gash lay just beneath the ribcage on his left side. His face grim, Kyr stretched his arms wide and began to rise into the air.

"Again?" said Leviathan with a harsh laugh. "You would give yourself for the blink monkeys again?"

"No," said Kyr, his voice rising in power. "Not again. ALWAYS!"

A blast of light and glory burst from Kyr's form like the brilliance of a newborn star. His wounds began to shine, erupting with living streams of red and blue flame. Garin fell to his knees in awe.

"THEN COME!" roared Leviathan, "and I will drag your living form into the deep for all eternity!"

In one fluid move Kyr cast himself from the edge of the precipice and dove toward Leviathan. By now his body was almost too bright to look at, a spear of silver light that trailed blood-red and cool blue flame in its wake. He struck Leviathan with the force of a meteor, shattering the dark scales of his chest, and the dragon screamed in pain. But, despite the wound, the beast's shadow grew into a great burning mass of darkness that swallowed the light, sank slowly into the abyss below, and was gone.

And Garin was left alone.

For a long time he stared downward into the sickly boiling depths of Tehom and contemplated what Kyr had done. Silent tears ran down his face. He said no words. There were none that were worthy of utterance.

"Child of Phaneros, why do you look beneath when the way is now open to you?"

The gentle voice startled Garin, and he raised his head to see a vision of a crown made of stars filling the sky on the far side of the abyss.

"I… I do not understand," said Garin, fighting back waves of sadness. "How?"

"Behold," said the voice softly, *"the blood of He Who Is Son of He Who Is beckons you…"*

Suspended in the air above the abyss were scintillating clouds of red and blue sparks, the last remnants of the fiery light shed by Kyr as he assaulted Leviathan. The clouds swirled together as Garin watched, their shapes merging and shifting until at last they settled into a pathway of stars laced with the blackness of the cosmos. The road stretched across the abyss before mounting upward through the center of the crown that still floated in the sky.

"Child of Phaneros, do not forget the words of He Who Is, Son of He Who Is. The night of the old creation is fast pasing and the dawn of the new is at hand. Ascend now to the City Imperishable and await the coming morn!"

Though he was still confused, the words kindled a small spark of hope deep in Garin's chest. Rising to his feet, he took a deep breath and set forth on the Sovereign Road. As he crossed the Abyss Garin took one last look down at the great crack that Daath's rebellion had opened in the structure of the cosmos, then turned his eyes skyward. A few moments later he passed through the shimmering golden crown, the world of Arethos fell away beneath him, and he walked again on the mountain of stars and darkness.

Here the road narrowed, crossing the sheer face of the mountain in a series of sharp switchbacks. Garin pondered this sudden steepness as he climbed, and when at last he realized what it meant a wide smile broke across his face; he was nearing the summit.

Atop the last switchback, the road turned abruptly toward a luminous crystal sphere that shone like a full moon: the final world. Garin did not hesitate when he reached it, but threw himself at the crystalline surface with abandon. For a brief moment all was soft light, and then Garin found himself on the ivory streets of a city of surpassing beauty. As he took in the glory of the place with awestruck wonder, a voice like a harp sounded behind him.

"Dear child, we are so glad you are here. We have been waiting for you."

Chapter 30: The Last Gambit

"Gedron, what you're talking about is unthinkable! It's open rebellion!"

Gedron sat across from Dyana at their kitchen table and watched the color drain from her face. He knew that he would have felt the same if their positions were reversed, but he had still harbored a secret hope that she would come to see his point of view more quickly. Evidently it was not to be.

"Dyana," he said with a mixture of exhaustion and impatience. "I would not involve you in this if it weren't absolutely necessary. Believe me, I know what I am risking here."

"Do you?" she said with a sudden flash of anger. "It's the first time you have talked to me all week. When you sat down, I thought perhaps you wanted to reconnect, especially in the face of all that has been happening. I knew -I thought I knew- how horrible you must have felt when the reignition failed. But now you tell me that the failure was deliberate and that you want my help to sabotage the next one? No, I don't think you do know what you are risking!"

Gedron took a deep breath, gathered his thoughts, and considered how to move forward. When he said that he had not wished to involve her, he had been telling the truth.

After leaving the Arx Memoria, Gedron had wracked his brain trying to come up with a way to alter the frequency of the vacuum sculptors' core filaments. On an engineering level this was relatively easy. The correction needed was relatively small, on the order of a few attohertz, and could easily be performed using the sculptors' primary calibration equipment. Yet barring a wholesale invasion of the Ouranos Radii's laboratories, this approach was effectively impossible. Then a new thought had occurred to him. Just as the strings of a musical instrument could be made to resonate to sound waves from an outside source, in principle the frequency of the filaments could be altered by a precisely tuned gravity wave. The more Gedron considered this possibility the more convinced he had become that it held the key to his dilemma. But he also knew that he could not enact it on his own. He would need Dyana's help.

"I swore an oath, Gedron," she said tersely, snapping him out of his reverie. "You did too."

"I know," said Gedron softly. "But think, Dyana, to whom did we swear that oath, those in control of our society or the people that make up that society? I know that we are living in the last days of a dying universe, but that doesn't mean that I, the Chromatocron, the Entrope, or anyone else should have the right to arbitrarily decide when end should occur."

Dyana's lips pursed together as she considered his words. Gedron could see the struggle in her eyes. Like him, Dyana had entered into her current position of authority within the Conclave for the best of reasons. He only had to bring those reasons to the surface.

"Dyana, I can prove to you that the intial attempt at reignition, had I allowed it to continue, would have wiped out half the Conclave," said Gedron. "And I can also prove to you that if the Heirophants use the vacuum sculptors the chances of supernova are unacceptably high. You are a gravitic scientist. At least let me show you the data."

After what seemed like an eternity, Dyana's shoulders sagged in seeming acquiescence.

"All right," she said. "I can at least do that much. Show me."

Gedron reached into his robes and brought out his personal infochryst. He sat it on the table and had begun to wave his hand in the gesture of activation when Dyana stopped him.

"No, Gedron, if you want me to look at this, I need to do it myself."

Gedron nodded, then pushed the infochryst across the table to her. Dyana gestured above it and a few moments later the device sprang to life, filling the air with simulations of stellar fusion, three dimensional charts of vacuum energy values, and graphics of projected entropy cloud activity. He watched as she studied the images, scrutinizing each with a critical eye. More than once he raised his hand to point out a salient feature only to be silenced. He understood; she needed to come to her own conclusions. After more than an hour she deactivated the infochryst and faced Gedron, her lips creased in a deep frown.

"All right," she said grimly. "I believe you about the first reignition attempt. Given this data how could I not. But what about the second attempt? I didn't see any information on that."

"There's a reason," said Gedron gently. "The rest of the data on this device was not supposed to leave the Omagehedron. If you look at it, you will be implicated in whatever comes next. Dyana, I've already counted the cost as far as my own life and career are concerned. Despite what you said earlier, I do know what this means." He paused for a second, then added: "If I show you the rest you will need to do the same."

Dyana's eyes narrowed.

"Gedron, first you tell me that you need my help in planning some sort of insurrection against the other Heirophants, and now that I am starting to think you may have a real point you give me a way out? Honestly, you are not making sense tonight."

Gedron sighed. "I'm sorry about how this is coming across. I truly want… no… I need… you to be with me on this. But I also don't want you to get hurt if we fail."

Dyana smiled briefly. "You can't have it both ways, Gedron. Go ahead, show me the rest."

Gedron nodded and reactivated the infochryst, this time bringing up a schematic diagram of a vaccum sculptor.

"The Ouranos Radii and Chromatocron have developed devices capable of locally modulating the strong force coupling constant. They call them vacuum sculptors, and they use a neutronium wire charged with mesons to modulate the virtual fermionic output of small laridian rings located at the device's ends. The virtual fermions shift the makeup of the underlying vacuum, which affects the coupling constant. The Heirophants are dispersing millions of these within Vai's photosphere and plan to use them to alter the binding energy of helium so that fusion will occur at lower temperatures and pressures."

"That would bypassing the need for a gravitic bombardment," said Dyana.

"Exactly," said Gedron. "But look at this."

Gedron gestured again and a summary of the most recent simulations runs appeared into the air above the infochryst. Dyana's eyes widened as she reviewed the data. At last she sat back, a look of shock and disbelief on her face.

"But why?" she said. "Why are they taking this path?"

Gedron took a deep breath as he carefully considered his next words. He knew that what he said next would be tantamount to blasphemy against the Conclave's deepest principles, but as he sat in thought an image of the

Entrope rose unbidden in his mind and he was surprised to realize that he no longer cared.

"Dyana," he said at last, "have you ever truly considered where the Axioms lead? I once thought that they offered the only way a society as diverse as ours could function. With each individual wrapped up in their own little world, their own little kingdom, conflict could be minimized and some version of harmony maintained. And if that were the extent of it, then perhaps all would still be well. But think about what the Axiom's say, Dyana! If there is no more to our consciousness than matter in motion then at the deepest level we simply do not exist! If our philosophy is true the each individual in the Conclave is nothing more than a little piece of nothingness desperately holding onto the mistaken belief that they are something real. Oh, we hide it well. We speak of everyone choosing their own path as if that solves the problem. But don't you see! If each path is right, and all paths go in different directions, then they all cancel out. If everyone creates their own meaning then in the end there is no meaning; existence simply doesn't signify anything."

Gedron paused for a moment, watching his wife's face as the implications of his words sunk in. "The last time the Heirophants gathered in Conclave," he added in a low voice, "I realized that the Entrope knew this, wanted this, to be true. I saw then that his goal is, and perhaps has always been, to see the Axioms through to their ultimate conclusion. He wants to unmask the lie that we actually exist by bringing this cosmos, or at least our part in it, to an end as swiftly as possible."

Dyana seemed visibly shaken, and for a moment Gedron felt guilty that he had precipitated this crisis.

No, he told himself, *there was no way to avoid this. Sooner or later she had to hear the truth. Sooner or later everyone will.* Still, he could not help but feel a pang of guilt.

"You sound like Garin used to before he left," whispered Dyana at last. Then her eyebrows furrowed and she looked at Gedron intently.

"Gedron, do you know where Garin is? Does it have anything to do with this?"

"I don't know," admitted Gedron sadly. "Trielle told me yesterday that Gedron was following a dream he had about something he said existed outside our world. She told me he went to our ancient homeworld trying to find a way outside of our universe. It sounded like madness to me, and frankly still does. But the axioms lead to madness as well, and at this point I think I'd rather Garin's madness be real than our society's"

"Not madness," said another voice, "truth."

Gedron turned to see Trielle standing in the doorway of the kitchen, a look of mingled exhaustion and exhilaration on her face.

"Trielle?" said Dyana, "where have you been?"

"To En-Ka-Re," she replied matter of factly. "Father, everything Garin spoke about is true. I saw the hidden valley where the Entrope has imprisoned the remnants of the Dar, though they call themselves the Sur Ekklesia now. I have met the *Alapsari* and the *Anastasi*. They are still among us, and, Father, they are not what you think they are."

Dyana looked at Trielle, her face suddenly tense with worry.

"Trielle, where is Garin?"

"It's hard to explain, mother," Trielle confessed. "And the parts I can explain you probably won't believe."

"Please try," pleaded Dyana.

336

"Garin is… outside…" Trielle said carefully. "I don't know any other way to say it."

"Before he left he said he was looking for a road outside of our dying universe, proof that the Axioms were false and that there is more to this life than matter in motion. I didn't believe him, but then he showed me the map from his dreams, and then we met Kyr."

Trielle sat down at the table and described their first meeting with Kyr and the fateful conversation that had taken Garin to Sha-Ka-Ri.

"Even then," she confessed, "I only half believed him. But when I traveled to En-Ka-Re, the *Anastasi* showed me the cosmos from the outside."

Gedron's mind spun with the implication of Trielle words. "What do you mean… outside?" he asked finally.

"I mean that they showed me what is beyond the space and time of our little dying pocket of a universe," she answered. "There's a mountain made of stars and darkness, and a chain of worlds stretching up to… to… I don't know what to call it. I only know that at the top of all worlds is something, or someone, that wears the form of a man and cares about us deeply. That's where Garin is, Father. He's climbing the mountain. And there's more. Their last High Overshepherd showed me a book written during the war that promises a last prophet would come before the end, one who would travel beyond the world and return with a last message to the Conclave."

"And they think that Garin may be this prophet they've been waiting for?" said Dyana, her voice hollow with disbelief.

"It isn't just a possibility to them," said Trielle. "The Sur Ekklesia are convinced that the book refers to Garin and are willing to break the siege of En-Ka-Re to make sure that he has a world to return to. And," here she paused as if weighing her next word carefully, "I'm convinced too. I know Garin is still alive out there and I know he is coming back, but we need to give him more time to complete his journey."

Gedron sat in silence as wheels turned within his mind. Trielle's words had awakened the deepest longings in his soul, and though he could not yet bring himself to accept her story he also could not escape the sense that, whether or not the tale was true, it might just be beautiful enough to die for. At last he broke the silence.

"Trielle, I want to believe you," he said at last. "I don't think I can go further than that right now, but if there is even a chance we can help Garin then we need to take it, especially when the alternative has a fifty percent chance of destroying us all."

Dyana nodded, her face a mix of conflicting emotions. "Gedron," she said hoarsely, "you said you needed my help to stop the vacuum sculptors. What do you need me to do?"

Gedron reached for the infochryst and called up the hologram of a vacuum sculptor with a gesture. Reaching into the image, he plucked out the neutronium wire at its heart and enlarged it.

"This filament is the key. As I said before, it is charged with mesons cause the device to produce an unbalanced field of virtual Kaons. It is these particles that alter the local strong force binding coefficient."

With another gesture Gedron opened up a window containing a complex waveform surrounded by a shifting landscape of equations.

"This is the de Broglie wave signature of the mesonic flux used to charge the filament," he explained. "In its current configuration the majority of Kaons are long-type, with a relatively slow decay rate. But Kaons violate CP symmetry, and with a small alteration in the waveform, the chiral balance of the virtual particles changes and the majority of Kaons become short-type. The change in decay rate weakens their effect on binding energy enough to effectively disable the sculptors."

Gedron called up a second window containing another waveform. He then brought his hands together and the two windows merged, neatly superimposing the waves one atop the other.

"As you can see, there is very little difference between the original waveform and the version we need. I ran a Fourier transform and was able to generate a harmonic correction that can make the alteration, providing we can find a way to introduce it into the neutronium strand. That, unfortunately, is a larger problem."

Suddenly Dyana's eyes opened wide with understanding.

"Gravity waves, you want to use gravity waves!"

"Specifically the Large Neutronium Antenna," said Gedron. "We use the LNA to read the gravitational waves produced by the suns and by the entropy clouds, so we know that it has sufficient range. If we could use it to produce gravity waves rather than detect them, we could use that wave as a carrier for the harmonic correction."

Dyana quickly reached toward the infochryst and called up an image of the Conclave. Within seconds the air above the table was filled with a whirling hologram of interlocked orbits. Dyana searched the hologram for a moment, and then grasped the image of a gas giant not far from the Guard, enlarging it until Gedron could see a pair of small asteroids in low orbit over the immense planet. Between them stretched a faint bridge, a rod of reddish material over fifty miles long that bound the asteroids together. Dyana gestured a final time and the hologram vanished, replaced by a schematic of the asteroids and the dully glowing column of crystalline neutronium that connected them. Specifications and readouts began to fill the air around the structure.

"These are the operating conditions of the antenna," Dyana said, indicating one of the readouts. "Gedron, what are the dimensions of the vacuum sculptor core filaments and the frequency specifications of the correction wave?"

Gedron reached into the image and opened up a subwindow containing the needed information. He watched as Dyana superimposed this data on the schematic of the antenna and then called up a series of complex gravimetric equations. It did not take the infochryst long to perform the calculation, and a few moments later a window containing the final results opened in the air above the device. Gedron stared at the numbers, an empty feeling in his stomach.

"Are there any other parameters we can change?" he asked, a hint of desperation in his voice.

"No," said Dyana grimly. "All the relevant parameters were in the initial run. It's not going to work."

"I don't understand," said Trielle. "I mean, I can see that the equations predict failure, but what factor is getting in the way?"

"Look here," said Dyana, indicating one term of the equations. "This variable represents the maximum frequency of the gravitational waves the antenna can generate. And here," she said, gesturing toward another term, "is the rate of signal decay per light-microsecond of space.

Trielle stared at the equations for a few moments. "Are you saying the antenna can't generate a high enough frequency to carry this particular signal without degradation?" she said at last.

"Basically," signed Dyana. "I've been doing gravimetrics almost my entire adult life, and I can't think of anything other than an explosively decomposing mass of neutronium that is energetic enough to create the carrier wave we need."

"How much neutronium?" asked Trielle, a thoughtful expression on her face.

"It would depend on how close the explosion was to the sculptors," said Dyana. "Gravity waves disperse fairly quickly." She paused for a second and then added, "If you were thinking of detonating the antenna, stop right now. Not only does it have too many safeguards, it is simply too large. The radiation from the explosion would be almost as bad as Vai going supernova."

"No," said Trielle, here eyes distant, "I was thinking about something else entirely." She paused for a moment, and then asked, "what if the explosion was in Vai's photosphere?"

"That close?" said Dyana in surprise. "I don't know how we could do it, but at that range it shouldn't take much more than a few tons."

"About the same amount of neutronium in a transport class laridian ring," said Trielle with a note of satisfaction.

Suddenly Gedron understood.

"You want to use our ether chariot, don't you?" he asked.

"That was the idea," Trielle admitted. "Mother, would it work?"

Dyana gestured above the infochryst, calling up another series of equations. Gedron watched as she scrutinized the scrolling rows of numbers.

"It should," she said at last, a cautious smile forming on her face.

Hope surged within Gedron, but then a new concern surfaced in his mind and that hope quickly died.

341

"This may work in theory, Trielle," he said, "but you have no idea how many safeguards are programmed into commercial grade laridian ring systems. I know how to circumvent most of them, but there is no way to destabilize the containment field without manual input. We can't just program the ether chariot and then send it into Vai. Someone would have to ride it in and detonate it by hand."

"I thought that might be the case," admitted Trielle. She hesitated a few moments, and then said, "I'm ready to go. I don't see that we have a choice."

A throb of pain beat within Gedron's chest, as if his heart were shriveling and dying within him. From the look on Dyana's face he could tell that she felt much the same.

"No," he said hoarsely, "This is my problem. I helped create it; I will solve it."

"You can't," said Trielle. "You need to be on the bridge of the Gog overseeing the ignition. Without you the Entrope will suspect something. Remember, our goal is not just to stop the vacuum sculptors, it's to buy Garin time. The Entrope and Chromatocron need to think that the vacuum sculptors are working. I've seen the space around Vai," she added. "I know that the etherreavers are already positioned for a gravitic bombardment in case it is needed. Once they realize the sculptors have failed they'll simply start the bombardment early."

Gedron slowly nodded. Though he would have given anything to change it, he knew her words were true.

"Then I'll go," said Dyana, her words thick with grief. "I am new to all this and a part of me still doesn't believe it, but I will not let my daughter go on a suicide mission!"

"Mother," said Trielle with a smile. "I don't think this is a suicide mission at all. You don't know the power of the *Anastasi*, but I've seen what they can do and I have their word that they will protect me if they can. Even if there was no chance of rescue, though, I am still prepared to go. I am sure Garin has already faced worse odds, and if I can do this for him then it is a gift I will gladly give."

She paused for what seemed like an eternity, then looked straight at Gedron, the force of her gaze burning through him like a laser.

"The Sur Ekklesia taught me something," she said in a low voice. "They taught me that no matter what the Axioms say the deepest truth in our cosmos is not the selfish desire to survive, but self-giving love. I've lived too long for myself, and if this sacrifice is what it takes to show my love for Garin then so be it. Now, let's go make the changes we need to the ether chariot. You need to show me how to load the counter-wave into the ring and how to disengage the neutronium stabilizers when the time comes. Besides, I have the distinct feeling that I may make it through this yet."

As Trielle rose, Gedron gazed at the face of his child and saw confidence mingled with doubt.

How much of this could have been stopped earlier if I had only swallowed my fear and voiced my true thoughts to the Hierophants?

Gedron sighed; it was too late now for regrets. Somehow, during her time on En-Ka-Re, Trielle had gained a faith in something beyond herself. For a moment he wished that he had that faith as well, but for now Trielle's would have to be enough for both of them.

"Come on Dyana," he said with resignation. "Let's go help Trielle. The ignition attempt is in twelve hours and we have a lot to do."

Interlude: The Harrowing of the Pit

Kyr dove downward like a shining spear, the shattered remnants of Leviathan dispersing about him in clouds of ash and cooling embers. Still, he knew that he had only destroyed his body. The true abyss still awaited.

Below him the deeps of Tehom churned with sickening slowness: endless waves of billowing darkness crashing amidst a sea of decaying gas and matter. The waves massed together as he drew nearer, transforming at last into a grinning visage of despair and chaos: the face of Daath. Its mouth opened wide, straining upward towards Kyr as if to swallow him. Then he was within the vast maw, and what light there was failed as the vast lips closed behind him. A few seconds later he hit the surface of the abyss.

He struck with the force of a thunderbolt and soon was miles beneath the dark waters, buried alive in the deeps of Tehom. The cold was like nothing he had ever felt before, a numbing suction more frigid than the void between stars that seemed to bleed the very life from his body. Yet still he dove downward. This was an ocean with a depth measured in light years, and he had far to go. He did not falter as the black waters congealed around him, growing thicker and thicker until the medium he traveled through was a trillion times denser than solid lead. All about him gaped the faces of the dead, an overwhelming flood of damned souls forever imprisoned in their own selfishness and pride. Their cries were almost a palpable thing, an endless aural tapestry of pain and rage, and above it all, just at the edge of hearing, he could hear Daath's black laughter. Finally, after what seemed like aeons, he reached his destination, a featureless plain of infinite darkness at the bottom of all worlds.

Tohu wa-Bohu: the primal void from which the worlds were called in the time before times. Here, not even possibility existed.

Kyr knelt down and began to grope through the muck and slime that covered the black plain, his hands carefully searching for the precious thing that he had lost. At last he found it: a white jewel half buried in the ooze. He carefully lifted up the jewel and it began to shine feebly, a pale glimmer of light amidst the endless darkness. Kyr smiled, and suddenly it was no longer a jewel but a woman dressed in torn robes. Her body was bruised and cut, and her heartbeat was faint and irregular, but she still lived. As Kyr gazed on her lovingly, she coughed and slowly opened her eyes.

"You came," she croaked.

"Yes," said Kyr tenderly. "How could I not, my Beloved?"

"But why?" she said in confusion. "After all I've done…"

"Because I am," said Kyr. "Now rest. There is one more thing I must do here, and then I will carry you up to my Father."

Kyr gently laid the woman down beside him and raised his right hand over his head in a fist.

"Spirit," he whispered, "pierce the void with wind and fire."

Kyr swung his fist downward, striking the black plain beneath with world-shattering force, and the deep convulsed. There was a noise like a thousand thunderclaps, followed by a deep grinding sound as a spiderweb of cracks shivered outward from the point of impact. Kyr watched as the centermost crack grew brighter and brighter until finally a slender ray of light shone through it, a brilliant beam from some realm of impossible radiance even more fundamental than the primal void.

It was enough.

From somewhere in the distance he heard the voice of Daath bellow in anger. Quickly he gathered the woman in his arms.

"Come, my Beloved," he said in a joyful whisper, "we rise."

Kyr stepped into the beam and pushed off from the black plain. Buoyed by the light, they began their ascent.

Book Five: A Rose Wet With the Final Morning's Dew…

Numenos

Chapter 31: Dark Resurrection

The Entrope lay on a cold slab in the Chamber of Rebirth awaiting the Rite of Dissolution, and his death. He had known this day was coming soon, but nothing in all his remembered centuries could have prepared him for the morning's events.

Less than an hour ago he had stood within the Chamber of the Pool, his body bathed in liquid flame as he awaited communion with the Presence. But when at last it emerged from the fires he knew immediately that something was deeply, profoundly wrong. Its human appearance forsaken, the Presence now was little more than a writhing mass of darkness and fire. The Entrope shuddered, remembering the Presence's unearthly roar of pain and the sudden, terrifying movement of its black fingers as they reached into his brain and poured that pain into him. The agony had been unbearable, as if a river of white-hot magma were surging through his entrails, searing and ravaging his body from within. Over and over again he had begged for release, and when, in a brief moment of lucidity, the Presence had responded, his condemnation had been swift.

"So, you think that such relief is a gift? I grow tired of your cries. Proceed to the Chamber of Rebirth and join me in the darkness. Perhaps a new body will give you the endurance to complete this task. If I am to fall then all worlds fall with me."

And then, without even a flicker, the fire had died, leaving the Entrope alone in the midst of the pool. Numb with shock at the abrupt dismissal, the Entrope had walked to the Chamber of Rebirth like an automaton, his actions barely registering in his conscious mind. Only after he had laid down within the memory extractor and commanded the

Irkallan Infochryst to begin the rebirth process did he truly become aware of where he was and what was about to occur.

Despite having been reborn countless times over the past millennia, each death made him uneasy. Oh, he knew that in an hour's time he, or at least someone sharing his thoughts and memories, would emerge from the bubbling biosuspension vat that stood next to the slab on which he lay. But what about this version of him? He wished that he could remember more from his past resurrections, but the memories all seemed to stop short of the exact moment of dissolution.

It is easy to maintain that your consciousness is a lie until it is about to be extinguished.

Then he pushed the thought from his mind. It did not matter, and it was too late to stop things now.

The Entrope watched as a delicate filigree of amethyst threads grew down toward him from the chamber's ceiling. Extensions of the Irkallan Infochryst, it was these threads that would access the deep neural tracts within which his thoughts, memories, and identity were stored. He lay motionless as the glassy filaments formed a cage around his head and soon felt the first unpleasant electric tingle of the extraction field as it penetrated his skull. Throughout the process he struggled to remain calm. After all, there was no point in awakening his new body in a distressed state. But one thing would not stop troubling him, a phrase the Presence had said when he stood within the pool.

"Join me in the darkness."

Despite the Entrope's frequent misgivings the Presence had been supportive, even encouraging, during his past rebirths. But not this time. There was a coldness and harshness in those words that left the Entrope with the unshakeable suspicion that the Presence had shared a deep truth that until now it had hidden from him.

356

Abruptly the electric tingle lessened and the slab beneath him began to warm. The last memory exchange was complete. Beyond this point, in all his myriad reincarnations, he could remember nothing. Who was he now? He knew that he was no longer the Entrope; that identity now lay in the miles of charged crystal that composed the Irkallan Infochryst. But he could not fully dispel the thought that in the past he had possessed another identity. Hadn't he had a name once? It had been millennia since it had been spoken, and suddenly nothing seemed as precious as that lost bit of knowledge. In vain he struggled to remember.

A burning sensation rushed through him as wave after wave of molecular disassemblers surged into his body from the slab. The burning was quickly followed by a creeping numbness as his very cells were torn apart, presumably to be used in the creation of his next incarnation. Within seconds his body was half-dissolved into the material of the slab, yet in the final moments of his existence the long sought after name came to him at last, and with his final breath he whispered it aloud.

"Larid, Ronath Larid…"

Then the last fragments of his physical form disintegrated and he was falling downward toward an endless vortex of churning black water. A thousand faces stared back at him from beneath the surface, and with horror Ronath Larid realized that they were all his own.

***

The Entrope came awake suddenly and fought to take a breath against the tidal surge of the ventilators that had pumped air into his developing body for so long. As if on cue the biosuspensive fluids surrounding him drained away, and the tubes and devices attached to his body

357

withdrew. The Entrope sat up and spent a few moments testing his new body. It was young and strong both physically and mentally, and he could already feel the misgivings of his previous incarnation evaporating like a bad dream at sunrise. The Entrope stepped out of the vat and walked to the memory retrieval device, where he gathered his crumpled robe from the now-empty slab. Donning the robe, he strode resolutely from the Chamber of Rebirth toward the transit tubes that would take him to the Omegahedron.

The time had come to reignite Vai, or erase all living souls in the Conclave, or perhaps both. It did not matter.

Nothing mattered.

Chapter 32: The City Imperishable

He was surrounded by vistas of supernal beauty: walls of alabaster and chalcedony topped by spires of unthinkably pure crystal, all crowned by a rosy brightness that blanketed the sky like a luminous cloud at sunset. But none of this beauty could compare to that of the being that had addressed him.

A towering figure stood before Garin. Its form was robed in purest white, and a breastplate of gold inlaid with pearls was upon its chest. Its noble face was as pure as a new snowfall and shone with a soft inner radiance. Atop its head sat a towering miter crowned with the image of a full moon. The figure smiled at him and reached out its hand in greeting.

"Welcome small one."

Its voice was a husky treble, almost matronly in its tone, and thought Garin felt sure that a creature such as this could have no gender he could not help but think of her as a woman. There was something familiar about the voice.

"I thank you for your warm greeting," he said with as much courtesy as he could muster. "Thought I have never been to this realm, I cannot help but think that we have met before."

At this the figure laughed with a sound like chiming bells.

"Met?" she said with a hint of good-natured sarcasm. "Do you not remember traveling through my domain in the world beneath? It was I that welcomed you to Arethos."

"Malkuth?" said Garin in bewilderment.

"Also called Kyriakos," finished the figure, as if eager that her full title be said.

"But how?" asked Garin, "Haven't I passed into another world?"

"Indeed," said Malkuth. "You have passed from Arethos, the world created to be the expression of our deepest thoughts, into Numenos, where we live and move and have our conversation. It is here that we are enthroned, and it is from here that we govern and serve the worlds beneath."

Garin marveled at this. Until now he had never met a being whose existence had spanned more than one world. No one, of course, except for Kyr. A sudden pang of sadness gripped Garin's chest, and his growing joy evaporated.

"Why is your face downcast?" asked Malkuth. "This is a realm of gladness and joy."

"I'm sorry," said Garin. "I was just thinking about Kyr. He gave himself to save me from Daath and is even now in the Abyss."

"He gave Himself for more than you," said Malkuth, "though if you were the only creature made he would have done no less. You are right to mourn, child of the lowest world, for it is Holy Saturday. But the time of His sojourn in the darkness will soon draw to a close and when the morn dawns you must be ready to meet Him. Come! The council of the Arethoi would meet with you before your ascent to the petals of the Cosmic Rose."

Malkuth turned and proceeded down the golden streets and Garin followed. Though Garin did not understand the meaning of Malkuth's words, by now he had grown used to the cryptic utterances of inhabitants of the higher worlds, and Malkuth's evident confidence in Kyr's return buoyed his spirits. As they moved forward it quickly became clear to Garin that he had entered this city near its outmost precincts, for with each step he took the magnificence of the structures around him grew. Soon they reached a glorious colonnade that ran for miles between rows of crystal skyscrapers. The inhabitants of the city, beings of light like Malkuth, thronged about them as they processed onward.

"It is not often that a child of the lower worlds visits the City Imperishable," said Malkuth with an almost apologetic tone. "Do not fear. The Malakim are curious, nothing more."

"It's alright," said Garin. "I'm not afraid."

And in truth he wasn't. Indeed, it was difficult to feel anything other than awe in this place. It was as if he walked in a vision of light, a dream that he wished never to wake from.

The colonnade at last ended at the gates of a diamond palace that soared to impossible heights. From the topmost point of the palace rose an emerald thread that spiraled higher still before vanishing into the rosy brightness above like a staircase to infinity. The gates were open.

Crossing the threshold, they entered a grand hallway with ceilings so high they were covered in clouds. Light shone from every surface and mingled with the mists above to fill the air with a myriad of rainbows that spanned the walls like arches. The hall led to a vast chamber paved with diamond and chrysoprase. In the center of the chamber was a raised dais on which sat thirteen thrones, all but two occupied by beings similar to Malkuth (though with differently colored breastplates). The twelfth was empty and the thirteenth was charred and cracked, as if it had been blasted by lightning. In the center of the dais stood a golden plinth on which rested an obscure object the size of Garin's fist. Then a bright flash of unearthly radiance drew his

361

attention, and he looked beyond the dais to see two additional thrones of titanic size. Set against the back wall of the chamber, these were occupied by beings of such glory and strangeness that Garin's mind could not arrange their appearance into a coherent image. The very attempt made him dizzy, and Garin closed his eyes momentarily to regain his bearings. When he opened them again, he saw that Malkuth had ascended the dais and taken a seat on the twelfth throne. Unsure what to do in the presence of such majesty, Garin knelt, his face downward.

"Do not kneel to us, son of the lowest world," said a deep voice. "Though our might dwarfs yours as a galaxy dwarfs an insect, we are fellow creatures like yourself. Only One deserves such honor."

Garin lifted his head and saw that one of the beings was now standing. His breastplate was of lapis lazuli and his miter was wreathed with a crown of stars. The being's hand was outstretched, as if beckoning Garin forward.

"Come forward, child of the low worlds. We would speak with you. I am Keter, the crown of life, known also Zeodotes and Chavath."

Trembling, Garin rose to his feet and ascended the dais. As he neared the object on the golden stand, he saw that it was a glassy sphere containing an intricate cubic pattern. He recognized it almost immediately.

"Is that the Cube of Cubes?" he asked, his fear vanishing as curiosity took hold.

"Indeed, son of the low worlds. You stand before the eidolon of the great cube, or perhaps it is better to consider the world below the eidolon and this the reality."

Garin approached the artifact closer and noted that a part of it near the center seemed fractured.

"The flaw that you gaze at is the effect of Daath's rebellion on the structure of the cube," said Keter. "Into its

362

perfect light he introduced a fragment of darkness and absurdity, and for that his place among the Two and Twelve was forfeit." As he spoke, Keter gestured to the shattered thirteenth throne.

Garin considered this for a moment. "Standing in the glory of this chamber, the fracture seems such a small thing."

"How could it be otherwise?" spoke a feminine voice. Turning from the cube, Garin watched as another of the beings approached them. Her breastplate was of shining platinum covered with stylized images of candles, and her miter was topped with a seven-branched candlestick that burned with brilliant flames. "Creation's wound runs deep but its wholeness runs deeper still, for without the wholeness what would remain to be wounded? The Joy of Creation will not be bound to those who wish to live in hate and sorrow, and the Music of the Cosmos cannot be silenced by those who refuse to sing."

Garin was silent for a moment. "And yet, from within, it seems a thing of great power. I have been in Daath's domain and seen the dark spheres in which he has bound the souls of those in his grasp."

"You misunderstand what you see," said Keter. "Daath has not the power to capture and bind souls. No, those who follow him are bound only by their own refusal to turn their faces toward the light and ask for deliverance. And yet they do not and will not. The hell-spheres are locked from within."

"You yourself know this," said the female being, whom Garin at last recognized as Tifereth, "for you called for such deliverance in the domain of my brother Gevurah, who is also called Rhadamanthos. There you confessed and turned from your part in the Shadow. You were willing to lose your life and instead received it back again as a pure gift, both there and at the edge of the Abyss."

"But what, then, of Kyr?" asked Garin. "He delivered me, but who will deliver him?"

This provoked a hearty laugh from Tifereth.

"He who is Creation's song, the Eternal Son of He Who is, needs no deliverance," said Tifereth with a smile, "for it is He that delivers all things from their bondage to darkness. It is Holy Saturday, and even now he descends to the deepest pits of Tehom to free his Beloved from chains of death and chaos. All moments of redeeming are included in this one act that transcends the worlds themselves. When a soul from the wounded spheres looks toward the light and cries out for help, it is His hand that saves."

As Tifereth spoke a great bell sounded, deep and rich. The twelve dropped to their knees in worship and the two incomprehensible beings enthroned behind the dais cried out in unison with such power that it seemed the foundations of the diamond palace would crack.

"THE MIDNIGHT OF CREATION HAS PASSED. THE DAWN SOON ARRIVES. CHILD OF THE LOW WORLDS, ASCEND NOW TO THE CRYSTAL ROSE ABOVE ALL CREATED POWERS. HE RISES! HE RISES!"

Keter arose and looked at Garin. "The time has come. Ascend now even as Metatron and Sandalphon have entreated you."

"I do not understand," said Garin.

"Above the City Imperishable stands the Cosmic Rose," explained Keter. "There rest the souls of the Kal Ekklesia, those who have died awaiting the coming of their deliverer. It is they that we were created to uphold and it is they that Daath has rejected in his rebellion, for they were meant to increase and we to decrease. At the far side of this

364

throne room is a door that leads to the Garden of Souls, the place in which this rose is planted. Go there quickly."

As if in response to Keter's words, a low rumbling sound filled the chamber, and an impossibly tall sliver of light appeared on the wall between Metatron and Sandalphon's immense thrones.

"I thank you, Arethoi, for assisting me as I traversed the Cube of Cubes," Garin said with a deep bow.

"It is our priviledge and joy, for within our realms we witnessed you awaken in the Beloved," Tifereth said. "Now go! There is not long now to wait."

As Garin descended the dais and walked toward the back of the throne room, he saw that the sliver of light was emanating from an open door. Countless stories tall, it was only wide enough for one man. As Garin approached the door, he stole a quick glance at the figures of Metatron and Sandalphon, and was again overwhelmed as his mind fought to comprehend the sheer otherness of what he saw.

Wheels within wheels made of unearthly metal...

Hundreds of unblinking eyes, each filled with lightning...

Vortexes of flame surrounded by rustling silver-white rings in endless concentric circles...

"YOU ARE UNABLE TO COMPREHEND OUR VASTNESS, AND RIGHTLY SO," said one of the beings (he could not tell which), "YET IN ANOTHER, FAR GREATER, WAY, IT IS WE THAT CANNOT COMPREHEND YOU: A CREATURE SMALLER THAN DUST, YET BELOVED ENOUGH BY THE LORD OF ALL BEING FOR HIM TO OFFER THE INFINITE DEPTHS OF HIS LIFE IN SACRIFICE. TRULY BLESSED, OUT OF ALL THRONES, POWERS, AND DOMINIONS, IS THE EKKLESIA."

Unable to frame an answer in response, Garin nodded and proceeded through the door. At first all was blinding light, but as his eyes adjusted to the brilliance he saw that he stood in a circular courtyard surrounded by ramparts of crystal. The ground of the courtyard was covered by a dark soil-like material that sparkled and flashed. Garin knelt down and scooped up the substance in his hands, and laughed in wonder as millions of tiny black diamonds coursed between his fingers. In the center of the courtyard was a great well, the bottom of which was lost in darkness far below. To the side of the well a stem of emerald thicker than a tree trunk rose from the diamond soil and spiraled upward into the pink haze of the sky. Leaves of translucent jade, wider than Garin was tall, sprung from the stem at irregular intervals, guarded by thorns as sharp as glass daggers. Garin approached the base of the stem and saw that a staircase had been carved into its upper surface. His path clear, he began to climb.

The ascent seemed eternal, the stem circling round and round like an endless spiral helix rising to unknown heights. Soon he had risen above the highest spires of the diamond palace of the Arethoi, and he could see the entire City Imperishable spread beneath him like a shining diadem. Above, the rosy haze that he had seen from the streets beneath began to gradually come into focus, at last resolving into a vast expanse of softly curving petals that extended to the furthest extent of his vision. Then the stem expanded into a profusion of glittering leaves and the staircase abruptly turned, diving within the glassy foliage before continuing upward between the roots of the vast petals. At last he climbed the final flight, and as the gleaming walls fell away Garin gasped in awe at the sight before him.

He stood upon a broad glassy plateau in the heart of a rose that dwarfed the city below in size. Row upon row of softly luminous petals stretched upward in gentle curves like the tiers of a mighty amphitheater beneath a dark blue sky. Each was covered with countless seats seemingly grown from their crystalline surfaces. At first Garin thought the seats were empty, but he soon realized that each contained the translucent form of a man, woman, or other sentient creature. Bright spirits like winged flames moved swiftly up and down each petal, ministering to the forms.

Garin walked to the edge of the plateau and approached the ghosts (for so he had come to think of them) on the nearest petal. The translucent beings regarded him intently, slowly lifting their hands in a gesture of greeting. Though they seemed weak Garin could see the vitality and memory that burned in their eyes, and he realized that in some ways they were more alive than those who dwelt in the Conclave. Still, their evident frailty troubled him. It seemed almost inconceivable that such creatures stood higher in the order of creation than mighty beings like Metatron and Saldalphon.

"These are the souls of those who have died in faith. Here in the Cosmic Rose of the Kal Ekklesia they rest as they await a better world and a better resurrection."

The voice was both strong and feminine. Startled, Garin turned toward it and saw a semicircle of thrones near the plateau's center surrounding a well similar to the one in the garden below. The thrones were carved of jasper and carnelian, and upon them sat men and women drawn from all races and species of the Conclave. These figures were far more solid in appearance than the ghosts, but a strange, almost luminous, quality seemed to hover about their faces, like moonlight shining in a clear sky. Then Garin noticed that one of the figures, a woman clothed in white and blue robes, had risen from her throne and was walking toward him. The woman reached out her hand as she drew near, and, to his own surprise, Garin reflexively took it and kissed it in a gesture of tender affection.

"I am called Mater Marya," she said gently, and Garin knew then it was she that had spoken.

Her face was an endless network of wrinkles, an ancient visage apparently millennia in age. Yet despite this she seemed to radiate an almost palpable aura of liveliness.

"I am Garin, of Phaneros," he replied.

"Oh, my grandchildren and I know you well, Garin," said Mater Marya. "We have watched your journey from our ancient homeworlds with great joy and are thankful that you at last walk among us. Ever you have been in the prayers and supplications of the Fathers and Mothers, and the countless hosts of the Arethoi have long anticipated your coming."

"So what I was told by the Arethoi is true," he mused. "The great ones I walked amongst in the city beneath were created to serve us."

"Why, yes," said Mater Marya with faint surprise. "But we would not say it like that. It is true that the highest calling of the Arethoi is to uphold and serve the creatures of the low worlds, but only so that we may in turn uphold and serve He Who Is. And even He has not exempted himself from this pattern, for it lies at the heart of His nature, and thus He Himself became a servant for our sake."

As she spoke those words, Mater Marya's eyes grew misty with tears, as if remembering a time from long ago. After a few moments she wiped her eyes and continued.

"You have seen the flame-spirits that dart amongst the ghosts. Those are the ministers of the Arethoi, sent to succor us until the time of re-enfleshment is at hand. For aeons they have served us in our vigil, but we do not have long to wait now, not long at all. Now come, there is one last thing that we must do before the moment of ascension."

Mater Marya led Garin to the foot of the thrones, then raised her head and called out in a loud, clear voice.

"Fathers and Mothers, Blessed of the Races, Heart of the Beloved, the last of our number has come. He is Garin of Scintillus, soon to be anointed prophet to a dying world. Love Him, my brothers and sisters, for he is the last, and after him comes the Apocatastasis."

The words struck Garin with the force of hammer blows. Suddenly he realized that the entire company seated there was staring intently at him, waiting for him to speak. Garin's mouth was dry. He did not know what to say.

"I am sorry," he said finally. "I have travelled the Sovereign Road from Phaneros in order to see the truth of things, for I have always been taught that nothing existed beyond our cosmos and that all would soon dissolve back into the void. I am thankful that this is wrong, and have learned much, but... I know nothing of being a prophet."

"Boy," said a wizened old man who sat in the throne nearest Garin, "what makes you think any of us knew what we were doing either? I too was called as a child, and spent most of my life living in the desert places of the world once called Sha-Ka-Ri, preparing the way of my master, and I dare say my mission was successful. Yet at no time did I ever know what I was doing."

Then his voice softened. "It is not your knowledge He requires, child. Indeed, He does not often choose those with knowledge, power, strength or wisdom to carry His words, but instead chooses the foolish to shame the wise and the weak to defeat the strong. Besides," he added after a brief pause, "we have saved this throne for you for the past ten thousand years. Would you have us waste it?"

As he spoke he gestured to his right, and Garin turned to see an unoccupied throne near the end of the semicircle. As if in a daze, Garin walked slowly toward it and placed his hand on its softly gleaming surface.

"It's warm," he murmured.

"It is not for you to be seated there yet, child," chided Mater Marya softly, "for you are not yet anointed and have yet to face the trials that you have been appointed to endure in the worlds below."

Then a soft susurrus filled Garin's ears. It was a sound unlike any he had heard before, as if ten thousand times ten thousand voices were whispering together in eager anticipation, and he turned to see waves of excitement rushing like wind through the ghosts seated upon the petals of the Rose. Suddenly the fire-spirits leapt skyward, wheeling through the heavens in concentric rings of living glory, and a soft light like the first gleam of the sun in the morning sky began to shine from the well. With joy on their faces, the seated Mothers and Fathers rose in unison and gathered about its rim.

"Join us at the Well of Eternity," said Mater Marya, her hand extended toward Garin in a beckoning gesture. "Join us as we greet the dawn."

"What is happening?" asked Garin in confusion.

"Why, surely you know," she laughed. "His long battle in Tehom is almost ended and the one you call Kyr rises from the deep to make all things new. Now come! Come and see the victory of my son!"

A smile on his face, Garin walked with Mater Marya to the edge of the well and, gazing within, beheld a wonder.

Chapter 33: On the Edge of the Night

The Worldships Gog and Magog hung like dwarf planets in Vai's darkened corona. Together they were a study in contrasts, the floral organic symmetry of the Gog contradicted sharply by the angular, irregular shape of the Magog. It was as if the ships had been constructed to embody the essential conflict inherent in the Conclave's philosophy: one the image of the meaning an individual life could make, the other an incarnation of the meaningless chaos from which that life arose and to which it would inevitably return.

Gedron stood amidst the towering infochrystic displays of the Gog's bridge surrounded by the engineers and gravitomechanists of the College. In the air before him hung a holographic schematic of Vai. The image depicted the vacuum sculptor distribution as a blue mist of varying hues and intensities that covered the star's photosphere like a blanket of luminous fog. This layer was itself cloaked in a fine mesh of green lines representing gravimetric readings from deep within Vai's radiative layer. Further out still circled the etherreaver fleet, shown as a ring of burning gold points that surrounded the star like a halo. Gedron studied the image, half-hoping to find some flaw in the seeding process, some drastic imbalance in the vacuum sculptor distribution that would render today's exercise untenable even for the Entrope. But the local concentrations of the devices appeared to be uniform.

"The distribution appears optimal," commented Yithra-Gor redundantly.

"Indeed, my friend," sighed Gedron.

371

Though he fought to portray an air of pride and confidence, it was hard to keep the sadness and exhaustion from his voice.

It had only been five hours since he and Trielle had finished their work on the family's ether chariot, but already it felt like an aeon. Again and again he had tried to dissuade her from her plan but she had held firm, stubbornly professing her faith that the *Anastasi* would somehow rescue her in the end. Gedron had wanted to believe her, wanted it more than anything else in the world, but he was not fooled by her confident words. He could see the doubt in her eyes and had left with the unshakeable conviction that he would never see her again.

"Shall I confirm with the Magog that all is in readiness?"

"Yes, Yithra," said Gedron, snapping back to the present. Yithra-Gor bowed deeply and strode off to a nearby workstation. A few moments later a hologram of the bridge of the Magog coalesced in the air to his left. Gedron always had an eye for aesthetics, and the décor of the Magog offended that sense in a myriad of ways. Like its exterior, the bridge of the Magog was stark in design. No sculpted infochrystic columns nor golden dais adorned its spare volume. Instead, the bridge was formed of a series of gunmetal grey spires fused together in impossible angles. A convoluted series of platforms composed of glass and imagnite joined these spires in a labyrinth of bewildering complexity. In the center of this chaos stood the Chromatocron and the Ouranos Radii, each dressed in the full regalia of their offices. Evidently a corresponding hologram was being projected in the Magog, for the Chromatocron turned his head to face Gedron and addressed him as if he were present.

"Is all in readiness within the Gog?"

372

"Yes", replied Gedron. "We have only to wait for the Entrope. He desires to be present on the Gog's bridge when the sculptors are activated."

"Then the time is at hand, for I am here."

Gedron turned to see the black robed figure of the Entrope stride onto the bridge accompanied by a squadron of his personal guards. They were clad in battle armor and carried crackling energy batons.

He truly does not trust me, thought Gedron.

Then Gedron frowned. The voice of the Entrope seemed somehow stronger than it had only days before. As if in response to his unspoken suspicion the Entrope reached up and pulled back the hood of his cloak and Gedron's eyes widened in surprise. Once gaunt and haggard, the Entrope's face was now as young and fresh as that of a newborn. Only his piercing gaze remained unchanged.

"Do not look so discomfited," snapped the Entrope. "Surely you knew that I must renew my body periodically. How else could I serve as the living repository of the Conclave's base philosophy?"

"I have heard rumors of such things, but it is another matter to see the reality," said Gedron. He paused for a moment, then added: "I see that you brought companions."

"We are both aware of your questionable actions during the last ignition attempt," answered the Entrope in a smooth voice. "I intend to assure that all proceeds as planned this time."

Though the tone was friendly the threat that lay beneath was clear, and Gedron could not avoid the sense that this younger, stronger version was more predisposed to the use of force than his previous incarnation. If Trielle was successful he would not need to do anything to stop the vacuum sculptors, but beyond that he did not know what might happen. So much here depended on things beyond his control.

"High Gravitist, I see that the Entrope has joined you," said the Ouranos Radii. "Is all now in readiness? Shall we proceed?"

"Allow me to make a final scan of the Vacuum Sculptor distribution to assure that it aligns much as is possible with the current gas densities within Vai," said Gedron.

"If you must," replied the Chromatocron dismissively.

Gedron nodded grimly and turned again to the hologram of Vai. Raising his hands, he gave a sequence of commands that brought the green gravitometric mesh into sharp relief. He knew that matching the gravitational readings with the sculptor distributions would do little to alter the outcome of the process, but that was not his true intent. He was searching instead for the telltale gravitational distortion produced by the explosive decomposition of a laridian ring: proof of Trielle's success, and of her sacrifice.

Gedron glanced quickly at the chronometric readout of a nearby infochryst. There were only six minutes left until ignition.

The precise time of reignition had been set days ago, and after some discussion he and Trielle had decided that the explosion should be timed for two to three minutes before the attempt. Detonate the ring too soon and they ran the risk of discovery by the vacuum sculptors' diagnostic software; detonate the ring too late and it would not be effective as too much of the underlying quantum vacuum would have already been altered. But if the other Heirophants activated the vacuum sculptors early then none of their careful planning would make a difference.

"Come now," said the Entrope. "Surely this exercise is unnecessary."

"It will only take a few more moments to complete the scan," said Gedron with feigned calm.

He had to buy Trielle some time. He had to make sure that her life would not be sacrificed in vain.

***

Trielle's ether chariot shrieked down a twisted corridor of spacetime, its laridian rings throwing off coruscating blue arcs of gravitic force. Trielle closed her eyes and mentally reviewed the control sequence that would inject the new waveform into the primary laridian ring and deactivate the containment fields. Once she broke through into normal space she would have little time to enact the sequence before the ship crashed into the photosphere of the star. Too deep within Vai's bulk and the force of the explosion would be prematurely absorbed by the dense gases.

What if Anacrysis is not watching after all? What if I fail? What if I die?

The thoughts intruded on her preparations, and despite her best attempts Trielle was unable to dissipate the swarming cloud of doubts flitting about within her mind. Suddenly she felt an overwhelming urge to turn the ship around and flee back down the wormhole to the safe confines of her home.

"And then what?" she said aloud, trying to regain control of her thoughts. "If the vacuum sculptors trigger a supernova then I die anyway, and so does everyone else I love." Then a low tone sounded from the console. She had arrived.

With a crackle of azure lightning Trielle's ether chariot emerged into Vai's chromosphere. One moment all was darkness and in the next she was flying through ghostly red clouds of dully glowing gas. Ahead of her stretched the photosphere of Vai, a seemingly infinite wall of churning brown and red plasma. Even within the chariot's shield the heat was intense. Her hands hovered over the control console. It was nearly time.

She waited until the wall was almost upon her, until the swirling gas seemed close enough to touch.

"Anacrysis," she cried out suddenly, "I hope you are watching, because now would be an excellent time for a rescue!"

Trielle's hands flew as she activated the control sequence. There was a sharp whine as the counter-wave was injected from the craft's spare mesonic battery into the neutronium of the ship's primary ring, followed by a shudder as the shielding fields were released. A sudden orange light flared behind her, and she turned to see a network of glowing cracks race quickly around the primary ring housing. All around her she could see the protective fields that held out the burning gases flare, crackle, and begin to decay.

"Anacrysis," she screamed, "where are you?"

The primary ring housing failed with a sharp report, flooding the ether chariot with blinding light. An acrid stench of ozone filled the air, and Trielle looked up in terror to see the first wisps of stellar plasma breach the failing protective fields. Suddenly she was surrounded by translucent golden wings. She felt an abrupt lurch, and the universe fell away. Beneath the translucent surface of the world-wall Trielle could see the brilliant flare of the ether chariot's detonation.

"I'm sorry you had to wait so long," said Anacrysis. "If we'd rescued you sooner we might have been detected.

376

We may yet need the advantage of surprise before today is over."

Trielle breathed a sigh of relief. Then her eyes widened as she saw, all around her, the massed armies of the *Anastasi*. They hovered just outside the crystal world-shell, legion upon legion of warriors resplendent in golden armor and bearing swords that burned like suns.

"This day," said Anacrysis grimly, "the siege of the Sur Ekklesia ends."

***

A sharp burst of light erupted from Vai's photosphere as the ether chariot exploded in a sphere of white-hot plasma. Thousands of tons of neutronium disintegrated within milliseconds, releasing their trapped gravitic potential, and a shimmering torus of force burst from the boiling sphere. The gravity wave raced outward, carrying the correction wave within its vibrations, and as it washed over the vacuum sculptors the neutronium filaments inside them resonated, shifted, and began to sing a different note. The wave weakened as it spread and quickly diminished to a point where it could no longer affect the devices, but by then a substantial fraction had already been defused. The once-brilliant orb of plasma faded to a sullen orange cloud of gas that was soon dispersed by the winds of Vai's chromosphere. In the end nothing remained save a drifting wisp of ash.

***

A tiny spike of green light disturbed the surface of the hologram, and Gedron felt a stab of pain in his chest. Fighting to maintain his calm appearance, he watched as the

377

light flared, rippled for a moment, and vanished. The deed was done; the sacrifice made. At that moment Gedron would have given anything to know that Trielle had somehow survived, even as his rational mind told him that it was a frank impossibility.

Please, bring Trielle back to me! Bring Garin back to me!

Gedron railed against an indifferent universe, crying out to the powers that Trielle had trusted her life to but he could not yet believe in, and received the expected silence in return. He stared blankly at the hologram, trying to imaging a world without his daughter and son. His eyes grew moist with tears.

"My apologies for the delay," he said at last said, all trace of emotion absent from his voice. "I am satisfied. We may begin."

Chapter 34: The Son of Highest Heaven

Far below the Cosmic Rose, the deep boiled with mounting fury. Stray bolts of light erupted from its surface and the black waters writhed in response, as if trying to keep some irresistible force buried beneath their weight. All at once the waters massed together into the chaotic visage of Daath. His eyes were wide with pain and his jaws were clenched tightly shut. Fiery light spilled between his teeth.

NO! YOU CANNOT HAVE HER!

With a crackling sound the terrible face froze into a mask of black ice; a last, desperate attempt to hold the burning radiance in check. But the light was too strong. There was a sharp crack like the calving of an iceberg followed by a cry of unearthly agony. The face of Daath split in half, and the surface of Tehom burst open in a fountain of glory.

***

Beams of near solar intensity shone from the Well of Eternity, bathing the Cosmic Rose in golden effulgence. With each moment the light grew in brilliance, until Garin was forced to step back and shield his eyes. Then, just as the glare became intolerable, Kyr burst forth from the mouth of the well, soaring skyward on a pillar of incandescence brighter than the core of a star.

His robes were as white as new-fallen snow, and his form was wreathed in dazzling rainbows. Gone were the marks of age; his skin was now flawless, bright and fresh as a child's. In his arms he carried a wounded woman clothed in tattered rags, and as he flew toward the heavens he raised the woman aloft and cried out in a loud voice.

"FATHER, I HAVE FOUND MY BRIDE! I AM COMING HOME!"

The woman body's caught fire as he spoke. In a rush of crimson and gold her wounds were healed and her once tattered raiment became whole and clean. Bright beams rained down from her dazzling form onto the petals of the rose, and when the beams touched the ghosts their bodies were renewed. As one the newly incarnate ghosts rose and lifted their voices in a thunderous cry of all tongues and languages.

"Xu Xorba!"

"Al-Masih Qam!"

"Christos Anesti!"

High above, the wheeling spirits of the Arethoi drew swords of lightning and joined their voices to the cry of the re-embodied ghosts, transforming it into a mighty hymn that shook the Cosmic Rose to its roots. Then Garin noticed a soft sound beside him and he turned to see Mater Marya weeping.

"I am so proud of him…" she whispered softly.

Together they watched Kyr's brilliant form grow smaller and smaller until it finally vanished into the deep blue heavens. Neither said a word. Neither needed to. At last Mater Marya looked down at him with shining eyes.

"It is time now, child," she said tenderly. "My son goes to make all things new, and you must follow him."

A soft wind rose as she spoke, stirring the dimming remnants of the column of flame on which Kyr had ascended into a gentle vortex of sparks. As the sparks spiraled downward they shifted and changed, at last hardening into a winding staircase of stars and darkness.

"See," said Mater Marya with a smile, "my son has left you a road, as he has before. Climb now to the Temple Above All Worlds and take up the charge that has been laid before you. He waits for you there!"

A sudden flood of joy welled up in Garin's heart, followed by the deep conviction that he at last had found what he had been searching for his entire life. His eyes brimming with tears, Garin embraced Mater Marya.

"I will go to him," he whispered. "I will answer the call to be the last prophet of He Who Is, and when my work is done I will return here to the Rose."

Turning from Mater Marya, Garin stepped out onto the Sovereign Road and began to climb. Soon the Cosmic Rose vanished beneath him and he was alone in the midst of the sky. Then the sky itself opened up and the world of Numenos fell away.

There were no other worlds left.

Chapter 35: The Final Stand

High-frequency radio waves streamed from the Gog and Magog, activating the countless vacuum sculptors scattered throughout Vai's photosphere. Within each sculptor minuscule laridian rings woke to life and began to pour out streams of virtual matter. Armatures whirled, channeling those streams toward the artificial extradimensional space at the device's cores, and as the virtual matter flux passed the vibrating neutronium filaments the base state of the surrounding vacuum began to change, slowly altering the binding energy of the strong force.

The effect was weak at first, but strengthened steadily as millions of the devices flooded the body of the dead star with altered vacuum. The surface of Vai took on a shimmering, ephemeral quality as the properties of space shifted, and deep within the star's core helium atoms began to overcome their innate electrical repulsion. Driven by pressure and attraction the helium atoms drew closer and closer. But not close enough.

***

Gedron stood on the bridge of the Gog, his eyes fixed on the hologram of Vai. He watched intently as the surface of the star wavered like a desert mirage: silently counting the minutes, waiting for the first faint eruption of fusion fire. Though his emotions were raw he maintained his impassive demeanor. No matter how he felt, he had to play his role to the end. Assuming, of course, that the explosion had disarmed the vacuum sculptors. At last, judging that enough time had elapsed, he raised his hands and called up a diagnostic readout of Vai's current state. Out of the corner of his eye he could see that the Chromatocron and Ouranos Radii had done the same.

Gedron silently examined each parameter: gas density, temperature, gamma ray emissions. The data was consistent with a lack of fusion events. A wave of relief surged through Gedron followed by a backwash of grief and shame. How dare he feel anything now but despair? His daughter and son were gone. Only the certainty that they would want him to carry on gave him enough strength to continue.

"This data is unfortunate…"

The words came from the holographic image of the Ouranos Radii.

"Yes it is," responded the Chromatocron crisply. "It appears the devices have failed."

"So it does," said the Entrope darkly.

Gedron could see the deep suspicion in the Entrope's eyes and tried his best to look discouraged, though he doubted his performance was entirely convincing. After a moment he turned to the hologram of the Magog's bridge and addressed the Ouranos Radii.

"I am not as familiar with the construction of the vacuum sculptors as you. It is possible to reset them for a second attempt?"

"Unfortunately not," replied the Ouranos Radii. "Once the devices are activated the neutronium core filaments rapidly become unstable, a side effect of their interactions with the virtual matter stream. By now the majority of them have almost certainly evaporated. If they have truly failed then a new population must be seeded for a second attempt."

Gedron nodded silently.

"What of the etherreavers?" asked the Chromatocron. "Are they prepared for a second gravitic ignition attempt?"

Gedron turned to a nearby infochryst and called up the glassy, feathered visages of Harut and Marut. There was a brief flurry of data, then Gedron turned to the other heirophants and shook his head.

"Harut and Marut are still in the process of reconstituting the neutronium forge's core programming, and they inform me that at least another several weeks will be needed," he explained. "That effectively rules out the use of gravitics at this time." He paused for a moment, trying his best to appear disappointed before finally adding: "Unfortunately we may be done here."

"Far from it," said the Entrope with more than a hint of iron. "High Gravitist, instruct the etherreavers and worldships to fire a concentric gravitic volley at Vai. Tell them to use the same settings as the first attempt."

A flood of terror swept through Gedron. Though he knew the Entrope had little interest in a successful ignition, he had not expected him to declare his intentions so openly. Quickly gathering his thoughts, Gedron attempted to defuse the situation.

"Entrope, without the neutronium forges we cannot hope to sustain the ignition. Surely the best plan is to wait until we can begin a proper attempt."

The Entrope strode towards Gedron, his face contorted in a sickly smile.

"And yet," he hissed, "we will not take that path. We will instead take the route of action. Instruct the ships to fire a gravitic volley."

"But surely you understand, the etherreavers can only sustain fusion if the ships continue their barrage indefinitely," said Gedron, still fighting to sound calm.

"Such an action will almost certainly generate an entropy storm orders of magnitude greater than anything we have ever experienced."

By now the Entrope was mere feet away from Gedron. His eyes burned with black fury, and his breath reeked with the fetid stench of decay.

"Of course I understand," whispered the Entrope. "Do you understand, High Gravitist? Our universe began billennia ago as a meaningless fluctuation in a cold, dark void, and soon it will end in another cold, dark void. Our consciousness is only an illusion, a thin veneer painted over the primal darkness that is the only true reality. You profess to hold the Axioms of the Conclave and yet seem to persist in the fixed false belief that our existence can somehow have meaning. All is void, High Gravitist, all is darkness, and it is time to pull away the veil. Therefore I will ask you one more time. Instruct the ships to fire!"

At that moment Gedron felt his entire life pivot around him. With terrible clarity he saw the decisions he had made laid out before him like a road, each mile taking him closer to the sterile abyss. He saw also the family he had neglected: his brilliant wife Dyana, Trielle with her incessant desire to know the truth, Garin with his relentless questioning of all he thought false. Then a soft whisper rose from his memory, a phrase spoken in anger by his dead daughter as he had argued his powerlessness to change his path.

Father, whatever you may think, you do have a choice...
And suddenly, he found that he believed her.
"I will not!"

The words rang out from Gedron's mouth with an intensity he would not have thought possible.

"I will not acquiesce to this madness, Entrope! These ships are under my command, and I will not order them to fire."

"Not anymore," whispered the Entrope.

Stepping back, the Entrope spoke so that the whole bridge could hear.

"The High Gravitist has denied the Axioms of the Conclave and has forfeited his right to be named a Heirophant. I hereby take command of this ship. Guards, please escort Gedron from the bridge!"

Three figures in black power armor strode forward, grasped Gedron's arms, and compelled him to step down from the control dais. For a moment he considered resisting, but as if in response to his unspoken thoughts one of the guards drove his energy baton into Gedron's gut. A surge of electrical energy crackled through him and he felt his muscles spasm and go limp.

"Now," said the Entrope a final time, "prepare for the requested gravitic volley."

For a split second the eyes of the gravitic engineers wavered and looked toward their former leader. Then, with a collective sigh, they complied. Commands rang forth from the Gog, broadcast to the fleet on wide-band radio laser. On the great infochrystic displays that ringed the bridge, Gedron could see the telltale glow of gravitic energy building around each etherreaver like an aurora. Crackling azure lightning arced between the irregular spindles of the Magog, and a familiar shudder coursed through the deck beneath him.

"Begin the ignition sequence," said the Entrope, and a million spears of blue fire stabbed toward the dead sun.

They never reached their target.

Gedron stared in shock at the display. He could clearly see the gravitic discharges, each a brilliant blue thread streaming from the ring of etherreavers toward Vai. But, strangely, each thread seemed to terminate thousands of miles from the star's surface. Gedron glanced at the Entrope. His brow was furrowed in confusion, and Gedron watched as he approached the holographic display and raised his hands in a command gesture: shifting and enlarging the area where a particular gravitic discharge terminated. In this view the beam was a torrent of cerulean flame that coursed through Vai's outer corona before striking a translucent golden sphere and dissipating. Then Gedron's eyes widened in surprise. Although his current position did not afford him the best view, he could just make out the glowing form of a man within the golden shell.

"Entrope! Who are they?"

Gedron turned toward the voice and saw Yithra-gor gesturing toward another infochrystic display, a look of terror on his face. His eyes on the display, Gedron watched as the blackness of interplanetary space was lit by a thousand bursts of brilliance. Each was a momentary rift into an impossible realm of perfect light, and through these rifts poured an army of winged creatures wreathed in fire and holding swords that gleamed like fragments of the sun.

"The *Anastasi*..." murmured Gedron with a sudden rush of hope.

The Entrope let out a snarl of rage.

"They have broken the siege," he roared. "I will crush them!"

"No," said a calm voice. "You have broken the truce, not the Sur Ekklesia, and I think you will find us a formidable foe."

A mighty wind filled the bridge followed by a blinding flash as a golden sphere burst into existence. The surface of the sphere shifted into two translucent wings that opened to reveal the shining form of a man in golden armor.

387

In his arms he held a young girl. Gedron's heart leapt when he saw her face.

"Trielle!"

"I'm here father," she said with a smile. "I told you Anacrysis would protect me."

"Seize the *Anastasi*!"

The angry roar of the Entrope quelled the joy of their reunion and Gedron watched as five of the guards rushed Anacrysis, their energy batons extended. But Anacrysis simply folded his wings in front of him like a protective shield, and the batons had no effect. After several failed attempts to subdue the *Anastasi* the guards changed their approach, surrounding him and Trielle instead.

"Creature! Traitor to your race!" roared the Entrope. "You have no idea what you have unleashed by interfering here. For ages I have been content to let your kind dwell in peace within the vales of En-Ka-Re so long as you did not trouble the greater workings of the Conclave, but now you have changed that. Did you somehow think to take us by surprise and free your people? Did you imagine that mechanisms were not in place to raze En-Ka-Re if even one of you dared show your face? Even now the laridian rings that surround your vale are charging for the assault that will end the lives of the *Alapsari* under your care. Your actions this day have condemned them."

Anacrysis laughed. "Condemned them more that your actions here? Do you think we are fools, that we have no way of knowing what is happening in the greater world? Your deeds this day condemn us all, Conclave and Ekklesia alike. No, Ronath, it is you who have broken the siege. Look around you and see that, even now, we do not attack. All we do it block the effect of your beams."

At the mention of his name the Entrope cringed.

"What?" laughed Anacrysis. "Did you not think we knew who you were? You forget the origin of our name then: *Anastasi*, the Risen Ones. You have died a thousand deaths alone and afraid in your secret chambers, Ronath Larid, in an effort to bring the cosmos with you. We have only died once but now live in the power of Life Himself, and death has no more dominion over us. Even those of the Ekklesia that have yet to die do not fear it, for death has lost its sting for all who dwell within her. No, we are not the prisoners here, but rather the people of the Conclave, whom you are your fellow Heirophants have kept in darkness for millennia. Now come, cease the gravitic volley."

"Oh, I think I will continue just a little while longer," said the Entrope smoothly. "You are right about one thing, creature. The Conclave is ours! It is ours to give it life and, when the time is right, ours to usher it into the darkness of the void. And, in the name of all those that do not wish to live in your insipid Dar Ekklesia, I declare that the time is now! Observe, creature! Your blockade is irrelevant."

Turning from Anacrysis, the Entrope gestured and the scope of the hologram changed, expanding outward until the whole of the Conclave of Worlds could be seen. Immediately Gedron understood.

"The entropy clouds…" he whispered.

The sheer force of the gravitic volley had profoundly destabilized the clouds, precipitating a storm far greater than anything Gedron had ever seen before. Their surfaces seethed with green flame, and sinuous prominences burst from their depths like hungry dragons, shredding planets to atoms in their wake. The storm's fury continued to grow until at last the entropy clouds erupted in a hurricane of poisonous green light, a cyclone of annihilation that

389

crashed down upon the worlds of the Conclave with relentless force.

"You see?" laughed the Entrope. "There is no possibility of stalemate here. Even if your army were to destroy our entire armada, the amount of virtual bosons already released by this last volley is enough to terminally destabilize the clouds. This cosmos is sick! Sick with the false delusion of its own existence! It is time to reject that lie. The people of the Conclave came from nothing, travel to nothing, and today, will become nothing again!"

Though Anacrysis' wings were still wrapped around Trielle like a shield, Gedron could see them droop slightly.

He knew the Entrope was right. Nothing less than a new source of solar wind could stop the storms now. He had taken his stand too late and now would lose everything. Everyone would lose everything.

"Garin is coming father… I know he is…"

Gedron heard the faint whisper of Trielle's voice, but had no faith left to believe her.

Book Six: And the Morning Come One More Day...

Chapter 36: Brightness of Uncreated Light

All worlds far behind him, Garin climbed the upper slopes of the cosmic mountain. The road was steep now, a sheer incline of crimson stars and deep darkness that cut back and forth in a series of sharp switchbacks. Flashes of lightning and crescendos of deep thunder blasted continually from the summit above, and the face of the mountain rumbled beneath in counterpoint. He was weary but climbed onward, propelled by the conviction that time was growing short.

As he drew near the summit a strange light began to shine around him, as if all creation was slowly catching fire. Then, after a near-vertical ascent that taxed the limits of his strength, Garin pulled himself over the final ledge. He had arrived; from here all directions were down.

Before him stood the Temple Above all Worlds, a vast cube of gold easily taller than the Arx Scientia. Its smooth surface burned with barely concealed brilliance, as if a source of light so bright that even solid metal could not stand in its way lay within. Two broad pillars stood in front of the structure, each carved in intricate relief with scenes from across the five worlds below. The Sovereign Road, now level, ran between these pillars to a tall gate set into the shining wall. The doors were ajar, and from within issued a music of such strength and majesty that he felt his bones would break beneath its force. As he listened, Garin realized that this was the source of the thundering he had heard as he climbed.

A sudden fear welled up within his breast. Surely there were things within that man was not meant to see. Surely he would die beneath the weight of their glory. Yet still his resolve held. He had come this far and would not turn back now. Garin strode forward and, with trembling hands, opened the door and entered.

The glory within was blinding, a light so bright that it shone through Garin's skin and bones as if they were glass. He stood upon a pavement of sapphire broken only by a great altar burning with seven flames that outshone the stars. At the end of the pavement was a throne of purest diamond, and the One that sat on the throne, the source of the radiance of that place, struck such terror into Garin's heart that he thought it would burst. Language did not have words to describe what he saw...

The form of a man, seemingly chiseled from pure unadulterated brilliance.

A cloud of darkness so deep that it burned with a radiant luminosity.

A pillar of consuming fire hot enough to reduce creation to ashes.

Around the throne circled ten thousand times ten thousand living creatures, each bearing forms that made the appearance of Metatron and Sandalphon in the world beneath seem common, and as they flew they all cried aloud to the One who sat on the throne, their voices joining in the thunderous chorus Garin first heard outside the temple.

"HOLY, HOLY, HOLY IS THE EVER-LIVING ONE; WHO WAS, AND IS, AND IS TO COME."

Before the throne stood Kyr, the woman still held in his arms.

"Father, isn't she beautiful..."

At once a voice sounded from the throne, a voice so pure and vast that Garin could no longer stand under its weight, and he fell down as one dead. For a long while he knew nothing, then he felt a hand on his shoulder.

"Rise, my son."

Garin opened his eyes and saw the luminous form of Kyr standing over him. As he stood, he noticed that the room seemed somehow darker. The burning Presence still sat on the throne, but now a thick cloud was interposed between them, shielding him from the intolerable light. The woman was nowhere to be seen.

"My Father and I have veiled our glory so that you might stand and live," said Kyr. "Now come, we have much to speak about."

"Where is your Beloved?" asked Garin. "I saw you carry her to the throne?"

Kyr laughed. "You have traveled long, but still do not know what it is you have seen. Have you not looked at yourself since you entered the domain of the Uncreated One?"

Garin looked downward and saw that he was clothed in robes of purest white, the same robes worn by the Beloved.

"I... I don't understand," said Garin in confusion.

"I know, my child," said Kyr gently, "but you soon will. You will see both who I am, and who you are. Now, are you ready for one last journey?"

Garin looked at Kyr's face and saw a joy that he had only known before in brief glimpses. Confidence surged within him, and with newfound strength he said, "Yes, I am ready."

"Then take my hand," said Kyr.

Garin took it, and the world around them vanished.

***

He was swimming in a limitless ocean of fire. All around him, above and beneath, blazing currents rolled with unearthly force. Yet, curiously, he felt no fear. Though the flames enveloped him with all their raging fury he was not burned. Rather, they caressed him with inviting warmth, flowing into him and kindling new life within his body. It was as if he had been waiting to enter this sea his entire life.

Then he perceived two great shapes swimming in the sea with him: one ponderous and old as the mountains, one bright and new as the sunrise. Words of fire issued from the swimmers: blazing syllables that rolled from their tongues, their movements, their very beings. And though it was expressed a thousand different ways, in the end all the words said the same thing.

My life for yours…

As Garin listened in wonder he saw that the endless conversation between the swimmers was the source of the ocean in which he swam. Each current, each movement of the endless fiery deep was a synonym, a story, another way for them to pour out their life and love to each other. In the same moment of understanding he also perceived another presence within the waves, every bit as vast and powerful as the swimmers yet somehow concealed behind and beneath the powerful currents. And between the three, at the very heart of their endless movement of outpoured life, stood a point of pure stillness that transcended all understanding, a tranquil eye in the midst of the infinite storm of love.

"Now you begin to understand," whispered a voice. *"But there us yet more to see. Come…"*

Garin felt a rush of upward movement and in a flash of fiery spray broke through the surface of the waves. As he swam forward he felt the sea bottom rise beneath him, and soon was standing on a great shoal, the flaming waters ebbing and flowing around his feet. With him on the shoal was an old man. His hair was as white as snow and a long beard trailed from his face. He was clothed in a white robe, its hem streaked with red stains from the fiery water, and his eye burned with unquenchable fire.

Wading beside the old man was a white-robed boy not much older than Garin. His hair was a rich black, and his face wore a joyful smile. Something about him seemed familiar to Garin, though he could not say what. As Garin watched the pair stopped, faced each other, and embraced with such vehement affection that he thought his heart would break.

"*My life for yours, my Son,*" said the old man.

"*And mine for yours, Father,*" replied the boy.

As the boy spoke Garin's eyes widened in sudden recognition.

"Kyr?" he whispered.

The boy smiled at him briefly, then turned to the old man.

"*Come Father, there is something I would show you.*"

The boy took the old man by the hand and led him toward a dark ribbon that coursed along the shoal's far edge. Garin followed, and the ribbon soon resolved into a swift current, its fiery waters laced with streaks of shadow. When the boy reached the edge of the shoal, he knelt down and pointed into the dark, churning waters.

"*My Son,*" said the old man gravely, "*all our desires are as one, for we both wish to breathe our being into the currents that surround us and give our love form and shape. But of all the currents in the infinite sea you have chosen the hardest.*"

"*I know, Father,*" said the boy. "*But look within. Can you see her? I love her Father!*"

Garin peered into the current and saw within the fire and darkness the face of the Beloved. Scars crossed her face and dirt soiled her skin, but a strange beauty still shone through.

397

"There is beauty in this world-current, but there is also pain," said the old man. *The one you love will hate you, despise you, reject you! In this world, my Son, you will be murdered by those you have made. Is this truly what you desire?"*

"I know all this," said the boy with a sigh, *"but I love her even as I love you. Even now I see all that she will do to me and yet I love her still; not because of who she is, but because of who I am."*

The boy paused for a moment, as if carefully considering his next words, then turned to the old man and spoke.

"I will enter this world Father. I will create it, love it, and die for it. And in the end I will bring my Beloved to you, Father, for I can think of no greater gift. From before always you have poured out your life for me, now it is time that I pour out my life for her, and in so doing pour out my life for you!"

The pair stood in silence for what seemed like an eternity, then a gentle tear rolled down the old man's cheek and he spoke.

"My Son, in you I am truly well pleased. Go, and bring many with you to glory."

The boy smiled, turned, and plunged into the current.

Then the scene changed again, and Garin found himself beside the boy as he dove deeper and deeper into the darkness. Down they went, far below the bright surface of the sea into the cold depths where nothing can live. The burning water seemed to open and unfold around them as they descended, until at last they hung in the heart of an icy void. With deliberate movements the boy stretched out his arms, took a deep breath, and cried out at the top of his lungs in a voice wracked with pain.

"LET THERE BE LIGHT!"

The last thing Garin saw as the vision faded was a drop of blood falling from each of the boy's hands into the now brilliant darkness.

***

"Do you now understand?"

The words shook Garin from his reverie and brought him to himself. He was back in the Temple with Kyr by his side.

"Somewhat," said Garin slowly, pondering what he had just witnessed.

"Mortal minds can not truly comprehend that which transpired between me and my father before times flowed," said Kyr. "But what I have shown you is an image, an eidolon, of that which passed between us in that far off age, and of what passes between us still."

Garin fell to his knees, overwhelmed by the sudden knowledge of whom he was speaking to.

"My Lord!" he cried out. "My Lord and my God!"

"You are right to give me those titles," said Kyr with a smile. "Indeed, you have called me Lord ever since we met, for the name I gave you in the streets of Scintillus means master in the ancient tongue of the Ekklesia. But I also have another name. In the depths of time, on a dark world, I gave myself to renew the life of the cosmos, and the time is soon coming when the cosmos will burst forth with the fruit of that life. When that day comes all will call me redeemer, and know me as I am. Do you believe this?"

"Yes," said Garin. "Ever since I dreamed of the map I have wanted to believe, but now that I have seen you as you are, I know the words you speak are true."

"Before that day arrives," continued Kyr, "a final time of repentance will be offered to the people of Phaneros.

For millennia now the Conclave has oppressed my Beloved, my Ekklesia. They have borne it with grace and dignity, waiting patiently for a time when my story can again be spoken among the worlds so that the people of the Conclave might understand, and in understanding turn and believe. But even now a battle rages within the heart of Phaneros, a battle that, if lost, will prevent this time from coming, leaving the souls of all within the Conclave imprisoned in the darkness."

As Kyr spoke, tears began rolling down his face.

"I love them, Garin," he said. "I love them so much. And now I ask if you will go for me? Will you return to Phaneros and be my last prophet, paving the way for the final restoration of all things?"

"I will," said Garin without hesitation, "though I do not know the words to say."

"Do not fear," said Kyr. "I will place my Spirit, the fiery ocean of love that burned between me and my Father before all worlds, within you. He will give you the words. Now, are you ready to receive this power, and this charge?"

"Yes," said Garin.

"Then stand fast before the throne," said Kyr.

All at once the veil was torn away and the glory of the Uncreated One burst upon Garin like a searing wind from the mouth of a blast furnace. Then the blazing form on the throne before him rose, and Garin heard words proceed from the heart of the fire.

"WHOM SHALL I SEND, AND WHO SHALL GO FOR US?"

"Here am I," said Garin. "Send me."

"THEN LET THE FLAME OF OUR SPIRIT TOUCH YOUR LIPS SO THAT YOU MAY BE PURIFIED AND EMPOWERED FOR THE TASK THAT LIES AHEAD."

As the words echoed through the temple one of the living creatures, a six winged dragon with scales of golden fire, flew from the throne to the seven-flamed altar. Taking a live coal in its hand, the creature flew to Garin and touched it to his lips and his forehead. A wave of searing pain surged through Garin's body, followed by an inrush of power so intense that he felt as if he would burst.

"GO!" thundered the Uncreated One. "GO AND BE OUR VOICE IN A TIME THAT HAS FORGOTTEN US."

"Yes," said Kyr. "Go, and herald the sunrise of a new morning."

Garin bowed deeply toward the throne, then turned toward the temple door and began to walk away. He knew he had a long journey ahead of him.

"My son," said Kyr, "where are you going?"

"To fulfill my mission," said Garin in confusion. "I must reach Phaneros before I can begin."

Kyr laughed.

"My child, in this place all worlds are present. The Great 'hedron, the Cube of Cubes, the Mount of Sacrifice, even the worlds of the Conclave are but a step away. Behold."

Kyr gestured to his left and the air beside him shimmered and parted, revealing the bridge of a worldship. The scene was chaotic. His father hung limply between two guards in black power armor. Trielle was there also, enfolded in the wings of glorious creature unlike any he had ever seen before. The cloaked figure of the Entrope stood proudly at the center, his arms outstretched in a gesture of command. And at its very edge, where the polished gold of the bridge met the glistening sapphire of the temple floor, rose a tall doorframe made of stars and darkness: the

401

terminus of the Sovereign Road. Taking a deep breath,
Garin walked forward and stepped through.

Chapter 37: A New Sunrise

"Entrope, over a hundred worlds have been lost thus far."

"Excellent," replied the Entrope. "Continue the barrage at the current intensity."

The expression on Yithra-Gor's face was one of abject despair, a mirror of Gedron's own emotions. Only a few moments ago the Entrope had instructed him to give a running update on the storms' progress. Yithra-Gor had reflexively looked to Gedron for assistance as he had done so many times in the past, but, held captive by the Entrope's guard, there was little Gedron could do.

Across the bridge Gedron could see the ring of guards surrounding Anacrysis. He knew that the *Anastasi* could easily overpower them had he been alone. With Trielle to protect, however, he was effectively trapped as well. And even if one of them could have broken free it was too late to stop the storms. In less than an hour they would reach the Guard, and, soon after, the inner worlds. All hope gone, Gedron closed his eyes and waited for the end.

"No, Entrope! You will not continue!"

Gedron's eyes snapped open. The voice seemed strangely familiar, yet rang with an intensity Gedron had never heard before. The Entrope quickly turned about in rage.

"Who dares gainsay me?"

"I do."

Gedron watched as a glowing crack appeared in the air to his right. The crack swiftly widened, opening like a door into a space filled with almost palpable brilliance. In the midst of the light Gedron could just make out the faint silhouette of a boy, and as the form stepped through the door and the light faded Gedron's eyes widened in surprise and joy.

"Garin!"

"Who is this?" said the Entrope in confusion and rage.

"My son, Entrope!" said Gedron with pride,

Garin turned to the Entrope, raising his right hand in a gesture of authority and strength.

"Entrope, hear the words of the Ever-Living One. Too long have you oppressed the people of the Sur Ekklesia, and this day your evil has become complete. Therefore you and your servants will be bound that the cosmos may have a measure of freedom before the end."

"You have no power over me," snarled the Entrope. "Guards, escort this child from the bridge."

The guards holding Gedron abruptly released him and he collapsed to the floor. As he watched them advance on Garin a sudden burst of determination filled him. He would not let them hurt his son. Taking a deep breath, Gedron struggled to his feet. Then Garin looked at him, smiled, and shook his head.

"Don't be afraid, Father. I can handle this."

Stretching out his right hand, Garin fixed the guards with a hard, piercing stare and gave a simple command.

"Stop!"

It was as if the guards had struck an invisible barrier. Though they struggled with all their strength, writhing and twisting in an effort to obey their master, they could not break through. Garin nodded and turned back to the Entrope, a grim look on his face.

"You say I have no power over you," said Garin. "Yet I tell you this day that you would have no power at all unless it was given as a gift by the Most High. Today, that gift is revoked."

Then Garin's eyes softened, and his next words were spoken in a gentle, almost pleading whisper.

"There is still hope for you, Entrope. I have been to the other worlds. I have seen your master defeated by Love Himself, and I come here to offer that love to the Conclave. Now, I offer it to you. Renounce your current path! Even you are not beyond redemption."

"If I am not beyond redemption then I hereby cast myself past its reach," hissed the Entrope. "I do not want your love. I desire only oblivion, an oblivion that will soon consume us all."

The Entrope turned as he spoke, glancing toward Yithra-Gor in a silent question.

"Another fifty worlds have been lost," he whispered.

The Entrope turned back to Garin with a wicked smile and said nothing more.

Garin sighed.

"You leave me no choice, Entrope."

Again he raised his right hand, this time extending it toward the Entrope, and the words that came from his mouth struck with the force of a meteor.

"Because you have spurned the offer of redemption you will be cast out of the life of the Conclave, imprisoned by the power of this decree in the dungeon you call your home for one hundred years, until the last times of the Ekklesia have come to completion."

The Entrope lunged at Garin with a roar, but his feet remained rooted in place. His face twisted in rage, and he cursed and spat at Garin.

"Go now," said Garin softly. "Leave this place."

The Entrope's every muscle tensed with resistance, but he could no more disobey the force of that command than he could the law of gravity. With slow, tense steps, the Entrope and his guards marched off the bridge and soon were gone.

"Father," said Garin, "there is much I need to tell you, but there will be time for that later."

"Perhaps not," said Anacrysis grimly as he stared at the holographic images of the entropy storms. "I know of nothing that can stop what the Entrope has unleashed."

"Garin, what can we do?" said Trielle. Gedron could see the fear in her eyes.

"Trielle, you believed in me as much as you could, even when I thought I might be mad," said Garin. "Hold onto that faith just a little while longer."

With measured steps, Garin ascended the control dais and turned to Gedron.

"Can you open a visual channel to the rest of the ships?" he asked.

"Garin, this ship can broadcast to the entire Conclave," said Gedron.

"Even better," said Garin with a smile.

Still weak from the shocks of the energy batons, Gedron staggered to a nearby infochryst and motioned for Yithra-Gor to join him. The pair worked feverishly, and after a few moments a ring of holographic images drawn from all the worlds of the Conclave sprang to life around Garin. Garin surveyed the images, briefly taking stock of each, then raised his hands in an ancient gesture of declamation and began to speak.

"People of the Conclave, I am Garin, son of Gedron Donar, High Gavitist of the Conclave. Not long ago I thought as you do, and my life centered on my own selfish desires. But I was given a glimpse of something more: the possibility that there might be realms beyond this dying cosmos in which we dwell, the possibility that the

406

world itself is rich with a meaning beyond that which we impose. I have come now to tell you that these are not mere possibilities, but the truth."

"Our world, our cosmos, is no accident, but was created in love by Love Himself. Yet in our selfishness we have denied Him at every turn. When He first came to us on Sha-Ka-Ri we slaughtered Him, and when He again came to us as Lord of the Dar Eklesia we made war on Him, banishing His people to a lonely moon circling a forsaken brown dwarf. And yet His love for us has not diminished. Again he calls for us to lay down our selfishness, our Axioms, everything that we have used to shield us from Himself, and receive our lives anew in return. For a day is soon coming when the cosmos as we know it will end and a new creation break forth newly minted from its ashes. I ask you now, when that last day comes on whose side will you stand? One hundred years will be given to you to make this choice."

As Gedron heard the words his heart was stirred to life. Then he looked again at the image of the entropy storms and a wave of doubt and despair crashed over him, drowning his newborn faith.

One hundred years? The storms will reach Scintillus within hours.

Suddenly he realized that Garin was looking at him, and he raised his eyes to meet his son's. Their gaze locked for a few moments, then Garin turned back to the ring of holograms and spoke.

"For many of you my words have created nothing but inner turmoil. You want to believe that there is something beyond the walls of space and time. You want to know that the hope I hold out is real and not just an illusion with which to pass the time until the final death of the cosmos. But you see the storm that rages around us, a storm that threatens to extinguish all life in the Conclave and, ultimately, you do not know whether I can be trusted. Therefore, I ask you this. What is more probable? That a new creation will be born after the world in which we live passes away, or that a boy can speak to a dead star and command it to burn!"

For long moments no one moved on the bridge. No one dared to. Then Yithra-Gor bent down to examine a nearby infochryst.

"High Gravitist! Look!"

The infochryst displayed the relative mix of helium and hydrogen within Vai's core. Gedron frowned. The values were changing rapidly.

"Something must be wrong," said Yithra-Gor.

"No," said Gedron with a sudden burst of excitement, "There is nothing wrong here. Yithra, order the fleet to stop the barrage and retreat to a safe perimeter. Two million miles from Vai should be adequate."

With slow steps Gedron ascended the control dais to stand beside his son. He looked to his left. The holographic connection with the Magog was still active.

"Chromatocron," said Gedron, "I would advise that you move your worldship to a safe distance. Check the core readings from Vai if you wish to know the reason."

With a wave of his hand he dismissed the hologram and called up a realtime image of Vai.

***

Deep within the core of the dead star a light began to burn, a crack in the surface of the cosmos leading to the worlds beyond. And from those worlds poured a fresh influx of hydrogen gas, the primal element of creation.

408

Higher and higher the concentrations rose, until at last a critical threshold was reached.

And Vai's core ignited.

The first prominence pierced the star's photosphere as the last of the etherreavers reached a safe perimeter, a brilliant arc of searing flame that leaped from the swirling plasma into the corona and crashed down millions of miles away. A few moments later there was another, and then a third. A billion blinding flares of light erupted across the photosphere as white-hot supergranulations flashed through the surface. The photosphere grew brighter and brighter as the temperature increased until, in a rush of golden incandescence, the plasma burst into flame, showering the Conclave with living sunlight.

***

Far above, in the Sepulcher of Suns, Hyperion Starfather knelt at the bed of his dying child. Beside him stood Vasya and Verduun, holding bread and wine in their aged hands. Suddenly Vai's eyes snapped open, their once dull surfaces flaring a brilliant gold. A nimbus of bright rainbows surrounded him, and in a wash of silver light the lines of age fled from his face like shadows before daybreak. With a shout he leaped from the bed, his youth restored.

Hyperion stood, a broad, glad smile on his face. Calling to his sons, he raised his voice in a mighty hymn of thankfulness. The night was not yet over, but now there was a brightness on the horizon.

The dawn would soon be here.

***

Gedron gazed in wonder as Vai burned with new brilliance. What once was a dead star was now brighter and more vibrant than its brothers. A broad smile grew on his face as he gloried in the light.

"High Gravitist, the entropy storm is abating."

Gedron turned toward Yithra-Gor and nodded.

"Yes, the renewed solar wind should be enough to hold back the entropy clouds." He paused for a moment, remembering Garin's words.

"At least," he said at last, "for a little while."

Calling Trielle to his side, Gedron knelt before his children.

"I need to apologize to you both," he said as tears ran down his face. "I have spend most of my life pursuing my own goals, but you have showed me a better way. I only hope that it is not too late to start again."

"There is time, Father," said Garin with a smile. "He has given us all time."

Then Garin turned toward the images of the Conclave that still circled the bridge, and his smile faded, replaced by a thoughtful, pensive look.

"I only hope," he said at last, "that the races of the Conclave see that time for the gift that it is."

Chapter 38: And the Rough Places Made Plain

Two days later Trielle stood beneath the glittering spire of the Arx Scientia with Garin at her side. The three suns shone steadily in the sky above. Crowds of students thronged around them as they headed to their classes. Not too long ago Trielle would have been among them, but no longer. Now she had a higher calling.

She watched as the endless sea of faces swept past her brother. Most seemed to recognize him but from there the expressions changed. Some smiled in admiration, some glanced away in confusion, many bore looks of outright hostility.

"It seems prophets have never been accepted in their hometown," said Garin with a wry smile. "Or at least, that is what I've heard."

"Who told you that?" asked Trielle.

"I read it in an old book," said Garin. "I'll tell you more about it someday, but right now there is too much to do."

Trielle studied Garin. It was as if he were a different person. She understood. One simply could not see what she had on En-Ka-Re and remain unchanged, and from what Garin had told her of his journey his experiences had been far stranger. Even now he would not tell her everything. She suspected that some of what he had encountered simply could not be put into words.

"Let's go Trielle," said Garin. "It's time to begin."

"May I go with you?"

Trielle turned toward the voice and saw her father emerge from the crowd. For the first time in weeks he was

411

not dressed in his formal robes. Then she noticed that he was smiling. He seemed almost relaxed, as if a vast burden had been lifted from his shoulders.

"Aren't you needed at the College today?" she asked.

"I would be, if I were still High Gravitist," he said. "I was released from my duties this morning by the Chromatocron and the Ouranos Radii. Yithra-Gor now bears the mantle of office. But even if it had not been taken from me, I confess I would have given it up. There are more important things to do now."

Trielle nodded. Though she knew how much work it had taken her father to gain that position, she could not deny the relief she felt. "So," she said at last, "where are we going, Garin?"

"Tyr-Fell," replied Garin. "I received word last night from the *Anastasi* that many from the outer worlds have gathered there.

A puzzled expression crossed Gedron's face.

"Tyr-Fell? Why there?"

"I'm not sure, exactly," said Garin. "The *Anastasi* told me its name means 'Hill of the War God' in one of the ancient tongues. They said it reminded them of a place they had known long ago on Sha-Ka-Ri."

Gedron nodded and began to walk in the direction of the Kinetorium.

"No, father," said Garin sternly. "I will not use the devices of the enemy to accomplish my mission. Besides, we have better means of travel."

Gedron turned and looked at Garin, a bewildered expression on his face.

"Chronocrys, Ramiel, Shardash, we're ready," said Garin loudly.

A sudden gale blew through the crowds, followed by a burst of light which faded to reveal three golden spheres. Then the spheres unfolded, becoming the winged forms of three *Anastasi*.

"Come, Garin," said Chronocrys with a smile. "The crowds wait to hear your words."

A female *Anastasi* approached Trielle.

"I am Ramiel, and this is Shardash" she said, gesturing to the third figure. "We will take you and your father to Tyr-Fell if you wish, but I must warn you that our method of travel can be somewhat disconcerting."

"It's all right," said Trielle with a smile. "I've done this before."

Ramiel nodded, then folded her golden wings about Trielle. There was a lurch, followed by a sudden sense of flight, and the universe vanished beneath her. When the shining wings opened a few moments later they stood in the heart of the deserts of Tyr-Fell.

One of the innermost of the rim worlds, Trielle was surprised it had survived the entropy storms. Windswept dunes punctuated by low stunted bushes and outcroppings of yellow stone stretched as far as she could see. A deep blue-black sky rose from the horizon to her right, only to be stopped in the midst of the heavens by the seething green wall of the entropy clouds. And all around her were the multitudes. Representative of almost every race in the Conclave, they had gathered here to hear her brother.

Suddenly overwhelmed by the task before them, Trielle gazed upward, tracing the arc made by the edge of the entropy clouds with her eyes.

It's somewhat like the Conclave, I suppose, she mused. *The line between light and dark runs through each one of us.*

A burst of wind and a flash of light announced the arrival of Garin and her father. As they stepped out from

413

the protective confines of the *Anastasis'* wings Trielle saw the mingled wonder and surprise on her father's face and laughed. Then she looked over at Garin. His eyes swept back and forth, silently surveying the crowd, and his features were clouded with an expression of deep concern. Her father evidently noticed as well, for he walked over to Garin and put his arm around his shoulder. Trielle could barely hear his whispered question.

"There are so many, son. What will you tell them?"

Garin paused for a moment, then turned to Gedron with shining eyes.

"I will tell them the story, Father: the story that the world tells itself."

Trielle watched with pride as Garin took a deep breath, climbed atop a nearby rock, and began to preach.

Epilogue:

     I write this treatise, O Theophilus, to give an account of the things that have taken place among us at the time of the Apocatastasis. Though none of us are now subject to death or decay, each year more and more come into existence who did not live through that terrible time. I thus write this record in the hope that those who did not experience it might read, and in reading, understand.

     In the decades following the rekindling of Vai, Garin and his family grew in strength and honor as prophets of the Most High. To them was given the charge to travel the final remnants of the old universe and tell the story of He Who Is, calling the people of all worlds to faith. It was a noble task, and many were won to the light. Yet the day came when the hundred years had past and Garin Donar was taken by death and assumed his throne in eternity. Those were dark times indeed, for the Entrope was loosed and allowed again to make war on the Ekklesia.

     The conflict was universal in extent. Many perished, and as the battles raged on the last stars were extinguished one by one, victims of the Entrope's weapons. Without their strength the entropy clouds could no longer be held at bay, and fiery storms swept across the dying Conclave. Soon all that was left of the Cosmos was the world of En-Ka-Re and a few lone asteroids. It was there, in the remains of the valley in which we had been imprisoned, that the last survivors of the Ekklesia gathered to make their final stand.

     I remember it well. A great mass of refugees huddled in the center of the plain, surrounded by the weapons of the Entrope. The skies above pulsed with billowing masses of putrid green fire, almost close enough to

415

touch. Then the Entrope himself ascended the mountain ridge and commanded that the last of our number be exterminated before the descent of universal night. I will not deny that we felt fear then, but as one we grasped the hands of those beside us, denied that fear, and prepared to die with a hymn of praise on our lips. It was then that He came.

The purity of His presence shone in the tortured skies like a newborn star. His robes seemed to be woven of light itself. A brilliant rainbow encircled him, its color as green as emerald, and his face burned like metal in a forge. He did not say a word, but stretched out his hand, and all at once His bride stood beside him. Then, in a way that to this day remains a mystery to me, she changed. Her form shone with a glory beyond anything I have ever seen or will see again, and when at last it abated a mighty city stood in her place: Hyrosol Neos, the City of the Most High.

It was shaped like a vast cube many hundreds of miles to a side, with walls of gold and foundations of precious gems. Its gates were open, and we watched in wonder as the shining form of He Who Is, Son of He Who Is strode to the threshold and shouted with words like thunder: "BEHOLD, I MAKE ALL THINGS NEW!"

In rage the Entrope ordered his minions to turn the might of their laridian rings upon the city, and a thousand spears of crackling blue fire rained down upon her. But the city shone with new light, and a tidal wave of golden radiance burst from her walls, dispelling the gravitic discharges like shadows in sunlight. I still remember the feeling as the light washed over me, a strange sense of dissolusion and recreation, as if the pattern that was my body and soul had somehow been lifted from my physical form and inscribed upon the fabric of the universe at a deeper level.

416

The golden light coursed through the valley, and I watched it change those of the Ekklesia as it had changed me. Then I saw real fear in the Entrope's eyes. Calling his servants to himself, The Entrope ordered one last, desperate attack. But within seconds the light swept over them and they dissolved into mist and were no more. At last the light reached the entropy clouds, and for an instant the golden wave hesitated, the forces of destruction fighting to contain the power of creation. Then, with a sound like the shattering of a world, the entropy clouds burst into a million shards of dissipating green fire and we gazed in awe at the ancient sky as one by one the stars came out.

Of life in the new creation you know well, O Theophilus. Our very being is written on the fabric of space and time itself, where neither death nor sickness can reach. The speed of light is no longer a barrier and the galaxy is ours to explore and inhabit, though each of us regards Hyrosol Neos as our true home. And still the great golden wave travels onward. Scholars speak of a time when it will reach our neighboring galaxies, and then we will have access to them as we do to our own. Yet amidst all these marvels our greatest joy is the simple knowledge that our lives have meaning and that we are loved. For those of us that remember the old order, when selfishness and pride dominated our hearts, such knowledge will always be precious. May it remain precious to you as well.

Yours in the Bonds of the Most High:

Yithra-Gor
1023rd Year of the New Creation

…and there shall be no more death, neither sorrow, nor crying, neither shall there be anymore pain: for the former things are passed away. And he that sat upon the throne said, "Behold, I make all things new."

-Revelation 21:4b-5a KJV

Glossary:

Axioms: The basic philosophical principles of Conclave metaphysics. The Axioms are typically expressed as three interrelated phrases: matter gives rise to consciousness, consciousness gives rise to meaning, and meaning is subject and subordinate to consciousness. The corollary of these principles is that meaning is imposed by conscious organisms on the physical universe and thus is not an intrinsic property of the cosmos.

Conclave of Ten Thousand Worlds: The Conclave is all that is left of the galaxy: 97,943 worlds arranged in a complex spiral of gravitically stabilized orbits within a 65,450 cubic light-minute volume. Conclave space is bounded by the entropy clouds and centered on the three suns, the last stars in the universe. The term "Conclave" is also used to refer to the society that has grown on these worlds and to their government, much as the name of a country can refer to the land as well as the people. They are ruled by a technocracy known as the Five Heirophants.

> College of Gravitists: The largest body of stellar engineers and gravitic scientists in the Conclave. Under the direction of the High Gravitist, the College of Gravitists oversee all orbital and stellar engineering projects and maintain the laridian ring network. They are based in the Arx Scientia and the Omegahedron.

> The Guard: A ring of brown dwarfs that orbit at a distance halfway between the three suns and the entropy clouds. Although not true stars, their combined particle

421

emissions are enough to partially stall the advance of the clouds. The guard is meant to be the last defence and protection of the inner worlds of the Conclave should the suns begin to fail.

Latis: Innermost planet and capital of the Conclave of Ten Thousand Worlds. Latis orbits closest to the three suns and is tidally locked, with one side bathed in perpetual noon. Its largest city, Scintillus, is the hub of Conclave government and science.

En-Ka-Re: A small world orbiting one of the brown dwarfs that make up the Guard. The surface of En-Ka-Re is pockmarked with craters from ancient wars. The world has no atmosphere except within the valley in which the Sur Ekklesia is imprisoned.

Entropy Clouds: The manifestation of a runaway cosmological constant, the entropy clouds surround Conclave space and threaten to destroy what is left of the cosmos. The mere touch of an entropy cloud induces the spontaneous unbinding of all physical forces, causing the affected material to explosively decompose into its component particles. At present the entropy clouds are held back by the radiation pressure and stellar wind of the three suns, with a lesser contribution by the brown dwarfs of the Guard.

Sha-Ka-Ri: An abandoned world at the edge of Conclave space, Sha-Ka-Ri is the first world of humanity and in ages past was called Terra and Urth. The Sovereign Road begins here in the heart of a dead city.

Vai: One of the three suns. Vai is one of the last stars in the universe. It is the first of the three to reach the end of its lifespan.

Vasya: One of the three suns. Vasya is one of the last stars in the universe.

Verduun: One of the three suns. Verduun is one of the last stars in the universe.

Voidstars: Conclave term for black holes. As gravitational singularities, voidstars represent the only form of matter immune to the entropy clouds.

The Cosmic Mountain: The great peak of folded multidimensional timespace that upholds the worlds. The mountain arises from the abyss of Tehom, and, at its summit, is crowned by the Temple Above All Worlds. The Sovereign Road travels up the length of the mountain, beginning at the lowest world, Phaneros, and ending at the Temple.

Arethos: The fourth world in the ascent of the Cosmic Mountain, Arethos is the world of virtue and formal causes. It is also called the Cube of Cubes by its inhabitants, the beings called the Arethoi. Notable locations include the domains of the Arethoi and the Abyss.

Materia: The second world in the ascent of the Cosmic Mountain, Materia is the source and wellspring of physical law and is the world of material causes. Also called the Great 'hedron by its inhabitants. Notable locations include the Peak of the Third Glory and the Xaocosmic Border.

Mythos: The third world in the ascent of the Cosmic Mountain, Mythos is the source of story and temporal flow and is the world of instrumental causes. It is structured in a series of concentric rings traversed by narrative arcs made visible called meridians. Notable locations are the House of Hyperion Starfather in the Sepulcher of Suns, the Mare Primum, the ancient city of Hyrosol Eld, the Shattered Temple, and the Mount of Sacrifice.

Numenos: The fifth and highest world in the ascent of the Cosmic Mountain, Numenos is the source of order and direction and is the world of final causes. It is divided between the City Imperishable and the Cosmic Rose.

Phaneros: The lowest world on the Cosmic Mountain. The world of linear time and phenomena, Phaneros contains the spacetime of the Conclave.

The Shadow: Also called Khuliphoth, the Kingdom of Shells, the Shadow is a great band of darkness that stretches up the side of the Cosmic Mountain like a wound in the fabric of creation. The Shadow begins at the Abyss in Arethos and ends in Tehom. The Sovereign Road crosses the shadow as it passes between Materia and Mythos.

The Sovereign Road: The father and king of all roads. The Sovereign Road stretches from the shattered remains of Sha-Ka-Ri in Phaneros to the Temple Above All Worlds, touching on all the worlds of the cosmos.

Tehom: The black churning sea at the base of the Cosmic Mountain. Tehom is the primal nothingness from which creation was summoned.

Temple Above All Worlds: The source and summit of all creation. The Temple stands at the peak of the Cosmic Mountain. Within is the altar and throne of the Uncreated One.

Datachryst: Small crystalline devices used for permanent information storage and archival.

Ekklesia: Name for the galactic empire that preceded the formation of the Conclave. The Axioms and Corollaries were formulated in opposition to the ideals and values of the Ekklesia.

Alapsari: Name for those races of the Ekklesia that have never experienced corruption. They are functionally immortal. At the time of the Conclave the majority of them have been hunted to extinction.

Anastasi: Name for those members of the Ekklesia that have been restored to physical life after dying. Anastasi recall their time while disembodied and their restored flesh has a different relationship to timespace than it had prior to death. Anastasi have the ability to fly both inside and outside the boundary of Phaneros' timespace and can travel faster than light. They do not require air or food.

Dar Ekklesia: Formal title of the Galactic Empire during its period of power and ascendancy. Also called simply the Dar.

Hyrosol Neos: Primary city of the Dar Ekklesia. Hyrosol Neos is shaped like an immense golden cube and, prior to the defeat of the Dar Ekklesia, was stationed near the event horizon of Sagittarious A* near the galactic core.

Kal Ekklesia: Name given to those of the Dar Ekklesia who have died. They rest upon the petals of the Cosmic Rose in Numenos, awaiting the final resurrection.

Sur Ekklesia: Name of the Galactic Empire during its time of imprisonment and exile by the Conclave. The bulk of the Sur Ekklesia dwells in a guarded valley on En-Ka-Re.

Etherreaver: Interplanetary ships capable of generating intense bursts of gravitic energy used for planetary and stellar engineering. Earlier designs were used extensively in the Philosoph War.

Ether Chariot: Small interplanetary craft used for transit. Each is equipped with a Laridian Ring system capable of both standard propulsion and wormhole generation.

Five Heirophants: The five ruling technocrats of the Conclave. Their titles are derived from the four forces of nature plus entropy.

Chromatocron: The Hierophant of the Strong Nuclear Force. The Chromatocron is the philosophical leader of

Conclave society and is charged with maintaining the social forces and attitudes that bind that society together. He is also responsible for maintenance of the three suns ongoing activity and output.

Entrope: An enigmatic figure whose origins are shrouded in mystery. Heirophant of Entropy, he plays no societal role but functions instead as a seer and oracle. Unlike the other Heirophants, the Entrope effectively becomes his own successor by a process of cloning and memory transfer overseen by the Irkallan Infochryst.

High Gravitist: Currently Gedron Donar, the High Gravitist is the Hierophant of Gravity. It is his responsibility to maintain the Laridian rings that keep the worlds orbiting each other without collision and serve as the main transit devices of Conclave society. He is titular head of the Gravitic College.

Ouranos Radii: The Heirophant of the Weak Nuclear Force. The Ouranos Radii oversees all commerce and is responsible for maintaining the Conclave's biocomputational and infochrystic networks.

Photocanth: The Heirophant of the electromagnetic force. The Photocanth oversees all Conclave energy production as well as the interplanetary entertainment networks.

Infochryst: Infochrysts are the primary computational devices of the Conclave. Grown by imposing neuroelectric patterns on the native crystalline lifeforms of Latis, infochrysts range in size from small personal devices to the

427

massive core infochrysts used by the Conclave's scientific and governmental institutions.

Harut and Marut: Infochrystic artificial intelligences used by the High Gravitist to control the neutronium forges.

Ionocaric Infochryst: The core infochryst of the Arx Memoria. The Ionocaric Infochryst functions as a metalibrary and data mining engine. It contains copies of every piece of written, filmed, or otherwise recorded material the Conclave has ever produced.

Irkallan Infochryst: Stationed deep beneath the Omegahedron, the Irkallan Infochryst functions as life support for the developing body of the next Entrope. Unlike most infochrysts, some of the Irkallan Infochryst's architecture is psychoactive in nature and is used to transfer memories from one Entrope to his successor.

Nagmochron Infochryst: The core infochryst of the Omegahedron. The Nagmochron device collates and analyzes all data it receives regarding societal trends and movements. It is capable of making long-term sociometric predictions with near perfect accuracy.

Radithesia Infochryst: A secondary infochryst that functions under the supervision of the Nagmochron device. The Radithesia infochryst monitors and analyzes entertainment systems' data from across the Conclave.

Ramachrond Infochryst: The core infochryst of the Arx Scientia. The Ramachrond Infochryst collates data from deep stellar probes and the Large Neutronium Antenna, giving it the ability to closely monitor the activity of the three suns and the entropy clouds. It is frequently used by the High Gravitist for stellar engineering simulations.

Large Neutronium Antenna: A gravitational wave detection device used by the College of Gravitists to monitor the activity of the three suns and the entropy clouds. It consists of two asteroids linked together by an immense bridge of crystalline neutronium tuned to the resonant frequency of the three suns.

Laridian Ring: A key technological innovation introduced early in the life of the Conclave, laridian rings allows for the near-effortless manipulation of the space-time manifold. Within each ring, spinning bands of crystalline neutronium are coupled with a membrane-like field polarized to the strong force to create space-warping beams of virtual fermions. Laridian rings are used extensively for transit, orbital stabilization, and stellar manipulation. The Conclave as it currently exists would be impossible without their use.

Neutronium Forge: Moon-sized space stations designed to gravitically extract the neutronium needed to create laridian rings from the cores of the three suns. The extraction process is overseen by the Harut and Marut infochrysts.

Once-men: Denizens of the corrupt city of Hyrosol Eld in the world of Mythos. In ages past the Once-men sold their souls to Lord Daath in exchange for power and are now trapped in a living death. During the process by which they became Once-men their eyes were replaced by living gateways into the Shadow.

Oneirochryst: A type of infochrystic device capable of interacting with most electromagnetically-based nervous systems. Oneirochrysts are particularly calibrated to extract, archive, and alter subconscious thoughts and dreamstates.

>Oneirograph: Portable data crystals used to store and view extracted subconscious thoughts and dreamstate information.

Philosoph War: The galaxywide war that lead to the downfall of the Dar Ekklesia and the founding of the Conclave. Also called the War of Unification in the sanitized version of history currently taught in the Conclave educational system.

Psychochryst: A type of infochrystic device capable of interacting with most electromagnetically-based nervous systems. Psychochrysts are particularly calibrated to extract, archive, and alter conscious thoughts, emotions, and memories.

>Great Psychochryst: The largest and most powerful psychochryst. The Great Psychochryst is used by the Heirophants while in conclave to create a shared thoughtspace in which their movements, expressions, and thoughts can be instantly understood. Via its interactions with the other core infochrysts, the Great Psychochryst also allows the Heirophants to directly manipulate societal and scientific data and to alter the large-scale activity of Conclave systems.

Scintillus: The chief city of the planet of Latis and capital of the Conclave. Built in the center of Latis's lightside, the city is bathed in the brilliant sunlight of a perpetual noon. Its buildings, grown from Latis' native crystalline lifeforms, are considered one of the wonders of Conclave engineering.

Arx Memoria: The chief library and information storage facility of Scintillus. The Ionocaric Infochryst functions as its core information processor.

Arx Scientia: The central institute for science and education on Scintillus. The College of Gravitists maintains a set of laboratories there. The Ramachrond Device functions as its core infochryst.

Kinetorium: The Kinetorium is the chief transit hub for the planet of Latis. In its center is an obsidian sphere containing a series of titanic Laridian rings. These rings are used to maintain the transit corridors that link Latis to other worlds and to stabilize the planet's orbit. Each world of the Conclave has at least one kinetorium.

Omegahedron: The central administrative building of Scintillus. The Omegahedron houses, among other things, the Throne Room of the Five Heirophants, the Nagmochron Infochryst, and a division of the College of Gravitists.

Vacuum Sculptor: A device designed by the Chromatocron and Ouranos Radii that is capable of altering certain physical constants within a limited area.

War of Unification: See Philosoph War.

Worldship Gog: One of the two flagships of the Conclave. The Gog is the size of a small moon and is built to resemble an open lotus blossom. Lined with thousands of Laridian

Rings, the Gog can generate more gravitic distortion than entire planets.

Worldship Magog: One of the two flagships of the Conclave. Though similar to the Gog in size, the architecture of the Magog is built along a more chaotic pattern and consists of irregular shafts of crystal bound together by imagnite struts. The Magog's gravitic distortion capacity is similar to that of the Gog.

Dramatis Personae:

Phaneros:

Garin Donar: Son of Gedron Donar, High Gravitist of the Conclave. His journey on the Sovereign Road is chronicled here.

Trielle Donar: Sister of Garin and daughter of Gedron Donar.

Kyr: An elderly man who first meets Garin and Trielle on the streets of Scintillus.

Gedron Donar: Father of Garin and Trielle, and current High Gravitist of the Conclave of Worlds.

Dyana Donar: Mother of Garin and Trielle, and chief gravitational wave analyst for the Large Neutronium Antenna.

Erskilion of Garuda: A member of the winged Garudan race and current Photocanth, Heirophant of the Electromagnetic Force

Tauron of Latis: A human colleague of Gedron's and current Chromatocron, Heirophant of the Strong Nuclear Force.

Silindii: A member of the Gelasian race and current Ouranos Radii, Heirophant of the Weak Nuclear Force.

The Entrope: The nameless Heirophant of the Force of Entropy.

Anacrysis: Young man whom Trielle meets in the Arx Memoria.

Tseramed: A human and Abbott of the Holy Order of Gatekeepers.

Xellasmos: A member of the Ferisian race, historian of the Sur Ekklesia, and resident of En-Ka-Re.

Yochenath: A human priest of the Sur Ekklesia and resident of En-Ka-Re.

Yithra-Gor: A member of the Gerellian race and Master Gravitomechanist of the Worldship Gog.

Materia:

The Perichorr: Denizen of the Great 'hedron and archetypal incarnation of the Electron.

First-Of-The-Bound: Denizen of the Great 'hedron and archetypal incarnation of the Quark.

Chromoclast: Denizen of the Great 'hedron and archetypal incarnation of the third symmetry of the Weak Nuclear Force.

The Exofuge: Denizen of the Great 'hedron and archetypal incarnation of Gravity.

The Mass: The antagonist of the Exofuge and assailer of the Great 'hedron.

The Shadow:

Daath: Once one of the Arethoi, he is now the enemy of creation.

Mythos:

Hyperion Starfather: Denizen of Mythos and sire of all the stars of the cosmos. He dwells in the Sepulcher of Suns.

The Mariner: Denizen of Mythos and navigator of the Mare Primum.

The Beloved: Sleeper in the crypt beneath the Shattered Temple and Kyr's betrothed.

Arethos:

Malkuth: One of the Arethoi. She is also called Kyriakos, the Steward of Sovereignty.

Gevurah: One of the Arethoi. He is also called Rhadamanthos, the Steward of Judgment.

Tiferet: One of the Arethoi. She is also called Kallos, the Beauty and Joy of Creation.

Numenos:

Keter: One of the Arethoi. He is also called Zeodotes and Chavath, the Crown of Life.

Metatron: One of the Cherubim and Lord of the City Imperishable.

Sandalphon: One of the Cherubim and Lord of the City Imperishable.

Mater Marya: One of the Fathers and Mothers of the Kal Ekklesia. She dwells within the Cosmic Rose.

Made in the USA
San Bernardino, CA
26 May 2018